# Lilies for Alex

## By Toni Wingrove

### Book one in The Rossi Mafia Trilogy

Released 13<sup>th</sup> January 2022

Facebook: @toniwingroveauthor

Instagram: toni_wingrove

Email: author_toniwingrove@yahoo.com

# Table of Contents

# Chapter One

The sun beats down from the mid-day sky, bathing me with her ethereal glow. Laying in the cocoon of the meadow, I splay my hands wide to run my fingers through the soft blades of grass. The vibrant wildflowers dance to their own merry tune, emitting their perfume and showering us with scent. Alex hovers above me with love radiating in his luminous eyes. His beauty surrounded by the halo of the sun. The gentle breeze kisses the leaves in the trees making them ring out with their motion. Leaning closer I feel his breath coat my face and I wait in anticipation as bells sing in my ears. The nearer he draws, the harsher the sound. His lips barely touch mine when the cacophony becomes unbearable to my senses.

Leaning over I silence the alarm, disgusted with the device for pulling me from the depths of my dream, robbing me of the taste of his lips. I miss Alex terribly when he works away, my dreams won't even spare me the anxiety I feel at our separation.

Laying in the softness of our bed, I soak up the warmth that surrounds me, inhaling his scent which is embedded in the weave of the pillow I'm currently anchored to. Sighing contentedly, I allow myself 5 more minutes to immerse myself in the aroma of my husband.

"What the hell is that...?" I say out loud, quickly retracting my foot from the unknown substance.

I've trodden in some dubious things at 6 in the morning, Lego bricks, which hurt like the devil or cars the boys had lined up on the stairs, unfortunately, though, it's none of those things. The dogs been sick over the kitchen floor, not a little bit, bucket loads.

Looking over I see Bear laying quietly in his bed, feeling sorry for himself, and perhaps a little bit guilty too.

"Hey big fella, not feeling too well then?" I say to my poorly boy.

It almost feels as if he answers me with his eyes, as I gently sit down in his bed for a cuddle. He willingly sidles over to lay his massive head on my lap. Looking into his eyes, I see he's feeling pretty lousy.

"Oh, Baby Bear, what are we going to do with you hey?" I ask him whilst tenderly stroking the soft fur on his head.

Looks like a visit to the vet for us today.

Bear loves John our vet, in fact he loves everyone. I never imagined us with such a massive dog. He's a mixture of giant breeds, including various mastiffs, and sometimes it feels like he's almost human with his antics. The downside of such a large dog is the mountains of hair and the slobber. Hanging from his jowls like shoe laces, a quick shake to his head and the trajectory is left up to nature. I've found drool hanging from light fittings, sofas, walls, ceilings, my work trousers, whatever's in its path is fair game.

I lay his head back down and hoist myself up in the most elegant manner possible. I didn't realise when you're about to hit 40 raising from the floor would be quite so difficult. I'm not that much overweight, maybe a few extra pounds. I remember having a svelte size 10 before I had the boys and I could gracefully rise from the floor in an ethereal manner. Sadly, gravity and time has done its worst and what was once pert, and firm has sadly jiggled down south and collected a few extra pounds on route. Thankfully Alex's love is still fierce.

Turning on the light I take a moment to admire my beautiful kitchen, it's every cooks dream. When we first viewed the house, I fell in love instantly. It was dated with brown swirly carpets and matching patterned wallpaper, but I could see through the hideous 70's décor to the bare bones and knew instantly that it would become a home. Alex wanted us to stay in London to be closer to work, I wanted the space and fresh air for children. I won.

Finding the mop, bucket and paper towels I tip toe back to the mess and kneel down to start cleaning. Every once in a while, I see him staring back at me, almost in an apologetic manner, I just smile and give him my gentle words of reassurance.

Once finished I do what I should have done to start with and put my sliders on to protect my feet. After washing my hands, I turn on the radio and coffee machine. Two of my favourite things in the morning. There is so much pleasure from sitting in a house that is still sleeping, sipping coffee and listening to music. I need to wake the boys soon for school, but I just need 5 more minutes to myself.

7 o'clock arrives too quickly and chaos descends on the house. Leonardo, or Leo as he prefers, is in his last year at school and looking forward to the next chapter in life, college. Living out in the sticks is great when they're young, but once they grow up it's a pain as transport isn't great. Thankfully he can get the train to college each day. Just one more thing for me to worry about.

Marco, or Marc, has two more years left and it saddens and scares me that our babies are growing up so fast.

Both boys are the spitting image of their Dad. Lustrous, thick black hair, golden skin and beautiful dark eyes. That's the first thing that attracted me to Alex, his eyes. Pools of dark liquid chocolate, velvety soft and meltingly decadent. You could get lost in them for hours, if not days. They say the eyes are the gateway to the soul, but his were the gateway to my heart. I fell in love with him instantly and we're still completely and utterly in love today.

Whilst the boys are frantically getting ready I check my phone for messages, I knew Alex wouldn't be coming home last night but I still worry. He stays over in town when he has to work late. As the manager of the nightclub Gia for the past 12 years, thankfully it's not often he works at night. Normally he oversees the running of the club during the day letting his assistant manager, Matteo, work the evening shift. When you're in your late 20's and the prospect of watching hundreds of scantily clad women strutting around, gyrating on the dance floor, it's obvious which shift he would choose. Matteo is a self-confessed man whore. On the few occasions

I've met him he's flirted outrageously. I'd smile and laugh at his antics. Alex would scowl.

Matteo's away so Alex needed to cover for a few days. He does it at least once a month, Matteo needs time off occasionally I suppose. I really don't like it when he's away all night, I know it's safe where we live, we have Bear to protect us, actually he'd probably lick them to death. The main thing I really can't stomach on the late shift is the state of his clothes, especially the blood splatter. His shirts get ripped when he has to break up fights and they're sprayed with little droplets of blood. I've said to him time and time again that that's the bouncer's job, but he still steps in and helps them. At 45 he should be more careful, but one thing I can assuredly say is my husband is fit, with a capital F.

Alex sent a message at 3am this morning, instantly relieved I quickly open it:

**LOVE YOU XXX**

I consider replying to it or calling him, but he's probably knackered. If I send a message, I'll risk waking him with the notification noise. I'll call him later.

With the boys dropped off at school I navigate back to the village. As a small country practice the vet operates a drop-in clinic during their morning surgery. I'm relieved to see there's only a few cars in the car park, hopefully we'll be in and out quickly and I'll be able to get to work. Thankfully I have the luxury of being self-employed which is a godsend.

John isn't working today, unfortunately, Chloe is. With a sigh of resignation, I take a seat and wait with Bear who is sprawled out on my feet. It's obvious he's still out of sorts as he isn't his usual buoyant happy self.

The two other patients sit in complete silence hoping the big bad bear won't notice them. They're cuddling their pets so tightly to their chests, almost cutting of their ability to breath. Mentally I shake my head at the typical reaction. Why are people so judgemental?

The primped and preened she-devil will be seeing him today. That's probably a little mean of me, I'm sure she is a perfectly lovely person, I didn't get the opportunity to find out when we first met her. She spent the whole appointment making doe eyes at Alex whilst standing at the examination table gently caressing my dogs' fur and running her fingers along my husband's arm, at the same time. I stood there totally dumbstruck. When I raised it with Alex after he just brushed it off by saying 'I didn't really notice her, I only have eyes for you' then kissed my forehead and walked off with Bear.

That's the way Alex has always been, he really doesn't see any of them. They could throw themselves at him and he'd gently push away their advances and deflect their flirtatious remarks. They could be stripped naked and he wouldn't see them. He tells me constantly that I am his everything, his whole life, his reason for living. He has only ever seen me.

I know a lot of people don't believe in love at first sight, I can only assume they're the ones who've never felt genuine love in its full and truest form. It really does happen. Your brain is electrocuted, the shock sends a current through your body and you can feel it, love. It runs through your veins and defines your soul, plans out your future and becomes your destiny. The moment two souls find their mate the whole world becomes theirs.

Bear and I have been waiting for about 10 minutes when Chloe bounces out of the examination room.

"Hello Mr Big Bear. Have you come to see Chloe for some big snuggly cuddles?"

It's official, I hate her. Bear looks at me, his eyes asking,

'Is she for real!!'

Sorry buddy. Suck it up. We're in this together.

I smile politely at Chole, although I imagine it's more like a sneer, Bear has a similar countenance, as we follow little miss tight buttocks into the examination room. A sterile table sits in the middle, I assume 'normal' pet owners gently lift their poorly babies onto it. I can't and won't lift two-ton Tessie on there. At 10 stone you would need a crane.

"Up we get then." She says in her nicey, nicey voice.

Can she really be that dumb? She actually giggles at her own stupid request.

"It's OK handsome. I'll Kneel down in front of you instead."

Seriously, I'm speechless. Just, wow. Words fail me.

After a very uncomfortable examination from the Flutterby Princess, Bear's given a clean bill of health. Apparently, it's something he ate. No shit sherlock. Smiling politely, we leave together, and I lead Bear back to the reception area to pay. The entire waiting room scoops up their pets, cradling them protectively in their arms, from the big bad bear. Bear couldn't give two figs about any of them. He just wants to go home.

We pull into the drive and I sigh with relief, glad to be home but most of all glad Bear isn't really poorly. Jumping from the car I make my way round to the boot and as it opens Bear is standing stock still staring into the trees at the side of the house. He's more alert now than he has been all day. His attention is fixed in the far distance between two trees. His body language screams 'something's not right'. His eyes don't waver from that one spot.

Quickly turning I lock onto a shadow in the distance. Blinking quickly to moisten my eyes but in that split second, it's gone. Scanning from left to right, trying to find the ghost of a shadow but nothing's out of place. Turning in a full circle and making a quick survey of the area I see nothing but trees. The moment's passed but it has left me hyper aware of our surroundings. It's eerily quiet.

The house sits on the edge of the village, backing onto woodland. There are no close neighbours, and nobody would have any reasons to walk through the copse of trees in our garden. I've always felt safe here, but I feel spooked.

I'm not 100% positive I actually saw anything, it was probably just a squirrel or rabbit. With a small shake to my head I turn back to Bear, giving him a loving scratch behind his ear before he jumps down and saunters towards the house.

## Chapter Two

Picking up the post as we walk through the door and I'm hit by smells that always comfort you and say, 'you're home'. The fresh Lilly's in the hallway, the fabric softener on the clean washing and the smell of Alex's aftershave. It's strange how a smell can transport you back to a memory. I remember when he kissed me for the first time. The feel of his soft lips against mine, his arms holding me close, the soft texture of his clothes. That feeling of being enveloped, totally surrounded by the smell of cloves and bergamot and freshness. Surrounded by Alex. I'll never forget that moment, he was so debonair I was in complete awe of him. His suit fit his perfectly toned physique, shoes shined to perfection, the crispness of his shirt and tie, his perfect hair and those captivating, enigmatic eyes. I was star struck that he singled me out. He could have anyone, but he chose me.

Checking through the post I see nothing urgent, just a few for Alex and mostly junk mail for me. Tossing it on to the Island in the kitchen, I check to see Bear has fresh water. Chloe suggested no food till later. Just plain chicken and rice.

"Sorry buddy, nothing for you yet."

With a disgruntled look at my words Bear trots over to his bed and promptly falls asleep. I turn the radio on, so he has some company. Strange, I don't remember turning it off earlier, must have been one of the boys.

Picking up my work diary and an apple I say goodbye to the snoring dog and head back out to the car, casting a quick look around, I'm still a little unnerved.

Heading straight to my little studio I mentally run through the work I have outstanding. I never imagined I would become all artsy. Somehow, I've made a profit from doing something I love. I've captured a small sector of the market for upcycled furniture. Alex couldn't see the attraction at first but once I explained that each piece is unique, how people express their individuality through their décor, he started to understand. I've never needed to work, but Alex understands my need to keep busy.

I mainly work on pieces customers bring to me. They have an image in their mind and try to explain it. As they describe the room and their design style I begin to build a picture in my mind. Mentally I walk through their homes and see what they're trying to achieve. They want unique, unique is what they get. I don't always get it right, and those mistakes are easily rectified. Some customers have very bizarre tastes. Each to their own I suppose.

I prefer to visit customers at home and view the piece in-situ, looking at the room as a whole I then have a feel for their design style, and what would work best for them.

The other side to my work is buying individual pieces of furniture and painting them how I like. Some are sympathetically done, others I just go mad on. Depends on my mood. Depends on the weather. Depends on the day.

Thankfully it's a final viewing today of the finished piece. I've caught up with my workload and I only have a few appointments later in the week. Two are people I've worked with before, they're easy as they trust my judgement. The other is a new family that have moved to the next village. I met her briefly and she seems nice, probably a bit too nice, but when you're new to an area you try your hardest to be friendly and fit in. The residents in our village only consider you a local if 3 generations of your family have lived there. Hopefully by the time I'm a great grandmother I might be accepted.

When we first moved to Bramley End we were stared at like an unusual species in the zoo.

Alex is of Italian descent, although he and his brothers were born in the UK, unfortunately though he is considered a foreigner by the people in this village.

His parents came to the UK when they were newly married. As the story goes they began by working for the family business and started with a small restaurant, which quickly expanded and grew under the guidance of Alex's father. Before his death 12 years ago, The Rossi family had grown substantially and now owns a significant number of businesses. Alex's older brother, Dante, runs The Rossi Company now. Gia is one of their more lucrative establishments, a nightclub aimed at the higher end of the pay grade. As a member's only club, people can show off their wealth and flaunt their status in life.

Gia is worlds away from the club Alex and I met in. A small dingy nightclub in town with a dodgy looking interior and furry carpet that stuck to your feet. There was the ever-present stench of sweat from the masses of bodies crammed into the too tight space. With no fresh air and definitely no air conditioning, the humidity rose as more people were packed into the confined area. The moisture hung from the ceiling and any make-up you wore melted and dripped from your face. It sounds awful, and it probably was, but when you're 19 and ready to spread your wings, dance till dawn, flirt, drink copious amounts of cheap watered-down vodka, it felt like heaven. No parents. No restrictions. Just freedom.

I remember seeing him from my vantage point at the edge of the dance floor. He was lent gracefully against the bar with 2 friends, who I later found out are his brothers. Holding a tumbler between his fingers with a shot of amber liquid which he swirled around and around. He stood out because of the quality that simply oozed from his every pore. The sheer magnitude of his presence was completely out of place and yet he looked comfortable. Like he belonged.

Most men were wrapped up in the obligatory black trousers and cheap nylon shirt. Not Alex. He wore a 3-piece suit with pride and from my standpoint I could feel the quality of the man. I remembered thinking in my drunken state how they looked like gangsters. I could almost picture him playing the idolised criminal in a movie.

Laughing to myself I still can't believe I actually asked him that. It pains me to think how embarrassing I must have been. Talk about opening liners. When a man of drop-dead gorgeous proportions approaches you, DO NOT blurt out, 'are you a gangster?'.

I hastily retracted my words and blamed it on the alcohol, making sure not to look up at the God who stood before me. I remember apologising and rambling on about men not normally wearing such fine clothes. I didn't dare remove my eyes from his suit clad torso, and what a torso it was, still is.

Alex stood there saying nothing. He placed his finger under my chin and slowly began to raise my head. My eyes followed the line of buttons from his jacket up to the smaller ones of his waistcoat, along the silky smoothness of his tie and past the impeccably tied knot. His Addams apple was where I first glimpsed the golden hue of his perfect skin. At the column of his throat I watched him swallow, the only outward sign of his nerves. Moving up on to his powerful jaw, the inviting shadow of his beard almost made me raise my hand to feel the texture of the bristles beneath my fingertips. My eyes continued their pleasurable journey north taking in his beautifully crafted lips, parted in anticipation. I felt his heated breath cover my face with the faint aroma of whiskey, and the masculine nose, with a slight break to the top, added to his absolute beauty.

Finally, they made their way to their intended destination.

Finally, they found their resting place.

Finally, I looked into the eyes of the most magnificent creature I had ever seen. His beauty and power combined resulted in this resplendent beast and I wanted to bathe in the magnificence of him.

Our eyes locked as an electrical current travelled between us, wrapping itself around, uniting us. A force that couldn't be seen pulling us into one another, tying us together, binding us permanently. We were both stunned into silence as the world around us disappeared and we were the only two people who existed. My breath stopped as our hearts began to pound in harmony. In that moment I knew I was his for eternity, and he would always be mine.

Mrs Somerset arrives at 10.45 to pay for her Gin Cabinet. A retro 60's style bow fronted wooden cabinet with etched glass doors and glass shelves. A piece she already had in their lounge, she wanted it to be more exuberant for the conservatory they were remodelling. As a big gin fan, she wanted it to shout out her personality. As soon as I saw it, I knew, and I was right. Painted in a beautiful shade of vibrant blue with hints of peacock green and gold accents, it turned out fantastically. I was so proud of the finished result when I called her that I asked for permission to post pictures on my social media pages. She was thrilled that her 'silly old cabinet' would bring a smile to people's faces. Her words not mine.

"I absolutely adore it." She gushes to me when I reveal the finished piece.

Working with enthusiastic people that appreciate my skills is an honour.

"I have passed your details onto a few of my friends Kate. I do hope that's ok and you're not too busy to help them."

I love her enthusiasm.

"Thank you, Mrs Somerset, I can always fit them in. Tell them to mention your name."

Mrs Somerset is thrilled and settles the bill. As her car is too small to take the cabinet, I offer to drop it over later today, possibly early evening, I can get the boys to help me. With a "Toodle-loo" and a wave over her shoulder, she vanishes from my studio in a waft of perfume and silk.

Leaving the studio mid-afternoon, I have just enough time to run around the supermarket and still make it in time to collect the boys from school. I'm not allowed to park anywhere near the gates as that's 'just not cool mum'. It's not like I drive a beaten-up old jalopy like my parents had. Theirs was dirty brown with rusty brown patches, a hole in the floor, where you could see the road whizzing underneath, and a brown Velcro interior that strangely smelt like cheese and felt oddly wet to the touch.

Alex is slightly paranoid about our safety. He ensures we drive around in the latest vehicle with the most airbags. I remind him constantly that we don't need anything that big, it's just the 3 of us during the day, but he insists. It wouldn't surprise me if it had some sort of satellite tracking us and bulletproof glass. I think he forgets we live in the countryside, not the town, bedsides what harm would ever come to us here?

Racing back home from school, I realise I haven't spoken to Alex yet today and try to call him from the car. On the first try the call drops off.

"Leo, can you try calling your dad please, I've got no signal." I ask.

Leo tries from his phone, which is ever present in his hand, he looks at me and shakes his head, his call isn't connecting either. He tries again, and then turns the phone towards me, there's no signal out here. Typical.

"Don't worry darling, I'll call him when we get in."

I just get some sort of grunt in response as he puts his ear phones back in.

"How was your day Marc?" I ask looking at him in the rear-view mirror.

Marc stares out the window, I know he heard me.

"S'alright s'pose."

Marc's been struggling at school this year. Not because he's at the bottom of his set, it's because he's at the top of all of his classes. It's not fashionable to be brainy. He damps it down for school and all his mates, but I know he loves to learn. He's always been that way. He would pick a topic and learn everything there is to know till he exhausts it. In primary school their topic was volcanoes, it scared me how much he already knew when the teacher started on the subject. During the first lesson Marc argued with his teacher that he had his facts wrong, and in fact over 80% of the earth's surface was volcanic in origin. His teacher said he was incorrect and wouldn't listen to him, silencing him whenever he tried to contribute to the rest of the lesson. That night Marc put together a folder of facts and figures and the following morning marched straight into school and thrust it into his teachers' hand.

As he turned to walk away he muttered;

"Maybe I should be teaching this class instead of you!"

I didn't reprimand him as he was in fact correct in his initial argument with the teacher, I also didn't tell him off for his comment as it's the sort of thing his Dad would say. I merely smiled, kissed him on the head and walked away. When you're a Brainiac like our son, you've got to stand up for yourself otherwise you'll get bullied, and not just by the pupils either.

Pulling back into the drive the boys help unload the shopping, dumping it all on the side in the kitchen. Leo wanders over to Bear to check he's feeling better and judging by the huge smile that is spread across both their faces, it's safe to say he has improved vastly. The bond they have is incredible.

"Don't get covered in dog's hair please." I absentmindedly say as I throw the cold food in the fridge.

"Can you quickly run and get changed, I need to deliver a cabinet to Mrs Somerset today."

The boys kick off their shoes and trudge upstairs as I take out my phone to call Alex. Still no service. We don't have a home phone, we've never seen the need for one. It's times like this I wish we did. I try sending a message in the vain hope it goes through whilst I'm driving.

We safely deliver the cabinet, with the boys doing all the heavy lifting, and place it in her conservatory. It looks amazing and I'm really proud that something I created will take pride of place. The room has been decorated to complement the cabinet, with two large chesterfield sofas in gold sitting opposite one other and a beautiful green and gold glass coffee table in-between. The thick blue rug adds a soft touch and the numerous plants in their golden pots finish the look.

We say our goodbyes and make our way back home.

## Chapter Three

Driving home, I hear those usual words from any teenage boy.

"I'm starving." They say in unison.

Nothing new there.

"I bought pizzas for tonight." I respond.

I love to cook but tonight I can't be bothered. The boys seem content to eat junk food, and I'm happy that they're happy.

They're good kids. A lot of parents struggle when their children hit the terrible teen's, but we've been lucky. Alex is very strict with them. I don't always agree with his parenting style, but we have two courteous well-mannered young men we are proud to call our sons. Alex's parents apparently were very strict when he and his brothers were growing up. His mother still scares me after 20 years of marriage to her son, not that I really know her. We don't see his family very often, I've asked Alex to invite them over, but he says they always decline with some excuse or another.

Pulling into the drive I spot an unfamiliar car just pulling up in front of the house. I pass them and drive up to the garage door and turn the car off whilst looking back in the mirror at the strangers in our driveway. As we all get out Leo looks to me with a questioning look. I return his gaze with a shrug of my shoulders and shake of my head. The boys are just as curious as me. I have no idea who they are.

The three of us walk side by side towards the uninvited visitors as they alight from their car.

"Can I help you?" I politely ask.

I'm glad that I'm not standing here alone, the incident from earlier in the day pops in to my head and vanishes just as quickly.

The man who was driving waits for his female friend to join him. The overall appearance of him is not a pleasant one. A greasy mop of hair is slicked to one side and what look suspiciously like sweat stains on his shirt beneath his crumpled suit, it makes me shiver in revulsion. The lady has a much cleaner appearance, dressed in her masculine trousers and shirt and smart looking jacket.

"Mrs Rossi, Mrs Katherine Rossi?" He asks.

With a quizzical brow, and somewhat apprehensively I answer.

"Yes, that's me."

"My name is Inspector Rite, this is my colleague Inspector Shaw. Could we speak inside?"

Alex has drummed it into me, and the boys, you do not let anyone into the house unless you know their business. It's our safe place, he always says, and we should keep unwanted people out.

"What's this all about?" I ask in return to his suggestion.

I see him look towards the boys in turn and then back to me again.

"I really think we need to go somewhere more comfortable."

The hairs on the back of my neck are starting to stand to attention. Something's not right. I can sense it.

Nodding to both boys in turn, I encourage them to walk into the house with a hand pressed gently to their lower backs.

"Leo, can you take Bear upstairs with you and Marc please?" I ask as we enter the hallway. The last thing I need is for the dog to attack a bloody police officer.

"But mum, what if you need us?" He asks in a low voice.

I look at my eldest son and realise in that moment he has transformed before my eyes into a man. He has gone into protective mode, emulating his father.

With a proud smile I say.

"It's OK, I'll holler if I need you."

With a reassuring smile I gently rub their backs and they walk up the stairs with Bear in tow. Both boys look back over their shoulders, both look scared, concerned.

"We can go in here." I say over my shoulder.

I purposely take them to the kitchen as I don't want them tainting any other part of our house.

Leaning my bum against the island, I place my right ankle across the top of my left and cross my arms firmly over my chest. My position screams closed off.

They both remain standing as I look at them expectantly. Inspector Rite clears his throat and flicks a glance to his colleague. It's in that moment, that glance, that look, I know my life is about to change. I feel the blood already draining from my face.

"I'm really sorry to have to inform you, but we believe your husband Allesandro Rossi was involved in a car accident this afternoon. He was pronounced dead at the scene."

I stare at the man stood in my kitchen, unable to take in his statement. I can't comprehend the meaning of each individual word spoken, I pray I misheard him. This is some kind of joke. They have the wrong person. I look from one to the other and back again, but their faces remain impassive, unmoving. They've got it wrong, it can't be Alex, it's a big mistake, huge mistake.

"You've made a mistake." I tell them emphatically. "There must be a mix up... he, we're, ....he, he can't be."

I stumble over my words, unable to articulate what I need to say. I can't seem to verbalise my thoughts, my feelings.

"You're wrong!" I all but scream in their faces, as I shake my head

Alex can't be dead, it's impossible, I would have felt it. If Alex had been killed his heart would have stopped, my heart would have split in two and crumbled, turned to dust. Our hearts beat as one, they're connected for all eternity. I would have felt his stop, as mine would have stopped in that very moment too.

The look that passes between them sends a shiver to my very core when I see the truth of it in their eyes. I look away from the two people that have entered our home and shattered our lives. I can't stand to see them as it makes it all real. If I look away, then they're not here anymore. It's just a nightmare.

Placing my hands on the island, I lean my whole weight through them, needing something to ground me. My breathing is becoming erratic as I drop my head to my chest, my eyes dart from side to side looking for answers. Swallowing back the bile that has risen, chocking on the scream in my throat, I need to concentrate on my breathing. Holding the island, I use it to support me whilst my world spins and tilts out of control. A feeling of terror runs through my veins. My breathing is becoming deeper as I hear the sob resonate within desperate to be released.

Lifting my head is the discomfort I need to distract me from the agony. The searing pain of the tears on my cheeks burn as they free themselves. I swallow again and again to withhold the cry of torture. Staring through the window I see only the images of our lives running on a reel through my head.

They have crushed me, devastated my soul. My very reason for breathing has been ripped away. They have destroyed my life, the shock of their words sending my body into distress.

"Can we call anyone for you?" Shaw gently asks from behind me.

I shake my head. No.

I don't want anyone except Alex. He would make this pain go away. He would hold me in his arms and soothe away the hurt, the distress, the crippling sadness. Softly whispering words of tenderness, protecting me, caring for me, loving me.

How can that all be gone?

My world has collapsed.

My heart has broken.

I will only ever be half the person I was.

The other half has been taken and I can never get it back.

I know I need to be strong, our boys need me. Alex's boys. For now, I just need to just think about me, protect me. The tears silently slide down splashing the worktop. The feeling of utter devastation settles over me. The burning in my throat intensifies as I desperately hold in the cry of pain, of distress, my body needs the release. It wants to be set free. I want to scream. I want to shout they're wrong. I want to smash my fists into the counter. Over and over and over. I want to let the hurt out.

How can this happen? How? My body begins to shake with tremors of despair, sorrow, holding in the agony that wants to be let loose.

I can't do any of those things. I have to hold it all inside. I need to stay strong. The boys need me to stay strong for them.

It suddenly hits me, oh god the boys, I have to tell them. It rests on my shoulders to break this devastating news. Shaking my head at the thought. They will be just as heartbroken. Alex is their hero. They idolise him. We are such a close family we've never needed anyone else. We have each other.

Had.

We had each other.

Now the boys only have me.

# Chapter Four

I'm aware of their presence still in the kitchen, I can hear them breathing. The ticking of the clock. The hum of the fridge. The sound of the boys upstairs. Looking up to the ceiling I can see them in my mind's eye. They're in Leos room. I can feel them sitting anxiously waiting for me to call them down. Their brains must have gone into overdrive thinking, what's happened. I know I need to tell them but I'm incapable of moving. I've forgotten how to speak. My breathing sounds forced. My heart has died but my brain has taken over control of my body. I want to curl into a ball and die. I want to be with Alex. I can't. I won't. They need me. I have to continue to live, for them.

Tears sliding down my face, burning a path, I hastily wipe them away with my hand. Turning I raise my chin strengthening my resolve and take a deep breath, centring myself, straightening my spine, I remind myself, I'm a Rossi. I'm Alex's wife.

"How did it happen?" My voice sounds strange to my ears. I don't need to know. I want to know.

"The accident occurred on the country lane connecting Honiton and Waters End. On initial inspection it looks like he lost control of the vehicle."

I watch as his mouth moves. I hear the words, but it feels like an eternity till they register. Everything is working slower. It takes a while for my brain to catch up. That can't be right.

"No, you're wrong, he doesn't drive that way. You've made a mistake."

Honiton would be at least 50 miles from his normal route. We don't know anyone there. He drives from home into London by the same route every time. Why would he deviate?

"Yes. We're positive" The female inspector adds.

"We need to ask you a few questions if you feel up to it. Can I make you some tea?" She asks.

Bloody Tea. How the hell is that supposed to help!

"What sort of questions?" I respond sharply. Confused at what direction this is taking.

"Shall we take a seat?" she says with her arm held forward, guiding me towards the dining table.

Robotically I follow. Numb. My mind a jumbled mess of emotions.

Sliding into the chair, I stare at the head of the table. Grateful neither of them sat in Alex's seat. A sob makes its way up from my chest and I fight to keep it in. I will not allow these people to see my tears. I will save them. I will shed them in private. My tears of love for Alex.

"We need the details for Mr Rossi's dentist."

Dentist. Why would they need that? He can't help Alex. Anyhow, we wouldn't get an appointment this late in the day.

"We need the records for identification purposes."

I'm totally confused. With a furrowed brow I look from one face to the other.

"But he's my husband. Surely, I would identify him, not Mr Spencer."

I'm feeling lost, a boat bobbing anchorless at sea. I know I should comprehend what they're saying, the fog in my brain just won't let me see it.

"What aren't you saying?" I'm becoming angry at the torture of this verbal dance.

Inspector Shaw leans forward.

"Unfortunately, Mr Rossi sustained multiple injuries on impact. It would have been quick. He wouldn't have suffered."

I know she's trying to be kind, but these are just words to them, like a script they roll out. Of course, he suffered.

"We need the dental records to positively identify your husband's body."

I turn to Inspector Rite as he takes over the verbal torture.

"I'm really very sorry but due to the impact it's our only positive means of identification."

I stare at him in disbelief, his words don't make any sense.

"So, you're not positive it is Alex." Hope sears through my veins.

"What makes you think it's him?" My head swinging from one to the other.

"We identified his vehicle and it contained a wallet with your husbands driving licence and cards inside." Rite informs me.

"Someone could have stolen the car. He could have been robbed." I forcefully retort as I make to rise from the chair.

Where's my phone? I'll call him and prove them wrong.

Inspector Rite raises his hand to halt me. He knows my thoughts, I can see it in the sympathetic look in his eyes.

"Yes, it is a possibility, but highly unlikely. I'm really very sorry Mrs Rossi." With the firmness of his reply I know it's true. His statement has completely crushed me all over again.

"Can we call someone to be with you?" Inspector Shaw gently asks as she reaches across the table to lay her hand over mine in comfort.

"No." Is my only reply.

I have the arduous task of calling Alex's family to inform them, but I need to speak with the boys alone first. They are my first priority. No-one can help me with this.

Rising from the chair I retrieve my bag from the kitchen counter where I dumped it earlier. Inside I find my purse with the card for the dentist. I know where it is as Alex asked me to make him an appointment last month. It hits me, I need to cancel his next appointment, I need to cancel a lot. A sob runs through my chest. Leaning against the counter I give myself a moment. I have a monumental task ahead of me. A journey I never dreamt I would ever have to take.

With a deep inhale of breath, I turn back to the inspectors handing over the card. My hands have a small shake to them belying the strong demeanour I'm trying to fake. Making eye contact with them I strengthen my resolve.

This is really happening. This has to be the shittiest job anyone should have to do. Walking into a happy home and ripping it apart with the words they speak. Shaw's emotions are clear on her face, but Rite is hard to read. This isn't the first time he has delivered this crushing blow.

"What happens next? What do I need to do now?" I ask.

"We'll be in contact tomorrow Mrs Rossi. Again, we're very sorry for your loss."

Rite rises from the table, scraping his chair legs as he goes.

"We'll see ourselves out."

Shaw looks at me with a sympathetic smile and rises more gently, following her colleague out the door. Their exit signalled by the click of the front door. A definitive click. A click which echo's through the downstairs. Reminding me how empty and alone I am. My whole world, what is left of it, is upstairs. I need to go to them. Break their hearts in the same way our unwelcome visitors did to me.

The enormity of the task hits me. The tears I have been holding back find their way out. Silent tears. Pain leaves my body with each single drop. How am I supposed to live without him? How do we survive this? How do we carry on?

The sound of the boys coming down the stairs wakes me from my musings. Wiping the tears from my face with the backs of my hand, wiping them down the leg of my jeans, allowing the tears to soak into the fabric. Taking a deep breath, I prepare to turn and face the hardest task of my life. The task of telling my boys their father has gone. Trying to remain strong for them but crumbling to dust inside.

We sit huddled on the sofa, my arm around Leo, rubbing his shoulder gently. His arms encircling my waist, anchoring me to him, ensuring I'm glued to him. Not wanting to let go. I gently run my other hand through Marc's hair where it rests on my lap. We have passed the hysterics stage. All of us. The disbelief. How their father could have been taken from them. The questions I couldn't answer. I feel numb. My throat burns. My eyes are swollen. My nose sore, my heart broken.

I'm struggling to breath as the enormity of our situation starts to sink in. When a quarter of a pie is taken, it is never whole again. We will never be whole. The silence in the room is deafening. A home usually filled with laughter is tainted with desolation.

Looking across the room I see Bear hovering. He knows something has happened, he senses it. Tip-toeing towards our small despondent group, he noses his way in and lays his head onto Leo's lap. Instantly both boys reach out to him, gently stroking is head. His eyes never leave mine, and I can see the sorrow reflected back in his orbs. He knows. With a nudge further into our unit, he firmly places his paw on Marc's shoulder, looking at us each in turn from his position on Leo's lap. He closes our circle. Completing the pie.

After a few minutes or it could have easily been hours I know I need to tend to immediate business. I need to inform Alex's family. I gently lay a kiss on each boy's head.

"I need to ring your uncles and nonna."

Reluctantly the boys rise to a more seated position to allow me to get up, tracking my every movement into the kitchen. I decide to make the call from the island as I can see the sofa from there. They can still see me, but they don't need to hear.

With shaking hands, I attempt to open my home screen, and on the 3rd attempt I'm successful.

Scrolling through my contacts I find the number I need.

Dante has always intimidated me. Tall and dark like Alex, you could mistake them for twins. The aura he pervades is menacing though, and completely at odds with Alex's relaxed manner. One look from Dante would unsettle the strongest of men. The wrath of his stare is not for the faint hearted.

I sigh deeply and press call. My hands shake as I hold the phone to my ear, hearing the tap-tapping of my earing as it knocks against the glass front. My nervousness ramps up as the call connects.

It barely rings once, and I hear the deep timbre of Dante's voice.

"Kate?"

Clearing my throat, I attempt to speak but the words are stuck. The tears start to build behind my eyes, ready to spill.

Clearing my throat again, I take a deep breath.

"Kate is that you?" He asks, with worry in his voice.

"Y-Yes." Deep breath, I can do this. I can do this

"I'm really sorry to have to do this over the phone Dante...."

I feel like I'm hyperventilating, I'm going to pass out. Slowing my breathing down, I need to take proper breaths.

"Alex has, he-he..." Blowing a large breath our through my mouth I try again.

"Alex died this afternoon. He-he was..." Breath Kate... In...Out...

"He was killed in a car accident." The words cut through me like a knife.

I'm desperately trying to keep my vision clear, I see black spots creeping around the edges.

I need to stay focused. I need to hold it together.

There is compete silence on the other end of the line, I can hear his gentle breathing, but no words. He needs time to process those words. I'm still trying to process it. Eventually I hear him take a large intake of breath.

"How?" He asks calmly.

"Apparently he lost control of his car. The police said it happened really quickly."

The silence between us is huge. Now that I have said the words, I feel wrung out. I don't have the energy to comfort him. I know I should, but my body has gone in to self-preservation mode. The little energy I have left is needed for me and the boys.

Suddenly I hear movement on the other end of the line. The sound of leather releasing its hold, shuffling of papers and the distinctive jangling of keys and snapping of fingers.

"I'm on my way." Not words I expected to hear.

Alex is close to his family, he should be, but we're not. I always thought they didn't accept me, didn't like me. For Dante to drop everything just to be with us, makes me question why we have this distance, why Alex kept us apart from them.

The sound of a hand smothering the phone muffles his next words.

"I need to leave. Now." Words not intended for me.

"No, Dante, please don't." I firmly say to get his attention.

I can't handle the pressure of people, especially in our home. Not tonight.

"I can be there in an hour." He says to me.

"Please Dante, no, I want to just be with the boys."

I drop my chin down to my chest. Exhaustion is taking over; my body is beginning to ache from the stress and tension.

"I'm really very sorry Dante." I quietly say.

His exhale of frustration is audible. Not many would dare say no to Dante.

Quite frankly I couldn't give a toss right now.

"I will call mamma and Benito."

I'm glad he's taking the pressure from my shoulders and listening to me. The thought of calling anyone else is beyond my comprehension.

"Thank you. I appreciate it." And I genuinely mean it.

He hesitates a moment before asking.

"Do you need anything Kate? The boys, how have they taken it? Do they need anything?" I'm touched by his concern for us when he must be as broken as we are.

Glancing towards the lounge, there are 3 sets of eyes on me.

"They're bearing up."

I don't have anything more to add. Not that I'm being rude, I simply have no words to sum up how they are feeling. Nothing can be bought to substitute their loss.

"Can I call you back tomorrow Dante? I'm sorry, I just, ....I don't want to talk right now."

Never a truer word spoken.

"Of course. We'll speak tomorrow." He instantly replies.

I'm about to hang up when I hear him speak softly.

"I'm really very sorry Kate. Really, I am."

I feel the devastation in his voice.

"Me too." Is my only response as I disconnect the call.

Verbalising the words has bought it all home to me.

My husband is dead.

My husband has been killed.

The words are like a dagger to my heart, slashing away with its vicious blade. Leaving me raw, bleeding inside.

It doesn't feel real.

It doesn't feel right.

I can still feel him.

I can feel his heart still.

It all seems like madness.

How can I still feel him?

## Chapter Five

It's oddly satisfying separating pre-cooked rice into individual grains in the bag. Standing with my hip against the counter, I methodically run my finger and thumb of each hand over the packet and divide the grains.

My gaze wanders to the darkness outside, my own reflexion bounces back to me. Eyes almost swollen shut, sore to the touch. My lips quiver involuntarily. Tremors wrack my body, magnified by the quiver of escaped strands of hair. I'm a mess.

Averting my eyes from the reflection, I close the blind, I can't bear to look.

Continuing to separate the rice I empty it into Bears bowl. Peeling the wrapper from the pre-cooked chicken I almost gag as the smell hits me. Turning my face to the side, I prepare his supper, trying not to breathe through my nose. Walking over to Bears feeding mat, I gently place the bowl down.

"Come on Bear. Supper time."

I know he will eat it, but he won't move yet from his sentry point by the boys.

We need to eat. None of us have any appetite but we need sustenance to get us through. I settle on sugar and milk. Filling the kettle, I search the cabinet and find a jar of hot chocolate. Spooning powder into three mugs, adding a dash of milk, I then go in search of biscuits. Smiling to myself, I would normally be horrified at hot chocolate and biscuits for supper. This is not normal. How could it be?

Laying everything on the table, I walk over to the lounge door.

"I've made a hot drink. Do you want to come and have some?"

I plaster a smile on my face to reassure the boys, it must work as they rise from the sofa and follow me back to the kitchen, with Bear in tow.

Taking our seat's, we simultaneously glance towards the head of the table, all having the same thought. I look away quickly before my tears start again.

Sitting in silence. No words are needed right now. We all need head space to process our thoughts. I feel like I'm here but not quite. Hovering above myself. Looking in on the scene like a voyeur. My body is present. Nothing else is.

Holding my steamy mug in my left hand, fingers entwined with the handle, I slowly dunk the biscuit into the frothy creaminess. Watching as it dips in and soaks up the chocolate liquid. My mind is entranced with this simple motion. The perfect symmetry you can create. Dry and wet. Two halves. Opposites creating a whole. The circle complete, regardless of the state of each half, entrusting the other to hold together.

My musings have caused one half to become saturated causing it to fall from its partner. Sliding away from its other half, away into the mug. Separating them for all eternity.

It's late. It's grown dark outside and I've sat here putting off the inevitable. I don't want to climb those stairs. Giving in to my need to sleep will signify the close of the day. The bed will feel too big, too cold. Sleeping there alone scares me. Once I'm alone and in private, I know my resolve will crumble. The barrier holding back the tears will break and the dam will burst. When the day concludes it brings an end to the last day that Alex was alive. Once the clock strikes midnight and the new day begins, I will bear a new moniker. No longer a wife and mother, I become a widow. The thought terrifies me. Widows are old. They have lived a full life with their love. They have laughed together, they have done everything together. Their lives long and full and memories become their constant companion. Alex and I created memories, but not enough. We weren't finished making them.

Opening the back door, I encourage Bear to follow me out. Trotting at his own pace he slowly makes his way out for a wee. Standing on the mat, leaning against the door frame, I look up to the clear sky.

The stars seem brighter, with no light pollution, all the constellations are visible to the naked eye.

I smile at the thought that Marc knows which is which. He knows all the names. I'm happy to simply stare at their magnificence. The gentle twinkling as they hang in the darkness, not too proud to shine.

Hearing Bear rustling in the trees, I turn to the right, trying to make out his form in the inky blackness. With the light from the house behind me, I hoped it would illuminate him. It doesn't. Leaning back in through the open door, I flick the outdoor light on. Twisting back around I look out towards the trees again but I'm still unable to see him as the light doesn't reach that far.

I hear the sound of leaves crunching and twigs snapping under his mammoth weight. I smile to myself. He must be nearly finished. A sound has me spinning to the opposite direction, I jump back in shock suddenly as Bear walks towards me from the left-hand side of the house. He's not looking at me, he's looking into the trees. His gaze is fixed where I heard the noise I thought was him. I see the fur on the nape of his neck stand to attention.

My brain seems too slow to process anything.

"Who's there?" I practically screech.

Of course, there's no answer.

I'm starting to shake.

"Bear come on. Quick."

I turn quickly, and grab hold of the door ready to shut and lock it as soon as Bear passes the threshold.

"Please Bear."

My voice is barely a whisper, but he must sense my desperation.

He walks inside at a quicker trot. I shut the door so firmly I'm surprised it doesn't go through the frame, turning the key in the lock as soon as the latch has engaged. I see my hands shaking. I feel the perspiration on my brow and the twisting knot inside of me. I'm practically shitting myself, I'm so scared. I didn't imagine that this time. Definitely not.

Taking the key from the door I slip it into my jeans pocket and rushing through the house towards the front door, locking that too. Fisting the keys in my hand I spin round. Lights are on in every room and all the curtains and blinds are closed. I sigh in relief. Whatever is outside can't see me, I feel secure with the feeling the material offers. I've never felt uncomfortable in our home before, I've never had a reason to feel scared. I always had Alex to chase those fears away.

The sun is beginning to rise marking the start of a new day.

The first day of the rest of our lives.

Sleep didn't come easily. My thoughts were consumed by Alex, and my dreams were haunted too. I need to get some air, I need to walk.

Pulling on my clothes from yesterday and grabbing the keys, I pad downstairs, Bear is still asleep in his bed. Walking around I open the curtains and blinds and slide the front door key into the lock, but don't unlock it.

It's a humbling feeling letting in the autumnal sun. Dust motes dance in the rays of light. Performing a perfect symmetry with their partners. Entranced by their movements I stand still and watch, trying not to think about anything. My head and body hurt. It feels like the remains of a hangover, without the wine. Normality is needed right now.

Turning on the radio I head over to the coffee machine. Normality.

Breathing in the aroma of the freshly ground beans I take my usual seat at the island. Normality.

Thinking about the day ahead. Not normality.

I quickly try to retract my thoughts, which then makes me think harder about the thoughts I don't want to have. Breathe. Breathe.

Bear is watching me from his bed, nervously, he thinks I'm losing my mind. Maybe I am.

With a despondent sigh I remain seated and finish my coffee.

Taking one task at a time, I may make it through. I need to take it minute by minute, which will become hour by hour and eventually day by day.

That feeling of Alex being gone hasn't informed my heart yet, I can still feel him.

As I rummage through for a piece of paper and pen, I'm bombarded with a flashback of Alex looking in this exact drawer. The junk drawer. Every house has one. Ours is full of pens, paperclips, elastic bands, staples, no stapler, old mobile phones, batteries. Everything you need in your life but doesn't have a home of its own.

I remember walking into the kitchen a few weeks ago, as he was stood staring into the abyss. Snaking my arms around his waist from behind and kissing the centre of his back, his smell invaded my nose, making me smile.

"What are you looking for?" I mumbled into his back.

"You." Was his one-word reply.

He spun round and held me close to him with his arms wrapped tightly. I remember soaking up the warmth of his embrace. My favourite place to be.

With a sigh at my wayward mind, I find the pen and paper.

*Morning Boys*

*I'm going for a walk with Bear*

***Back soon***

***Love you lots jelly tots***

***Mum***

***Xxxxx***

Checking the time on the clock, I add 8.10 to the top of the note, I don't want them to worry.

"Come on lazy bones."

Bear rises from his bed and wanders towards the back door. Retrieving his lead from the hook, I put on my old wax jacket and walking boots. Finding a woolly hat in my coat pocket I pull it low over my ears, the sun may be shining but it's going to be bitterly cold out there.

I pull out the key which is in my jeans pocket still. After unlocking and opening the door, I quickly look around checking the area and turn back to close the door and lock it.

We walk through the garden and out to the open fields, purposely avoiding the wooded area. I'm still a bit creeped out. My imagination must have run away with me last night. Maybe it was a deer or a fox.

With a deep inhale of breath, we take our normal path through the fields. It's so open I start to feel free allowing the weight to temporarily lift from my shoulders. Walking around the field we come out on to the lane. With no cars around I allow Bear to wander off the lead and he's happy for the reprieve. Coming back on ourselves we enter the top of the field near the house. Checking my watch, I see we've been out for almost an hour. My feet start to slow on our return trip. Not from fatigue. The dread of returning and facing the task ahead is slowing me down. I'm not ready to return to reality but I have to. They need me.

As we near the house I spy two large black cars sitting in the driveway. Unfamiliar cars. We're both muddy from our walk so I head towards the back door. Inserting the key, I open the door inwards and gasp at the sight before me.

Standing with his back to me. an arm wrapped around each of the boys, hugging them to his chest, I see his 6ft 3-inch height, muscular frame, broad shoulders, dark lustrous hair and golden glow to the nape of his neck. Stumbling back slightly I clutch a hand to my chest as my jaw begins to quiver. I'm seeing things. I must be. It can't be. Taking a sharp intake of breath, I have to hold the door frame tightly. My body begins to sway as a sob rips its way past my lips. He slowly turns towards me and I see. I have to blink rapidly to clear my vision as the dark spots begin to descend. It's not him. I can't believe my mistake. The trick my eyes played. The cruelness my brain has performed.

Standing before me hugging my boys is Dante, Alex's older brother. From the side of him I see a movement and my eyes quickly dart over. Benni rushes forwards with his arms outstretched, ready to catch me if I fall. I can see from his eyes that he has spotted my mistake. Swallowing deeply to keep the emotions in, I move my eyes to the floor. I need to ground myself. I need to school my emotions. I don't want these people to see me break. I don't really know them. I never imagined they would be here in our home. I never imagined they would come to us. I always got the impression they didn't want to know us. That they didn't want to fully be a part of our lives. Why are they here now?

Benni reaches my side and encourages me through the door, gently closing it behind me, holding my arm as if I were infirm. I don't want to show any weakness in front of them, so I simply smile a thanks and detach myself from his grasp. The aroma of coffee invades my nostrils along with the smell of food and I have to quickly swallow as a feeling of nausea overcomes me. Sick from my grief.

Breathing in through my nose and out through my mouth I centre myself and start to take in my kitchen. Dante is stood with an arm around each of my boys. I'm uncomfortable with his closeness to them, I don't really know him. I swallow the lump in my throat and hide my fear. He unnerves me. Alex and he are almost identical, in looks and physique. I'm still shaken from my mistake at his identity.

Benni hovers close by, with a sad smile on his face. Benni is more familiar to us, more approachable. Alex and I have spent more time with Benni then Dante. Happy by nature he is easy to like.

The sound of others has me turning my head in their direction. Mrs Rossi, Alex's mum, sits at the table. A look of total devastation covers her face. I need to remember that they are Alex's family too. He didn't just belong to us.

Standing behind her are 2 men that I don't recognise. Intimidating in their presence they silently watch the scenes unfold.

Maria rises from her chair elegantly and moves my way. She is a wonder to behold, her grace is magnificent. She may be in her late 60's but she has the composure of somebody half her age, I've always felt intimidated by her. Dressed to perfection she wouldn't look out of place walking in Florence or Paris or Kensington.

With a lace handkerchief twisted in one hand, she walks towards me with her other hand outstretched. Laying her soft palm against my cheek she looks deep into my eyes with a look of sorrow and understanding. This magnificent woman lost her husband too. She feels my pain. She understands my loss like no one else in this room can. With her one small touch she has shown me more kindness than I've received from her in 20 years. Alex didn't want us to get too close to his family. He made us feel that they weren't nice people. He wanted to maintain a distance and I never questioned him. They were his family he knew them best.

"La mia bellissima figlia."

I've never learnt Italian fluently, merely picking up a few words and phrases over the years from Alex. I frown in response to her, showing my lack of understanding.

"I talk to you in English."

She gives an encouraging nod, taking my hand leading me to sit at the table.

"How are you bellissima?"

I should be asking her that. Her son has died, and she's more concerned for me.

With a deep intake of breath, I answer her honestly.

"Heartbroken."

What else can I say?

Nodding, she offers me a sad smile, patting my hand with affection and understanding.

"My beautiful Allesandro. He is taken from us."

We are united in our pain. The loss of someone we both loved dearly.

Dante walks over to the table and takes a seat at the head, I hear a quiet gasp from behind me. No one sits in Alex's seat. It's reserved solely for him.

"You can't sit there." Leo informs him emphatically. "That's my dad's chair."

A look of shock registers on Dante's face. His demeanour displaying his displeasure at being called out over his choice of seating. I'm proud of Leo for standing up for his dad and standing up to this intimidating man.

"I apologise Leonardo. It was not my intention to dishonour your father. You are the head of this house now. This is your seat."

Rising from the chair, Dante moves around the table to sit opposite Maria and me. He looks at her hand still holding mine, then to his mother and them to me. A strange look crossing his face.

"We need to discuss the arrangements Kate."

I know I need to organise his funeral, I didn't expect Dante to be so forthright. I thought I would have a little more time before anything needed to be set in motion.

"What were Alex's' wishes?" He asks.

Many years ago, we discussed the morbid details of our demise, both assuming we would go simultaneously. We wanted to be buried together, side by side in the local cemetery for all eternity. Neither of us wanted it to be a morbid affair. It would be a celebration of our lives. The love we had shared over the ages of time. He was adamant he didn't want a fuss.

I relay this to Dante with my head bowed, avoiding his icy glare. Maria halts her caressing of my hand and I see her shoot a look to Dante from my peripheral vision. This is not what they expected. I know they want to say more, I can feel the hesitation in the air.

Looking up I stare Dante in the eye.

"I will honour my husbands' wishes. He will be buried here at Bramley End. This was his home."

I see the look of displeasure on his face. Inside I strengthen my resolve whilst mentally straightening my backbone. I will not back down.

"Si." Is his one-word response.

"I have to wait to make any arrangements. The police wanted to speak with me again."

Dante shoots a questioning look to his brother and I follow his line of vision. Benni has stood back and said nothing but his presence a balm to my nerves.

Benni furrows his brow and shrugs his shoulders with an imperceptible shake to his head. Looking back at Dante I see his nod of understanding. They're having a silent conversation. Private dialogue only they can decipher. What are they saying, what are they discussing?

Looking back to Benni I ask.

"What? What's the problem?"

Benni drags his eyes from Dante and plasters a smile on his face. A smile I notice that doesn't reach his eyes.

"They probably have routine questions for you."

"Like what?" I fire back

I see his brow furrow slightly. It's a trait that Alex has. Had. Alex used to do that. I know he is just about to lie to me.

"They will just want to find out his movements for the day. Try to plot his route. That sort of thing."

"Why would they need to do that?"

I genuinely want to know why the inspector needs to speak with me again and I'm curious as to how Benni will answer.

"We will not worry now. We wait for them to visit. Dante will sort it out." Maria pats my hand affirmatively, putting an end to the matter.

I'm not happy for Dante to 'sort it out'.

Looking back at Benni I press him further,

"Why would they need to know his movements? I have no idea why he was near Honiton that day."

"Honiton?" Dante asks, almost aggressively.

Spinning my head back to face him I nod in answer to his question.

"His car crashed on the road between Honiton and Waters End."

The look Dante fires to Benni is demanding. Quickly turning my head, I see Benni's face devoid of anything. He shows nothing outwardly.

He simply shrugs his shoulders.

"I have no idea."

He does, I sense it. He knows something. Something he isn't willing to share with me, or is he hiding it from Dante. My head hurts from the conversation, so I sag back into the chair.

The boys have remained quiet throughout our discussions, choosing to stand by the island with Bear at their feet. I sense that Bear's not comfortable with all these strangers in our home. In particular the two men he is watching intently. They haven't moved or spoken.

Leo walks towards the table and stands behind my chair. I can sense he wants to ask something but feels intimidated by the family's presence.

Swivelling in the chair I look up to him expectantly, encouraging him to speak.

"Is..Is.. umm... Isn't Honiton close to the airport?"

As soon as he speaks a feeling of dread covers me. Looking up to Benni I raise my brow in question.

"Why would he be near the airport?"

Benni balks slightly belying his poise.

"I doubt very much he was going to the airport Kate." A small smile lifting his lips ."He wouldn't go anywhere without you."

I can tell by his response I won't get any more answers from him.

## Chapter Six

My stomach rumbles to my embarrassment. I haven't eaten today.

"We eat. Come bellisima."

Maria gestures towards the food laid at the table. There's enough to feed an army. Fresh fruit platters and the aroma of flaky pastries invading my nostrils. I inwardly groan. I can't eat. It's not fair. Alex doesn't have the luxury of eating these beautiful delicacies.

"Eat." Maria encourages.

Turning to look at the boys I nod in encouragement. Marc walks to the cupboard to retrieve plates and returns to the table hesitantly. He hasn't said a word. He is uncomfortable with these virtual strangers too.

Sitting as close to me as they can the boys timidly take a pastry each. Gingerly I pick up a piece of melon and nibble at the edges.

I see Dante lift his head to the two silent guests and flick his head towards the door in an act of dismissal. Following his silent order, they start to move towards the hall. With a furrowed brow I turn back to Dante.

"Where are they going?"

Dante turns to me, trying to disguise his irritation.

"They are checking your security." He responds tartly. "You will be alone now. We need to ensure your safety."

His answer tramples on my heart at the reminder of our loss.

"It is not safe for you to be here. They need to check you have enough security to protect you."

With that he looks back to the two men and gives a more determined flick of his chin. Silently warning them to heed his demands.

"The house is already secure, Alex made sure." I quietly say.

We were always Alex's number one priority and our safety was always at the forefront of his mind. When we moved into the house he had the windows and doors changed to the most secure locks, along with a state-of-the-art alarm system with motion sensors. I've never used it. Never seen the need. Maybe now we should.

Dante simply nods at my response. Marking an end to the subject.

Maria fusses over the boys ensuring they eat something. Secretly I'm glad. As she is their last remaining grandparent, I've always thought the boys needed a more familiar relationship with her. Alex felt they didn't need anyone but us. My parents passed long before they were born. Both died simultaneously, no doubt from their hedonistic life-style.

Rising from the table I make my way to the coffee machine. Taking a cup from the cupboard I turn and wiggle it in silent offering at the party assembled at the table. With several shakes of their heads, I turn and place the cup under the spout pressing the button. Happy for a moments space. I lean my hands on the counter and bow my head down taking a deep breath. Despondency takes over me for a few moments.

I feel, more than hear, someone move close to my side. Their arm leans up to the cupboard above me.

"How are you?" Benni all but whispers into my ear as he removes a cup.

I'm not sure why he tries to hide his question from his mother and brother, but I appreciate it.

Taking my cup from the machine, I angle my head slightly to allow him to hear my words more clearly.

"Scared. I don't know how I can go on without him."

Benni places his cup under the spout with one hand and gently rubs my shoulder with his other.

"I don't understand how he can be gone." Turning more fully to Benni. "I can still feel him. Here."

Pressing at my heart with my balled fist tears leap to my sore eyes, threatening to spill.

Unable to look him in the eye any longer I begin to turn away.

"It's going to be OK. We'll take care of you all." He all but whispers.

How can he say that, how can he say such a thing? His flippant words crush me.

I turn a scowl towards him showing my hurt and displeasure at his words and walk back to the table, coffee in hand, noting Dante's gaze fixed on Benni and me. The look that crosses his face makes me falter in my step. A look I can't decipher, but it's almost suspicious. Glancing back over my shoulder, Benni has plastered an unaffected look on his and turned back to finish making his drink.

After the boys have eaten, I suggest they might want to take Bear outside and feed him. It's obvious from Leo's demeanour he doesn't want to leave me alone. Marc can't get up from the table fast enough. Grabbing his clean bowl and food from the pantry Bear plods along behind Marc and out the back door. Leo is still sat at the table and I silently communicate that it's OK to leave. The pressure in the room is palpable. I wish I had the luxury of immaturity and could walk away too.

As the back door shuts I open my mouth to speak as one of the two men walk back into the kitchen attracting Dante's attention immediately.

"Boss, Rite's here."

With a frown I look back to Dante and he simply nods. Rising from his chair, he straightens his sleeves and looks down to me in a condescending way.

"I will speak with him."

Temporarily flummoxed I sit there as he makes his way towards the door. Snapping out of my inertia I rise from my seat. Maria grasps at my hand to stop me. Looking down at her, I simply remove my hand from her hold.

"Thank you, Dante, but that won't be necessary." I hear a small gasp from Maria and I swear Benni chuckles.

Looking toward the nameless man, I raise my eyebrows in expectation.

"I believe it is my house and I will see to any visitors."

Striding past him I make my way to the hall.

"Good morning Mrs Rossi."

Nodding at Inspector Rites greeting I gesture my hand towards the lounge. I'm not happy to allow him access to any other parts of our home, but the kitchen is currently a bit busy for my liking.

Sitting in an armchair, I motion for him to take a seat.

"What can I do for you Inspector?" I simply ask on an exhale.

"How are you today Mrs Rossi?" His question seems lacking in any compassion. I don't like this man. He delivered the words that annihilated our world.

I choose not to answer and continue to look at him with raised brows. I'm not sure what he was expecting but I will not show any emotions to this man.

Everything about him unnerves me. Secretly I wish Dante had dealt with his questions. Sitting on my velvet sofa in his cheap suit and scuffed shoes he looks totally out of place. I'm not a snob, never have been, never will be. But the look he portrays is not one of a professional man. In my stricken grief yesterday I didn't notice, but he has a look about him that I don't trust. I've always told the boys that we have an inbuilt sixth sense. If you don't feel comfortable with a situation, trust your instincts. It will never let you down.

I sense a presence behind me and hear the footfall on the floor.

"How can we help you Inspector?" Dante's voice is low but menacing.

The inspector looks up and almost balks at the imposing figure standing behind me. Laying his hand on my shoulder over the back of the chair, he stiffly shows our solidarity.

"I am Dante Rossi, Allesandro's brother, and in turn brother-in-law to Mrs Rossi." Emphasising his claim with a pat. I'm not sure what his statement is meant to achieve but it's clear it's been understood. The inspector looks at me and then back up to the imposing figure of Dante.

"I wanted to check Mrs Rossi was OK after the devastating news yesterday."
I can tell he's lying my spider senses are still tingling.

Dante moves around my chair and stands over the inspector, blocking his view of me. I hear rather than see the Inspector swallow.

"I...I just, umm, have a few, err, uhm, questions for Mrs Rossi." He stutters, Dante's imposing figure unnerving Rite.

"Ask them." He responds bluntly.

Alex was often that way with people he didn't know or trust. The thought makes me smile slightly inside. Looking around Dante's body Rite finds me.

"Do you know why Mr Rossi would have any reasons to be near Honiton yesterday?"

His question kills the small seed of happiness I had, plummeting me back to this hell.

"No, I don't." My head is spinning with unwanted thoughts. "Perhaps he needed to see somebody or there was a diversion, I have no idea." I really don't. I've been racking my brain and I can't think of a single reason why.

Reaching out to Dante I touch the back of his leg in a silent plea for him to move aside, begrudgingly he does, and sits down on the sofa next to the Inspector. The inspector becomes even more uncomfortable, shifting slightly to extend the void between them. Looking at them from my vantage point these two men are from totally different realms. I never noticed how different Alex was to other men. Ordinary men. I was always too consumed with his presence. I never saw anyone but him.

Viewing these men side by side, a man who was Alex's double, against the inspector, I start to see a wealth of differences. The cut of the clothes, the quality of the shoes, the physique, the hair, the poise. Alex had all these traits and they suited him with his warm character, happy outlook. Features I absolutely adored. On Dante they are imposing, intimidating, almost menacing. He holds himself in a way I never saw in Alex. How can two men be so identical in their looks and yet eons apart in their countenance.

"Was anybody else injured?" I find myself asking.

I'm not strong enough yet to learn all the details, but my conscious mind hopes no one else was hurt.

With another audible swallow the inspector looks at Dante first, then me.

"No, there wasn't."

My curiosity has started to get the better of me.

"How did he crash then? What caused it?" I had convinced myself somebody else had caused the accident. That they were to blame.

Once again, the inspector looks at Dante before he answers.

"It appears he lost control of his vehicle on the bend. We suspect he was travelling at high speed."

Dante and I snap a look to each other, our look confirming what the other is thinking.

"That is impossible!" Dante spits at the Inspector, "Allesandro was never careless in his driving."

Alex was always careful. He was a proficient driver. Constantly he would ask me to slow down, especially on the school run as he knew how distracted I could get. This just doesn't make any sense. Alex was the safest of drivers. I trusted him with my life. Our boys lives. He would never take any risks.

I'm hesitant at my next question, hope waving at me as she stands in the background.

"Are you 100% sure it is Alex?"

I glower at the Inspector as I feel Dante's hard stare on me. I know it's cruel to raise this question in front of his brother, but I still can't believe he has died. I still feel him.

"I'm really sorry Mrs Rossi, but the dental records have confirmed it this morning."

And there goes hope, turning her back and walking away.

Something is niggling at me. I can't put my finger on it, but something just isn't, well, right.

Putting it down to my grief, I look at the Inspector in anticipation of his questions.

Seeing the Inspector to the door, I feel my shoulders slump. For a small window of time I thought they had made a mistake. The pathologist confirmed it is Alex, smashing that window to pieces.

With one hand pressed against the closed door, I brace my arm to take the weight of my heavy head. I want to just stop it all just for a moment. Stop the world from spinning to give me a second to catch up. It appears, the inspector's words, that Alex was speeding along the Honiton Road and he took the bend too fast. There is a lack of skid marks approaching the bend which I'm finding a bit odd, surely Alex would have braked as he saw the bend approaching. Consequently, the car ploughed into a large oak tree. Due to the speed they suspect he was travelling at he was killed on impact. Alex's car is similar to Dante's, large, safe, expensive. There are so many flaws to this I'm struggling to believe it's real.

Walking back into the kitchen, the boys have returned and naturally Bear is in tow. Sitting at their feet I see him eyeing one of the nameless men.

"Who are you?" I ask, sod manners, this is my home.

With a shocked look on his face he turns to Dante.

"He is an associate of mine." Dante intones.

"Why is he here? In my house." I return deadpan.

Dante looks me in the eye. I can see he is deliberating what to say, I lift my eyebrows at his silent contemplation.

"He works for the family."

"As what?"

Dante is beginning to get pissed off at my questions.

"Today he is my driver. He is also in charge of security."

"Why doesn't my dog like him?" The question confounds him.

"Bear doesn't like him. In fact, he's not comfortable with either of them. Why?"

I've always lived by the motto, 'If my dog doesn't like you, then neither do I'. It's always served me well.

Bear chooses that moment to walk over and stand in front of me. Protecting me. He senses my need for him.

"I am sorry your dog does not like my men." With a fierce look he half turns to the nameless two. "They will wait outside." Dismissing them instantly.

The air in the kitchen is uncomfortable. Dante may be in charge of the Rossi company. He is not in charge in our home.

"I think it's time we left." Benni pipes up. "We'll leave you alone for now."

"No, they come with us. They come back to the house." Maria seems distressed at the prospect of leaving us here.

"Thank you, Maria, but our place is here." I'm not leaving. This is our home. This is where I feel closest to Alex. I need to be here.

"Come mamma. We will see them again soon." Dante encourages his mother from her seat. "Do you need anything before we leave?" Dante holds his mothers' arm as he turns to me to ask.

"No thank you Dante. We'll be fine."

Fine is possibly the worst word in the English vocabulary. Fine is a word you use when you really aren't fine but you're trying to comfort the person who is doing the asking. Soothing their integrity. Allowing them to walk away on the misconception that you are in fact fine. All the while you are breaking apart inside. With the word fine, they can walk away with a clear conscience.

Once they all leave, I set about clearing the mess in the kitchen. Simple tasks. Normality. The fridge is stocked with trays and dishes of home cooked food. I'm slightly taken aback at the presumptuousness of the act. Enraged they had the audacity to think I couldn't feed my own family. After a moment of anger, I let it pass and see it as the act it was meant as. Love. They are simply showing their love and support in the only way they know how. We don't have a close relationship. They have no way of knowing what it is we need.

What I really need right now is for someone to hold me. Tight. To clasp me in their arms telling me it's all going to be OK. Making the hurt go away. Alex would have made the pain disappear. He always made everything right. I need to learn how to do that for myself now. I need to hold us together as a family. I need to become the force that he was. I need to become the protector. I need to become strong.

## Chapter Seven

A few days after the family descended on us I receive another visit from Inspector Rite. The sight of his dirty car pulling into the drive has me sighing in dismay. I've answered his questions. What more can I tell him? I have no idea why Alex was there that day. It doesn't matter how many ways he asks the same question the answer will always be the same.

Telling Bear to stay in his bed I walk into the hall ready to open the door. Thankfully the boys have gone out for a while. They need a slice of normality in their lives right now, and they certainly don't need to hear any more of what this man has to say. Both boys are visiting friends in the village and will be home for dinner. They need to talk through their grief with someone other than me. They need to do normal things teenage boys do. I'm jealous of them. I can't escape it.

Opening the door, I look at the Inspector with raised brows. My silent question at his return is clear on my face. With a fake smile he walks up to the door. I make no move to invite him in and lean my hip against the door jam. It's damn cold out here. I would rather freeze than allow his presence to taint our home further though.

"Good morning Mrs Rossi, or can I call you Kate?"

I don't like his familiarity. I don't like him.

"Mrs Rossi is fine." Is my simple reply.

Rite stops walking forward, understanding registers on his face that he isn't welcome inside.

"I wanted to talk to you about your husband's family."

Now that's not what I expected him to say.

"What about them?"

"Are you aware of their connections in London?" As he asks his question my phone rings from the back pocket of my jeans. Taking it out I see Dante's name. Rejecting the call, I turn back to the inspector. My reply is on my lips as the phone in my hand rings again. Something in me says I need to answer his call. Sliding my finger to answer I look at the inspector, silently telling him to wait.

"Hello."

"Kate are you OK?" He sounds rushed, unlike the composed Dante I have come to know. His question asking far more than the actual words.

"Yes.... Why?" I'm curious at the coincidence of his call. It's almost as if he knows I'm uncomfortable. How the hell did he know to call me at this very moment?

"Are you sure you are OK Kate? You do not sound yourself."

"Can I call you back in a minute or two? I've got a visitor right now."

"Who?" I get a sudden sense that he knows who's standing at my door. Turning slightly, I stare into the security camera facing the door. A sudden cold runs down my spine. Dante told me one of his nameless was in charge of security.

"Are you watching me?"

The delay in his response is my answer. If I could see him I would witness the same traits Alex had when he was just about to lie to me.

"Don't lie to me Dante." My voice may come across as quiet but the authority in my words is clear.

"It's for your own safety. We need to know you and the boys are safe. You are on your own."

I appreciate his honesty; however, I do not appreciate him invading our privacy.

"What does the inspector want?"

Looking at Rite, his distress is apparent in his stance. He knows it's Dante.

"I'll call you back." Disconnecting the call, I glare at the man before me.

"What do you want Inspector?"

Shifting his feet, I can see he is formulating his next words.

"How well do you know your husband's family Mrs Rossi?"

Not sure where this conversation is going I choose not to answer. I have no desire to say anything unfavourable, I hardly know them, but they have shown how much they care.

"What is it you're asking?" I retort.

I see him shuffling again. Not sure if it's from his discomfort or the cold. I wrap my arms around my torso trying to conserve some heat. It really is cold out here. It doesn't matter how cold it gets though, he isn't welcome in our home. I wish I had the security of Alex wrapped around me.

"The Rossi family have many connections in and around London." He imparts a knowing look. "Connections of an un-savoury nature."

My confused look is my only reply.

"Your husband was believed to be involved in a number of businesses."

This I already know. Alex ran their nightclub Gia and helped Dante within the Rossi company from time to time.

"And how is that linked to my husband's death?" I really have no idea where these questions are leading.

"We are investigating a number of illegal incidents that have led us back to the Rossi family. Do you have any idea of the true nature of your husband's business?"

I must be really missing something here. I have no idea what.

"He was the manager of Gia, the nightclub owned by the Rossi company." I can't be clearer. How can managing a nightclub be of interest to the police?

My phone begins ringing in my hand. Looking down I see Benni's name. Seriously. Did Dante call him. Is he going to question me too?

"Yes Benni?" I say into the phone in exasperation. "What do you want?"

My question comes across as harsh and a little rude, but right now I've had enough of people questioning me.

"Just checking you're OK. Dante called me."

I knew it. There is being protective and there's being an arse.

"I've already told Dante, I'm fine. I'll call him back in a minute. The inspector was just leaving."

I aim a pointed look at Rite. Understanding of his dismissal clear on his face.

Disconnecting yet another call, I look back to the Inspector.

"Is that all?"

I have no desire to talk to anyone anymore. His banal questions are pointless. They won't bring my husband back. What's the point in them?

"I'm sorry to have disturbed you." It's obvious he's not. "That will be all. For now."

His final words come out almost as a threat. I really don't like this man. He un-nerves me.

Turning away from him, I go to close the door. As he walks away he turns back, flicking a quick glance to the camera and whispers.

"Be careful."

I turn my head to the camera and then look back at him, but he's already moved away.

Making a cup of green tea to warm me, I sit at the island to sort through my thoughts before I return Dante's call which I abruptly ended. My stomach has been tied up in knots for days. Since Alex died. It's hardly surprising. The thought of eating makes me nauseous. I thought I would try a simple tea to settle my stomach. It seems to be working. I can't go without my morning coffee though.

With my hands wrapped around the cup for comfort, Dante's name flashes up on my phone. It's like he knows I've just sat down.

"Yes Dante." I say on a huff.

"What did he want?"

Blunt. Direct. To the point. I'm getting used to his mannerism. Polar opposite to my caring husband.

"I'm not really sure." I answer him honestly.

I hesitate before I divulge what the inspector said. I would have told Alex straight away, but something makes me delay with him. I have to remember that he is family, even if he did invade my privacy.

"How long have you been spying on us?" I jump straight in.

Previously I would never have had the guts to be so forward. I've got nothing to lose.

"I told you Kate, it is for your security. We need to know you and the boys are safe."

"How long Dante?" More forceful this time. I'm really not holding back.

He hesitates for a moment, and I can tell he's starting to get annoyed at my directness.

"Since we visited. The day after Alex died."

I appreciate his honesty.

"Are you having me watched too?"

I have to know how far his security reaches. I know I've seen something on two occasions, but I've had a sense of being watched. It may be the security system, I really have no idea.

"Watched? When?" He responds forcefully.

OK not the response I expected. Dante has no idea what I'm talking about.

"It's nothing. Don't worry." If it's not Dante, then who is it?

"When? How often? Where?" Dante rapidly fires his questions at me. I'm a little taken aback at his forcefulness. I take a breath in and remind myself that he's not in charge of my life. I am.

"It's probably nothing. Forget I said anything." I don't think my response will appease him, so I head straight into my conversation with the Inspector.

"Rite questioned me about Alex's job." Leaving that there, I hope Dante will fill in any blanks.

He doesn't.

"What did he say?"

So, we're going for questions rather than answers.

"Just that. He asked me if I knew what he did."

I don't mention his questions about the family. I will let that sink in and see what conclusions I come up with myself.

"You know he worked for the family business." It's more of a statement but sounds strangely like a question. "He has run Gia for many years."

"You seem distressed when he was talking to you. You were uncomfortable".

Yes, I was uncomfortable with Rites presence, but more so at the thought of being watched.

"Why do you have a live feed of my door?"

I'm curious as to what his response will be. Will he fob me off again?

"As I've said before. We need to make sure you are all safe."

In that moment I get a sneaking suspicion that there is more. Something he isn't saying. My phone notifies me of another incoming call, checking the screen I see it's Marc. There's also a message from Leo.

"I need to go. We WILL talk about this later."

I hang up on Dante for a second time and accept the call from Marc.

"Hey what's wrong?"

Marc has been to visit a friend he's known since birth. I trust the family. Alex was always suspicious of everyone. I could never understand why.

"Can you come and get me please?"

Exhaustion sounding in his voice.

"I'll be right there. See you in 5 minutes."

"Thanks mum." He hesitates for a moment then says. "Love you, please drive carefully."

That hits home hard.

"I will. Love you more. Bye."

Hanging up I quickly read the message from Leo. He wants me to pick him up too. Firing off a quick text to say I will be there after I collect Marc, I grab my car keys and head for the door.

"Back in a minute Bear. Just going to get the boys."

I know I sound mad talking to him, but he does understand. He does.

Pulling out of the drive, I take a quick glance to the trees. Nothing. What did I expect? I'm being paranoid. I laugh to myself thinking that Dante probably has a drone following my every move, or a tracker on my car. Actually, hang on, how would I know if there is a tracker. Where do they hide them? Thinking back to the day they visited, one of the nameless went outside. Could they have stuck a device on my car. Now I'm really getting paranoid.

Pulling up to Marc's friend's house, I call him to say I'm outside. I'm not being rude. No that's a lie. I am being rude. I really don't want to hear sympathetic words. I'm finally getting my head around the situation we're in, I don't need someone knocking me back down again with their commiserations.

Marc answers on the first ring.

"I see you. I'm just coming." And with that the front door opens.

Rushing down their pathway Marc jumps into the front seat. Not looking back. That's not good.

"Too soon?" My simple question is more of a statement.

Putting on his belt and adjusting the seat he responds with a nod. I give a cursory wave over my shoulder to his friend's mum and pull away. Marc is silent on the way to collect Leo. This is really not good.

Leo is out the door as I pull into his friends drive. I unlock the doors and he jumps straight in the back seat. Not a single word of complaint about him being the oldest and how he should sit in the front. Nothing.

"Thanks mum." I hear him mutter.

We drive back to the house in silence, the radio playing to fill the void. I realise then that they are struggling. They haven't been back to school this week. More for my own selfish reasons than theirs. We need a change of scenery after the funeral. We need to take this last hurdle together before we can start the process of healing. Start to build our new lives as a smaller unit. A different dynamic.

Dinner is a quiet affair. Not bothering with the dining table, we sit around the island eating parmigiana that Maria left us. The freezer is fully stocked with every conceivable dish possible. Neighbours have been kind, dropping off their offerings along with their condolences. Some of it was very welcome. Others not so much. When a member of your family dies people crawl from the woodwork and show false sympathy, trying to befriend you just to get all the gory details. Most of those people would cross the street to avoid Alex. They had never even given him the time of day, and now they act like he was their friend. If only they had taken the time to get to know him.

The boys offer up small snippets of conversation about their days, but it's obvious how tired they are. They offer to clear up, but I let me off. They need to recharge their batteries. They need some time alone.

I stand up to start clearing the mostly uneaten food and Leo walks up and holds me tight. As he's taller than me he rests his chin on my head, I hear him sniffle.

"I love you." I say into his chest.

He will grow to be tall like his father. I hope he inherits his other traits too.

Marc joins us, and Leo opens his arm to include him in our hug.

"I love you both so much."

We stand there, the three of us, holding on tightly to each other. Using each other as an anchor. I will not cry. I will not cry. We're doing alright. We're strong. We've got each other. We just need to get through the funeral in a few days. We can do this. We have to.

After a while Bear decides he wants to be a part of our huddle and noses his way in. A laughter emanates from all 3 of us. The first true laughter we have had for some time. A laughter that is needed right now. Really needed.


## Chapter Eight

Waking early every morning isn't easy. It makes the days so much longer. Whilst I'm asleep I can escape the truth for a few short hours. In those hours Alex still visits me though. Memories of our time together mixes with our dreams we had for the future. My heart still hasn't got the message that he's gone. I still feel him. All the time. Maybe it will hit me after the funeral.

Dragging myself from bed, I quickly shower and go downstairs to make a coffee, putting the radio on as I go. Normality. Sitting on my usual stool at the island I look around and survey my house. The funeral is tomorrow, and I need to move some of the furniture to make way for guests. I chose to have the wake at our house. I don't know why. The mess is going to be horrendous. I just wanted it to be here. Looking around I see a few sentimental items that need putting somewhere safe. They may be of no great importance to anyone else, but they're important to us. Finishing my coffee, I let the dog out and then feed him. He has been so neglected lately. We all need to get away. A change of scenery would help us all. Placing his bowl on the outside patio I look up towards the trees. There's nothing there. Bear shows no interest at all. Leaving him to eat I move back into the kitchen to find a box.

Leo and Marc come down the stairs as I'm placing items into the box. A look of horror on their faces.

"What's going on?" Marc asks whilst Leo looks around.

I didn't think these maudlin items would have registered with them. What teenage boy notices decorative items.

With a small smile on my lips I reassure them both.

"It's ok, don't panic. I'm just boxing up the important stuff to keep it safe."

The look of relief on their faces make me appreciate them more. They know how important the small things in life are.

Carefully the boys help me pack away objects. A stone from the beach we took Bear for the first time. A photo of us all at a theme park on a ride. A shell with a hole the shape of a heart. A caricature from a holiday when the boys were young. To others these objects are inconsequential. To us, they are more important than gold. I decide to put them in Alex's study. I don't know why, it feels like he will look after them for us. I haven't been in there since he died. I couldn't bring myself to unlock the door. It was his domain. I can do it now. I can.

Placing the box on the hall table I go back to the kitchen to get the spare key from the junk drawer. I have to talk to the police as I need Alex's personal effects returned. I don't want to talk to them yet, maybe next week.

The boys are making breakfast as I walk into the room. I see it's a competition. How much cereal can you get in a bowl without it spilling. Marc goes to get the milk from the fridge as Leo walks over to the drawers for spoons.

Rummaging through the junk drawer Leo stands next to me, patiently waiting to get to the cutlery drawer above it. I find the key, starting to close the drawer, when Leo stops me and pulls out a phone. I noticed it the other day when I was looking for a pen to leave them a note. I just assumed it was something one of the boys had thrown in there. I didn't pay it any mind, Leo on the other hand is looking at with a lot more interest.

"Who's is this?" He asks, turning it over and back again. He looks up at me expectantly.

"I thought it was yours, or Marc's." I respond turning my head from Leo to Marc and back again.

"Why would we have one of these. They're crap."

Maybe I should take more notice of technology. As long as it works, I'm not bothered by what model it is. Alex always bought our phones, insisting the boys had the latest model. I would simply be handed a new phone every year when the contract was renewed. Never really thought about it before. Another thing I need to know how to handle.

"I don't know then." I say looking at the device in his hand.

"Where do you think it came from?" He asks still looking at the device.

Pressing the button on the side, Leo tries to turn it on, but the battery is dead.

"Do we have a charger for that model?" I ask Leo.

A shake of his head is his only response. If it's not the boys', and it's definitely not mine, then it must have belonged to Alex. That doesn't make sense though. Why would he have another phone. I really don't know what to think.

"Leave it in there till we can find a charger that fits it." I inform Leo.

I'm just as intrigued as he is. I want to know what it contains.

Placing it back in the drawer Leo then closes it and opens the one above to retrieve spoons.

Putting the key in the lock to Alex's study feels wrong. This was his space, his domain. He would occasionally work from home and the study was for his sole use. Since the boys were young and could walk they would barge into any room with an open door, shouting and singing and trying to get attention. With so many calls to make he kept the door closed to reduce their interruptions and noise. He just never got out of the habit. Even I would knock and wait. I would never dream of going in without his permission. To go in there now without him present feels like I'm trespassing.

Holding the key in place I can't bring myself to turn it in the lock. I'm not strong enough yet. I can't go in there.

Slowly taking it out, I tuck it in my pocket and turn around to pick the box up from the hall table. I'll put it in the wardrobe. It will be just as safe there.

The boys are both stood in the kitchen doorway watching me. I try to give them a reassuring smile, but it's not very convincing. Leo gives a subtle nod to his head, putting his arm around Marc as he guides him back to their cereal. I'm grateful. They're there if I need them.


It's been a long day, but I'm not ready for it to end as tomorrow will come too soon. I called the funeral directors earlier to ensure everything is in place. They have been amazing. Mr Bond has been both efficient and professional whilst being sympathetic. He took care of all of the arrangements. I would have been completely lost with it all. Once the death certificate was completed they set everything in motion as Alex had to be collected from the police morgue via private ambulance. Mr Bond asked me for the clothing I wanted him to be buried in. The thought had never occurred to me before. What do you bury someone in? I chose a beautiful grey suit with a crisp white shirt. It was already pristine, but I decided to wash and iron it again for him. It would be the last opportunity I would have. I deliberated long and hard about his underwear. Would the embalmer be male or female? Would they dress him? Would they handle him with the care and love I would?

The thought of another woman dressing him broke me. I was sat in the wardrobe with a pair of his boxer shorts screwed up in my hand sobbing uncontrollably. The boys found me wiping my tears on them. I couldn't explain to them what had triggered my tears. It would be too hard. Too personal. They just sat on the floor on either side of me as we held each other tight. They didn't ask any questions, for which I was more than grateful.

The notice for the funeral was placed in the appropriate papers informing people of the details. We decided we only needed one car to follow Alex in the hearse. When I called Dante to inform him, his displeasure was evident. I've since learnt he has ordered 2 more cars. I apologised to Mr Bond as I imagine Dante wasn't too polite with his request.

The flowers were easy. Since we have been married Alex has bought me fresh lilies every week without fail. I would place them around the house on any available surface. The florist is creating a beautiful wreath of Lilies. The boys wanted DAD in bright coloured flowers. They thought he would appreciate it. It would make him smile.

The village church always has an amazing display of flowers, so it will look beautiful. I gave the church a donation towards their next display.

The vicar has been incredibly supportive. I was unsure if Alex could be buried here in the village. Although he wasn't actively involved in the Catholic church, Alex was still Catholic. The vicar informed me that The Vatican no longer required burial in a Catholic cemetery. I understood it might upset his family, but I wanted to keep Alex close to us. Maria isn't happy at my decision when she called me this week. I explained to her, as I did to Dante, these are Alex's wishes, they have to honour them.

My only real task was to organise the wake. We chose a local catering company who will come in and set everything up whilst we're at the church. I asked the boys to choose the buffet menu. They needed to feel a part of the organising. They've opted for a simple affair of sandwiches and finger food. I don't know how people can eat at funerals. I know I won't. They also offer a stocked bar service including wines and spirits. I just pay for what people drink. I have no idea how many people will come to say their goodbyes. There's only two people that I need, and they will be sat at the front on either side of me.

Dante has phoned twice to check on us. I've spoken to him more this week than I have in the whole of my married life. He has this impression that I'm a weak-willed women incapable of holding things together. That I'm on the brink of collapse. My god I miss Alex and I will crumble at times, but the boys and I will stay strong together. I told him I will take things one day at a time. It confounds me what he thinks of me. Where did this impression come from? He doesn't know me.

Maria called to check on us too. It was a difficult conversation for 2 reasons. One, because she slips into Italian and I can't understand what she's saying and two because she's used to getting her own way. It's obvious Dante takes after his mother. She tried relentlessly to get me to use their local church. Applying pressure, informing me it was a family church, how difficult it would be for extended family to attend, the catholic connection, she was relentless. I stayed firm.

Benni has called a few times. Unfortunately, I've been too busy to speak with him at length. He always seems to call when I'm leaving the house, or I'm cooking or driving.

I appreciate their concern but it's quite alien for me and the boys. We've never had any interaction with any other family. It's always just been the four of us.

## Chapter Nine

It's a crisp sunny autumnal day when I open my eyes. The sort of day I ordinarily love. The sort of day to wrap up warm, pull on your boots and just walk. The sort of day you take in the changes around you as the summer says goodbye to allow Autumn to take its place. The sort of day you watch the leaves drop from the trees. The sort of day the birds are busy feeding from the remaining berries in the hedgerows. Today is not that sort of day. Today is my husband's funeral.

Looking at my reflection in the mirror I see changes in the image looking back at me. I look older. I feel older. The lines on my face are prominent revealing the untold heartache I've been through. My hair is showing signs of grey weaved in with the blonde highlights and my natural brunette strands. My hazel eyes reflect the depth of pain I'm in. I feel drained. I'm almost at empty. I've kept it together as much as I can in front of the boys. Tried to show them I'm strong and they can depend on me. They need me to be their pillar. Their anchor in this horrendous storm.

"Let's just get through today." I whisper to the shadow watching me.

I can hear the family have arrived and I'm procrastinating. If I hide up here till the cars arrive then I won't have to face them. It won't be real. The boys are down there though. They need my support.

On a huge exhale I descend the stairs. The house is filling with people I've never met. For all I know they could be smartly dressed burglars.

At the bottom of the stairs I look into the kitchen and see Maria holding court. There are two older ladies standing at her side, closeted in hushed conversation. They're all speaking in Italian and gesticulating frantically. Looking towards the dining area the boys are surrounded by two older men and Benni has an arm around each of them. From the boy's body language, they're comfortable in Benni's presence. Both look at him in awe as he includes them in their conversation. The caterers are currently unloading boxes from their van via the side door, making numerous trips back and forth. Turning towards the lounge I see Dante speaking quietly with the nameless two. Their attention solely on him. I hear softly spoken words float towards me, again in Italian. I'm glad no one has noticed me yet. I think I would break.

Sneaking out the front door I stand on the step and take a minute to myself. To breathe in the cold crisp air. To take in the silence. Today is going to be hard. It's going to be hard for the boys and I need to stay strong to keep them strong.

The gentle whoosh of the door opening behind me alerts me that I'm no longer alone. I don't have any energy spare to turn around.

"Hey Kate." Benni softly says from behind me.

I lift my head up in acknowledgment of his greeting.

"Do you need anything?"

"My husband." What other answer is there.

Benni tenderly places his hand on my shoulder rubbing lightly. I hear the exhale of his breath.

"I can't understand how he's gone." I say, turning to face Benni, his hand dropping to his side. "I can still feel him." I thump my closed fist to my breastbone. "Here."

Benni looks down to the floor, unable to meet my eyes. He slightly shakes his head, defeated.

"I don't know what to say Kate. I'm sorry."

I feel awful for my selfishness. He's lost his brother.

"Me too." I say as I walk past him back through the door.

As soon as I step inside the house Dante's head whips round, looking at me, then over my shoulder through the open door. The look he gives his brother is fierce. I can't even begin to understand what it means. Quite frankly I couldn't give a rat's arse right now.

Walking away I leave them to have their wordless discussion. I'm too tired to even care.

Taking a large breath to fortify myself I walk in to my kitchen. Yes. It's MY kitchen. My house. Mine. They are the intruders. Not me.

Heading straight for the coffee machine Maria tries to intercept me. I simply put my hand up in the universal sign for 'wait' and carry on with my task. I feel the stares at my back and the silence in the room is overbearing.

With my head held high I place my cup under the spout and press the button. The sound of the beans grinding is deafening. Then the aroma hits me. I'm going to be sick. Breathe. Breathe. In. Out. Do not show weakness.

Tilting my head slightly away from the smell I wait as the coffee is delivered into the cup. I know as soon as I turn around all eyes will be on me. Breathing through my mouth I take in another breath and prepare myself for the scrutiny of my silent audience.

Lifting the cup, I make my turn and see the sympathy in all of their eyes. Shit. Not what I need. I can't handle sympathy right now. I need to offer a convincing display. I can crumble on the inside, but the outer walls need to remain in place. They can't see me break.

I look at the boys in turn, silently asking if they're OK. A small smile touches the corner of Leo's mouth and Marc nods. I can't speak to anyone right now. I need to space. I need to escape.

Head held high I walk away from the kitchen counter and straight out the back door. No one has spoken a word, and no one has tried to stop me. The caterers move aside as I exit, and I nod my thanks back to them.

It's cold out today, although the sun is trying it's hardest to warm me. My black dress and jacket aren't of adequate thickness to keep the chill at bay. I can't stay out here long. Holding the mug between my hands I'm grateful for its warmth even if I can't drink it. The grief has hit me hard now. Seeing everyone here has made this all very real.

Lost in a daydream I hear footsteps from behind. The mug has long gone cold, and I feel a chill inside snaking its way up my body.

I know what they've come to tell me. I heard the cars arrive a few moments ago. I pretended they were for someone else. Tried to deny I even heard them.

"Come Kate. We need to go." The voice softly says.

Dante holds out his arm to me in support as I turn around. Placing the cold cup on the patio table I place my arm through his as he escorts me inside.

"Do you have a coat?" He asks on a frown. "You are very cold."

As he says it the realisation hits me, and I shiver slightly.

"I've got it." Marc says from the doorway.

Walking forwards with the coat held out in offer to me Dante takes it from his hands and helps me instead. Everyone is watching me. Turning my head in his direction I nod my thanks and walk forward with my spine straight and my head held high.

"Are you ready boys?" I ask.

Both boys nod their answer and walk towards me. I take hold of both their hands and squeeze them tight.

"We can do this." I quietly tell them. "We've got each other."

Another nod is their only response and I realise they are holding back their tears too. Scared to open their mouths in case the flood gates open.

With another squeeze to their hands I release them both and make my way out the door to my husband, who is waiting for me.

The hearse shines in the weak sunlight and the lilies are beautiful on top of the coffin. The wreath on the side with the brightest flowers spelling 'DAD'. A single tear escapes. I will allow that one. I will allow Alex to see my heartache at his loss.

Reaching to the top of my head I take my sunglasses off and put them firmly in place.

"It's time to go Alex." I whisper.

The church is lit with the fragile light of the sun. Looking through the window of the car I can see hundreds of people in the graveyard waiting for Alex to arrive. The door of the car opens, signalling our need to exit. Taking a moment to compose myself I look over to my amazing boys. Leo and Marc look frightened at what's to come. They've never been to a funeral before. My parents died before they were born. Their funeral was a cheap affair at the crematorium. Firstly, attending my mothers and less than six months later my fathers. I was in my early twenties and had no idea what I was supposed to do. I felt like a child trying to make arrangements I knew nothing about. Alex helped when he could. I had no other family and their so-called friends where of no help.


Walking up to the church I see people hesitate, unsure as to whether they should approach and offer their condolences. I recognise friends and neighbours, but the numbers are mostly made up of strangers. These nameless people all looking at us with sympathy.

Heading into the church I remove my glasses and feel a cold run through me as I shiver in my wool coat. Taking a seat in the first pew I hear, rather than see, the congregation follow suit. The organist is playing a haunting melody and the gentle humming of voices carries up to the vaulted ceiling.

Sitting in silence I hold the hands of Leo and Marc trying to pass on the strength they need from me. Dante escorts his mother to the pew on the opposite side, followed by his brother. Her tears are visible, Dante has a look of pain on his face and Benni looks away as I see his with a blank expression. We all deal with death in different ways.

The melody changes signalling the arrival of my husband and we all rise as one is respect. The vicar begins his slow march down the aisle escorting Alex, the pall bearers carrying him upon their shoulders. I watch avidly as he is transported towards the front of the church, along with everyone in attendance. Following his path, I glance through the mourners, catching a few of the nameless faces look towards me and away again quickly. I'm glad that we're at the front, I won't have to school my face to pacify anyone.

As his coffin is laid on the catafalque and a silence surrounds us all the vicar silently asks us to sit. His motion signalling the beginning of the service. Signalling the beginning of the end of us. The end of Alex and me. The end of our family. Maybe now my heart will get the message. I still feel him because his body is close although in my head I know he has gone.

Standing at the graveside holding the boys to me as tightly as I can. Watching the coffin be lowered into the earth is the hardest part of today. Knowing he is in there and I can't touch him, feel him, talk to him anymore. The ground will consume his body and he will belong to her now. Not me.

Taking a single lily, I kiss it gently and throw it into the ground.

"Good bye my love. Goodbye my heart."

The boys take a flower each and similarly kiss it and throw it in too. Their tears are silent, tracing a path down their faces. Dripping from their chins. Landing on their shoes.

Maria, Dante and Benni each take a flower throwing them gently into the grave.

"Goodbye Alex." I say for the last time.

Taking their hands in mine, I turn and walk away with Leo and Marc. The ground is soft beneath my heels as I walk over the grass towards the waiting cars.

"I'm very sorry for your loss Mrs Rossi." The driver says as we approach.

I nod my acknowledgment as he opens the door.

Marc slides in first, me next and Leo last, showing his protectiveness in that one small act. Leo has grown so much. Taking their hands again I look at them in turn.

"Let's go home."

The driver pulls away from the church and takes us back to our new normality. Our new lives without Alex. Our home without him.

The caterers have set up an amazing display of foods and drinks and I thank them for their hard work. My head feels like I'm trying to swim through fog. I know there are people around me but they're all a blur. I need to take a few minutes to compose myself.

Bear is sitting quietly in the corner of the kitchen. He knows. Walking over I crouch down and give him a hug. I don't care about the hairs right now. I need to feel him, and he needs the reassurance as much as I do. The sound of cars arriving drags me away and I make my way into the hall. I have no idea what the protocol is with funerals. Do I stand and greet people? Do I thank them for coming? As I enter the hall Dante walks through the door with his mother on his arm.

"Bellissima."

That one word is all it takes for her to break down. Walking directly to me she envelops me in a hug. A hug that at this time is more than welcome. A hug that shows her love and compassion, her understanding.

Slowly I raise my arms and return the hug, fiercely. I didn't know till now just how much I needed an embrace from another human. The warm contact that brings you a brief respite of solace. I've hugged the boys more these last few days than I have in years. Giving to them what Maria is giving to me now.

Dante gently places his hand on my back.

"Come, you need to sit."

He's right, I'm ready to collapse. Maria releases me from her arms but takes my hand and guides me to the sofa in the lounge.

"We sit." She instructs, and I do as I am bid.

I feel like a child. A child being cared for by an adult. My parents weren't overly caring, and I'm not used to maternal affection, but at this moment in time, it's what I need.

Maria sits with my hand in hers stroking it gently with her other. The softness of her skin is a balm to my nerves. Looking into her eyes I see her strength and I pray I can duplicate it. I can see the people arriving, but Maria holds my hand. It's like a lifeline that we both need. That connection to another human who is suffering the exact pain we are.

"La mia bellissima figlia. How strong you are."

I feel like a fraud. I'm not strong. I'm crumbling to ash on the inside. What she sees is a façade. A wall I've erected to stem the flow of sympathy. If it can't get through the wall, it can't hurt me. I need to protect myself. I need it to protect the boys.

"How are you?" I ask to deflect her statement.

The look that flashes across her face is the same as the one reflected in the mirror.

Her sigh is audible. Words are pointless.

"I need to find the boys." I offer, patting her caressing hand.

Standing I feel myself wobble, becoming light headed, I quickly grab hold of the nearest thing as my vision blurs and becomes black. The whooshing sounding in my ears from my thumping heart. I feel a cold sweat break out over my body. Nausea making my mouth flood with saliva. I quickly swallow down the saliva, breathing in through my nose. The object I'm leant against moves, causing me to tilt.

"I've got you."

The object grabs hold of my arm and places another arm around my shoulders guiding me back down to the sofa again. Breathe. In. Out. In. Out. The darkness starts to retract, my vision becoming clearer. I look up to see Benni hovering over me. A look of concern on his face palpable.

"Are you OK Kate? What do you need?"

Swallowing I continue to regulate my breathing. My nausea slowly subsiding.

"I, um, I need some water please." I reply.

Benni turns and strides into the kitchen, returning moments later with a glass.

Handing it to me, I see my hands shaking uncontrollably. Droplets of water spill on my lap. Leaning forward Maria places her hand over mine and guides the glass to my lips.

"Lentamente." She says taking the glass back. "You drink slowly."

Her demand is firm but kind. Sipping with her guidance I start to feel better and nod to show I'm finished.

"Thankyou." I say in a quiet voice.

"When did you last eat?" Benni asks.

The look on my face is the only answer he needs. I haven't been eating properly. The grief eating away at me. The guilt I feel that I can sit at a table with the boys and enjoy food and company was too much to take.

With a restrained huff he turns and walks back into the kitchen.

"You need to take care. Leonardo and Marco need you." I know she's right, so I nod gently to Maria.

Returning with a plate of food Benni offers it forward to me. Taking it from his hand I thank him and take a nibble. I can't taste anything. All I taste is dust. With Maria watching me like a hawk I finish the sandwich and start on the small canapes. My stomach starts to protest but I know I need sustenance.

"Grief is hard, especially when you are mamma."

Maria knows how hard it is to grieve for your husband, whilst still being a mum.

## Chapter Ten

Sitting on the sofa I look at the people milling about my home. I recognise a few friends and neighbours, casting sympathetic looks my way whilst shrinking away from the members of Alex's family. Sitting here as a virtual stranger to most of them I can see how intimidating they could be. All wearing the finest cut clothes, with their dark looks, conversing in Italian, I'm a little intimidated too. I never saw Alex as intimidating. I just saw the man that I loved.

Maria has disappeared in search of food or a drink or something, I'm not sure what she said to me as she rose. I'm sat here alone. I don't know where the boys are. I saw them walking about earlier being introduced to various uncles. I haven't got the energy to worry. They are both here, safe. I know they can't come to any harm.

After a short while Benni approaches and sits on the edge of the sofa.

"Better?" He asks.

I nod my head with a small smile to my lips. I do feel better. I need to eat. I need the strength.

We sit in companionable silence both watching the people milling around us. I feel he wants to say something, and I leave him to sort through his words. Whatever he wants to say is going to hurt. Eventually he turns his body towards me and takes an inhale of breath.

"There are some legal matters that Dante wants to go through before he leaves today."

I look at him with a furrowed brow. What legal things?

Benni interprets my facial response correctly.

"There are some matters that we need to talk through with you."

That makes even less sense.

"Dante wants you to know your position."

"Just spit it out Benni. My head can't take this." Blunt is my only approach. I have no idea what he is trying to intimate.

Clearing his throat again, I begin to see a different side to Benni. He has always been happy and carefree, like Alex. He seems almost nervous. Why would I be making him nervous, or is it Dante?

"Dante would like to speak with you after your guests have left."

"He would, would he?"

The look of shock on Bennis face at my retort has me feeling guilty. I smile at him and simply shake my head in a silent apology.

People start to leave, each offering me their condolences, a hold of the hand, a kiss on the cheek, or plural in the family's case. Maria approaches me with her hands out stretched. Instinctively I hold out mine to take them. It feels so natural. She stands and looks deep into my eyes. I feel like I'm being assessed for something, god know what though. She gives an assertive nod as if she has made up her mind, and I've passed what-ever silent appraisal has taken place.

"I do not know why he kept you from us. You are strong mia figlia."

Leaning forward Maria grasps me and hugs me to her fiercely. Leaning back and taking a hold of my shoulders she smiles and kisses both my cheeks.

"I have said goodbye to Leonardo and Marco. I see you all soon. You come to the house."

There is little point in arguing. We will cross that bridge when we come to it. Turning, Maria walks towards the front door where one of the nameless two is standing with the car door open. He is obviously a chauffeur today. 'I wonder if they hire him out' I chuckle to myself.

The quiet is a welcome reprieve. I can hear the caterers quietly going about their business, which reminds me that I need to pay them.

Taking a large breath in I roll my neck to release some of the pent-up tension and walk into the kitchen.

The lady who runs the small catering company is stood by the dining table with her back to me. She is quivering slightly as Dante towers over her. He is talking in a hushed voice. I see him hand her a large amount of money which she accepts, nods and scurries away. As she moves Dante sees me watching their interaction. He has paid her. I don't know why this angers me, but it does.

"What do you think you're doing?" I ask, the anger simmering near the top of my voice.

With a shocked look on his face Dante looks away to check if anyone is close by, mine following, to find we're alone.

Bringing is eyes back to me I can see he is trying to control his anger. His nostril flaring, displaying his restraint. I have no idea why? It's a simple enough question.

Taking a huge intake of breath, he looks at me in a menacing way. I'm sure that scares most people, but it won't scare me.

"I will thank you NOT to interfere in my business Dante. As much as I appreciate yours and your family's assistance, we don't need you."

The shocked look on his face is a picture, and if I wasn't so damned angry I'd laugh at it.

We are locked in a silent duel. Neither of us backing down. I'm sure as CEO or whatever he is he feels the need to intimidate his employees to do as he bids. Not me. I'm my own person.

"I have managed on my own perfectly well these last 20 years when Alex had to work. I'm sure I can manage perfectly well for the next 20!"

With my scathing remark I turn toward the door and come face to face with Benni and the other of the nameless two. The look of shock at my words registers on their faces. I feel like a bitch for my harsh words on the day of their brother's funeral, but I will not back down.

"I'm going to check on the boys." I quietly say to Benni as I pass.

He nods his head and steps back out of the way.


The boys are both in Leo's room playing video games.

"Hey." I say softly as I enter.

Both boys look up and nod their heads in greeting. I can see them trying to hide their pain. Bear lays at their feet, looking up at me and laying his head back down again.

"Everyone's gone except your uncles."

It feels weird calling them that, but the boys have a right to a relationship with the two men closest to their dad.

"Do you need anything? Dante wants to have a chat with me before he leaves." I

 keep the reference light as I'm not sure what 'legal matters' I need to discuss with him, and I have no idea why he is concerning himself with our private affairs anyway.

There are a few meetings I have to set up to discuss our financial position. I thought I would start with the bank and see what we owe on the mortgage. I don't earn hardly anything, maybe a few hundred pounds here and there on commission pieces. We might have to sell the house and move to something smaller. The holiday home in Cornwall will need to be sold too. I have no idea what the financial situation is with that. There are so many people to inform of Alex passing away. The thought is slightly overwhelming. I need to contact the insurance company about the car. Find out the situation with life insurance. The list is endless. When someone dies they should give you a little pamphlet that says:

With a list of all the people that need to know.

The boys turn back to their game with a nod of acknowledgement. They have bought up a tray of leftover food and enough pop to fill a bath.

"I'll come and see you after they're gone."

With a kiss to both of their heads I move off into our bedroom. My bedroom. It's my bedroom now.

Heading into the walk-in wardrobe I avoid looking at Alex's side. Removing my suit and hanging it up I then proceed to don my preferred attire. Pulling on my favourite jeans and a jumper I slide my feet into a comfy pair of shoes and pull my hair up into a messy bun. Taking the cotton pad, I begin to remove the armour I painted on my face this morning. Once my face is void of all makeup I rub in face cream and apply a natural lip gloss. This is me. This is the real me. I feel fortified by the return of me.

Straightening my spine, I hold my head high. This is our home and I will not allow another man to walk in here and presume to take control.

Walking down the stairs I see Dante and Benni in the lounge talking quietly. They appear to be in some kind of hushed argument. Clearing my throat, they both turn at once.

"You wanted to speak with me Dante." I say displaying a confidence I don't actually feel.

"Please." Dante says gesturing for me to enter and sit down. It seems a little presumptuous to offer me a seat in my own home, I raise an eyebrow at him.

"There are a few things we need to discuss Kate. Please sit." Again, with the authoritative voice.

Walking in I choose the armchair. It gives me a sense of control choosing this seat over the sofa that Dante is indicating to.

"Did Allesandro share your financial situation with you?"

I'm not sure I'm comfortable discussing this with Dante.

Benni sits on the sofa, leaning his elbows on his knees with his head hanging low. He gives off a vibe of feeling uncomfortable.

"Um, well not really." I stammer "Alex dealt with all the financials."

I honestly have no idea of anything. Alex took control of all matters relating to money. I don't even know what we owe on the mortgage, let alone who our telephone contract is with. I figured once I find the strength to enter his study I would find my answers there.

Dante looks towards Benni, but he still hasn't raised his head. Looking back towards me he goes on.

"What do you know?"

Well that's just it. The optimum question. What do I know?

With a vacant look on my face I shake my head in answer to his question. I really have no clue where to start.

"I'm sorry to raise this today but it must be done."

Taking a seat next to his brother his face morphs into business mode. Dante is a busy man, I should be grateful for any help and assistance he can give us.

"Allesandro appraised me of your current financial state of affairs. You and the boys will have nothing to worry about."

Isn't it strange how when someone tells you not to 'worry' about something, you automatically start worrying.

"What do you mean?" I ask.

"You own the house. There is no mortgage." Dante clarifies gesturing around the room. "Allesandro paid for the house outright when he bought it."

The look of shock on my face must be a picture. My jaw almost hits the floor.

"How? Where on earth did he get that kind of money from?" Wow, just WOW!

"We were so young when we bought this house, I.. I.. I just assumed we got a mortgage. I remember signing papers."

I remember at the time being distracted at the prospect of moving into our dream home. Raising a family in this amazing house that we would turn into our home.

Turning his head again to Benni, I see Benni gives a small nod of approval. Dante turns back to me formulating the words he wants to say. I've never seen Dante like this. He's almost hesitant.

"Allesandro was very wealthy." Waving a hand between himself and Benni. "Our family have been very fortunate in our, umm, business dealings."

Come again??? I look from Dante to Benni and back again.

"Alex was rich?" I need to simplify this for myself.

"Yes Kate. As a family we have been fortuitous. Subsequently Allesandro has enjoyed his familial share of those, umm, investments."

Something isn't adding up. My spidey senses are jumping about.

"What investments?"

Dante looks uncomfortable. Benni is pale. For an Italian man, it's not a healthy look.

"What investments Dante?" I ask again.

Straightening his back, he plasters the look of a CEO back on his façade.

"We have many establishments, as you know, Gia being Allesandro's main concern."

I see him swallow. Why is he nervous. Keeping quiet I wait for him to continue.

"We are also involved in, well, other areas of business."

Looking him dead in the eye I see the tell-tale signs of withholding information. Alex tried but I always saw through it. I don't look away. Tilting my head, I raise my right eyebrow in silent question. Nothing. He doesn't give me anything. I could ask but I know it won't be the full truth. I probably wouldn't understand and quite frankly it's none of my business.

"Okay, so the boys and I are safe. We won't need to leave."

The thought makes me insanely happy. I didn't relish the thought of having to move away from the house that holds all our memories.

"Uum do I need to have the deeds or documents or what have you changed?"

Dante shakes his head.

"No Kate. The house, it is in your name. Allesandro bought it for you."

And there goes my resolve. I look down to my lap unable to make eye contact. The tears are welling and I'm not sure they will remain in place. Swallowing hard a few times I finally get them under control.

"When?' I quietly ask, my head lowered.

"When you first bought the property. The papers you signed were the deeds to the house. It was always about you Kate. He wanted you to be happy. Always."

I hear compassion in his voice. My heart is beating fast and my head is feeling light. This really is my house. Lifting my head, I look around me and see it in a whole new light.

"He bought it for me." I whisper to myself.

Dante remains quiet allowing his news to sink in. I run through a stream of emotions but mostly I'm astounded, we've owned this house all these years. Shaking my head slightly I look back to Dante.

"Why didn't he tell me?"

I'm hurt that my own husband couldn't confide in me, his wife, but his brother knew. What else didn't he tell me?

Dante looks towards his brother again and I see Benni shake his head.

"I do not know Kate." He's lying. "There are a few other properties also in your name."

OK, I'm glad I'm sitting down. I haven't had a drink all day, but I could really use a glass of wine about now. I need to keep a clear head though. Pursing my lips, I nod my head and indicate with my hand for him to continue.

"They are of little importance at this time." He dismisses with a shake to his head. "You will come to learn more as we move forward. They are mostly businesses, of which you will still receive the profits." Holy cow!!

"How many businesses are we talking about?" I'm surprised I still have the ability to speak I'm so shocked.

"I do not have all the details with me. I will be happy to talk to you at another time. Please do not worry. They will all continue to operate."

He nods his head indicating an end to that part of the conversation. A small thought pops into my head, he may know.

"I, um, I don't suppose you know anything about the cottage? The, umm, the one in Cornwall."

For the last 10 years the boys and I have spent various school holidays and weekends there. Leo and Marc caught the surfing bug early in life. We could have travelled around the world, but Alex was often too busy, and I preferred to stay in the UK. Cornwall offered the best solution for all of us.

Dante nods his head.

"Yes, but it belongs to the Leonardo and Marco jointly."

The boys love the cottage. It's not terribly big, with a wonky chimney, titchy rooms and small garden, but they love it. From the back gate they can carry their surfboards down to the beach and spend the day in the water. It's their little slice of heaven. Alex realised how much it meant to them, and for that I will love him just that little bit more.

Swallowing hard, I nod my understanding, and turn to look out the window. From my seat I can see the trees in the garden. Something catches my attention and I crane my neck to see it better. Squinting I try to see what it was, but it's gone. That's if it was even there. Shaking my head, I turn back to Dante and Benni, both observing me with a furrowed brow.

"What's wrong?" Benni speaks, for the first time.

"Oh, it's probably nothing, but I just, well I thought I saw something out there again." Looking back out the window to check if it's still there.

"It's probably just a deer or something. It spooked me and Bear last time."

Shaking my head a little to dispel the thoughts, I focus back on Dante ready to recommence our conversation, he, however, isn't. Hastily rising from his seat and taking his phone from his pocket he starts to walk away.

"Please excuse me, Kate." He throws over his shoulder.

Looking back to Benni I ask the obvious.

"What's wrong with him?"

Benni simply shrugs his shoulders in an act I've seen the boys do hundreds of times.

"Maybe you should take the boys down there for a few days. You could all do with a bit of a break."

I assume he's referring to the cottage. Smiling at his suggestion, I have to agree with him. I had the same thought a few days ago.

The boys would enjoy a bit of headspace. I know I could. With their winter wetsuits they could still surf or just laze about the cottage with a blazing fire and a movie or two. The more I think about it the more I like the idea. I'm sure the school will be understanding. We wouldn't need a lot. Just pack up a bag each, and Bear of course, and jump in the car. I could get the boys to do an on-line shop whilst we're driving down, actually maybe not. We need to eat real food at some point.

Turning back to Benni I see him regarding me as I formulate my plan. I give him a small smile and nod of the head.

"I think we will."

Looking around the house I see the mess and wince at the thought of clearing up before I can leave. With a sigh of resignation, I know I've got to clean as I won't want to come back to a dirty house.

"I could get someone in to clean while you're away." Benni offers.

As nice as that sounds, I'm not comfortable with a stranger coming into our home doing something I'm capable of.

"Thanks, but I'll do it tomorrow. The boys and I can set off the day after."

With a plan formulated in my head it makes me feel good. I can't look too far into the future, once we're down there we'll just take it one day at a time. The boys could even keep up with their schooling on-line. With a decisive nod to myself, yes, that's what we'll do. That way we're not restrained by time.

Dante returns to the lounge giving Benni a discreet nod.

Re-taking his seat he looks at me.

"We can discuss details further at another time."

I'm glad as I don't think I can process anything more today.

"You will all come to stay at the house."

We'll do what? We've never stayed there. I don't want to.

"Actually." I start, looking towards Benni and back again. "I'm going to take the boys away for a few days. I think we need the break."

With a frown Dante makes it clear that he doesn't agree, he almost seems panicked.

"Where?"

"I'm going to take them down to the cottage, their cottage. They need a distraction for a week or so."

"Is that safe?" He asks in response.

I don't understand how it can't be safe. We've spent whole summers there, alone. It's a quiet little village where nothing happens, or does he mean the drive down?

"We'll be fine. We've done it before on our own. Alex never had a problem."

I'm beginning to become uncomfortable with Dante telling me what to do. He's not my husband.

Looking Dante straight in the eyes I make it clear that I won't be swayed from my plans.

"I think it's a good idea Kate." Benni states with an encouraging nod towards me.

Dante turns to look at Benni and they share another silent conversation. Benni must convey something that reassures Dante as he turns back to me and simply nods in agreement.

"When will you leave?"

Looking around again I wave my hands to signify the mess.

"I'll get all this cleared up tomorrow and go the day after."

It's not that bad but I can't leave it. I wouldn't be able to relax whilst we're away. With the boys help we can get it done in a couple of hours. Once we're done we can get packed. They will be excited to go. It will be nice for them to have something to look forward to.

"I will need to let their school know." I say, more to myself.

"I will tell them."

You will, will you? He doesn't even know what school they go to, or does he? I'm beginning to wonder.

"Thank you, Dante but I will call them. That's my job. I'm their mum." With my speech I rise from the chair indicating the end to our conversation. Benni rises with a slight smirk to his face and Dante follows with a scowl to his.

"Thank you both, to all the family, for your help and support today."

I'm beginning to get chocked up. I swallow down the lump in my throat and start to walk towards the front door. They both follow recognising their dismissal. At the door Benni grasps my shoulders and kisses both my cheeks gently.

"It will all be ok." He whispers in my ear.

I step back to look at him with confusion evident on my face. How is it all going to be OK?

Dante then moves towards me too, in a stiffer manner. He leans forward and kisses both my cheeks without actually making contact.

"Do you need anything before we leave?" He asks.

I do a quick think through.

"No, we're all good thanks. Oh actually, I um, I assume I can still access bank accounts and other stuff?" The thought hadn't occurred to me before now. "I need to let the bank know. They won't freeze our account, or anything will they?" I'm starting to panic a bit.

"No." Simple and to the point.

"Well then, no we'll be fine. I only need a little bit of cash for diesel and food anyway." I've never lived an exuberant lifestyle, preferring the simple things.

Dante removes his wallet and takes out a stack of notes, all £50's. I frown at him as he goes to pass it to me.

"Take this." I raise my hand in a no gesture and step back.

"No, thank you Dante, I have enough money of my own from my work."

Dante continues to force the money forward, but I simply cross my arms and take another step back. Realisation dawns on his face. I'm not taking his money. With a bewildered look at me he returns the money to his wallet.

Benni opens the door and leaves, I'm sure I hear him chuckle. Dante casts one last look at me and follows Benni out. One of the nameless two is standing by the car with the door open. As Benni steps back to allow Dante to enter first I see a stunned look on Dante's face. He really isn't used to people saying no to him. Benni smiles back at me. The first true smile I've seen all day.

## Chapter Eleven

I'm suspended in that moment between slumber and wake. That moment that keeps you warm in the embrace of sleep. The moment that all is right with the world. The moment before realisation steps in and reality comes crashing down into your brain. The moment before you fully comprehend what your life has become. It's in these moments that I can still feel him. My heart still sings in tune with his. I thought it would realise the other half had been taken once the funeral was over. My heart seems a bit slow in grasping it.

Rising from bed with a sigh I see it's still dark outside, it's barely 7 o'clock. The sound of the boys moving about shows their eagerness for our planned trip. They need this. We spent the day yesterday cleaning and putting things away, packing our bags and emptying the fridge. We don't need much food, I know the cupboards down there are stocked with basics that we could survive on for a week at least. Dressing in my usual attire of jeans and jumper, I quickly make the bed and straighten the room ready for our return. Grabbing my warm coat and boots I make my way downstairs. Bear is looking at me upside down, lazing in his bed tracking my movements.

"Morning my gorgeous boy, ready for an adventure?"

Struggling to right himself he rises to a standing position and wanders towards the back door. I let him out and consciously avoid looking towards the trees. I don't need to spook myself this early and it's still dark out.

The boys thunder down the stairs, dropping a backpack each by our luggage in the hall, no doubt crammed with phones, tablets, chargers. All the essentials for a teenage boy.

"Do you want to eat before we leave? It's a long journey."

It should only take us about 4 hours. I hope.

Walking to the larder they each grab a handful of cereal bars and bottles of water.

"These will do." Leo responds.

I grab a couple and put them in my pocket for later. I don't want to risk Bear being car sick, so I avoid feeding him his breakfast. Taking his bowls, I wash them in the sink and leave them to drip dry.

Bear pushes the door open with his nose and wanders back into the kitchen, excited to see the boys up and about this early. Marc kneels down and hugs him around his neck.

"We're going to the sea Bear."

Bear is oblivious to his words but senses his excitement. He's going to enjoy the freedom of the beach too. Luckily there aren't that many people on the beach this time of year. Just a few die hards.

Locking the door, I walk through the house checking all the window locks. The boys have taken the car keys and loaded our bags onto the back seat next to where Marc will sit. I smile at their consideration for Bear, giving him enough space to lay down flat in the boot. Leo returns and swaps the keys for Bears bed I'm holding, taking it out to the car. They really are good kids. I'm proud of them both.

Taking one final sweep around the house, I pick up my bag and lock the front door. We need this time together. We need to learn how to live as just the three of us.

Getting in the car I look at my passengers and smile.

"All ready?"

I get nods and even a snuffle from Bear.

"Let's go."

The drive down is easy. There is hardly any traffic about and the monotony of driving helps my brain to relax for a while. The miles pass by quickly and as Bear seems content to sleep I don't bother to stop. Approaching the Tamar Bridge the excitement in the car goes up a little. We're nearly there. I decide to stop at a supermarket before we get to the house to buy fresh ingredients.

Parking the car in the furthest corner from the store entrance, I open the boot to let Bear out to toilet in the shrubbery. He takes an age sniffing out the exact spot to cock his leg. A few people have approached this area to park, seeing the beast roaming around they soon divert their cars and park further away. Eventually he has finished relieving his bladder and jumps back into the car.

"Not long now." I tell him, giving him a kiss on the head and a scratch on either side of his jowls.

"I won't be long." I tell the boys through the boot. "Open the windows a bit please Marc." Shutting the boot, I hear the back windows slide down.

The supermarket is fairly quiet this time of day. In the summer it is packed with holiday makers, buying their produce for picnics on the beach. That's normally me. It's so different in the colder months. I manage to run around grabbing all the essentials and a few naughty treats too. Before long I wheel the trolley back towards the car. Leo jumps out when he sees me with a smile and unloads the trolley in the back seat, surrounding marc with shopping bags. Laughing at Leo, he bats them away and positions them in the footwell and the spare seat. Leo returns the trolley as I jump back in the driver's seat.

When Leo gets back in and buckles up I look at them both. They are wearing similar smiles. It's nice to see. With a returning smile I start the car and move out of the car park.

We don't have far to go but in Cornwall I learnt their miles are significantly different to anywhere else in the world. They measure them as the crow flies, not by the tarmac. It may say 15 miles to your destination but with all the bends and turns it's more like 30.

The village comes into view and I see them both lean forward to get a better look. Taking the last few turns we finally arrive at the cottage.

Parking outside the front gate on the road I sigh in relief. It's a welcome sight. Built of old stone in the 1800's it was originally a miner's cottage. A simple 2 up 2 down design with the bathroom downstairs in a small extension off of the kitchen. It's our retreat from the chaos of the world.

It doesn't take long to transport our bags and shopping the few steps from the gate into the house. The boys ferrying most of it whilst I unpack the cold stuff to put in the fridge.

"Who's hungry?" I ask on their last pass through.

Bear looks at me along with the boys. All of them then.

Filling up Bears bowl with food and water I set them by the kitchen door.

"Sandwiches?" I call out, getting a duo of yeses in return.

We curl up on the sofa with our lunch and listen. The sound of waves crashing in the distance is comforting and familiar. I feel the stress of the last few weeks starting to lift a little. I can't escape completely but it's nice to just get a break from it all.

"Do you want to go surfing in the morning?" Leo asks Marc.

They start discussing the waves and tide as I drift away with my thoughts. Sitting on the comfy sofa with my feet tucked under me I start to look around. Although it's small this house has always felt homely. It would probably sound callous if I said it aloud, but I'm glad Alex didn't come here very often. I'm grateful not to have the constant reminders of his absence from our lives. We can pretend we're on our usual holiday with just the three of us. Oh, and Bear of course.

The gentle chatter of their voices hums in the back ground. I'm tired. Really tired. The fatigue has hit me now. I've been running on reserves these last few weeks. Placing my plate on the floor, I take the blanket from the back of the sofa and wrap it around me. I'll just shut my eyes for a few minutes. Just a few.

I wake to the smell of food cooking and a good-natured squabble between the boys. It's dark outside and someone has lit the wood burner. A few side lights are on and the curtains are closed. No wonder I've slept so long. It's really cosy and warm. It feels like the cottage has wrapped herself around us protectively. Rising from the sofa with a stretch I see Bear laid on his back in front of the fire with all four paws in the air. I doubt he'll move again tonight.

Wandering towards the kitchen I see the small dining table has been pulled away from the wall and laid for the three of us. There is a pan of pasta boiling and a sauce heating in another. The smell of garlic bread emanates from the oven. The boys are attempting to grate cheese which is what's causing the squabble. As fast as Marc grates, Leo is eating it. I smile at the scene. Happy but saddened too. They have grown up so much. Matured. Alex will never get to see this. Shaking the thought from my head I pad into the kitchen.

"Something smells good." I say.

Both boys turn to me with a smile on their face.

"We've made dinner." The pride in Marc's statement is evident.

"I'm starving." I really am, I realise. I haven't been eating much lately, the proof in the fit of my clothes. "What have we got then?" I ask, although it's obvious.

Marc rattles off what he's done, and Leo nods his encouragement at him.

"Thank you. Both of you."

After draining the pasta, losing a few bits in the sink, he proceeds to serve three bowls. Leo takes the garlic bread from the oven and cuts it before placing it on the little table.

"This looks and smells amazing." It does.

The chatter is light hearted as we all tuck into our meal. The pasta is slightly overcooked, but I would never, ever criticise or complain. I realise in that moment that I have a smile on my face. A true genuine smile.

After clearing away the mess and feeding Bear we decide to watch a DVD. I haven't even been upstairs yet to unpack.

"Give me a while to unpack and put my jimmy's on." I tell the boys as I head up the little staircase.

Heading into my bedroom at the front of the house I'm suddenly struck by the smell. I have no idea how it's even possible for it to have lingered this long. Alex hasn't been here in ages. He was too busy to come with us over the summer. He said something about putting plans into action or something similar. I just assumed it was the renovations for Gia. Thinking back, I can't actually remember what.

It doesn't make sense for his aftershave to linger, unless he left some clothes last spring. Opening the wardrobe, I see why. His coat is hanging in the wardrobe. The smell so potent as if he'd worn it only yesterday.

Taking it from the hanger I hold it to my face, inhaling as deeply as I can. The smell floods my head with visions of him. I can see in my mind him wearing this coat when we went out for an evening. I was cold, so he took it off to drape over my shoulders, filling me with the warmth that clung to it, sharing the heat from his body. I remember that night, looking up at the stars in the clear sky as we wandered home after a meal out.

Replacing the coat on the hanger I slide it in with the other various clothes I leave here. Taking a fortifying breath, I close the wardrobe door. Closing off my haunting thoughts.

After shutting the curtains, I quickly change into my pyjamas and pull on a pair of thick fluffy socks. We have a movie to watch. The boys are waiting for me. I shake my head to dispel the anguish and make my way back down the stairs.

Bear is still laying in the same position, snoring really loud. Smiling at him I make my way into the kitchen taking a bowl from the cupboard and fill it with popcorn. We all need the normality of a night in with a film. I'm actually looking forward to it.

We've been in Cornwall for a few days and have settled into a routine. We wake late every day and I take the dog for a walk along the beach while the boys surf. I don't know how they can bare to be in the water. It's freezing. I'm happy for the time alone with my thoughts. I don't allow myself the luxury of dwelling on Alex though. It would be too easy to be sucked into the whirlpool of memories. The time alone allows my mind to be free of all thoughts and responsibilities for a short while. Bear is loving the freedom. He can run without his lead, darting in and out of the sea with each crashing wave. When hunger hits us we all traipse back indoors for lunch and settle down to play board games all afternoon. After we make dinner together in the evening we change into our pyjamas and watch a movie with the fire roaring. We all appreciate the simplicity.

This morning I need to grab a few groceries from the shop in the next village. I can't be bothered with the hassle of the supermarket. It's too far and I only need bread and milk and a few other bits. Leaving Bear with the boys at the cottage, they are both laying on the sofa catching up with their friends on social media.

"I won't be long." I tell them all. "Is there anything else you want?"

They both throw a few suggestions my way, mostly pop and sweets. At the mention of chocolate, I start to crave a bar of dark bitter chocolate too.

Climbing in the car, I crank up the heating and put on my heated seat. It's beginning to get really cold. The clocks are due to go back soon signalling that Winter is on her way. Cornwall in the winter can be very harsh. With lashing rain and driving winds, it can be pretty unforgiving.

As I wait for the car to heat up I spy something that looks out of place in this sleepy little village. I suppose my car could be classed as luxury, it's not unusual to spot others like it in the summer months, but there aren't that many prestige vehicles in this village, especially out of season. It's not renowned for encouraging holiday makers here. We were lucky to buy this cottage. Practically falling down, none of the locals were interested in the cost of the renovations. We managed to buy it at a reasonable price and a local team renovated and practically re-built it. Because we used trade's local to the village we were almost given their approval.

The car is parked across the green. As we've only used the back door to access the beach I haven't noticed it before. Large, black and shiny it stands out against the sun beaten cars of the locals. Something about it seems familiar. It probably belongs to a relative or friend of our neighbours, I've probably seen it in the summer months.

Putting my seat belt on I pull away and start mentally running through my shopping list. There is a fantastic local butcher near the shop and an amazing little bakery too. We haven't had the obligatory pasty yet, that will be a nice treat for lunch, and maybe a steak for dinner tonight. I'm hoping the shop has salad to go with it. It's nice to feel hungry again. My appetite is starting to return. I need to be careful I don't take it the opposite way and binge eat.

The shop is fairly empty, only a few people getting their essentials before hunkering down in their houses for the rest of the day. Grabbing a basket, I set about loading it with healthy and distinctly non-healthy goods. Picking up the sweets the boys like and a bar of chocolate for me too. There is a small pet food section where I find a treat for Bear. No doubt it will be gone within seconds. There isn't much salad, but I take what I can. Picking up anything I can remember from the list and make my way over to the till. The lady serving remembers me asking questions about the boys and the dog. She doesn't ask about Alex. As he didn't spend much time at the cottage it's not surprising. Secretly I'm glad not to have to answer questions and explain. Down here it's normal for it to be just the three of us.

After packing my bags and paying I thank her and make my way out of the shop. The butcher and baker are just a few shops away, but the bags are heavy, so I walk to the car to drop them off. Opening the boot with the key fob something catches the corner of my eye. Placing the bags in the boot I turn my head and see the rear of a car driving away. Not that unusual but the streets are practically deserted. What has got my attention is the colour and the style. It's black and shiny and luxurious. It's also the same car that was parked near the cottage earlier. A cold shiver runs through my body. Is it a coincidence? I'm not convinced it is.

Closing the boot, I lock it and walk towards the butcher. Standing at the front of the shop I look into the window but not at the produce on display. I stand stock still and look at the reflection of the road behind me. After a few moments I start to feel stupid at my own anxiety. There's nothing there. It must all be in my imagination. With a shake to my head I open the door and make my way in to the empty shop.

The bakery is busy, so I wait in the queue of people. The smell is amazing and so tantalising. Looking around I try to decide what to buy. Leo likes traditional pasties, Marc likes cheese and onion and I love their steak and ale. The queue slowly moves forward, and I look over the cakes in the window display. The thought of a cream scone is tempting but their Cornish cake is pretty good too. As my eyes flick between the cakes I look up to the stands of displays and naturally rove my eyes across the front window passing something out on the street. I flick my eyes back quickly and I see it in the far distance. Sitting in the front seat is a man. He's obscured from view by the glare to the front windscreen. He's sitting perfectly still, waiting, inside a car. A large black luxurious car. At that very moment the server calls out to get my attention. I hadn't noticed the line had moved on and it was my turn. I look up as she calls out to me and quickly whip my head around to the window again, but all I can see now is the empty road outside. Shaking away my suspicions

I turn to the server to order. I'm not sure why I've seen the same car three times, but it's unnerved me.

On the drive back to the cottage I spend far too much time looking in my rear-view mirror to be considered truly safe and I'm glad when I pull up to the gate at the cottage. There is nothing there. Nothing has followed me. Why would anyone be watching us. I'm just being paranoid, Captain Sensitive. With a shake to my head I jump out of the car to retrieve the bags and make my way inside. It's only when I close and lock the door do I realise how much I'm shaking.

The days turn into weeks which pass in a blur. Each one the same as the last. The new dynamic of the three of us as a family settling around us. I know we're living a false hood here in Cornwall, pretending it's a holiday. The only thing missing is my usual check in with Alex when he wasn't too busy to talk. Looking back, we hardly spoke with him whilst we were away. I'd get a text now and again saying he loved us, or how much he missed us, but it felt like we were totally detached from him whilst we were down here. He encouraged us to go away as much as we could. I understood he was busy, and he didn't want us just sitting about at home whilst he was busy working. I always appreciated his thoughtfulness. We were his number one priority. It's sad that he missed out on so much, the first time the boys surfed on their own, night time swims, bar-be-ques on the beach. All memories that only the three of us share. He loved seeing the photos, always promising he would be there on our next visit.

I know we need to return to real life and I'm dreading telling the boys. To see them smiling each day has been a godsend. I never thought they would.

As we're all watching TV snuggled on the sofa and chairs with blankets I decide now's the time to say something.

"We need to go back soon."

I leave the statement in the air for them to process. Neither of them looks my way. I feel their despondency in the atmosphere.

"I know you don't want to, neither do I, but we have to go home. We can't stay here forever."

Leo drops his shoulder, that feeling of misery seeping from his body. Lifting his head, he looks over to Marc.

"We know."

Nothing else needs saying. A sadness descends on our little group. We all continue to look at the television, with none of us actually seeing it. We all realise that reality is just about to come crashing down.

## Chapter Twelve

We've been back home for a few weeks and have tried to adjust as best we can. The boys went back to school the Monday after we returned from Cornwall. The school have been amazing, and a counsellor is on hand for them to talk to. They've been given a small amount of leniency with regard to their attendance, but both boys have soldiered on and attended every day since their return.

I've picked up on work where I can as a means of distraction. When I'm sanding or painting my head is filled with the job in hand. It's when I stop that it all comes crashing back again. It's in those moments that I have to catch my breath before it allows the grief to leak with my tears. Neighbours and friends have continued to be supportive but have respected our need for time and space. Alex's family haven't been quite so respectful. The calls have become constant since our return. I feel ungrateful at their on-going concern for our welfare, but it feels wrong to develop any relationship with them now that Alex is gone. I have never fully understood why Alex wanted us at a distance from them. Whenever I would ask he would distract me, and the subject would be forgotten. I can see they are forceful in their strength and love, they have shown us their kindness. A kindness I assumed they didn't possess. When he did talk about his family it wasn't in a favourable light.

This morning I decided to start on a new piece. I dropped the boys at school and made my way to a charity furniture outlet a few towns away. I can feel a margin of excitement bubbling at the prospect of finding something I will like. The furniture is donated to the charity and sold on from a large warehouse. You never know what you will find there.

Pulling into the car park my excitement level rises a little. Waving at one of the volunteers I make my way into the warehouse and I'm immediately greeted with mid-century furniture, Formica topped tables, 80's designed bookshelves, beds, badly painted pictures. The warehouse is huge, and it can often take me a few hours to walk around. My head is planted solely in the warehouse and it takes me a few moments to realise that my phone is ringing. Taking it from my bag I see that Dante is calling. On a sigh I answer him.

"Good morning Dante."

"Kate, good morning. Are you well?" As formal as ever.

"Yes, thank you Dante, and you?" I need to maintain a politeness I remind myself.

"Are you away from home?" Odd question.

"Yes, why?" I've learnt that directness works best with Dante.

"I believe the Inspector has called at your home again."

He is still monitoring the camera at the front door I realise. There's no point calling him out on it. We both know the truth.

"When will you return home?"

My excitement has just dropped a little at my impromptu shopping trip, but in that same moment I remind myself I'm my own boss. I set my own schedule.

"Later, after I pick the boys up." I say with a bit more bravado and a decisive nod. I'm proud of myself.

"We need to talk." Not the words I wanted to hear.

"What about?"

I'm not cutting my day short for something inconsequential. This is the first time I've wanted to go out of the house. The first day I put on jeans without paint splatters. The first day I felt like me again. Knowing Dante, it will be to discuss something stupid like the boys and how they need to be around the family more or Maria wanting us to stay for a weekend. My sigh must be audible to him over the phone.

"About Allesandro."

My heart stops momentarily at the sound of his name and begins to beat again to its rhythm that was always in sync with his.

"Why?" My question is quiet, but I know he heard me.

"We can't discuss family matters over the phone. It is not safe."

There's the use of that word again, safe.

"You will come to the house this weekend. Mamma is expecting you all."

My shoulders drop in defeat. I know I can't get out of visiting them any longer. I've put them off with excuses, but now I've run out.

"When do we need to be there?" My tone displaying my displeasure and despondency.

"There will be a car to collect you this evening."

"What? Why?" Why so soon, and I'm more than capable of driving to the outskirts of London, besides I need my car in case we need to escape.

"My driver will collect you."

"What about Bear?" I throw at him.

It's obvious from the delay in his response he'd forgotten about him.

"If we come so does he."

I'm almost smirking at the thought of our lumbering big, hairy, sloppy, messy dog in their pristine home. Barrelling through the rooms with their dainty tables and object d'art carefully placed, laying on their satin sofa's. I hope he's thinking the same and retracts his invitation. Juvenile it may be, but I push on.

"The boys would never dream of leaving him at home. We know he can be a little slobbery, but he is very lovable. Just don't get too close to him in your suit though."

Pinching my lips together to stem the laughter I patiently wait for his response.

"That is fine. He may stay in the security office."

Well that back fired.

I realise I can't get out of this now. He was my only excuse for not going. I am curious though. What does he need to talk to me about? What do we need to discuss about Alex? We had no secrets, well none except for the house and the cottage, oh and some business he owned, apart from that, we told each other everything.

"OK." I relent. "What time?"

"5pm there will be a car to collect you all. Good bye Kate."

As he is just about to hang up I quickly shout down the phone.

"Make sure it's a big one!" And with that I disconnect my call.

The warehouse has several pieces that I like. I'm torn between an 18th century book case with three large drawers and shelves with leaded glass doors above. The structure is sound and there's no woodworm. All the components are there but it's been sadly mistreated. The other item is a French style 19th century sideboard. The heavy brown colour making the piece look sad and neglected. There are no signs of woodworm but there's a lot of scratches, thankfully none are too deep.

I'm stood leaning against the sideboard making my deliberations when I hear a voice I recognise. I can't place the voice in my mind and as the furniture is stacked high in places I can't see the owner. It niggles my brain that I can't fathom who owns the voice. She sounds familiar, but I can't think why. She is talking to another person, and her voice fades away as they walk down the aisle next to mine. Shaking my head, I stop trying to figure out who it is. I'm sure it will come to me later.

Bending down I start to look inside the cupboards of the sideboard and have a good poke about to check it's structurally sound. There's nothing worse than working on a piece that starts to fall apart under a sander.

"Hello, Mrs Rossi?" The familiar voice asks from beside me.

As I straighten I hit my head on the inside roof of the cupboard.

"Shit!" Rubbing my head, I extract myself from the mouth of the sideboard. As I straighten I recognise the voice immediately.

"Inspector Shaw. How are you?" The inspector looks completely different, dressed casually in jeans and a jumper, standing next to her is another woman.

"Are you OK Mrs Rossi? I'm really sorry. I didn't mean to startle you."

The worry on her face is evident, transporting me back momentarily to the last time we spoke. Plastering a smile on my face I try to reassure her.

"I'm fine, don't worry."

"How are you?" She asks with true feeling but some trepidation.

"We're getting there. Thank you for asking and thank you for your kindness that day." The Inspector blushes slightly.

"I was merely doing my job Mrs Rossi." She appears very nervous.

I see her friend start to shift, and the Inspector diverts her attention towards her.

"We need to be going." She states. "Take care Mrs Rossi. Really do be careful."

The way she says it makes me slightly uncomfortable. And with that they walk away.

As they make their way to end of the aisle I spy her friend lean in to her and hear my name drift in the air. The Inspector nods her head whilst she whispers back. The words only meant for her friend, but they head directly towards me.

"Yes, Rossi Syndicate." It's not said in an admiring way. It's said with true fear.

After purchasing both cabinets, the prices are so reasonable it would be silly not to, I arrange with one of the volunteers for delivery to my studio next week. Ideas for their transformation whizzing through my brain as I tuck my purse back in my bag.

Sitting in the driver's seat the Inspectors words resonate through my brain. Rossi Syndicate. I knew the Rossi family had built quite an empire, but the word Syndicate is what bothers me most.

Retrieving my phone, I type in Rossi Syndicate and await the results. I don't profess to understand all the results but it's obvious the family have a LOT more businesses than I original thought. Their reach stretches from nightclubs to bars, strip clubs, which I shiver in repulsion at, and casinos. There is no mention of the family members though. Scrolling through I see Gia as one of their main operations.

A newspaper link catches my eye and I begin to read the article, which is a report of a police raid at Gia last year. Alex never said anything about it. Surely something of that magnitude, he would have told me. The police warrant was issued on suspicion of laundering. There is no further information, but I'm pretty sure it has nothing to do with washing.

Scrolling further through I see no additional information on the raid or its outcome. My next search is for the word Syndicate. I know the dictionary definition is a group of individuals who combine to promote, but it seems an odd choice of word to describe a company.

The results for Syndicate are typical of the internet, offering links to various shady looking groups. Something is needling at the far reaches of my brain, but I can't quite grasp it.

Closing down my phone I sit in the car park of the warehouse and sort through my thoughts. Why wouldn't Alex have told me there was a police investigation at the nightclub. Maybe a competitor was trying to play silly games and gave the police false information. They would have needed evidence though.

My head is starting to hurt with all the considerations and ideas running around. Looking through the windscreen I start to settle my mind by planning what we need for the weekend; clothes, shoes, Bears bed and food, evening wear? God do I need to get dressed up to have dinner? I slam the door shut to those thoughts and start the engine. They will have to take us as they find us. I will concede and wear something other than jeans. They should be grateful for that at least.

Pulling out of the parking space I drive towards the exit and do a quick scan to check for any cars before I pull out. During my quick search in both directions it takes my brain a moment to catch up with what my eyes have just clocked. Tucked in a side road further into the industrial estate is a car. Not unsurprising considering the number of people who work in the various factories and warehouses, but what is standing out and glaringly obvious is the make and model. The large black shiny car is the same make as the one in Cornwall.

Pulling into the road, I carefully navigate my way through the network of roads and finally exit the industrial estate.

Looking into my rear-view mirror, the road is empty. I sit at the junction for a moment to allow my heart to return to a normal rhythm. I can feel my hands shaking on the wheel, so I release them and shake them out before taking it again. Indicating I turn the opposite way to home.

It takes 15 minutes longer to get home than usual, and I'm happy to see the road leading into the village. I didn't see the black car again, in fact I didn't see much traffic at all. I laugh to myself at my own stupidity. There must be hundreds of black cars on the roads. Finally pulling along the drive I sigh in relief at the sight of home. Our safety, our sanctuary.

Walking in through the door Bear barrels up to greet me in his usual exuberant way. He loves it when you scratch him under his chin. It has to be the exact right spot, or he will move his head around until you find it. He seems even more needy than usual. I feel bad for neglecting him so much lately.

"I'm sorry Bear, I promise we will go out more next week."

Ignoring me he continues to sit and receive his head rub.

Flicking the kettle on I sort through the mail I picked up after Bear has had his fill. The amount of junk they send out is criminal.

Why do I need a stair lift?

No, I'm not quite ready for food delivered by Alan or one of the team who ensures a kind and courteous service. I wonder if the food actually does look like that?

There is the mobile phone bill, which I know is paid by direct debit. I need to talk to the company and cancel Alex's contract. It was all in his name, I assume I write with a copy of his death certificate to let them know. The thought of that word cuts through me every time.

Swallowing down the lump in my throat I quickly shake my head to dispel my wayward thoughts. The last one is the bank statement.

Sitting with it in my hand I come to a realisation that I've never actually opened a bank statement. Whenever they would arrive I would leave them on the side for Alex. Why have I never opened a letter that was addressed to both him and me? Alex always told me I didn't need to worry myself with those things, that my number one job was to raise our boys.

Whenever I went shopping I just used my bank card, never thinking about the amount. If I needed diesel I just filled it up and used my bank card.

The kettle flicks off which wakes me from my reflexions. Walking over to the cupboard I take down my favourite mug, the boys bought it for me last year for Christmas as a joke. It has a picture of us all on it, including the dog. Putting in a green tea bag and topping it with water I take a cautionary sip. I need it a bit sweeter today. Digging out the honey I stir in a spoonful and return to the island with my sweetened tea.

It feels wrong opening the letter but it's my job now. Sliding my finger under the seal I take out the folded sheets and start scanning through. I don't know what it is I'm looking for, but I see the various transactions over the last month, both here and in Cornwall. I'm shocked when I see the amount I spend on a weekly basis itemised like this. Maybe we need to start economising. I know Dante said Alex was rich but if we keep spending like this we will soon be poor.

Picking up my mug of tea I blow across the top and take a sip. The sweetness and aroma soothe me until I reach the bottom of the page and almost spray it across the kitchen. Carefully I place the mug down, as I don't want to risk breaking it with the shock. Scanning over and over again, double checking the account name and numbers. Definitely our joint account, both Alex and my initials and surname are correct, and I remember most of the transactions listed. My eyes stray to the final balance one more time and realisation sets in. We are really, really, REALLY rich. Counting the digits back from the decimal point several times. I'm looking at a lot of numbers. I know six zeros is one million. I'm looking at 7 of them.

Gently placing the paper back on the island, I sit in stunned silence and stare. How the hell do we have so much money? Where did it all come from? It doesn't make sense that we have so much. Laughing to myself, I can't believe I was so worried about buying both pieces of furniture this morning. I could probably afford to buy the whole warehouse.

## Chapter Thirteen

After collecting the boys from school, I decide to break the news of our little jolly away. Leo seems OK with it.

"Cool, will Benni be there?"

"I don't know, I didn't really get a chance to ask." That's an understatement.

Marc is a bit quieter, but I'm not overly worried, it's his nature. Taking his tablet from his school bag he puts his ear phones in and loads something and starts listening intently. I frown at him in the rear-view mirror, but his attention is totally engaged. Turning my eyes back to the road I see Leo typing on his phone from my peripheral vision. It's nice to see them both acting like normal teenagers. I know losing their father is going to come back and hurt them over and over again, but as their mum it's nice for me to see them trying to get on with their normal lives.

Pulling into the driveway there is an enormous SUV sitting in the drive. Both boys' heads pop up from their devices to take in the gargantuan truck, then quickly turn my way in question. Laughing to myself I realise Dante had heard my closing words to him. Trying desperately not to snigger I get out of the car and walk over to the driver as he emerges from the colossal beast, having to use the step that emerges from underneath to reach the ground. I'm surprised he doesn't get a nosebleed from being so high up. Desperately trying to rein in my thoughts I smile at one of the nameless two, recognising him from his previous visits.

"Mrs Rossi." He says in greeting, with respect in his voice and a sort of bow.

I stand there just looking at him. What an odd thing to do. I love history and the courtliness of manners in their greetings, but this is definitely not the 1800's. Turning to the boys I see their wide-eyed looks are similar to mine. Turning back to the nameless one I smile politely as he rises from his bow and turn on my heels towards the house. My eyebrows must be near my hairline in shock. The boys follow me but the nameless one stays by the car.

Unlocking the door, I flick a look to the boys and then to the nameless one and back to the boys again. Is he going to stay there? I ask them in silent question. Both Leo and Marc shrug their shoulders with a small shake to their heads.

Looking around the boys I try to get his attention, he is stood stock still, but his eyes are frantically scanning the area. I turn and look in the direction he is, but there's nothing there.

"I , um, I ,err, I don't know your name, sorry." I say trying to capture his attention.

He quickly turns to me and with a shocked look he responds.

"Richie. My name is Richie Mrs Rossi. I'm sorry."

What's he sorry for? Odd one.

"Well Richie, do you want to come inside and wait? We need to grab a few things before we'll be ready. Dante said the car wouldn't be here this early."

The look of mortification on his face makes me feel bad for saying anything.

As he is just about to speak I put my hand up to stop him.

"Actually, I'm glad you're here, you can help. Hope you don't mind?"

I plaster a smile on my face and continue inside. The boy's barrel past me and I hear Richie's footsteps on the gravel. Walking into the kitchen I hear the front door close.

"You can come in here." I shout, and I hear him following my voice.

I try to reassure him with a smile, he looks so nervous.

"I need to get the dog's things together. Could you grab his bed and sack of food please?"

Richie nods and walks towards Bear's bed, picking it up with one hand and grabbing the sack of food with the other. As he starts to leave the kitchen Bear comes padding in stopping Richie in his tracks. I know they've met before when he was here with Dante, but I can't understand why Bear is staring him down. Richie's nerves have just gone up another level.

"He's probably wondering why you've got his bed." I try to inject a bit of humour

"Come here Bear." The dog tilts his head, so I know he heard me.

"Now Bear." I say with a bit more force.

Bear slowly turns his head from his prey and wanders aimlessly over to me. I can see Richie physically start to relax, his shoulders moving down from their kiss with his ears as his body unfolds from itself. Bear nudges my hand and I give him his obligatory rub as a well done for following my command.

I packed us all a bag earlier and now that the boys are changed we can leave. Double checking the back door and all the windows, I grab my bag from the island. On a moment's whim, I don't know why, I open the junk drawer and retrieve the crappy phone that Leo found in there. Shoving it in my bag, I do a quick scan and leave.

Setting the alarm and locking the house I move towards the car. Bear is in the boot looking out the back window. I can see the drool already. The boot is fully carpeted, I hope they've got a good hoover as his fur will be everywhere before we've even left the driveway. Ho-hum, not my problem. That's what boot liners were made for.

The boys have jumped into the cavernous back seat and Richie is stood by the door. I start to worry, am I supposed to get in the back with them, or do I sit in the front? It's a bit like getting in a mini cab. Do you get in the back and feel like you're being chauffeured whilst trying to avoid eye contact in the mirror, or do you get in the front and sit in stilted silence feeling like you've invaded their personal space? I move towards the back door and stand with my hand on the door.

"Are we all in?" I ask.

I know they're old enough to get in the car by themselves, but I'm buying myself a moment to decide where to sit. Holding onto the door, I shut it and go to the passenger door at the front. With a shocked look Richie walks towards the door but I beat him and open it myself. Climbing in I see a worried look on his face. Oh god have a chosen the wrong seat. Well I can't move now. This is another reason why I wanted to drive myself, to reduce stupid stressful situations like this. Aaarrrrhhh.

Driving along the twisting lanes the silence is oppressive. I'm used to the sounds of the boys squabbling or arguing over what music to play. They both seem to appreciate the seriousness of the situation.

Turning slightly in my seat I look at our silent driver.

"How long have you worked for Dante?" I ask.

The enquiry seems to take Richie by surprise. The look of shock has me wanting to retract my question.

It seems like an age before he answers.

"5 years." Man of few words just like his boss then.

I suppose if you're around Dante all day long his mannerisms will rub off on you.

Turning back, I continue to stare out of the window at the road ahead.

After an hour of silence, we eventually pull off the road and a pair of imposing gates rise up to greet us. I'm starting to have serious reservations about this. Pulling up to the gates they begin to open. I didn't see him press anything and he bypassed the intercom. Looking up through the windscreen I spy a security camera.

Somebody must have seen us arrive. The gates slowly open inwards and we move forward along the tree lined drive.

Looking around I take in the landscape and catch a glimpse of two men walking along the perimeter of the grounds. As quickly as I see them they seem to melt away into the surroundings.

Turning a final bend, the house comes into view. Both Leo and Marc lean forward to capture a better look. Holy cow!! It's enormous.

On the few occasions we've met with his family it has been in public settlings and sporadically at an apartment in the city. I thought that was big. This is the Rossi family home. I'm stunned. The imposing white façade is held up by 6 columns. The huge windows rise up on three levels and stretch across the front of the building. The place is enormous.

"Wow." I hear from the back seat.

Wow is right.

Standing on the stone steps is Dante looking austere in his black suit and Maria visibly twisting her hands. She looks nervous. I don't know why, I'm the one who should be. Maybe it's the prospect of our ickle tiny, teeny weeny dog being let loose in her magnificent home. Actually, I'm really worried now.

Richie stops and a suited man steps forward. Taking the handles to both doors at the same time he opens them simultaneously and steps back to allow us to disembark. I grapple with the seat belt and take my bag from the footwell. I can hear the boys moving about in the back, but I can't take my eyes from the magnificence of the house.

Dante moves forward with his mother on his arm. He gives me a moment to take in one last sweep of the vista before he addresses me.

"Thank you for coming Kate."

I didn't realise I had an option.

"Good afternoon Leonardo, Marco. I hope you are both well."

The boys are displaying similar looks to me and simply nod their heads in answer to their Uncles question.

Over the years I've dragged the boys around various country estates trying to force a bit of culture and history into them. I've never had a reaction like this from either of them. I suppose it's different when you know the people who live in the colossal mansion.

I hear a bark from the car which quickly wakes me from my trance. Smiling to Richie, I walk towards the boot.

"Can you let him out please?" I ask.

I'm actually dreading letting Bear out. The lawns are perfectly manicured and the flowers that are still holding on look flawless. One cock of his leg and there will be brown patches and wilting plants. I silently pray that he will behave.

The boot begins to open, and I don't have time to grab his collar and put his lead on. Bear hurls himself from the boot and stalks off towards the immaculate carpet of grass. Please, no. At least wait till Dante and Maria aren't looking. My prayers are ignored. Bear walks over to a beautiful piece of topiary, sniffs it a few times and then ever so slowly lifts his leg. My shoulders drop to the floor with my despondency and heat floods my face. The smug look on his face displays his merriment. He knows exactly what he's doing. He could have chosen anywhere to wee but he chose there. He's started now and there is no way I can stop him. Turning back to Dante and Maria I see a horrified look on both their faces. Why did I insist on bringing him?

"I am so sorry." I start.

What else can I say. They will probably throw us out and have nothing more to do with us all. Richie and the other man are both displaying similar looks but theirs have a touch of fear to them too.

Sucking up my mortification, I stride over to Bear with his lead in my hand and give him the most severe look I can muster. I don't need to say anything as he can read my body language and he knows how angry I am with him.

Kneeling down I clip the lead on and whisper to him.

"Why did you do that?" I point towards a wooded area and continue. "You could have gone over there!" I point another way. "Or there" And another. "Or there".

I think Bear starts to realise his error and lowers his head in shame. I immediately feel bad for chastising him. If he was at home he could go where ever he wanted. I shouldn't expect him to know any better. He keeps his head lowered as I lead him back to the party of stunned faces.

"I'm really, really sorry. I, I err I umm." I swallow down, I have no idea what I can say to rectify the situation.

"Do not worry." Maria's calm voice cuts through my ramblings. "He needed to go!" She says with a shrug to her shoulders and her palms out flat. "When you got to go, you go."

I could honestly kiss her right now. Dante still looks disturbed. He is appalled that our dog has just violated his topiary.

With my head lowered I walk and stand next to the boys. I should be scuffing my toe in the dirt or something as the situation has become a trifle awkward. Actually, I'd better not as I might misplace some of his perfectly placed stones. The boys move in closer, I'm not sure if it's to protect us or out of fear. I'm the parent I need to protect them.

Dante clears his throat and starts to tell the door man to take 'The Dog' to the security office. My head snaps up immediately at his command. Pulling the lead back, and subsequently Bear, I stand in front of them all and stare him straight in the eyes. I'm not sure why I take this stance, but his command was said in a less than friendly way.

"Where is he taking him? I want to see where he's going."

I will not allow a man I barely know order my dog be taken away by a man I've never seen before.

The door man stops his movements towards us and looks back to Dante for instruction. Dante tries to hide his look of irritation. Considering my words, he nods to the doorman.

"I will accompany you."

Although the words are said to me, he is still looking at the door man. Whatever message was conveyed, he acknowledges with his head and walks with purpose around the building and out of sight.

"Come."

His one-word command is issued. The boys follow me as I lead Bear behind Dante, like follow my leader, to the Security Office.

The office looks like something from a spy film. One wall is covered in monitors, I can see various views of the house and grounds, plus several businesses I assume The Rossi family own. Two men in identical black suits sit at the desk watching movements on the monitors. The gentle hum from the various computers and the panting from Bear are the only sounds to be heard. Dante walks and stands behind one of the men and whispers in his ear, he immediately rises turning to face us.

"This is Mrs Rossi, Leonardo and Marco. You will look after their dog whilst they are staying." The words are said in more of a command than a request.

"Bear, h..h...his name is Bear." Marc stammers.

I smile at him with pride.

"Yes, Bear." Dante informs the man.

 "We need to get his bed and things from the car."

I'm not sure who I'm aiming it at. I appreciate this is Dante's home, but he's our dog and I want to see him settled before we leave him here.

With a flick of his head the man acknowledges Dante, turns towards the door and leaves.

With just one man left at the desk the view of the monitors becomes clearer. I stand scanning the images, taking in the beauty of their home and gardens portrayed on screen. I can see the outside of a few clubs, showing both the front and rear exits, and, judging by the gaudy décor, a strip club too. I'm just pleased there are no images from the inside on display. The boys are very aware of girls, but I think they're a bit young to see that! On the bottom row are images of residential properties, one is very familiar.

Looking up to Dante I see him watching my reaction. Surely this is an invasion of our privacy. There must be laws against him monitoring our house.

"Why is that there?" I point at the image. I might as well be blunt.

The boys look towards me and quickly back to the bank of monitors. I can hear from the intake of breath when they see it too.

"You need to be kept safe."

Really, that word again. With an exhausted sigh I challenge him.

"Dante, we live in a sleepy little village in a sleepy little county. It's more than safe, and besides, I do NOT need you watching our every move. It's creepy and probably illegal. I want you to stop it. Immediately."

I use my firm Mum voice and judging by the shocked look on his face it might have worked. I see the man monitoring the screens tilt his head a little to get us into view. He can't see Dante's face, but his body language is shouting quite loud.

Standing tall I stare him down when a scowl crosses his face. Give me your best shot. I could do this all day buddy. Not moving I remain in place waiting for him to either explode with rage or concede defeat. The little tick at the corner of his eye tells me more than he realises. He is fit to burst. Alex and both the boys have it, I realise now that it must be a family trait.

"Rimuovi l'immagine ma mantieni attivo il feed."

I assume he has admitted defeat as the image of our home disappears from the bank of monitors. The man keeps his head down as Dante is REALLY annoyed now. I could smile and do a little dance of triumph, but I won't. Keeping a bland look on my face I nod my thanks.

Marc tugs at my arm trying to get my attention, turning I look at him and wait for him to speak. He motions for me to lean closer so he can whisper in my ear. He has a look on his face I can't fathom. Leaning in towards him he cups his mouth around my ear so only I can hear.

*"He's only turned the picture off the cameras are still working."*

Straightening up I look him in the eye, a slight frown on my face. He nods at me, and I know he understood. I'm trying to figure out how he's learnt Italian, when he says one word.

"Tablet."

My beautiful, amazing, intelligent boy. I nod and offer a huge smile to him. Marc has just become our secret weapon. Thinking quickly as I turn I look at the man at the desk.

"Excuse me." I tap him on the shoulder when he doesn't respond.

He turns slowly and a little cautiously.

"You ned to cut the cameras off completely. I believe you've only turned off the image." I smile at him with the sweetest smile I can muster. Busted.

The man and I both turn to look at Dante. There is almost steam coming from his ears. With a clenched jaw and pursed lips he turns his head to the waiting man, whilst keeping his raging eyes on me, and nods, once. Turning back to his monitors he keys something in to the keyboard and the screen goes from grey to black.

## Chapter Fourteen

We settle Bear with the two security men, each of us giving him a big hug and extra scratches. He lays down and promptly falls asleep. I'm still a little uncomfortable with leaving him here. I'll pop back in a while to check on him.

Once we are all stood again Dante leads us from the security office, no less angry, back to the main house.

"I will take you to mamma."

Following on behind him we enter the house and escorted to a downstairs room. The elegance of the room is in every piece of furniture, swathe of material and painting. The cornflower blue of the walls is inviting and offers a majestic feel whilst still being homely. Now I can understand why Bear is in the office outside.

"Mamma." Dante says to the cavernous room.

Maria rises in a regal fashion from her chair and walks towards us, with both hands stretched out in greeting. Taking both of my hands she pulls me to her and kisses both my cheeks. Stepping back, she keeps my hands captive as she looks me over. Her smile ever present. Dropping me, she moves on to the boys and does the same to each of them. A feeling of love pouring from her actions.

"Come. Sit." She says, tugging on Marc's hand which she has grasped firmly in hers.

Maria takes a seat in the middle of the sofa, pulling Marc next to her whilst patting the seat to encourage Leo on the other side. I opt for the seat opposite and watch as my boys are gently manhandled by their grandmother.

Maria seems happy to sit and look at the boys in turn, but I can see them squirming under the intensity of her gaze. I need to rescue them, even if it's just from her visual scrutiny.

"How are you Maria?" I can't think of anything else to ask.

I don't really know this woman.

Maria turns her eyes to me and I see the boys both physically relax in that moment. With a gracious smile she responds.

We sit for half an hour chatting about nothing in particular. Every time she started to look back to the boys I would question her about a painting or piece of furniture to keep her attention on me.

"Ah the time it has passed quickly. We must wash for dinner." Maria says as she rises from her seat still holding both boys' hands. With the biggest smile I can muster I rise too and start to follow her from the room.

Standing outside is another man in a suit. Exactly the same as all the others I've seen. It must be a uniform, I think to myself.

"Per favour, portali nelle loro stanze." Maria says to the man.

He offers a stiff bow and looks towards us.

"I will see you at dinner. We dine at 8pm." And with that Maria walks further into the house.

"Please follow me." I hear and quickly turn to the waiting man.

Smiling up at him I nod, and we follow up the stairs. We pass the first-floor landing, rooms laid out on either side of us, their doors open except for one. A similarly suited man is standing outside and watching our movements, his hands braced behind his back. The two men acknowledge each other with a silent nod, and our guide moves on up the next flight of stairs.

The staircase arrives at the centre of the u shape again and it is obviously the sleeping quarters for the family. Taking us to the left we are escorted to a suite. The door opens into a lounge area with two doors leading off on either side. Looking through the door nearest me, I see it has two single beds and on them are the boys' bags.

"You're in here boys." I say and they both come barrelling past me.

I turn to go to the other room and the suited man is still stood there.

"If you need anything Mrs Rossi, dial 9 on the phone and someone will come to assist you." He says whilst pointing to the telephone on the side table.

"Somebody will collect you and escort you down to dinner."

My frown must be obvious. With a slight smile he answers my question.

"It is a large house. It is easy to get lost."

That does make sense I suppose. I smile at him as he begins to back out of the door. With his hand on the door he looks at me and I sense he wants to say something, but he merely smiles, and closes the door behind him.

My bedroom is huge with a king size bed looking out over the expansive grounds, the claw foot bath shares the same view from the bathroom. My bag has been set neatly on the bed, a mild panic starts as I start to unzip it. I've only bought one dress with me. I just hope it's enough.

The boys appear settled, the tv is on and they're lying on their beds with their devices in hand. Leo is in a frantic messaging frenzy, I assume to tell his friends where he is. Marc is on his tablet with his headphones on again. Walking over I gaze over his shoulder. He looks up at me and smiles as he removes his headphones.

"That was VERY clever of you earlier." I state.

The beam on his face sets mine off.

"How long have you been learning this?" I ask pointing to the language app on his tablet.

Marc shrugs, almost in embarrassment.

"For a few weeks."

His brain is like a sponge. It soaks up every ounce it can. I'm not surprised now that he could understand what Dante said. Placing my hand on his arm I look at him sincerely.

"Can we keep this between us? I think it's better for now."

I can't quite explain it, but I would rather keep this from the family. If they know we can understand everything they're saying they may be more careful, and we wouldn't have caught Dante out earlier.

It's clear that Marc isn't comfortable with the deception and I feel bad for asking.

"You could be our secret spy." I say, knowing his love of mysteries and spy thrillers.

The smile that breaks out on his face says it all.

"I could write down everything they say in Italian." He says, then a frown crosses his face. "But in English of course."

I smile my agreement and rise from the bed.

"You need to shower and change before we go down for dinner."

The look of horror on their faces is comical.

"Just wear whatever you want that's clean." And with that I leave the room.

I deliberated over using the bath but opted for a shower as I need to wake up fully and the bath would make me drowsy. I might try it later before bed. Fully revitalised I stand and look at the black dress laid out on the covers. Chewing the inside of my cheek I realise how shabby it looks against the beautiful cream damask. It's either that or my jeans. It's too late to start worrying now.

Pulling the dress over my head, I fumble around the back for the zip, just catching it between my finger and thumb, and dropping it again just as quickly. Trying and failing again and again. Alex always helps me with zips when we're going out.

The thought slams into my brain and literally knocks me off my feet. I realise that today is the first day I haven't thought about him constantly. It sounds ironic, as we're staying in his family home. Sitting on the end of the bed my shoulders drop as I clasp my hands between my knees, staring into nothing. A feeling of guilt overcomes me. How can I have gone this long without him consuming my thoughts? I feel dreadful that I allowed him to slip from my mind for hours. Today felt like a normal day, with Alex at work and me with the boys. I know I will never recover from his death fully while I still feel him. Why do I still feel him? Despondency overwhelms me, a weight pushes down against my shoulders. How could I have forgotten he's gone?

The table must seat at least 16, the shine reflects the chandelier glowing above. Laid out to perfection are numerous dishes with two ladies dressed in grey uniforms ferrying back and forth to the kitchen for more. Dante sits at the head with his mother to his right. I was shown to the seat on his left and practically dragged Marc into the seat next to me. I might need him to translate. Leo is sat between Maria and Benni and seems more than comfortable.

We've all made an effort tonight, well for us at least. We're happier lounging in front of the fire with plates of food chatting or watching a movie.

Dante is in his usual pristine attire of dark suit as is Benni, although his is a little less austere. Looking between the two I realise that Alex always wore a suit too. The thought has me wrinkling my brow as I look from one brother to the next. Come to think of it, Alex rarely wore jeans or casual clothes. Every day he would dress in yet another suit before he left for work. Even for a casual meeting with his brothers.

Looking again I begin to see them in a very different light. Why do they always choose suits? They are more than just clothes to these men. It's armour. The clothing sets them apart from all other men. I know why they wear them. It's to set a precedence. An air of authority. A feeling of superiority they allows them to metaphorically tower over others. Realisation crashes into my brain, flooding it with thoughts that I can't keep from my face. They are superior, and not just in their manner. Their actions and their lifestyle place them in a higher realm. This family is different to the masses. I never saw it before, I was never invited to.

Turning my head, I see one of the many nameless faces standing guard at the door. There are a lot of men here, they all wear the same attire, the same look to their faces. Turning back to the family convened around the table, I start to really see them, for who they truly are. I was blinded by their air of authority, and grief clouded my vision, but I can see them now. They are superior, that is obvious by our surroundings but it's in their demeanour, their poise, their attitude. Those men are here to protect them, to guard them.

Oh my god! Why didn't I see it before? They're guards. All of these men are guards for Dante and the family. The drivers, the security, the two men I saw walking the grounds, the man outside of the closed door on the landing.

Turning back to the table Dante and Maria both watch me intently. Both sporting similar looks of unease. I can't make eye contact as my mind runs through all the times I've seen these men. All the words about safety from Dante. Alex's need to keep us protected. What do they need to protect us from?

Dinner is served as I try to school my thoughts. The conversation around the table is light thankfully. Benni and Maria are happy to converse with the boys, but I occasionally feel Dante's eyes on me. Looking up to him I offer a smile as I lift my water to my lips. If I keep my mouth busy I won't need to talk.

Thoughts whirl around and around my head. Why, being the main one. Why do they need this level of protection, why do they need so much security, why is Dante constantly worried about our safety? Why, why, why?

Is it because of their success and the vast wealth which they have obviously accumulated? I inwardly shake my head, I don't think it's that. The words I heard the Inspector say in the furniture warehouse come racing back to me. Rossi Syndicate.

Remembering the web results the jigsaw pieces that are spread out start to merge. A picture begins to form in my mind. I really am that naive.

Picking up my napkin from my lap I lay it on the table and rise.

"Would you excuse me a moment please."

My heart is pounding. I need to get away from their gazes. I try to keep realisation from my face.

Dante and Benni share a look as Maria speaks.

"Are you well Kate?"

I smile and nod.

"I'm fine thank you, I, err, I just need to nip to the loo quickly."

Scuttling away from the table, I barely make it to the door when a nameless suit stands in front of me, practically blocking my exit. He is sporting what I assume is his version of smile.

"I can escort you Mrs Rossi."

Why do I need escorting? Determined not to look back I plaster on a fake smile.

"I'm fine thank you. I'll just run up to my room."

Scooting around him I quickly ascend the stairs passing the first landing at speed. The door I spied earlier is still firmly shut. No-one is standing outside now. No one is guarding it. It hits me in that moment that it's Dante's study and the guard is there to keep him safe.

I sense someone behind me, following. Hastily I continue to the second-floor landing, quickly closing the door to our suite behind me. I retreat to my bedroom and seal myself inside before my thoughts tumble out any more.

Pacing from one side of the room to the other my brain starts to run through past events like a film. Have I really been this blind? All these years and I suspected nothing. His actions never led me to think anything untoward was happening. I've been kept completely oblivious to the true nature of this family intentionally. Alex kept me and the boys away deliberately and I'm beginning to realise why. With his surname there is only one reason, The Rossi Family Syndicate.

Taking the phone from my bag I frantically type *Rossi Family Italian Syndicate* and the results are instantaneous. They all come back with the words *Organised Crime* attached.

I feel sick. Really sick.

My eyes dart about the room looking for sensible answers. It all seems so far-fetched. I feel like I'm in the middle of a drama when in fact this is my reality. How could Alex have been part of a family involved in crime and I had no idea? How could I not have seen it? I already know the answers. Alex kept us away for a reason and now that reason is abundantly clear. It wasn't because we weren't good enough for his family. It's because he was afraid for our safety. The security systems. The lack of contact. Conceding and allowing us to live far away. He wanted to keep us safe. Thoughts crash into my head, the danger he must have faced, the things he must have seen.

My pacing is leaving tracks in the plush carpet, but I need to keep moving to keep up with the thoughts as they invade my mind. Understanding hitting me over and over and over again. The money, the expensive cars, the clothes, the houses, their lifestyle. It all makes sense. No normal family could afford this standard of living. Even the CEO of a conglomerate of companies would struggle to sustain that level of decadence in their everyday life. I swallow down the painful thoughts as they each take their turn in my head. All of this power, all of this money, I'm terrified of how they acquired it, and it's not just theirs. Our home, our lifestyle, our bank account.

A knock from the outer door shakes me from my realisations and I can hear my name being called. I'm not sure I'm ready to face these people but I can't hide up here forever. Oh my god the boys. I've left Leo and Marc downstairs. Panic starts to set in. What do I do?

Breathing slowly, I need to calm my nerves. I need to put on the naïve face I've been wearing for the last 20 years.

With sweaty hands I open the bedroom door, unsure of who I'm going to find. I think I'm going to throw up. The saliva invades my mouth and tremors shake my body.

"I'll just be a....."

Slamming my hand over my mouth I run back into the bedroom and just make it to the bathroom before I lift the lid of the toilet. My knees slam to the floor as my entire stomach is emptied within. Over and over I continue to be sick till there is nothing left, the dry heaving crippling my stomach. The sweat from my brow dripping onto the toilet seat as I lay my head on my arm.

The footsteps I hear from the other room hasten when their owner must see my position.

"Kate, are you OK?"

Do I look ok! I would be screaming if I could.

Benni squats down next to me and places his hand on my forehead. Rising again I hear the tap run before he returns to me and places a wash cloth over my brow and runs it around to the back of my neck.

"Are you done?"

With a slight nod he places his hands under my arms and lifts me, flushing the toilet as we rise. I'm guided to the sink where I place my hands in the vain hope they will take the weight of my weary body.

Filling a glass, he hands it to me and I catch his reflection in the mirror. The look of concern and worry reminds me of Alex and in that moment I feel the excruciating pain of his loss. Benni is replicating Alex's actions completely. He would care for me like I was his angel, his whole world. I was his everything. The tears silently glide down my face as I look away. It's just too painful.

Taking the glass from my hand Benni leads me back into my bedroom.

"I think you need to lay down for a while."

I get the feeling he means for more reasons that just being my being sick.

I nod and kick off my shoes. I need to get to the boys, but I'm wiped out. I'll just lay down for 5 minutes. Re-charge myself. Once I can walk without collapsing, we're getting Bear, packing up our stuff and leaving. Alex kept us away from these people and their activities. He purposely isolated me and the boys to keep us safe and secure. All these years he has wrapped us in cotton wool to protect us and we've voluntarily walked straight into the Lion's den!

## Chapter Fifteen

The low winter sun is desperately straining to share its rays, bouncing light around my unfamiliar surroundings. Soft sheets encase me, the weight of the comforter reassuring. Laying there for a few moments I take in my surroundings when reality hits home. I'm in the bedroom of the Rossi House and it's morning.

Rising from the bed carefully, my stomach revolts and I have to steady myself on the bedside cabinet for a moment. Once the wave of nausea passes I pad to the bathroom. My reflection shows a gaunt, haunted woman, who is drained. The dark circles around her eyes reflecting untold pain. Turning away I use the toilet and clean my teeth, almost gagging as the brush hits my tongue.

My dress is creased, and my hair is a matted mop. Finding my bag, I dress in my usual apparel and run a brush through the knotted mane.

Opening the bedroom door, I can see across the lounge area, the boys are still asleep. Leo with his arms stretched above his head, Marc curled in a ball on his side.

Taking a breath to fortify myself I move towards the door to the suite. I know I need to see the family. I also know I need to hide my realisations from last night. The sooner we can leave the safer we will all be.

My first priority is to check on Bear. As I open the door I sense rather than see the guard outside. Without bothering to look I simply mumble a good morning and move towards the staircase. My shadow follows me and tries to get my attention.

"Good morning Mrs Rossi. Are you well this morning?"

It's not his fault how I found myself in this position and my manners forbid me from being rude.

"Much better." I say and continue down the stairs.

"Would you like me to show you to the breakfast room?" He asks, flanking my movements.

The thought of breakfast has my stomach rolling over. Swallowing down the saliva, I shake my head.

"No thank you. I'm going to see Bear."

If I can find my way to the front door, I'll be able to get some much-needed air on my walk over to the security office.

"I will escort you."

His response leaves no room for negotiations and it's issued more as a command than a suggestion.

Pausing on the landing he almost barrels into my back but stops in time and steadies him-self on the hand rail. Taking a fortifying breath, I try to take in some much-needed courage.

Turning to face him I see it is the guard from last night. The look on his face confirms it was a command and I know I won't be allowed to wander freely.

With a small smile, to hide my nerves, I nod and begin towards the final staircase.

The front door is opened as we approach by yet another guard and my sentinel follows me through.

I can hear his barking as we approach the office and the sound has me worried immediately. Bear isn't a barker. The only time he barks is if he's in distress or he senses we need protecting. Alex trained him to react to trigger words if I was ever out alone and needed him to scare someone off.

Breaking into a run I fly through the security office door and the sight before me breaks out the biggest smile I could ever hope for.

My beautiful cuddly, lovable, adorable Bear has two guards cowering in the corner of the office with a look of pure fear on their faces. He's displaying an amazing set of teeth in his huge jaws and the sounds he's making between barks is deep and aggressive and obviously scary to those who don't know him. His whole body is poised for attack. I remember seeing him in this exact same pose when training with Alex using various weapons.

Pinching my lips together to suppress my laugh I walk towards him. My guard grabs hold of my arm to restrain me and Bears head whips around and sees me being detained. The growl echoes throughout the room and my arm is promptly dropped.

"Mrs Rossi, I think you should move behind me." My prisoner offers.

My smile gets bigger and laughter is slipping away from me.

"It's OK." I tell my guard and move towards Bear.

"Hello my beautiful boy. You're so clever protecting mummy." I speak to him in my mummy loves Bear voice.

Walking straight up to him I crouch down and throw my arms around his neck. Bear instantly changes back into a placid loving dog and pushes his nose further into me.

Leaning back, I hold his head in my hands and look him directly in the eye.

"You don't like being in here do you." I all but whisper to him.

Bear simply pushes back into me again for a cuddle. Sitting myself on the floor I keep one arm around his neck and direct my glare to the two men in the corner, I'm shocked that Bear has reacted to them so violently.

Looking from one to the other I realise I haven't seen them before. Both men stand stock still not moving their eyes from Bear, with their identical suits it's obvious they are Dante's men.

The taller of the two stands with his hand inside his open jacket. His body moving with each deep inhalation. As he breathes in his hand is revealed and I can see something in his grasp. Breathing out and the jacket hides it from my sight. Waiting anxiously for his next breath and I see his deep inhalation opening it further, the object becoming much clearer. It takes a few more of his movements for realisation to set in. I've never seen one in real life but there is no mistaking the shiny black grip or the protruded handle, of a gun.

Holding a little tighter to Bears neck I swallow the lump in my throat. Seeing a gun on TV is nothing like real life. I feel a slight wobble to my chin as the thought rushes across my mind.

"Were you going to shoot him?"

The menacing words that echo around the room have come from my mouth. I'm furious. Shit scared, but furious. How dare they threaten my baby.

Using Bear, I quickly stand and face the man down.

"Were you?" I all but shout in his face.

The unknown man looks to my escort for help, when he doesn't respond he quickly looks at me again. My anger rising to astronomical levels now. I've gone into protective mode with no concern for my own safety, I need to protect Bear.

"FUCKING ANSWER ME." My volume scaring me. "NOW!!!"

I think I may have officially lost it.

I'm standing in an isolated room, alone, with three men who are all probably armed, on the remote estate of my estranged brother-in-law, who, by my reckoning, is part of some crime syndicate. Way to go Kate.

My thoughts aren't exactly lucid right now. My logical brain has upped and left. I can feel I'm losing the plot, but I have no idea what to do to stop it. I'm just spiralling, spinning and I can't stop it.

Bear moves his body fully in front of me into a protective stance. I am so glad to have him with me, I feel safer, he senses the threat in the air as much as I do. There is no way they will let this go. I've just screamed at an armed man. Oh shit!

Quickly looking at my escort I see his eyes drilling holes into the tall man. The sound of running from outside the open door has me quickly turning my head. I have no idea what the outcome of this will be, but I need to protect Bear. I can hear at least 2 people running our way and my nerves are skyrocketing.

Looking quickly from the open door, to my escort, the men in the corner and back to the open door, trying to judge my possibility of escape. The footsteps are directly outside now and I know my window of opportunity has gone. I didn't think I could out run these men, but it was a chance I was willing to take.

Breathing rapidly my heart is beating through my breast and I feel like I'm starting to hyperventilate. I need to calm myself down.

Breathing in through my nose and out through my mouth I wait for more scary men to burst through the door. The way my escort was looking at the man gives me a glimmer of hope he would help me. But would he?

The sound of bodies barrelling through the entrance has me spinning towards it. All imposing and displaying menacing looks, they scan the office, primed, ready for attack. Dante is at the front of two other men, chests heaving from their exertion. Looking from his men to me then back to his men again assessing the situation. The two guards behind him looking for any potential threat as I shrink back slightly from the shock of their entrance. It's in that moment I see their hands are raised and each of them hold a gun pointed directly at me.

"Che cazzo sta succedendo?"

The sound of Dante's voice wakes me from my shock. He hasn't raised his voice but it's still a menacing sound.

All three men in the office look at him in fright. I have no idea what he's said but even I'm scared.

When they don't answer him fast enough he turns his scowl on me and Bear.

"What is going on?"

Swallowing my fear, I know I have to answer him. Pointing my finger to the man I speak.

"HE was going to shoot my dog!"

I decide to show my anger as opposed to fear. I'm majorly freaked out by it all, nervous as hell but I'm still boiling mad.

Swinging his head to the man at the end of my finger, his nostrils flare in anger.

"Spiegare!"

The man starts to gabble on in Italian, pointing wildly between himself and his colleague and then towards the dog and finally at me. The look on his face makes me wither, I can't understand a word they're saying which frightens me even more.

Finally, my escort speaks up in a calmer tone, I assume giving my side of the story, as Dante looks back towards me slightly less darkly.

"Are you hurt?"

I offer him a confused brow. Truthfully, I thought I'd be dead by now, but I'm far from hurt.

"I'm fine." I answer pointing my finger at the man again. "It's that moron there. He was going to shoot Bear."

Bending slightly, I start stroking his head before I continue.

"He was just doing his job, he was protecting me. He sensed danger."

Dante nods once and answers.

"Buona."

I know that means good, but what's good about this situation?

Looking from me he pins the man to the wall with his glare.

"You will apologise." His tone indicating there is no room for negotiation. "Now."

I hear the audible swallow from the man as he drops his gaze.

"Si Capo."

With his head slightly lowered he begins his apology. I half-heartedly listen as I'm still processing what he said to Dante.

'Si Capo.' Those two words I do know. They mean 'Yes Boss'.

Standing in the office I feel like I'm watching as an outsider. These men visibly bow down in Dante's presence. The respect for him is visible but what I also see is fear.

I sense eyes on me as I take in the scene before me, my escort watching me intently, reading my facial expressions and body language, assessing my every reaction as the situation unfolds.

It's all become much, much clearer. I knew Dante was their boss, stupidly I thought he was a CEO who had a hand in small time crime, but with those two words my biggest fears are true.

Capo is the Italian word for boss but it's also the name used for the highest-ranking member of a mafia syndicate.

Realisation starts to hit, I really am in a precarious situation. I don't think Dante would hurt me or Bear, but I don't know this man standing in front of me that well. I've witnessed his anger when people around him don't comply to his wishes, he's even directed those eyes at me when I've dared to defy his requests, or should I say command.

My warden still watches me intently and a look passes over his face, I would almost say friendly, but I'm so scared I could be mistaken. He gives an imperceptible nod as my mind comes to its conclusion correctly. That nod telling me that I've come to an accurate assumption. I don't know who this man is, but at this moment in time he is my one ally, my possible saviour in a situation I never dreamed I would ever find myself in.

Dante is speaking to the two guards in Italian, his tone calm, but I'm not convinced he is. Turning from his men he looks me directly in the eye and then down to Bear. Bear has sat and watched the whole situation pan out along with me and has definitely picked up on the 'bad guy' vibes too. Running my hand through his fir to relax me, more than Bear, I need the contact with him right now, I need to draw from his strength. Looking back up to me Dante seems to come to a decision, I can see it cross his face.

"We will go to my study. The dog may accompany you."

Too bloody right he will, I'm not leaving him with these assassins.

The two security guards won't look at me directly, they stand with their heads high but their eyes downcast. My friendly sentinel gives me a half smile and gestures for me to exit the security office first. I don't even know his name but I'm grateful for that small act of kindness. I smile at him in thanks and begin to leave, Bear naturally follows me. We walk back to the house in silence, with me leading the way, to the front door with Dante close behind. I lean down to stroke Bears head and cast a sly look behind to check if my new friend is in the procession, I can't quite make him out without it being obvious, but there are several men behind Dante. I turn my head back to the house and approach the front door as a guard steps forward to open it for us all.

Swallowing down my apprehension I enter the door and grab hold of Bears collar. The last thing I need is for him to run rampant through these halls. Stopping in the entry way I spy Maria in the same room we sat in yesterday, watching intently. She stands in her proud upright position showing no signs of weakness. Her eyes leave me, and I assume make contact with Dante, as I see her give a definitive nod of her head.

"It is time." She says to him.

I know she could have spoken to him in Italian but I'm assuming it's for my benefit.

Time for what?

What is it?

Oh shit, does she mean it's time for me to die. Every thought I never thought I could have is currently running through my head. What the hell am I supposed to do. I need to get us all out of here. Would they really hurt me, us? We're really in trouble now.

Sitting in Dante's study my hands are clasped tightly between my knees, my jaw is clenched so forcefully I might crack a tooth. Dante is on the phone which I'm grateful for. It gives me a few minutes of reprieve but waiting is ramping up my nerves. I can feel myself physically shaking. Maria is sat in the other chair facing Dante's large wooden desk in her usual resplendent manner. She appears relaxed but her anxious hands clutch onto the lace handkerchief. Bear lays at my feet and I'm glad for his cooperation. He appears relaxed, but I know he's not.

From my peripheral vision I can see my friendly warden standing behind watching over us all with his hands grasped behind his back and legs set slightly apart.

Hanging up the phone Dante looks to his mother and a silent question is answered, with a nod of his head he looks down to his desk sorting through papers. I don't think he's actually looking for anything, he's buying himself some time, trying to formulate how to begin, looking up at me finally, with a determined look.

"I imagine you have a few questions Kate."

That's an understatement, a few. My first one being, will I survive this interview?

"Mmhh hhhhmmm." I can't speak.

Not moving his eyes from me he continues.

"I mean this with no disrespect Kate, but you are not Italian and may not fully appreciate our lifestyle. The Rossi family are very well respected by many families that we have associations with, this has enabled us to thrive and become successful in our business endeavours."

Respected is one word, I'd call it fear judging by the people who work for them, plus I know they have a large number of businesses, I found them on my internet search, but are those businesses a front for what my mind is conjuring. All I know of this lifestyle, as he puts it, is what I've seen during our stay. The opulence is overwhelming, the amount of guards here to protect them seems excessive if he was only 'successful in business'. Thoughts run around my head, picturing scenarios ranging from the ridiculous to the completely bizarre. . Will he confirm my fears, or will he maintain they operate a genuine business?

"As an old Italian family we are lucky to have the recognition of many people. Unfortunately, there are a few who do not regard our situation in life."

I can see he is struggling to articulate. His face gives away nothing though.

"As a family with vast wealth we require extra security, which you have noticed I believe."

I nod my head slightly.

"The men are here for our protection, and that protection also includes you and Allesandro's boys. I would like to offer my sincerest apologies for one of my men upsetting you this morning. He stepped out of line and made you feel uncomfortable by jeopardising the security of your family. He will be dealt with for his actions."

Dante's words are sincere and scary. I nod as I can't offer anything more.

Fiddling with the pen in his hand he flicks a quick glance to his mother and back to me again.

"What would you like to ask? I see you have questions."

My initial thought is for my boys but I'm almost too scared to bring them up.

"Where are Leo and Marc?" I ask, my voice just above a whisper.

Looking to his mother, Maria answers as she turns towards me with a genuine smile.

"Leonardo and Marco are with Benito. I believe he is having breakfast with them before they take a tour of the grounds."

That conjures up images in my head. Shit are they safe. The worry must register on my face as Dante quickly answers my unasked question.

"We would never hurt them, none of you. They are safer here than anywhere else."

I feel myself calm a little at his words. It is the truest statement I have ever heard him declare. I visibly relax, my shoulders dropping with relief.

"Kate we would never harm the boys, they are our future."

What the hell does he mean by that?

"I have no children of my own. They will take over the family business when it is time."

What business though? Would he be a real CEO of a genuine company, or something else?

"Alex was not happy to have them involved when they were so young. Leonardo is coming of age, we need to look to his future."

Alex kept us apart from the family for a reason. Is this the reason why? They want to use our boys as pawns in their game.

Maria turns to face me, handkerchief still clenched tightly in her hands.

"The family business it is handed to the eldest son of the next generation. Leonardo is the eldest and he will take over when Dante is ready to step down."

The look she gives tells me their minds are made up on the matter. Doesn't Leo get a say? What about his dreams? What about Marc? What if we'd had girls?

I'm so damned angry, Alex knew this. Why didn't he discuss it with me? I thought we shared everything but I'm beginning to realise how wrong I was.

No-one says anything as I process her words.

A gentle knock at the door echo's through the silent room. Dante permits them entrance, another example of his control.

One of the grey uniformed maids lays a tray on the mammoth desk and beats a hasty retreat. I wish I could too.

Maria busies herself with pouring coffee for the three of us, handing me a cup and saucer with a steady hand. As soon as I take it the cup clatters and the contents spills. Maria simply smiles takes the cup back and places a napkin underneath to mop up the coffee.

Dante sits back and watches me over the rim of his cup as he drinks the strong black liquid, no sign of nerves, the only sound is their drinking and the tinkling of china as it's intermittently set back in its rest.

"Why do you have so many men here?" I blurt.

I don't recognise my own voice, I know it came from me by the look they both send my way.

Dante resets his cup and places it gently on the desk. I don't think he's going to answer at first, but he slowly raises his head staring straight at me.

"I think you may already know the answer Kate."

Holding my gaze, he continues.

"It is obvious you have come to some, how would you say it, conclusions on your own."

He lets his words sink in and I know I haven't covered my shock so well.

"What are those conclusions Kate?"

Oh shit, I've got to actually say it. What if I'm wrong and I've blown it all up in my head and he's actually the CEO of the Rossi company and they need all these people to protect them. What do I say, what don't I say? Shit, shit, shit.

Sometimes keeping quiet is the safer way to learn more but I can see that I'm out of luck on that option.

I try to formulate my words to cause the least amount of offence if I am completely wrong. One thing I don't want to do is anger this man. Hesitating a moment, I decide it's now or never.

"I assume Syndicate is a key word for the family business?"

I know it's an odd place to start but the Inspector's words are at the forefront of my mind. She was really nervous, and that word seemed important.

"It is." Man of very few words now.

Swallowing, I arrange my next question in my head before I verbalise it.

"The Rossi company, or Syndicate, are involved in more than just, eerrm."

Breathe Kate, breathe.

"Legitimate businesses."

The last two words coming out on a rush of air.

"Correct." He is not making this easy for me.

Breathing deeply, I know he's waiting for me to say more, that way he won't incriminate himself with details I don't have. He's going to stay quiet, he won't help me vocalise my suspicions.

In for a penny in for a pound!! I dive straight in, they'll either confirm my thoughts or I won't be leaving this house alive. God, I hope I'm not wrong, our lives depend on my next words.

"The Rossi family are part of an organised syndicate. The guards," I wave my hand in the general direction of our silent sentry, "are your men. They um, enforce your requests, commands," still flapping my hand at him, "do your bidding, protect you, drive you around, arrange, um things, and well other stuff."

I actually have no idea what they do. An afterthought suddenly hits me. I raise my head high and straighten my spine. I'm still furious.

"And eliminate potential threats. Like my dog."

I hear a quiet snicker from behind me and judging by the flick of his furious eyes and clenching jaw, Dante did too. The noise behind me immediately stops and Dante returns his gaze to me.

"Yes, you are 'somewhat' correct."

I didn't expect him to admit to any of it. I expected quite the opposite.

"Did Allesandro ever talk to you on how the family operate?" Dante asks dubiously.

He knows Alex never discussed this life with me, I have been completely blindsided by it all. I'm not sure how to answer without giving him the ammunition to blow our whole marriage to pieces. If I say I knew but ignored it all, then he will think poorly of me, if I say I didn't then he would think badly of Alex. I'm in a no-win situation. Luckily, he doesn't require an answer as my shocked face is answer enough.

"We," he points to himself and Maria, "are aware you were not born into this life and understand you may struggle to comprehend our regime. Allesandro was raised to work for the syndicate, as was I and Benito, our whole lives were in preparation to survive and exceed."

I've never heard Dante speak so earnestly.

Taking a sip of his coffee he replaces the cup and turns it by the handle till he is happy with its final resting place. I'm fixated on his exactness. This small act shows the true Dante. His need for perfection, for control. When you command such a vast empire I presume you need to keep order, even in the small things.

With his finger and thumb still holding the handle I can see him formulate his next words. I get the feeling they're difficult, but for me or him though?

"Allesandro couldn't leave you alone." He says to his cup.

I hear the sincerity in his words.

"Once he met you he couldn't walk away."

I remember when we first met, the pull was tangible and magnetic. Alex disappeared a few days later and I thought I'd imagined it all. When he reappeared again in my life I saw it was real and his decision was firm, he would stay forever. He promised he would never leave me again, but he broke that promise the day he died.

"Allesandro was torn Kate."

I can see Dante is affected by his own words.

"He knew his position in the family and his obligation to honour it, but he also made a promise to you that he would never break."

My heart is aching desperately for my husband. I had no idea he had struggled. He was such an honourable man, he would have torn himself apart to fulfil both promises. Tears start to well, I can't maintain eye contact with Dante any longer. His words are hurting me, cutting so deeply. There is so much about my husband that I had no idea about.

"His love for you kept him strong Kate."

I have to swallow down my emotions, he doesn't know how much I appreciate his words.

"Why didn't he tell me?" My quiet words come out.

I need to know why my husband lived this double life. As his wife I would have supported him in anything. Nothing would have stopped me from loving him. He's been gone nearly 3 months and my love for him is still as strong. I can still feel him beating in my heart.

"He didn't want to lose you. You had no knowledge of our life, or family, he felt it would be too much for you."

A small smile crosses his face as he recalls a memory.

"Do you remember what you said to Allesandro when you first met?"

I frown for a moment, recalling my private memories of our first meeting in that dingy club. How my eyes feasted on him, my heart was lost instantly. It takes me a while of searching my memories when it falls to the front of my mind. Dante smiles when he sees I've remembered.

"I asked him if he was a gangster." I say, just as embarrassed now as I was back then.

Dante nods at me confirming the memory.

I remember Alex's face remaining impassive as I dropped my gaze from his in my humiliation.

"Your question upset him. He never wanted you to see him as a bad man. He wanted you to always look at him with love in your eyes."

My chin begins to wobble, Maria takes a large intake of breath with a stutter, her handkerchief being twisted violently. I can feel how much his words have affected her too.

I don't know how to respond to Dante, I nod my lowered head in reverence to his statement.

My heart is in tatters, how much more can it take? I feel it beating violently in my chest and my stomach flutters with the feet of a thousand butterflies. I place my hand to my tummy to stem the movement as it lets out a loud gurgle.

I'm mortified. I can feel all eyes in the room on me.

"I think I need to eat something."

Maria leans over and pats my knee as Dante rises.

"My apologies Kate, I was not aware you had not eaten yet."

The direction of his voice changes and is aimed at my silent sentry on the wall behind me as he continues.

"Why was Mrs Rossi not offered breakfast?"

The tone of his voice isn't exactly friendly. Quickly lifting my head, I take in the look Dante is throwing at the guard, I immediately jump to his defence.

"It's my own fault, I wanted to check on Bear first. It's not....."

I have no idea what his name is, I screw up my brow and turn to face my friendly jailor.

"I'm really sorry but I don't know your name." I state with a smile.

My guard looks down at me and offers what I now realise is his version of a smile.

"My apologies Mrs Rossi, I'm Franco." He states with a bow to his head, I smile my thanks for his courtly response and turn back to Dante.

"Franco was good enough to take me directly to Bear after I declined his suggestion of escorting me to the breakfast room first."

This man has shown me unexpected kindness in this insane world I've suddenly found myself in. I do NOT want him being chastised by Dante for my bloody mindedness.

Turning back to him I smile and simply say,

"Thank you Franco."

The shock of my words in his defence flashes across his face before he schools his emotions in front of his boss.

## Chapter Sixteen

We make our way downstairs and enter a bright sunny room. The yellow of the walls reflects the winter sun making the room feel cheery and warm. The sideboard offers a number of covered dishes sitting inside warming trays. Dante orders fresh coffee and begins to fill his plate. Bears is sniffing intently at the food, his head almost touching the trays.

I'm not an emotional eater and with the information overload I've just endured I'm surprised I can stomach anything, I know I need sustenance though.

I lift the first lid to see the selection beneath and begin placing bacon and tomatoes on to my plate. At the next tray I remove the lid and the aroma hits me, instantly making me gag. I hurriedly replace the lid to the eggs, placing my hand over my nose to stop the invasion on my senses. Turning my head away from the offending smell I spot Maria watching me intently. I try to smile at her before I continue to move along the sideboard selecting mushrooms and brown toast before I take a seat at the large round table.

A lady in grey enters and proceeds to pour coffee for Dante then Maria, when she reaches me I place my hand over the cup to decline her offer. After the 360 degree somersault from the eggs, coffee might just tip my stomach over the edge. Stress from information overload is doing my digestion no favours at all.

The conversation around the table is light and I'm grateful to them both. I need to process what's already been dumped in my head before I can take in any more.

Buttering a slice of toast, I see Maria watching me intently, tracking my every mouthful. I feel under scrutiny with her gaze.

"Where do you think the boys are?"

I ask the table in general trying to lessen Maria's examination.

"Benito is showing them the grounds. Perhaps they will go swimming." Dante offers.

I smile with my response.

"The boys love the water."

Maria is still regarding me intently, I'm beginning to feel uncomfortable now. Placing her cup down precisely she links her hands in front of her on the table top.

"Are you well figlia?" She asks.

I nod in response as my mouth is currently busy chewing toast. She nods her head slowly, but her mind is clearly on something.

Dante witnesses his mother's reaction and stares directly at her, but her attention is firmly directed at me.

A frown appears on Dante's brow as he follows Maria's gaze and back to his mother again. I have no idea what has caught her attention, but I have a feeling something has occurred to her, and her alone.


Bear follows me from the front door with our new friend Franco. Looking around my surroundings I see them through different eyes. Now that I really look I see all the clues laid out right before me. Guards patrol the grounds in pairs along the perimeter of the huge boundary wall. No-one could get inside, or out, without being detected due to the number of cameras tracking every movement. Every man is vigilant, fully aware of their surroundings. The security office tracks every one of their businesses too. The guns, the cars, the scary looking men, all in black. How did I not see it all before?

Turning to Franco I smile to hide my thoughts.

"Where's the pool? Do you think the boys will still be there?"

Franco returns my smile with his own version and talks into his shirt cuff in Italian. Whoever he is talking to obviously responds as he holds his other hand to his ear. Looking to me he smiles and nods.

"Grazie." He says to his cuff again and lifts his arm to indicate the direction we need to go.

"This way Mrs Rossi."

I smile my thanks and begin to walk along the pathway with the faded heather . Franco trails behind me so I slow my steps for him to catch up, but he remains behind. Stopping I turn and look him directly in the eye.

"It would be easier if I followed you." I state.

He begins to quickly shake his head and I raise my hand to halt his refusal.

"Or we could walk together." My face showing I won't deviate from my suggestion.

Franco thinks about it for a moment, even checking for observers to our conversation. Finally, he yields to my suggestion and walks to my side. Standing still I look up to him.

"That's better and I would prefer it if you called me Kate. Mrs Rossi is Alex's mother."

The look of shock on his face is comical.

"I'm sorry but that is not possible." He checks no-one is in close proximity before he continues in a whisper. "Dante would kill me."

He says it so straight-faced the colour begins to drain from my face, when I unexpectedly register a smirk playing at the corner of his mouth. Turning back towards our intended destination he flings over his shoulder.

"This way Mrs Rossi."

The sound of his soft chuckle carries in the air.

I can hear the boys as we turn the corner and the glass house containing the pool comes into sight. The shouts of delight are a balm to my shredded nerves. Realistically I know Alex's family would never hurt us, but my head is still telling me we need to be careful. My bravado is enough to get us through this weekend, hopefully.

Marc spots me through the glass doors and waves frantically. I wave back as he runs along the side of the pool and cannon bombs, splashing its two other occupants. The sound of laughter from Leo and Benni puts a massive smile on my face. Franco opens the door for me to enter first and closes it quickly again behind us to keep the heat in. It is tropical in here. I feel the sweat forming on my brow instantly. Quickly removing my coat, I then start taking the cardigan off too. I'll be down to my underwear if I stay in here much longer.

"Hey boys." I shout over the raucous noise.

All three occupants of the pool wave back.

"Hi mum." "Hey mum." "Hello Kate." I get all three responses at once.

"How long have you been in here?"

Judging by the amount of water around the pool, it's quite a while.

"Ages." Marc shouts as he lifts himself out of the water in an arc to land splat on his back, splashing his brother and uncle.

The look of sheer joy on their faces is amazing. They needed to be children for a while. Let the stress and worries they're carrying be washed away with the water.

I'm starting to really overheat now, and I can feel my head starting to swirl. I place my hand on the back of the chair I dumped my coat on to steady myself. Bear begins to nuzzle my hand as he senses somethings not right. I don't want to interrupt the boys' fun, I need to get out of this heat.

"Is everything OK Mrs Rossi." I hear Franco gently say from my side.

He obviously witnessed my little swoon. I nod my head through the fudge swirling in my brain.

"I'm just a bit too hot in here."

Plastering on a fake smile I walk towards the edge of the pool to get the boys attention. I feel Franco standing directly by my side.

"It's a bit too hot in here for me. You boys have fun. I'll see you later."

Leo and Marc both wave and start splashing each other again. Benni looks at me with a questioning look.

"I need to get some fresh air, I'm fine."

I see Benni pass a look to Franco as I turn to collect my coat and cardigan and head for the door. If I don't get out soon I'm going to pass out. Black circles are swimming in my vision and my body feels really heavy. Shit, shit, shit. I need to get out of here quickly. I feel the cold air hit me as someone opens the door. My arm is taken, and I find myself being guided away from the glass house. The sound of a metal chair being scraped across stone and the gentle push to my shoulder lets me know I'm safe. Sitting with my head between my knees I take in huge gulps of the cool air, grateful to my saviour.

"Thank you Franco."

I don't look up, I know it's him.

I hear Franco speaking gently in Italian, but I can't stay focused long enough to figure out what he's saying or why.

After a few minutes of rest, I risk raising my head and hope the Wurlitzer has stopped so I can get off. I keep my eyes on the ground and slowly bring myself up to a sitting position. The ground holds my focus, so I can keep myself tethered to one point. Eventually I feel myself begin to shiver and my coat is taken from my lap and placed over my shoulders.

I'm beginning to feel better, so I raise my head fully to thank Franco again but it's not him.

Dante stands to my side with a concerned look on his face and next to him is Maria with a knowing look to hers.

"I have called the family doctor. He will be here momentarily."

I don't need a doctor, but I know better than to try to argue with this man, especially when I feel this weak.

"Come. We will escort you inside."

Dante looks over my head and I feel two sets of arms link with mine to raise me from my perch.

We negotiate our way to the front door where it is opened swiftly, Dante escorts me inside and I feel my other arm being taken as we climb the stairs. Once we reach the second landing and the door to our suite comes in to view a voice behind us gently speaks.

"The doctor is here."

Before retreating again.

Sitting me on the edge of the bed I feel fatigue like I've never felt it before. Well I have but that was years ago. I go to toe off my shoes, but Dante bats my hands away and lifts my legs on to the bed. Maria takes a blanket and lays it over me.

My mother was never very maternal, she only cared about her next high, be it drink, drugs or whatever she could consume to achieve that. She never had time for a simple kind act such as laying a blanket across her daughter as she put her to bed.

Sitting on the edge of the bed Maria looks down at me with a smile and places her hand across my brow. Her kindness bringing forward my emotions. The look she gives me is one I have never seen before, but I know what it is as I give my boys that exact look every day.

A gentle knock sounds at the suite door and Franco leaves the room to answer it. The sound of their conversation carries with them as they both enter the room.

With a respectful bow to his head Franco vacates the room again and shuts the door, leaving me alone with Maria, Dante and a stranger.

"Kate this is Dr Manessi our family doctor, he will see to you."

Dante nods to the doctor and turns to leave, Maria stays in position with her hand still across my brow. I go to sit up when my shoulders are gently pushed back down.

"No, you must lay still." Maria speaks quietly but I know it's a command.

The doctor approaches me with a sincere smile.

"What's been going on here then Mrs Rossi?" He asks.

As I'm just about to answer Maria speaks to him in Italian. I thought he was here for me.

The doctor looks a little perturbed at Maria but remains silent as she continues to speak. He looks over to me with a frown, I have no idea what Maria has told him, but he quickly places a smile on his face.

"I will ask again, Mrs Rossi, Mrs Kate Rossi, what have you been up to?" He gives me a little wink and moves forward.

"I think I should examine you." He offers and then adds, "In private."

I'm grateful to him as I'm feeling crowded by Maria and her need to answer for me.

It's obvious Maria isn't happy as she stands and looks from me to the doctor. She walks to the door in her elegant manner and before she closes it she looks back and offers a small smile. I'm glad she's not offended.

"Now Mrs Rossi, I hear you had a fainting episode."

"Please call me Kate. I went in to the glass house to see the boys in the pool and the heat was too much. It's nothing really."

"Well I'll be the judge of that hey." He says on a smile.

I feel a little bit foolish. They didn't need to call a doctor, I just needed fresh air. I'm not sure what to say, and this doesn't seem to deter him.

Removing a blood pressure monitor from his bag he attaches the cuff to my left arm. The cuff expands as I lay there and watch the numbers rise. Taking his stethoscope, he places it around his neck. When the machine signals it's finished he glances at the reading and makes an indeterminate noise. Placing the stethoscope in his ears he begins to listen to my chest, moving it around till he's happy. Taking my wrist, he places his fingers against my pulse whilst studying his gold watch tick along.

Another 'hhmmm' and he places my arm gently on the bed. Moving his equipment, he sits on the edge staring at me with pursed lips, taking a full assessment.

"Why do you think you fainted?"

I didn't actually faint, did I?

"It's silly really, after being outside in the cold the change in temperature in the glass house made me light headed."

He doesn't seem convinced with my explanation.

"What did you feel?"

"My temperature went up and my vision became distorted."

A small nod is his only response.

Chewing his lip, I can see him thinking through the episode.

"I'm a bit concerned as your blood pressure is quite high. There's no sign of any chest infection and your heart sounds healthy."

He pauses for a moment deliberating.

"I hear your appetite is affected by certain foods."

Maria! What exactly did she tell him?

I don't know what I can share with this man. Can I confide in him? What does he know about the Rossi family? Surely, he can't break the Hippocratic oath if I divulge any sensitive information to him. Shit.

"I ummm, I've been under a lot of stress lately."

I know that's a huge understatement, but it is vague enough not to get anyone into trouble.

I look down at my hands, my wedding and engagement ring shining brightly.

"My husband was killed in a car accident. This is our first visit with his family. I err, I've been told some things today that have been, well difficult to process."

The last few months have taken their toll on me. I know I've been letting myself go a bit, always putting myself last, I needed to think of the boys first.

"I've been physically sick with grief. Losing him has torn me apart."

Twisting the covers in my fingers I try not to let my emotions overtake me.

"I know I need to take better care of myself."

I don't need a professional to tell me that. This happening today has been a wake-up call to me. I need to make myself a priority.

"How often have you been sick?" He asks softly.

I think back over the last few months and realise it's quite a lot. I hadn't grasped how deeply my loss had affected my health. If I ate better it might help but my appetite has been up and down, that's when I actually remember to eat.

"My stomach has been unsettled since Alex died."

"May I?" He asks indicating to my stomach.

Laying myself flat, he pulls the covers down as I raise my shirt. Breathing on his hands he flashes me a smile.

"They may be a little cold." He says on a laugh.

Smiling back at him I relax my head into the pillows.

I feel the pressure as he presses his hands gently into my tummy. He palpates around when I feel him pause.

"Would you mind unbuttoning your jeans please?" He asks.

I flip the button and lower the sip halfway, he tucks the corners of the opening in on themselves and begins his examination again. I feel him pressing but not too firmly. It's not uncomfortable but I'm starting to feel awkward.

Taking his hands away he pulls up the comforter to preserve my dignity. Taking my wrist, he watches the seconds pass on his watch again.

I open my mouth to speak but he shushes me.

When he's finished he lays my arm down as he chews his lip.

"May I ask, how old are you Mrs Rossi?"

"39." I say dubiously.

"What was the date of your last period?"

I've never had a regular cycle. Thinking back, I realise I haven't had a period for a while. I know that's not unusual at my age with the menopause around the corner. Add with the grief and stress it's hardly surprising. It hadn't really crossed my mind. I hadn't missed them.

The doctor watches me as I try to remember.

"It's been a few months, but I can't say exactly, I've had a lot on my mind." I offer in way of explanation at my lax attitude.

"I understand." He says, with genuine sympathy.

I can see his mind is working through a possible diagnosis.

"With my age I thought I was going through the change, and the stress of losing Alex it has all affected my cycle.

He nods at my words, his lips pursed again.

"I'm really very sorry for your loss. How long ago did Alex pass away?"

"It's been nearly three months now."

It hurts so much admitting he's been gone that long my heart still beats with his.

"Were you and your husband close?" He goes on.

His questions are becoming a little too personal. Dropping my gaze, I answer with a nod.

"Alex and I were very close."

Memories of the love we shared bombarding me.

"I know this is very personal Mrs Rossi, Kate, but can you remember when you were last intimate? Was it with your husband?"

How dare he. I would never be unfaithful to Alex. I would only ever allow one man into my heart or my bed. Anger rises in me at his presumptuous question. Looking at him sharply he pulls back slightly at the fierceness on my face.

"I would never be unfaithful to the man I love."

The doctor appears happy with my response and smiles at my words.

"Love is a gift that should always be cherished Mrs Rossi."

I nod in agreement as his words take the sting out slightly from his earlier question.

"I would like to take some blood and a urine sample please. I will do a full screen to check what may be the matter."

Rising from the bed he digs into his bag and removes various tubes, cups and needles. Pulling on a pair of gloves he ties a plastic strip around my upper arm as he flicks at the vein. Pushing the needle in he starts to fill various vials. When he has filled them all to his satisfaction, he unties the strap as he removes the needle, pressing a piece of cotton wool to the puncture wound.

"Hold this please."

He takes my other hand and places it over the juncture and bends my arm.

Putting the needle in a yellow tub, he begins to write my name on each tube. I unfold my arm to check the bleeding has stopped. He places a plaster over the area and unsnaps his gloves throwing them in the container too.

Passing me the sample jar he nods towards the bathroom.

"If you could fill this please. I would rather you didn't lock the door in case you become unwell again."

Makes sense I suppose. Lifting myself from the bed slowly, I pad to the bathroom and close the door without locking it.

Holding the sample bottle with tissue paper the doctor holds open a plastic bag and I drop it straight in. My name is written on the side but it's not my address.

"Um I don't live here, that's not my address." I point out.

"Yes, I know. It's easier if we use the Rossi House as your address for now. Can I take your mobile number that way I can talk to you directly?" He asks with a knowing look.

I appreciate his forethought. I call out my number which he adds to his own phone.

"I'll call you in the morning with the results Mrs Rossi. We'll know more then. In the meantime, I want you on total bed rest and a proper diet. Avoid alcohol and caffeine please."

I almost laugh as I don't really drink, and I've gone off of coffee, but bed rest!! That means I'm at the mercy of Dante and Maria. A thought suddenly occurs to me.

"Tomorrow's Sunday."

"Yep. That would be correct." The doctor flippantly answers me.

"How can you get the results on a weekend?"

I've never heard of anyone getting lab results on a Sunday.

The doctor laughs and looks at me.

"That Mrs Rossi is one of the many luxuries extended to your family name."

What can I say to that!

"Can I just add your number to my phone so I know it's you calling in the morning?"

I go to grab my bag from the floor as a wave of light-headedness comes over me.

"Careful there." He admonishes, bending to pick up my bag and taking my arm to lead me back to the bed.

"Thankyou."

I dig through my mammoth bag and my hand wraps around the device, seeing it's the cheap phone I throw it on the bed and rummage again till I find my real phone. Entering his name and number he then issues his strict instructions for bed rest and nutritious food again and bids me goodbye.

With my head still swimming, I lay back and close my eyes to stop the nausea from overtaking me.

## Chapter Seventeen

Opening my eyes, I see the sun has moved position signalling the day has passed me by. I must have been exhausted to sleep during the day, and by the looks of it, most of it too.

Gingerly lifting myself to a sitting position I see a drink and snack has been left on the cabinet. I'm really hungry and go to take the plate when I sense someone nearby. Looking over to the door I spy Dante sat in a chair. He offers a tentative smile as he rises straightening his cuffs.

"How are you feeling Kate?" Real concern in his voice.

I do a quick assessment and realise I do feel better.

"Better thanks, just hungry."

Taking the plate, I sit back against the headboard and eat the fruit and crackers. Leaning over again I take the juice and almost drink it in one. The freshness quenching my thirst I didn't realise I had.

"The doctor was helpful I hope." He says standing at the end of the bed, obviously uncomfortable.

I should be embarrassed at my incapacitated state but right now I couldn't give a damn.

"He took some blood, I should get the results tomorrow. Thank you for calling him."

I'm grateful I didn't have to battle with the receptionist at my own surgery for an appointment.

"You are family Kate. It is your entitlement."

I'm a little embarrassed by his words.

"Did he give an initial diagnosis?"

Thinking back, he didn't. He asked about Alex as well as some very personal questions.

"No, I'll know more tomorrow."

Dante nods, I can see it pains him that this isn't something he can control.

"How have the boys been? Do you know where they are?"

A real smile flits across his face.

"They are well. Please do not worry Kate. I believe I have already confirmed they will come to no harm here."

I'm stuck in this bed and need to trust that he will keep his nephews safe.

Dante looks down and I see him frown. Following the direction of his stare I see my phone and next to it, face down, is the cheap mobile from home. Walking around to the side of the bed he indicates to the device.

"May I?"

I nod in agreement as he picks up the mobile and turns it over in his hand. A thoughtful look on his face. After several minutes of scrutiny, he looks at me with a questioning look.

"I found it at home in the kitchen drawer. I'd forgotten it was in my bag. It needs a charger as the battery is dead."

Dante offers a nod to my words.

"Who does it belong to?"

"We've got no idea. It's not the boys."

Another nod and he looks back to the device, a pensive look on his face.

"I have a charger. If I may I will charge it for you."

I don't really have a choice, we can't charge it and I am curious what's on it and who it belongs to.

"Thanks, I'd appreciate it."

Dante carefully places it in his pocket and questions me some more as to my comfort. When he's ascertained I don't need anything he leaves me to rest with a promise to send the boys up later.

As Dante leaves a lady in grey enters carrying a tray and a smile for me.

Placing the tray on the bed she fluffs my pillows before placing it on my lap. There is a domed plate cover, another juice, a tablet, a book and a home decorating magazine.

"We hope you are feeling better Mrs Rossi."

I smile my confirmation as she lifts the dome lid.

"The doctor suggested a simple meal. I hope chicken soup is to your liking."

The smell is amazing.

Checking over her shoulder, making sure we're alone, she taps her finger to the other items on the tray. Lowering her voice slightly she goes on.

"I thought you might like something to help pass the time."

A slight blush colours her cheeks. I'm so touched by her thoughtfulness, she must mistake my silence for displeasure as her face begins to fall. Quickly I reach out and take her retreating hand.

"Thankyou." I say. "I really do appreciate you thinking of me."

The blush creeps up her cheeks again and a smile lights up her beautiful face.


The soup is amazing. I really am hungry. When I'm finished I put the tray on the cabinet and pick up the magazine. I can't concentrate long enough to read right now, so flicking through the pages suits my mood better. The conversation with Dante earlier flashes through my head, I'm still in shock that my husband led a double life. I'm scared of the future for me and the boys. Will they let us walk away and continue with our mundane, normal life? I don't think they will. I know they wouldn't hurt the boys but if they choose a different path will things become difficult? I'm starting to understand now why Alex kept us away.

Dante and Maria are used to people doing as they say. The life they have is so far removed from ours. Leo would be in danger, so would Marc. The thought drives a knife to my heart. They're just babies. The only time they've been exposed to this life is in movies, and with them you have the luxury of turning it off. Once they get sucked into this life there's no getting out. Who will protect them now that Alex is gone? Dante will use them as pawns in this game he plays.

I don't know what to do. Thoughts go round, and round, scaring me more the deeper my mind delves into what their lives will become. Despondently I lay my head back trying to slow my heart rate. My babies can't live this life. What do we even know about life in a syndicate? I can't even imagine the depths of depravity they have sunk to, what exactly are they involved with, what was Alex involved in? Is this life like the movies with contract killing, illegal trade, oh my god, drugs, people trafficking. My head feels like it's about to explode.

"Knock, Knock." Someone says from the doorway.

Looking over I see Benni leaning his shoulder against the frame, witnessing my mini meltdown. I can't be bothered to plaster a fake smile on. My head is like mush.

"Come in." I say sullenly.

Benni gives me a half smile and walks into the room, nodding towards the bed.

"Please." I answer his silent request.

Sitting on the edge of the bed he turns to face me.

"How are you doing?"

Do I answer honestly or lie?

Giving me a look, I know he will see through my BS if I tried.

"Honestly, pretty crap. I'm stuck in this bed feeling like shit while my boys run riot in a house I don't know trying to process a complete information overload from your brother whilst discovering my husband wasn't exactly the man I thought he was. So, I'd say all in all pretty shit."

Benni gives me a nod and small smirk.

"How are you?" I ask back deadpan.

Benni laughs at my question and pats my leg.

"I know it's a lot to take in. Imagine having to live this life from birth!"

I smile at his response. Benni is a good guy.

"How did I not know?" I ask him.

I've been going over that question in my head. How the hell did Alex hide this all from me?

"His love for you was so important. It was everything to him." Benni answers with a smile.

"It tore him up having to live a double life."

It still doesn't answer how I didn't know. Did I ignore the signs, were there any?

"What happens now?"

The question has been burning a hole in my head.

"Is Dante serious about Leo having to take over? It's obviously not what Alex wanted for him. If he did he would have introduced us to this life earlier." I say flailing my arms around.

Benni chuckles again, my actions clearly amusing him.

"It's not as bad as you are probably imagining right now. Yes, there are aspects to the business that are a little unsavoury, predominantly it is all legitimate businesses. Yes, we have to be careful, rival families do try to move in and take over the areas we control, but it's not like the movies. We don't have mass shoot outs in disused car parks." Laughing to himself at the images he depicts.

"How the hell would I know Benni? Alex kept us away from all of this for a reason."

Benni looks down at me with a smile.

"We don't need to worry about those things now. You're not well and the stress isn't good for your health. Rest, be waited on, enjoy the luxuries that are here. Luxuries that you are entitled to enjoy. You are a Rossi. Leo and Marc are both Rossi's. We're your family Kate. We all love you and want to be part of your lives and you to be part of ours too."

Rising from the bed he straightens his jacket, clearly wanting to say something more.

"You're all safe here. Relax and rest while you have the opportunity."

Walking away from me and my jumbled-up thoughts.

The boys come and find me a while later, both full of their adventures. Not only have they swum, they've learned archery, been in the gym, played video games with Benni and one of the guards, watched a movie in the cinema. Cinema, in a house. This is so far removed from our lives I'm struggling to comprehend it. They're just getting changed as dinner is soon. I've been left with strict instructions to stay in bed and a tray will be bought to me. All those years I've carried a tray to the boys when they've been ill, I never realised just how much it was appreciated. Laying here I'm completely dependent on the family. I've only ever lent on Alex, this is all new territory for me.

The lady in grey from earlier comes into the room with a smile. She looks to be in her mid-twenties and has the most beautiful complexion. I envy her youthful looks.

"Hello." I greet her as she enters.

"How are you feeling now Mrs Rossi?" She asks placing the tray on the bed before she plumps my pillows again.

Leaning back, she places the tray on my lap and lifts the dome.

The smell is amazing. The rich aroma of tomato sauce with aubergines and pasta wafts up from the plate.

"Pasta a la Norma, Mrs Rossi. I hope you like it."

"Thank you it smells amazing." It really does, and I can't believe how hungry I am again.

Looking up to the lady with a smile I speak.

"I'm afraid I don't know your name."

"Sofia." She responds timidly.

"Well Sofia, thank you for looking after me so well today." My words are genuine.

Her blush from earlier creeps on to her face again and she seems shocked by my gratitude.

"It is my pleasure Mrs Rossi."

"Kate, please." I say.

Shaking her head, she frowns.

"Thank you Mrs Rossi, but that wouldn't be permitted."

I feel bad for putting her in this position. I don't know the protocol here.

"I apologise Sofia, it wasn't my intention to make you uncomfortable."

Sofia appears grateful for my words and offers me a smile and a bow to her head.

"I will come back and collect your tray in a short while. Enjoy your meal Mrs Rossi."

And with that leaves me to enjoy the nicest food I've eaten in a very long time.

The sun is shining through the windows, but I can tell it's cold out. The white cotton blanket that covers the ground shows winter has taken her hold. Standing at the window I wrap my cardigan around my pyjamas. I feel so lazy. Normally I would be up, washing on, walked the dog, dinner cooking. Just because it's Sunday doesn't mean I get a day off. Alex and I would share breakfast together whilst the boys slept in. I miss those mornings. The comfort we would get from simply being in the same space. Words weren't always necessary. Just knowing we were together was enough. It's those lost moments that I will miss him the most.

The ringing of my phone brings me out of my reverie. Picking it up from the cabinet I see Dr Manessi's name on the screen.

"Good morning Doctor. How are you today?" I ask cheerfully, and I realise I am. All this rest must have been what I needed.

I hear his chuckle down the line.

"I'm supposed to ask you that."

Switching my phone to the other ear I sit back in bed and pull the blankets around me. Not for warmth, but for comfort.

"How are you Mrs Rossi? Are you resting?"

I smile at his question, all I've done is rest.

"Yes doctor. I have been lazing in bed since you left yesterday. Sofia has brought me healthy wholesome food and is tending to my every need." I throw at him flippantly on a smile.

His soft laugh carries along the line again.

I hear his intake of breath, changing him instantly into business mode.

"I got your results back a few moments ago. Are you able to talk openly, are you alone?"

His question makes me suddenly apprehensive.

"Yes."

"It's nothing to worry about, please don't fret." He quickly offers.

Why didn't he say that first?

"Your blood shows that you are slightly anaemic. I would like to prescribe an Iron supplement for you to take."

"Can't I use a more organic approach?" I ask before he can continue.

"Yes, you could but I think it's imperative to get your Iron levels up as quickly as possible."

Strange, I thought he would have preferred the natural approach, most doctors would tell you to change your diet.

"Mrs Rossi, there is a reason for this deficiency. There's no easy way to tell you but your urine sample was tested, and there were high levels of HCG."
HCG, where have I heard that before? I'm wracking my brain when I miss what he says.

"Sorry Doctor I missed that can you repeat it please?"

"I said you're pregnant Mrs Rossi."

I'm stunned into silence. I'm nearly 40, how can I be pregnant?

After I had Marc there were complications and the doctor informed us that we wouldn't be able to have any more children. We never used any precautions, we didn't think we needed to.

I'm pregnant. It feels like a little miracle. Why now? Alex won't get to meet his child. The child he created. Touching my tummy, I feel a tear slide down my cheek. His child. I know why it's now. It's his parting gift.

"Are you OK Kate?" The doctor asks, clearly aware that I'm in shock.

"Are you sure?" I ask quietly.

"Yes. I thought I could feel something yesterday which is why I wanted to get the test run quickly. I would like to get you in for a scan as soon as possible but I would say you're between 16 and 20 weeks at a guess, but things are different for each pregnancy. I want to check the baby is growing properly."

I'm pregnant. Holy cow. I'm pregnant. I thought I'd started the menopause, but I was pregnant.

"I assume this is being kept between us for now?" He asks.

I hadn't thought past the 'I'm pregnant' stage.

"Yes, I think that's best." I don't need the added complication of Maria knowing, or Dante.

"OK, well I have a plan, bear with me. I'm going to ask Dante to have you bought to the clinic. I will say that I want to take more bloods that have to be tested immediately to rule anything further out, and for your own safety I would prefer to do them today whilst we are closed. I have an ultrasound machine here and we can take a look. How does that sound?"

Today. Oh my god, it's all happening so fast.

"OK, yes please if we could."

The car dropped me at the entrance of an impressive looking building. Franco got out first to check the surrounding area before escorting me inside. Dr Manessi asked him to wait in the outer office, I could tell he wasn't happy. I thanked him for his concern and assured him I'd be fine. Dante insisted he accompany me and that the boys should stay at the house, for which I'm grateful. They almost had to physically restrain Maria when she was adamant I would need her here.

The room has a professional feel with a homely twist. The furnishings are obviously expensive and decorated tastefully. Nothing like any hospital or doctor's surgery I've ever visited.

"Right, let's have a look shall we." Dr Manessi drags my mind from my perusal of the surroundings.

I lift my shirt and unbutton my jeans as he lays a blue cloth over my clothes, tucking it slightly inside.

"This may be a little cold." He says squeezing the clear gel on my tummy.

Using the wand, he presses slightly, and the distorted image appears on screen. The familiar black and white image looks like snowflakes in my belly.

Before long the image I'm seeing is a familiar one. I've seen it twice before.

"Oh my god." My hands fly to my mouth in shock. It's really real.

Dr Manessi smiles at my outburst and turns back to the monitor once more.

"Yep definitely a baby in there."

The outline is so clear. I can see the head, arms and legs moving, what looks like the heart. It's my baby. Our baby.

Oh Alex, we made a beautiful baby together. I see the doctor taking measurements, but I'm mesmerised by the magnificent sight before me. After a while Dr Manessi turns to me with a wide grin.

"Everything looks really good. All the measurements show a healthy foetus. You are about 20 weeks along."

I'm shocked. How didn't I know? When I was pregnant with the boys I was violently ill. I knew the moment I fell pregnant as everything changed. I couldn't eat, drink or smell anything for fear of throwing up. The sickness was horrendous for the first six months.

"Your percental chance of Downs would be higher due to your age, but the measurements show it to be low. There is still a chance of Downs and we could perform an amnio, but I'm sure you know the risks involved."

Shaking my head no, I don't need one. Whatever the outcome, this is a gift from Alex.

The doctor appears relieved and with a sneaky grin asks, "Would you like to know the sex?"

Smiling, I nod. I'm so far along, of course he can tell me now.

"Well Mrs Rossi I'm very happy to tell you it's a girl."

I burst into tears and a split second later the door bursts open with Franco filling the frame, gun raised.

The doctor looks at him, at me and back at him again. Crying whale like tears, I'm grateful to the doctor for speaking for me.

"As Mrs Rossi's personal guard can I assume you will keep this 'Personal' information to yourself?"

I hear a 'Si' before the door clicks shut.

I can't even be angry at the invasion of my privacy, or the risk of Dante finding out before the information has properly sunk in. I'm ecstatic, I'm also sad, Alex can't be a part of her life. Her. I'm having a girl. A daughter. I know how it will be already. She'll be spoilt by the boys. Showered with love. Alex may not know her, but she will definitely know him.

Franco gives me his version of a smile as he opens the car door for me, clutching the picture in my hand I slide in. I'm in total shock. Elated. My emotions are high from the news. Sad that I can't share it with the man who helped create her though.

The doctor wants to refer me to an obstetrician he knows. She runs a private practice, and he informed me that as part of the Rossi family I would be expected to use her, apparently  Dante will be getting all of the bills.

I don't know what I think about that, I feel like I'm being swept along. The NHS were amazing when I had the boys. I presume with my age it might be safer, and I know I can afford it. I won't be beholden to Dante.

Arriving back at the house I try to dampen down my smile. I don't want anyone to know before Leo and Marc.

Exiting the car I stop and look up at Franco to speak but he beats me to it.

"You have my silence." He whispers.

I nod my thanks and smile up at him. Turning to walk inside I stop as I remember the doctor's words. Turning back to Franco I swap my smile for a frown.

"You're my personal guard?"

Franco nods.

"When and who decided that?"

Franco seems a little uncomfortable as he answers.

"I volunteered. Mr Rossi wanted some-one to oversee your personal security during your visit and possibly into the future. I hope I haven't overstepped propriety Mrs Rossi."

I'm pleased it's Franco, as he's shown me kindness, but I'm not sure how I feel about Dante organising security for me. What's next the boys having personal body guards 24/7?

"Thank you for your honesty Franco."

I realise how much I trust this man. This is a discussion Dante won't like. I won't be moved around like a pawn on his chess board. When we go home later today our lives will return to normal. Of that I'm 100% sure.

## Chapter Eighteen

I walk towards the house with Franco trailing me, again. The door is opened by another guard and I'm immediately greeted by Maria with a concerned look.

"Is everything well Kate?" She asks, twisting her ever present handkerchief.

"Thank you, yes it is." I reply as I hear the boys and Bear running from the back of the house.

I smile as they race to see who can reach me first. Bear wins as usual. Both boys break out into a massive smile and Bear is looking for contact, nudging at my hand.

"Mum, you're back." They both lean in for a hug and I relish their rare show of affection.

"Are you better now?" Marc asks concerned.

"What was wrong?" Leo asks before I can respond.

I look towards Maria, "Would you mind if I talk to the boys in the lounge a moment please?" It pains me to ask. This is not our home. Maria doesn't look happy but affords me a smile regardless.

Closing the four of us in the room, praying Bear won't knock something over in his exuberance, the boys look anxious and I can't blame them. The last time I needed to talk to them I shattered their world. Shaking off my sorrow for a moment I walk over to the sofa and indicate for them to sit too. Bear follows suit and lays across my feet. When we're all comfortable I take the grainy picture from my jacket pocket. Holding it out they both glance at it and back to me.

"Do you know what this is?" I can't contain my smile.

Both shake their heads.

"This is an ultrasound image."

Both wear similar blank expressions.

"An ultrasound takes pictures of your insides. This one is inside my stomach."

Still blank.

Pointing to the gem in the middle they follow my finger as I draw her outline.

"This is a picture of your sister."

I let that settle in their heads for a few moments. Marc leans forward tilting his head left then right. Leo stares straight at it in awe.

"I had no idea, but your dad and I created her before he died. He didn't know but he left us all with a final gift."

The silence in the room for once is peaceful. Both boys staring at the picture. Leo takes it from my hand and Marc follows the image with his eyes then leans in closer to him, his shoulder against Leo's arm.

"She's an angel. Our very own angel." Leo says.

Tears immediately spring to my eyes. They love her already, I hoped they would.

"When will she be born? Marc asks.

"In May darling." They're desperate to meet her.

"Hello Angel." Leo says stroking the picture.

Angel, what a beautiful name. Stroking my hand over my tummy I look down with a smile.

"Hello Angel." I say to her.

Angel Allesandro Rossi has a nice sound to it.

We sit together for ages discussing the baby. What will happen, what room will she sleep in, can they help decorate, can they get the pram with the really big wheels for off-roading, will she like dolls? On and on, their enthusiasm is infectious. I could listen to them forever.

After a long while, I'm beginning to get hungry and decide to go in search of Sofia. The boys know not to say anything yet and go off to the pool, with Bear in tow of course. I remember it's Sunday and they have school tomorrow, so I let them have their fun.

Walking through the hallway Sofia appears and is as shocked to see me as I am to see her. Laughing, I walk over.

"Hi Sofia, could you help get me something to eat please?"

With her usual smile she answers.

"Of course Mrs Rossi. Anything in particular?"

"A sandwich or something would be great thank you."

"I'll bring it to your room, you can rest till it's ready."

Placing my hand on her arm I thank her and begin to climb the stairs. I hear footsteps following, I don't need to turn to know who it is.

"I'm just going to my room for a while Franco." I say on a smile.

I hear his chuckle as I continue up the stairs.

Waking from yet another nap I realise I'm a rubbish house guest. Taking a shower, I dress and go in search of Maria. As I descend the stairs I see Dante in his study. He catches me looking and waves me in. There's no guard outside today. Walking into the room I sit in a guest chair and offer him a smile as he finishes on the phone.

"What did the doctor say?" His question jerks me from my daydream.

I'm torn. I'm not sure if I should say anything to him but realistically he does have a right to know. Firstly, because it's his niece. His deceased brother's unborn child. Secondly, according to Dr Manessi, he's sending all bills to Dante. When he gets an invoice for an ultrasound, he might get an inkling.

I'm adamant that the boys and I will be returning to our normal life as this is all a fantasy and as much as they want to control our lives, I won't allow it. I'm not scared to say no to Dante. Alex was strong enough to tell him we weren't to be a part of this life, and so can I be. I will protect my children, all 3 of them.

"It's nothing bad, in fact it's the opposite." My smile ever present.

Taking a deep breath in I need to tell him. I have no idea what his response will be.

"I'm pregnant."

The look of shock is not what I expected and is absolutely priceless. I can see his frown line start. I need to clarify that it is his brother's baby by the look that is starting to appear.

"Alex and I didn't try but we created a precious little baby." I say stroking my tummy. I am so grateful to have her.

"A beautiful baby girl." Looking up to him I continue. "Angel Allesandro Rossi. She will take Alex's name in his honour and his memory."

I'm getting choked up but clearly not as much as Dante. He rises from his chair and goes to shut the study door. Returning to the desk he chooses the chair next to me and not his usual throne.

"Allesandro did not know?" He asks clearly in shock. "He will have a daughter."

He looks like he needs a minute to process. The tables have turned. It was me in shock yesterday.

I can see his mind starting to work frantically and he looks almost pained. What is he thinking, planning?

"He did not know? You did not know?"

I'm not sure why he's asking me again.

"No Dante. We were told we couldn't have any more children after Marc."

I'm a little embarrassed to say it out loud.

The cogs are spinning out of control in his head, I can feel it from my seat, I just know the speech about safety is on his lips.

Pulling the ultrasound picture from my cardigan pocket I lay it on the desk and flatten it with both hands.

"Meet your niece."

His head tilts from left to right like Marc's did earlier.

"Angel." He says, exactly like Leo.

It feels like forever before Dante looks at me to speak.

"I am happy for you."

I know he wants to say more so I stay silent. I have an inkling what his next words will be.

"We will need to improve security for you. It would be easier if you moved to the house."

And there it is, I knew it was coming.

I'm not leaving our home. We've been safe there, happy, why do we need to leave now? I need to know.

"Why? Why now? The boys and I are safe there."

I can see him putting together his argument in his head. I won't be swayed.

"You have come to understand some of our dealings. There are people who would hurt all of you to get to me, to get to the family."

"Hasn't happened before. Why's now different? Nobody knows our connection to your syndicate thing."

I can see the exasperation on his face.

"Kate, you need to understand there are some very nasty people in this world. You are nothing to them. If they eliminate you and the boys, the Rossi syndicate dies also."

I'm struggling to process that word, eliminate.

"What, like kill us, the boys, me? We haven't hurt anyone. We're nothing to do with the family. This is our first visit with you, ever."

How the hell did my life get like this? Oh yeah, I married a man I loved so much I was blinded.

"People watch our every move, they would have seen you arrive here. They will have identified you all, where you live, your lives, the boy's school, your business. Allesandro was careful in keeping your identity secret from any possible threats."

"Great, so you're telling me that we've lived safely in ignorant bliss all these years and one visit with you and our lives are now suddenly in danger. Gee thanks Dante. Wish I'd known this before. I would have kept a distance. Kept things as they were." I'm fuming.

"Kate, you need to understand you are my responsibility now."

"Responsibility my arse. I don't need you looking out for me and the boys. I've managed perfectly well. When Alex worked away over-night I managed to keep us all alive." I sarcastically throw at him.

Oh my god. When Alex worked away over-night. Do I want to know?

Looking at Dante he knows what my next question will be.

"What did he do when he worked away Dante?"

By the look on his face, I'm not sure I want the answer.

Looking down with a shake to his head I'm dreading the words that will come out.

"You don't need to know Kate. It's in the past."

How dare he? I have a right to know what my husband was involved with.

"Tell me."

The silence stretches between us. Eventually his eyes meet mine.

"Sometimes it is necessary to conduct business outside of the law. Allesandro had a natural talent for getting people to talk."

A frown of confusion is clearly on my face.

With a huge intake of breath, he rises from his seat next to me to re-take his throne. It's obvious he's uncomfortable discussing this with me.

Sitting down, he wheels his chair closer and lays his forearms on the desk, joining his hands.

"Since birth we have all received training to protect and defend, Allesandro excelled at it. He became talented in the art of information extraction. When we needed to find out information, Allesandro would step in. His techniques weren't always orthodox." Dante winces on the last word. I assume for my benefit he's giving the PG rated version.

"What do you mean?" My question is painful to ask.

"Believe me Kate, it is better if you did not know the details. You wouldn't understand, you were not raised in this lifestyle. Also, if you do not know, then you can't lie when questioned."

My imagination is going wild, Alex was never a violent person. He was gentle and kind, funny and loving. The man I'm currently imagining is far removed from the man I married.

My head is going over different scenarios, I've seen films where people were tortured, and the look on the persecutors face was pure glee. Was that who Alex really was and we saw a fake version, or was it the other way around, and he played that part in order to survive.

"Why do you live this life? Why didn't Alex just leave, walk away with me and the boys?" I ask.

"Sadly, it is not that easy. When you are born into a syndicate family you are sworn by honour, there is a code we have to live by. As an outsider I do not expect you to understand, but we do it out of respect."

"Surely you have a choice?"

Shaking his head, no.

How could Maria and his father have condemned their boys to this life. As a mother I will do anything to protect my boys from harm.

"Well I do have a choice Dante, I'm not one of you and I choose not to live this life. My boys will not be committed to a life sentence of crime and corruption. They have the right to choose their own path in life. I will not condemn my children the way your parents did."

Standing from my seat I make for the door. I'm getting my family and we're leaving here.

"Kate, I will allow your words to slide as you are family, but you cannot leave without discussing your security."

I'm not sure if it's a threat, but the tone scares me to a halt. My shoulders are rigid, the stress running through my body can't be good for the baby. I need to think of her. I'm not giving in, I'm compromising.

Turning back to Dante I see the shutters drop over his emotions. There will be no swaying him on this. With a heavy heart I walk back to the chair and lower myself. I expect a smug look to appear on his face, but it remains stoic. Jumping straight in, I might as well try to control our future.

"I will agree to additional surveillance cameras, and the house is currently fitted with alarms and secure locks, I'm not sure what more we can install."

I must be way off the mark judging by Dante's frown and gentle shake to his head.

"No Kate. You will need security protection. Guards."

I'm struck dumb. Guards, like he has? Following my every move. I don't mind Franco here in the house, but I'm not too keen on strangers following me and the boys. Will the boys need bodyguards at school? Their school thinks we're weird enough as it is.

"What exactly do you mean? Exact details please Dante."

Moving a few papers around he finds what he's looking for.

"As I said previously, it would be easier if you lived here, at the house." He raises his hand to halt my words of refusal. "However, it would be possible to remain in your home with some minor changes."

I see him scanning a list on the paper before he looks up again.

"You will need 24/7 security detail. Neither you nor the boys will be unescorted at any time outside of the house. One of my senior guards volunteered to escort you today."

"Franco?" I ask.

"Yes. I have instructed Franco to organize your security, he will oversee all the guards required."

"How much will this cost me?" I know Alex left us financially affluent, but I can't waste it.

With a frown Dante answers simply. "Nothing."

This is just getting too much for me to process.

"As part of the family you should have previously been under constant guard. Allesandro would not allow it. Keeping you invisible to our enemies was difficult to maintain but now you are visible. All of you."

And there goes our quiet simple life.

"Where will they stay? The guards." I ask.

"I believe there is an area above the garage." He says as he pulls out what look like drawings to our house.

Twisting my head slightly to see better I realise they are. It's a blue print of our home. With a shake of my head I lean back. I have no idea how he got it, and I doubt he would tell me.

"We will convert this space to accommodate a security room and sleeping quarters for the guards."

Right, glad you've decided on how my house should be re-modelled, should I let the guards pick out their own fabric and furnishings too?

Dante misses my perplexed look as he continues to study the drawings.

"Was you just going to go ahead with this, or did you actually intend on informing me?"

I'm probably pushing all the boundaries right now, but my life suddenly feels like it's in his hands.

Dante either misses my sarcasm or chooses to ignore it.

"The work will begin this week. I have arranged for a contractor to visit tomorrow. Franco will manage the arrangements."

Looking up at me he adds.

"I believe you have 2 spare rooms. The guards will use one to sleep and one for surveillance."

I don't even bother arguing with him. I know it will get me nowhere but angry and frustrated.

"It would be easier and safer for you to stay here until the work is completed." He offers.

I'm angry at the lack of control I have, and I'm desperate to get back home, but his words do make sense. We lived in the house whilst the renovations were taking place and it is not a nice environment to be in. The constant noise, and disruption is a nightmare.

Dante sits quietly as I run through both scenarios. Live in The Rossi house, and be waited on but uncomfortable and feel like an intruder or go back home to our sanctuary which we will have to share with strangers whilst the renovations are made to the garage loft.

"I'll get back to you on that." I say.

I need to talk to the boys.

"What do I tell the boys? What have you said to them already?"

I get no facial reaction from Dante.

"We will discuss this with them together."

I knew this time was coming and I'm not sure how they will react, I don't know how much information we will tell them.

"Please remember that Alex was their hero. I don't want their memory of him tarnished." I need Dante to understand how much they idolised him. "Please don't give them the whole truth." I say almost pleadingly.

I'm struggling to comprehend who that man was.

"I agree." He responds.

How many shocks can the soul take before it combusts. I just hope the boys can take more on their young shoulders.

## Chapter Nineteen

As I sit and try to visualise what our lives will become, Dante makes a call. If Dante is correct and we are in danger, what will the future look like. I don't know if he's just saying these things to control us, but what would be the point? We've never featured in their lives before, what advantage would there be now. He claims it's Leo and Marc's heritage. They will be expected to take over the firm, but as they've no knowledge of it, how can they? Thoughts are spinning round and round making me dizzy and quite frankly scared for them when a knock on the door breaks the cycle of black thoughts and Benni saunters in.

"You rang my lord!" He says in a jovial voice.

The boys follow him through the door and on seeing me, both offer up a smile.

"Hey boys. Everything OK?" I don't know why it wouldn't be. We're only staying at the home of the head of an Italian syndicate in imminent danger from unknown sources.

They both nod and look to Dante as he clears his throat.

"Bring a chair please." He says in general to our new guests.

After much shuffling, and banging of their obviously very expensive furniture, we form a semi-circle in front of his desk.

"How have you enjoyed your stay?" He asks.

The look on his face says he truly hopes they've enjoyed their time here.

The boys both offer their gratitude and even Benni seems to have enjoyed our visit.

"I am very glad. This is your family home too. You are both, all," he indicates to all three of us, "welcome anytime you want to visit."

I can see Benni nodding in agreement. I've misjudged these men somewhat. They have missed out on so much as the boys have grown up. I appreciate why Alex kept us away but sitting in this room are the two men who should be closest to the boys. I'm struggling with this push and pull inside of me.

"Your mother and I need to talk about your future."

I shoot Dante a look. He promised me he wouldn't say too much initially. Dante gives the faintest shake to his head as he goes on.

"I am concerned for your safety now that you father has passed away. I am a busy man, as is your uncle, and we cannot watch you all the time. Your mother has performed an excellent job, but now with another baby she needs to take care of herself more."

"I can look after me and Marc, and mum." Leo pipes up.

I trust he could defend against the typical school bullies, but the faceless enemy Dante described is far worse.

"I agree Leonardo. You are more than capable of defending both your brother and mother but unfortunately there are greater risks to you now."

The confused look on the boys faces has me worried what they may ask. I know Dante doesn't like being interrupted but these are MY children.

"Since Dad died I've discovered a few things that may put us in danger. There's a risk people will try to harm us because, well there's no easy way to put it but we're very rich. Because of the money the Rossi family have and also us, they would try to hurt us. What your uncle is saying is we need men like they have here to watch us, keep us secure. I need you both safe to help protect your sister."

I hope by using the baby they can understand my need for them to stay out of harm's way.

Dante gives me a grateful nod of thanks and turns to his audience again.

"I have spoken with your mother and we will make changes to your home for security to live there. I have offered your mother an extended stay while the renovation is carried out."

The sneaky sod. Dante knows I'm not impressed with his underhanded approach to get his own way.

"We have two options boys." I interrupt. "We can stay here, and you would have to get up really, really early for me to take you to school every day."

"Or they could be tutored." Benni pipes up quickly.

Are they both in this together?

"Or we could move back home and live in a little bit of mess while work is going on."

"We can do most of our school work on-line I suppose. Just need to get the teachers to load it to our homework pages."

And there goes my last chance of getting out of here, thanks Marc.

Benni is wearing a smug grin and I can see Dante is happy with this solution too.

"If we're staying I need a few things from home." I say to the room in general.

Benni hands me a pen and paper and a satisfied nod.

The sound of the door crashing open has all whipping our heads round as Bear saunters in uninvited. I smile at his unexpected entrance but not surprised. Wherever the boys are he wants to be too.

Looking back to Dante to apologise I see him half standing from his chair with his hand inside his jacket poised, looking at Benni I see him in a familiar pose. I realise that these men would defend us, keep us safe, lay down their life for us. It's a lot to take in. This isn't a life we're used to where every sound or movement is a threat. I'm really struggling to come to terms with it all. Thankfully the boys only see Bear as their uncles re-take their seats.

Maria is ecstatic that we have decided to stay for a while. I don't think she fully comprehends that we are actually going home at some point. Fussing over us all, issuing commands to their staff concerning our stay. If I don't reel her in, she'll be redecorating the boy's room to their taste.

"Maria, we're only staying while the renovations are going on."
"Si, but you need to rest now you are with bambino." She lovingly gazes at my mid-drift. Well that answers that question. Dante or Benni have already told her.

"You stay here, live here with us. We will take care of you, all of you."

Shaking my head, I know this isn't the time to start that particular battle, but she needs to know.

"Dante said it should only be a week or so, then we are going home."

Benni looks over to the boys with a mischievous grin and a raise of his eye-brows.

"Are you two ready?"

I'm not sure I like that look.

"Where you going?" I need to know.

"Off to have a little fun." He says with a laugh in his voice.

The boys scurry off after Benni leaving me in the lounge with Maria and Dante. Turning I ask him the same question.

"Where are they going?"

Dante tries to hide his smile when he turns to me.

"They are safe Kate."

Now my interest is piqued.

"Where are they going Dante?" I press him again.

With a sigh he deigns to answer.

"They are learning to shoot." Quickly raising his hand to halt my outburst. "They will not be using real guns."

Like that's any better.

"We have an area for target practice. They will be using guns with paint bullets."

I suppose that's not so bad. Normal people go paintballing for fun.

"My guards will be their targets."

Great, live targets.

Shaking my head, I give in. Maybe I'm being a little irrational over it. The boys should be allowed to have fun. I hope the guards have protection though because knowing my boys they will aim for their most personal parts.


Dante isn't happy that I wanted to collect our stuff myself. He laboured the point about his men being capable of retrieving everything we needed, I wasn't so happy about his men delving through my underwear drawer. It's not that I'm hiding anything but the only person to see my knickers was my husband and that will never change.

Franco is sitting in the front seat and one of the nameless two is driving us back home. I mentally run through what we need. The boys need their school tablets and bags, clean clothes, definitely underwear, a warm jacket each maybe. I need to get more poo bags for Bear, a few toys to keep him amused. I smile to myself at the thought of the guards playing tug of war with him. I wonder how many men he could take down? Franco sees me smiling and turns more fully with an enquiring look, I shake my head and he turns back to face the front. Me, what do I need? To start with something a little more formal for dinner, I feel a bit under dressed around them. I hope they don't expect me to change my style to fit in with them. This is the way I am and they will have to accept it, crinkles, wrinkles, jeans and all.

The drive passes quickly and before I know it we're parked in front of the house.

Franco turns to face me.

"Please wait here a moment Mrs Rossi, I would like to check it is secure." He says as he holds out his hand for my keys.

Digging them from my bag I hand them over, not in submission more in shock. Why wouldn't it be secure? Franco catches my confused look.

"It is my job to keep you secure. Please allow me to do that."

He exits the car and before he shuts the door he leans back in. "Please stay there. I will come back to collect you."

Walking up to the door I realise he doesn't know the code for the alarm and go to open the door, but the driver shakes his head.

"He doesn't know the alarm code." I say by way of explanation.

"Please stay seated Mrs Rossi. Mr Rossi shared the code with Franco before we left."

Great and yet another thing that Dante thinks he can control. When we get back home for good I'm changing it. Well maybe not me, I'll find the manual and get Marc to change it.

Walking towards the door I see him scanning the area for possible threats. Is he expecting old Mrs Jenkins to jump out of the bushes with her cat in one hand and her rolling pin in the other. Both very lethal weapons.

Opening the door and de-activating the alarm he pulls his gun from his jacket and moves inside. He really does think there's a possible threat. With the door being monitored by Dante's people I doubt anyone could get near to it. I hope the postman's OK.

We have been sat for 10 minutes at least, the driver scans the area constantly which is making me really nervous. I mimic his movements looking for threats. I have no idea what he is looking for and I'm getting more and more uneasy as the minutes tick by. Remembering the incident months ago I swivel in my seat to look out the back window, but I can't see the trees properly. My driver must sense my movement and turns also.

"Is everything OK Mrs Rossi?" He asks.

I instantly feel silly and turn back with a reassuring smile. His head whips towards the door and I follow too. Franco is exiting the house and the driver begins to climb out of the car.

"Please wait here a moment Mrs Rossi." He says and shuts the door.

I hate being ordered about and exit the car anyway. Walking up to Franco the driver throws an unhappy look my way and then says something in a low voice. Franco looks at me with a quizzical brow and then towards the area of trees, but they are hidden from his vantage point. As he can't see anything he approaches me.

"We can go in now Mrs Rossi."

I'm getting pretty miffed at being told what to do.

"Gee thanks." I say sarcastically.

I love our house and that feeling of comfort wraps itself around me. The flowers have started to wilt, and I make a mental note to throw them away. Home is our safe place and these men aren't part of it. They feel like intruders. Ignoring them I make my way upstairs running through my mental list.

It doesn't take me long to gather our stuff together and I return down the stairs. Franco runs up and meets me half way, taking the bags from my hands and walking back down again. I know I'm pregnant, but I can still carry them. With an unhappy sigh I make my own way down. Something doesn't look right, and I realise quickly what it is. The door to Alex's study is ajar. I know I never unlocked it, I haven't been in there since he died. I put the keys back in the junk drawer as I have a tendency to lose things.

I continue down the stairs with my eyes firmly on the door, apprehension building up, half expecting someone to jump out. I know Franco did a sweep of the house but with the door locked he wouldn't have known where the keys were. My uneasiness is climbing as I descend. Franco comes through the front door scaring the bejesus out of me. Clutching my hand to my heart to stop it from trying to break free.

"Are you OK Mrs Rossi?"

I consider not saying anything, but my curiosity is winning.

"Did you go in there?" I ask indicating the door with my head as I have one hand wrapped around the banister in a death grip and the other still holding in my heart.

"Yes. I did a full sweep."

"How did you know where the keys were?" I ask.

His perplexed look is his only response.

"It was locked. I haven't opened it since Alex died." That wave of sadness washing over me when those two words are said in the same sentence.

Franco shakes his head.

"It wasn't locked Mrs Rossi."

I know I never opened it and the boys have respected my wishes in this matter.

I shake my head and Franco instantly goes in high alert. Speaking into his cuff in mumbled Italian the driver suddenly appears through the front door. A look passes between them, Franco obviously issuing silent commands and the driver pulls his gun from his jacket and walks towards the study door. Franco indicates for me to stand behind him, as the driver moves to the left of the door with Franco and me to the right. Franco nods slowly three times and on the third count the driver grasps the handle and throws the door open wide. He instantly steps into the doorway and swings his gun from left to right and quickly behind the door. His eyes scanning everywhere. He moves into the room with his gun following his eyes up, down, around cabinets, under the desk. I can see his body is rigid and poised. Turning back to Franco he nods.

Franco looks to me and nods too and we start to enter the room. The feeling of invading, trespassing overcomes me, and my emotions are battling with my head. The smell of this room is totally Alex. I can see in my mind's eye him sitting at his desk, talking on the phone, scribbling at paperwork, tapping away on his laptop. I look around the room and take it all in. I can feel Alex in this room, more than anywhere else in the house. It's masculine to a tee but the small personal affects he has on the shelves give away the soft nature of my husband. The drawings the boys would present him with so proudly. A clay model that is supposed to be him but looks more like a potato. All of these memento's show Alex as the father that we knew and loved. I see our wedding picture sitting proudly as I move around his desk. We didn't have a large wedding, we kept it very low key but the happiness that radiates from our smiles is powerful. Sitting in his seat I'm aware of my two transgressors watching my every move. Not bothering to look up at them I offer my words.

"I haven't been in here since Alex died."

Their silence to my statement is welcome.

Holding onto the arms of the chair, I run my palms up and down trying to feel him. The leather is cold to my touch and I sag, disheartened. I didn't expect it to still be warm from his touch. It's been months.

I run my hands over the surface of the desk trying to soak up its memories through my fingertips. Alex loved this desk. Solid in the most beautiful cherry wood. It has a few imperfections after all these years, but who doesn't.

As I'm tracing the grain a thought strikes me as odd. Somethings missing. I look over the surface wracking my brain. I know there's something missing. It's like that game you play with the kids. You have a number of things laid on the floor, hide them with a cloth and when they're not looking you take something away and they have to remember what's gone. Marc was brilliant at it, Leo just wanted to play peek-a-boo with the cloth.

I keep my arms spread over the surface, almost leaning my upper body on the desk, when I realise what it is.

"Alex's laptop is missing."

I thought I'd said it in my head but Franco and the driver step forward slightly indicating they heard me.

I remember two days before he died bringing him a coffee whilst he worked after dinner. He was tapping away when I entered, hardly knowing I was there. His concentration was focused solely on the screen. As I approached him, cup in hand, he almost jumped at my presence and on seeing me lowered the lid of the laptop and turned his chair towards me with a large smile on his face. I walked over to his inviting lap, placed the coffee on the coaster and cuddled into his embrace. The memory is so vivid like it was only yesterday. If I had known what our lives would become, I would have stayed in that room with him all night, cradled in the protection of his arms.

I feel the tear that has escaped, I'm not embarrassed at these men seeing it. If they knew Alex like I did they would still be mourning his loss too.

Franco nods to acknowledge my words, points a look to the driver and leaves the room. I hear his voice from the hallway in a low timbre. I can't hear his words fully, but there's no point as he's speaking in his native tongue.

The driver stands still, not looking at me directly, which offers me some form of privacy. Swallowing down the lump I rise from the chair and make my way from the room. It's too difficult being in there.

Walking into the kitchen I go about clearing my head of melancholy thoughts and gather the last few things we need. The dog poo bags are a must, as I'm sure Maria doesn't want craters all over her perfect lawn. Opening the junk drawer, I'm shocked at the mess. I can't believe the boys would leave it like this. With my hand delving through the rubbish I realise that the spare keys were in here. I retract my hand quickly like there's a venomous snake hidden inside and step back from the offending drawer. I sense the driver has approached and can feel him looking over my shoulder.

"Is everything OK Mrs Rossi?"

I turn to look at him, but he's a lot closer than I realised so I take a side step.

"The keys to the study were in this drawer." Looking over his shoulder, as if I can see the lock from here I ask. "I assume the lock wasn't forced?"

He shakes his head no, but exits the room, I assume to double check.

The house is old, and we opted for original looking solid wood doors. There are only a few with locks and they are 5 lever mortice locks, so we could unlock them from either side in case the boys accidentally locked themselves in. The spare keys have one for every lock in the house.

Their voices carry into the kitchen as I stand there like a spare part. This is all unknown territory for me. It's then I realise that someone has been in our house. I feel violated. Looking around I try to gauge if I can tell who it was, if they've left any clues. Obviously, whoever it was, was a professional. Dante's security would have seen them on their surveillance, unless they did actually cut the feed. I'm such an idiot. Why did I tell them to?

Franco and our driver return both sporting unhappy faces. They probably blame me for telling Dante to stop watching the house. He was only trying to keep us safe, which is ironic as we're in this predicament because of him.

"I think we should go Mrs Rossi. Do you have everything you need?"

I shake my head and grab a bag from under the sink and start stuffing a few bits in I need for the dog. Looking around the room with new eyes, I feel uncomfortable which has never happened before. The thought of someone coming into our personal space is disturbing.

As I'm packing the last few bits the driver walks towards the back door and checks it. He nods to Franco, I don't know if that means it's locked or if it's been tampered with.

"How did they get past the alarm?" I ask.

I can tell from their faces they don't know, and I won't get any answers from them.

The driver takes the carrier bag from my hands and indicates for me to precede him out the kitchen. I look towards the backdoor once more before I exit the room.

Sitting in the back of the car again I shiver at the thought of a stranger in our home. I'm baffled. How the hell did they get in? Alex made sure we had the best locks and security to keep people out, but it doesn't seem to have stopped them. Only the four of us have keys.

There's no sign of forced entry and the alarm doesn't show that it's been tampered with. I need to check the boys haven't lost their keys and not told me.

Franco hands me my keys and I place them back in my bag. They're pointless now. They've got in once, they can certainly get in again. When we get to the Rossi house, I'll call a local locksmith and get them all changed, and I will even bow down and ask Dante to turn on the live feed to the cameras again.

The drive back is silent and smooth. Franco constantly monitors our surroundings and checks the vanity mirror periodically to see if we're being followed. I assume we're not as he appears relaxed. I'm not. This is not what I'm used to. Constantly checking over your shoulder, people breaking into your home, stealing laptops. Why didn't they take anything else of value? My jewellery may not be flashy but it's still worth money. A thought runs through my head and I dismiss it instantly. Dante wouldn't do these things to frighten me in to coercion, would he?

## Chapter Twenty

The gates loom up before us as we approach and open immediately. They swing back in a gentle sweep like two dancers on ice. The road is quiet, no cars, no people. Just silence. At first it feels eerie but once the gates shut behind us I feel a wave of security wash over me. I didn't realise I was so tense until they closed. I can't come to depend on the family. I need to re-establish that feeling of security in our home. That will be a little more difficult knowing that a stranger has been inside.

At the entrance, Franco exits and immediately opens my door, I nod my thanks and make my way up the stone steps. Another guard opens the door as I enter.

"Thank you." I say as I enter.

The house seems quiet, I'm used to the sound of the boy's music, or a tv playing somewhere in the house. I see Sofia pass through the hallway and she stops when she sees me.

"Afternoon, do you know where the boys are?" I ask.

"I believe they are in the pool Mrs Rossi."

Again. No surprise there. It's going to be so difficult for them to leave here. They're getting used to all these luxuries.

"Thank you." I say and move on to the staircase.

On the first floor I see a guard outside of Dante's study and decide now is the time to broach the subject of the cameras and my grievous mistake.

As I approach the guard stands slightly taller, not quite a menacing look, but definitely not friendly. It's then I realise it's one of the men from the security room.

"Is Dante available please?" I ask.

I feel like a child approaching the headmasters office. It's so surreal having to ask to see someone inside a home.

"He is busy." His curt reply, obviously still not happy with me.

"Could you inform him I wish to speak to him. It's urgent." I emphasise the 'urgent'.

Reluctantly he turns and knocks gently on the door. It seems like an age when eventually Dante says "Accedere."

The sullen guard enters and closes the door swiftly behind himself, closing me out. Yep definitely still upset.

Moments later the door opens again, and I'm expecting him to shut it, when he gestures for me to enter. He begins to follow me in when I turn and look at him. What does he think I'm going to do?

"Leave us." I hear from behind me.

Hiding my smile, I close the door blocking him out.

"Do you have a minute please Dante?" I ask.

He's a busy man and all of my melodrama can't be helping.

Dante nods and indicates for me to sit. Taking the seat I had earlier I look him straight in the eye. Alex always told me to look people in the eye. You can tell if they are lying and it shows you are honourable.

"I would like to apologise." He looks taken aback by my opening statement.

"I'm sorry I told you to take the surveillance feed down to the house."

I assume that Franco or the nameless one has already informed him of the intruder as he doesn't seem shocked by my words.

Looking at me directly in the eye, I know his words will be true.

"You asked therefore I did."

Probably the only time he has ever done as asked and it's backfired.

"Please could you ask your team to re-install whatever they need again."

He nods, and I assume it's already been done. He said Franco is in charge of security I'll check with him later.

I jump straight in with the burning question.

"Do you have any idea who broke in? As they've only taken the laptop I presume it had something on it that it shouldn't have."

The last part is more statement than question.

He sighs deeply which shows he's thrown.

"I will be honest Kate, I do not know what Allesandro had on it."

I see him chewing the inside of his cheek, almost showing his weakness, when he stops suddenly and sits up straighter.

"Do you know when Allesandro used it last?"

The earlier memory flashes through my mind and I relay the details to Dante, leaving out the more personal parts.

He slips into deep thought as I sit in silence. It's obvious there is more to this, and I'm getting worried. What was Alex involved with, and if Dante doesn't know it can't be good.

"Do you think Benni might know?" I offer.

He looks surprised at my suggestion, picks up the phone and orders them to find his brother. The silence is awkward as we await Benni's arrival. He knocks on the door and just saunters in without permission.

"You summoned me." He struggles to contain his smile.

Dante doesn't look pleased at his quip, and Benni doesn't look bothered at his brother's ire.

"Sit." Oh, he's proper peed off with Benni.

Benni sits down and throws me a huge smile.

"The boys are in the pool, and before you say it," he holds up his hand, "there are guards keeping an eye on them."

They are both fantastic swimmers, I'm not worried. I'm touched by his concern for them and his forethought in their safety. That bloody word again. Safety.

Turning back to Dante he smiles at his brother, Dante doesn't return his smile.

"The cameras are being turned back on at their home." He starts.

Benni turns to me and his eyebrows shoot to his hairline.

"I asked him to." I confirm before he turns back to Dante.

"We need to establish how somebody gained entry. There are no signs of a break in, and they only stole Allesandro's laptop."

It's not a look of shock on Benni's face, I can't quite figure out what it is.

"Do you know what it contained?" Dante asks.

Benni purses his lips. Is he thinking or is he trying to stop information from spilling out?

He shakes his head slowly. He's lying, Dante thinks so too. He fires his brother a look and I hear Benni gulp. He knows he has to say something, and for his sake I hope it's the truth.

Clearing his throat, he looks down at his lap for a moment, breaking the dagger like stare from his brother. With a large sigh he begins.

"It could be one of two things. Alex had some, err, evidence," he throws his brother a pointed look, "from the incident with the Colombo family."

Dante obviously knows the details as he nods his head up and down slowly.

"Was the video on the laptop?" Dante asks, and Benni confirms with a nod.

"Is there another copy?" He asks.

This time Benni shrugs his shoulders.

"Alex said he would keep one for," he hesitates and his eyes glance towards me, "security."

Dante frowns and his head tilts slightly in a thinking pose. I have no idea what this information or video is, and I stop myself before I ask a stupid question.

"I assume he kept a copy or sent the file to someone." Dante says before he continues to think.

Benni sits quietly allowing him.

I remember Alex sending stuff to me all the time. My insurance details, breakdown cover, tickets. I would always lose the paper copies. It became our standard thing. I've even got video's he's forwarded of the boys and Bear.

"Could it be on a phone?" I ask, my question raising both their heads in shock when it suddenly comes to me. "That crappy phone." I say to Dante.

He frowns for a moment before remembering.

Opening the drawer, he retrieves the phone I had in my bag. It's still dead.

"We need a charger." He says with eyes directed at Benni.

Benni takes the phone, turns it over to look at the port, then rises from his chair and leaves.

Dante seems deep in thought and I feel like I'm invading his space, I go to rise. I can talk to him later as I can see he's busy, his head shoots up and looks at me.

"Please stay." He says, more a command than a request.

After a short time Benni returns with a charger and plugs the phone into the wall, and the other end into the phone.

"It may take a while." He offers.

Re-taking his seat, he leaves the phone on the sideboard to charge.

I can't contain my curiosity any longer. I know the saying curiosity killed the cat, thank god I'm not feline.

"What's on the video?" I know they will either lie or I will hate the truth. I don't know what I'm hoping for the most.

Sharing a look, Dante nods to Benni, giving him permission to speak. Turning in his chair he offers me a small smile. I can see him trying to decide how much to tell me. They've opted to tell me the truth.

"For many years we have been in conflict with the Colombo family. This disagreement spans many generations. Nobody knows the true reasons for the quarrel. Historically it was just slander and name calling up until our fathers rein over the family. The Colombo family changed into new leadership shortly after Dante took over the head of our family and the clash continued under Lorenzo Colombo."

"Quel bastardo figlio di puttana." Dante spits.

I don't know a lot of Italian words, but I think I can figure that one out.

Benni looks at his brother and nods. Turning back to me I can see the disgust for this Lorenzo evident on both their faces. To get Benni so riled up he must be a nasty piece of work.

"Since Lorenzo took over they've upped their game from slander to stealing. A year or so ago we noticed a few shipments were incomplete. We assumed it was the suppliers. Alex, umm, helped us to find out."

Benni looks uncomfortable admitting Alex's role in their business. I dread to think what those shipments contain. I dread even more thinking how Alex helped to get the information.

"Once Alex discovered the goods where being taken after the suppliers had shipped there were two possibilities. It was either disappearing during shipping or after the goods had landed at the docks."

Dante remains silent throughout his speech.

Taking a deep breath Benni goes on.

"The boats were searched on arrival by Alex and myself but we couldn't find any evidence of stashed goods. After we, umm, questioned the boat hands and captain, it was obvious they were loyal to the Rossi family and weren't taking anything. Most of the men and their families have worked for us for generations. We felt we could trust them."

That makes sense I suppose. If your family has been involved in their business that long surely you would be loyal. I understand that loyalty is a badge of honour in Italian families.

"We had to look at the dock hands. Alex hated suspecting these men as they have always been loyal."

I can see how much it distresses them both. To the Rossi family loyalty is everything. They've built their empire on these people. Even as an outsider I can understand.

"Alex questioned each man in turn, when we started to see some discrepancies."

He hesitates, probably unsure how much he can tell me. Looking back to Dante, who gives him a single nod.

"When the stories of three men didn't gel with the others, we knew something was amiss. One man in particular seemed uncomfortable with our questioning, more than the others."

He looks slightly guilty, I assume from their actions. He swallows before he continues.

"Alex took him to a warehouse we own."

He's really uncomfortable now.

"We use it to……" He chews his lip, thinking of the appropriate word to use "Extract information from people."

Images run riot in my head. What like I've seen in the movies? Do they beat them while they're chained up? Brandish them with hot irons? Torture, maim, cut bits off?

My stomach revolts with each sick thought. These acts I can't stand to imagine, my husband inflicted on people. What if they were innocent?

Oh God, has Alex actually killed?

The colour must have drained from me as Benni quickly leans forward to grasp my arm.

"Kate?" He asks.

I can't speak. Swallowing saliva over and over trying to quell the sick feeling rising within me.

"Are you OK?"

I sit as far back in the chair as I can. I don't know if it's to get away from these men or to escape my raging thoughts.

I sense movement and a glass of water is placed in my hand.

"Drink this Kate."

I hear Benni's voice, but my vision is blurring. Taking great gulps of air, I try to stay conscious. A cold sweat breaks out and runs down my back.

"Kate, drink it please." Dante's commanding voice next to me shakes me from my paralysis. Holding the glass in both hands, I tentatively sip the water, relishing the coolness.

"I need some air."

Someone walks to the massive sash windows before I hear them opening, one, two then three.

The cool air washes over me, cooling the sweat on my skin. I breathe deeply appreciating the air that fills my lungs. Taking slow breaths in through my nose, blowing it out through my mouth, my sight beginning to clear.

After a while the cool fresh air begins to chill me, placing the glass back on the desk, I tug my sleeves over my hands and wrap my arms tightly around my waist.

I hear the sound of two windows closing before Benni returns, facing me, leaning forward with his elbows resting on his knees.

"How are you feeling?" He asks. "I know it's all a bit of shock, but it's not as gruesome as you probably think."

He looks slightly awkward saying those words and I know instantly he's not telling me the truth. It is as bad as I'm imagining it.

"Kate you need to understand, this is the way we operate. We have to be forceful to maintain control. If we don't, people will think we're weak and move in to our territory. We have to walk a fine line, sometimes our actions aren't exactly legal, but they are necessary."

I'd assumed as much but him vocalising my thoughts has solidified it in my mind.

How could I have been married to a man who performed such atrocities on another human being? That man is a stranger to me. He's not the hero our boys worshipped, nor the gentle, kind and loving man I fell in love with. I don't know who he is.

"We have worked hard to keep our family at the top." Dante injects. "Both our father and grandfather ruled vigorously to keep control. Our territory remained protected under their guidance. With that power they kept people safe, not just the family, our workers enjoyed the sanctity of security by association. Our only problem has ever been Colombo."

"Kate, Alex wasn't a bad man. He believed in justice. He only did those things to right any wrongs." Benni adds.

"But the wrongs are illegal anyway." As a law-abiding citizen this is all foreign to me. How can a family control so much?

Dante and Benni share a look before Dante returns to his seat.

"What you need to understand Kate is we offer products that people want to buy. Our 'goods' are clean. We make sure to supply the best quality; other families have deaths on their hands from their supplies."

"Drugs?" I ask quietly.

"Yes Kate, among other things."

I've never taken drugs and can't understand the need or the mentality of an addict. I appreciate they struggle with their addictions, their need to escape reality, their want of the high. Most people come home from work and open a bottle of wine and in some respects, they're addicts too. We're all addicted to something I suppose, but feeding their addiction is wrong. If the drugs weren't available, they wouldn't be able to buy them.

Benni must read my thoughts.

"If we didn't supply them they would find somewhere else to buy. A few years ago, there was a spate of drug related deaths linked to Colombo's supply. We guarantee our products are clean, pure even. If they bought elsewhere their risks are much higher."

I can sort of see what he's saying. Addicts aren't loyal, they'll buy what they need wherever they can get it, but if the Rossi keep them fed with cleaner drugs they are marginally safer.

I know I'm trying to justify their actions in this immoral trade. How the other family can live with the deaths on the conscience is beyond me.

"Alex didn't need to enforce control much. Because of the respect afforded to the Rossi name he was able to remind people verbally rather than...."

Benni doesn't finish his statement, he doesn't need to.

"Has this been his role the whole time we've been married?" I'm struggling to put my words together. I already know my answer by the look on his face.

With my arms wrapped protectively over my tummy I think of the man I knew. The father of my children, our boys adored him. He walked on water in their eyes. Not once did he raise a hand to them, he abhorred violence. We didn't punish them physically, there were more efficient ways. Taking away their prized possession was much more effective. He hardly ever raised his voice, the quieter he spoke the more they listened. How can such an amazing man be this chilling, ferocious enforcer they speak of?

I've asked before, but I really need to know.

"How was I so blind? Why didn't I know, why didn't he tell me?"

Dante goes to speak, but Benni beats him to it.

"He loved you so much Kate. He wanted to keep your admiration, your respect, your approval. You were his everything, he couldn't lose that."

This is all so messed up. I don't think I've even broken the surface of the levels of crime and depravity. As Dante said, it's better if I don't know all the details. It's not healthy and probably not ethical, but I can't think about any of this anymore.

Rising from the chair, both men stand too.

"I need to lay down for a while."

Benni goes to speak.

"Just give me time to process, well everything, please Benni."

Opening the door to leave, Dante speaks.

"He was a good man Kate."

I know he was, but which version? There were obviously two sides to him.

# Chapter Twenty-one

The boys are laying on the sofa in our suite when I open the door.

"Hey mum." They say in unison.

I feel terrible, I've hardly spent any time with them. After the day I've had, I just want to curl up on the sofa and sleep.

Sitting down in the chair, we all sit in silence watching the movie playing on the screen. Bear snores loudly from the floor, twitching occasionally then settling again. The boys are laid top to toe on the sofa with their heads turned towards the screen. If you took away the unfamiliar furniture, it would be a very familiar scene from home.

I have no idea what to do or what to think. We've been sucked into a life so far removed from ours I can hardly comprehend it. I don't know what to think about my husband. Alex Rossi is a completely different person to Allesandro Rossi. How can both live inside one person coherently? How did Alex live with himself, committing such heinous crimes. My shoulders sag from the weight bearing down on them, I can't imagine what his felt like.

I'm starting to understand why Alex kept us away from this life. I will love him till my last breath, but I can't respect the man that Benni described.

The shock and my emotions are running high and I'm hurt by Alex's actions and lack of trust in me, offended and troubled by it all.

The cosiness of the room warms me and the close proximity of the ones I love relaxes me. I'll shut my eyes for 5 minutes. I need to give my head and heart a break from the strain. This tension, these conflicting feelings, all of it is too much.

"Mum, it's nearly dinner time." I hear Leo's voice, but it sounds distant.

"Mum, you need to wake up." I feel him gently shaking me as I open my eyes.

"I'm awake." I say, stretching my arms and legs.

The chair may be comfy to sit in but not for sleeping in.

"What's the time?" I ask.

"Half six." Marc pipes up from the sofa.

Dinner is at seven, we need to get a wiggle on. Standing straight I move my neck from side to side to release the kinks.

"I need a quick shower."

I notice the boys are washed and dressed. Their thoughtfulness doesn't go amiss, they let me sleep as long as possible.

"I'll be as quick as I can."

Walking in to my room I close the door and strip off. I run my hands over my tummy. Now that I know, I can feel the life inside of me. Gently caressing around my abdomen in circular motions I marvel at the miracle I have safely cocooned. I don't know what the future will look like for us all, but one thing is for definite, I will keep my children safe and secure, even from this family if I have to.

Dressed in a loose top and trousers, I wave the mascara over my lashes, coat my lips in a clear balm and put my hair up in a messy bun. It's taken me less than 15 minutes and I'm back in the lounge again.

"Ready?" I ask, and they both stand.

Bear opens one eye to see who dares to disrupt his slumber before closing it again.

We walk down the stairs and in to the dining room where we find Maria and Benni. Maria looks apprehensively at the table and I follow her line of sight. Spread out is a traditional English roast dinner. Roast beef, roasted potatoes, various vegetables, what I imagine is a giant Yorkshire Pudding, all be it a little deflated. The food is so far removed from their usual fare.

"Thank you Maria, this all looks amazing."

I appreciate the effort she has gone to, I really do.

"We did not know what to cook, but I believe this is your traditional Sunday dish."

I can imagine her request sent their kitchen into a frenzy. The effort they have gone to just to please us chokes me up.

"It is all wonderful." I just about choke out.

The boys lean over the chairs eyeing it all, almost inhaling it.

"Yeah nonna, it's great." Leo says, ever the gentleman.

We take our seats as Dante enters the room. His look of confusion is a picture.

"What is this?" He doesn't sound angry, just confused.

"I want them to feel comfortable Dante." Maria's statement shuts Dante down immediately.

The dishes are handed around, the boys pile their plates high, Dante and Maria take much smaller portions, unsure. Benni seems happy with any food he's given.

We all tuck in and the look of surprise on their faces has me looking down quickly at my plate to hide my smirk. The boys are comfortable chatting and shovelling food in. The feel around the table is relaxed, complete opposite to my earlier meeting with Dante and Benni. We feel like a normal family sitting down for a normal meal in a very not normal house.

"How do you feel figlia?" Maria asks, shaking me from my reverie.

Chewing and swallowing quickly before I can answer.

"I'm good, thank you Maria. Really good. And thank you for all of this, it's delicious."

The smile on Maria's face helps me forget for a moment the bizarre world we've found ourselves in.

The conversation around the table is comfortable. My fears of it veering into talk of criminal activity are never realised. When they start to ere into anything business related, Maria shoots them a look, and they change the subject quickly. Their respect for Maria is phenomenal. These men are daunting and rule a criminal empire, but one look from their elderly mother and they re-vert back to little boys. It's quite amusing to watch.

"You will contact the school tomorrow?" Dante asks.

I'd forgotten, this weekend has been full of revelations and my brain has been fried. I need to let them know the boys will be working remotely.

"Yeah, I'm sure they'll be fine once I explain."

Dante gives me a firm look. Is he concerned as to what I will say?

"I was going to say we are staying with friends, as we have to have emergency repairs done at home."

He seems satisfied with my pretend excuse for the alterations. In a quieter voice I add.

"Plus, I need to arrange for the locks to be changed before we can go home."

I'd forgotten to tell him earlier my proposed plans to change all the locks whilst we're staying at the Rossi house.

Checking the boys aren't listening, Dante leans closer.

"It has already been dealt with."

Here we go again, Dante's need for control.

"It is my job to ensure your safety."

He leans back clearly finished with our conversation, and begins speaking with his mother, effectively halting any further comments from me.

We all move into the lounge, where coffee is served, I instantly decline. I can't stomach the aroma and it's not good for the baby anyway.

"May I see my nipotina?" Maria asks almost hesitantly.

With everything that's happened today I'd forgotten to talk to her about the baby.

Smiling at her request I begin to rise as the ultrasound picture is in our suite. With a sheepish look Leo puts his hand in his pocket and takes the picture out.

"I have it here nonna." He says and goes to sit next to his grandmother.

The two of them sit with their heads bent studying the image in her hands.

"What is your due date?" Dante asks.

"The beginning of May, it's so exciting." Marc responds, clearly eager for time to pass quickly.

Dante turns from me and begins talking with him, I assume about his sister as I hear the words 'protect' and 'honour'. I see Marc nodding along with Dante's every word.

Benni plops next to me on the sofa, with his arms stretched across the back, completely relaxed.

"I love roast beef." He says with a huge grin.

"You ate enough." I retort, and I hear him laugh softly.

"Don't tell mamma, but I get a bit bored of pasta."

Laughing at his words, I relax back into the corner of the sofa.

"I'm telling on you. You're going to be in so much trouble with your mum." I'm desperately trying not to laugh.

Benni isn't so successful. He lets out a full-on belly laugh, his whole body vibrating as his shoulders move with the motion. Dante and Maria both look our way but soon return their attentions to their partners.

Eventually Benni settles down.

"I don't want to ruin your good mood, but we need to continue our conversation from earlier." He says.

I know I didn't get all the details after I became stupefied with shock.

"When the boys are settled with their school work we can talk then." He adds.

I'm not looking forward to it at all.

"It's important you have all the details Kate. I know you think Dante is overtaking your lives with security." He gives me a knowing look. "But once you understand the dangers you face, you'll understand why it's required."

I can't argue with him. From what I've learnt so far, I know it's a necessary evil.

"Ironic though how we lived all these years oblivious and safe and the moment we visit, we're suddenly in danger." I say.

Keeping his voice low Benni goes on.

"Alex was really careful to keep you all hidden. Don't take this the wrong way, but most of our associates don't know he was married with a family."

His words shock me. I never insisted he wear a wedding ring, he always said he wasn't a fan of jewellery.

"I can see you're shocked but it was the only way to guarantee you remained invisible."

Alex really did take care to ensure our safety. I'm not upset, quite the opposite.

"So, we only became visible when we arrived here this weekend?"

Benni hesitates before he response.

"We should continue this conversation tomorrow."

I throw him a look of disgust.

"No, we should continue this conversation now."

My words offering no room for movement.

He doesn't look quite so comfy now, I couldn't give a damn.

Lowering his voice even further he almost whispers.

"Alex suspected they had discovered your identity months before he died."

Shit, this is not what I wanted to hear.

"Who?" I quietly ask, but I have a suspicion.

Dread is running through my veins.

Benni glances to the other occupants of the room to check our conversation is still private.

"The Colombo family." He says.

"Lorenzo Colombo?" I ask quietly. Benni nods his confirmation.

"What does he want with us?"

We don't know anything. I didn't even know my husband had a secret life before this weekend.

"Colombo is a sick bastard." He spits in disgust. "He would do anything to hurt the Rossi family. To him you're weak, unprotected." He raises his eyebrows at me. "And therefore an easy target. He preys on the vulnerable as they put up less of a fight."

My hands tremble at his words.

"What will he do?" I ask quietly.

"Believe me, you really don't want to know!"

Judging by his sickened look, I don't.

"Dante has your best interests at heart. He may come across as cold and un-feeling, but he cares for you all deeply. Now with another baby, a Principessa, he will become even more protective, it's his job as head of the family too."

I sigh deeply, there is no way to escape this life, no getting out now. It looks like we are governed by Dante's rules and it's not a position I ever wanted to be, neither did Alex.

"It's not so bad once you get used to it." He offers. "After a while you stop noticing the guards around you."

I don't know if I will ever get used to someone constantly following me.

It looks like we will all have to learn to change our lives, our ways, and I need to know just how depraved this Lorenzo is, what danger we are potentially in.

"What else did Alex find out? Did he know what Lorenzo's plan was?"

Benni nods, chewing his lip apprehensively.

"What did he find out Benni?" I all but demand.

He hesitates, checking the room again before he speaks.

"The video he has, had, on his laptop was of a man who worked for us. Colombo had gotten to him, threatened his wife and children. What he was stealing from each consignment was for Colombo, more and more with each shipment. When Alex had a little 'chat' with him, he was prepared to give up information he had if Alex spared his life."

Swallowing I try to stay calm.

"The man had heard Colombo's plans to kidnap you and the boys and, well, keep you for a while. In exchange he would expect the Rossi family to hand over our drug routes and territories."
Kidnap!!! Tremors wrack through my body.

"The man gave up all the information we needed on Colombo. Incriminating information. He supplied evidence of Colombo's involvement in a spate of disappearances. It seems he has a very keen interest in trafficking. From what we can establish the rest of the Colombo family aren't happy with the direction he's pulling their family. Trafficking for the sex trade is not an area we have any interest. The Rossi syndicate are vehemently against it and it's an unwritten rule that most of our associates won't touch it either. Colombo has gone against his families wishes and they're not happy."

Was that going to be my fate? Holding my belly tight I ask the fundamental question.

"How do we stay safe? What will stop him?"

"Dante has been meeting with other families that Colombo has crossed too. One family in particular, a young girl was taken. There was no actual evidence it was Colombo, and they can't accuse him without calling an all-out war. The man Alex questioned supplied us with names, dates, facts, all pointing directly to Colombo himself. The video evidence is what the other families needed to officially take Colombo down."

"What happened to the girl?" I ask hesitantly.

"She didn't survive the ordeal he put her through."

"Benni." We both turn to see Dante's glare.

Nostrils flared with the exertion of controlling his breathing. His body held tightly, controlling the anger within. His look is furious.

Benni doesn't cower, he doesn't melt from the intensity of his glare.

Turning his eyes from Benni he looks at me with sympathy. He knows that Benni has shared this horrendous information with me. It all makes sense now. Dante's commands for safety, all the guards, bringing us here to the Rossi house. We really weren't safe at home.

A thought suddenly occurs to me, so I turn to Benni.

"Do you think they've been watching me, us, all this time?"

Memories invading my mind, seeing shadows in the trees, Bear's reactions to the woods, cars following us both at home and in Cornwall, that constant feeling of being watched.

Benni breaks his staring stand-off with Dante to turn to me.

"We do." He nods in case I don't hear his words.

"They were in the woods." I say more as clarification for myself than for him. I did see something, I'm not going mad.

The week has gone by with me jumping at every noise, my nerves are in tatters. The boys have noticed my unease, and I've simply told them it's because we're in a strange place. They seem satisfied with my explanation. My mind has run through every unexplained incident. Why didn't they attempt to take us before? I'm grateful they didn't, and I'm indebted to the Rossi family for their intervention on our behalf. When I didn't know it was truly to keep us safe I couldn't appreciate their actions but now I feel ungrateful for my behaviour towards them.

Dr Manessi called on Tuesday to tell me that he had arranged for an appointment at the obstetrician's office to meet with the midwife. I'm dreading leaving the compound. This house, which I feared, has now become my safe haven. A sanctuary for me and the boys to stay safe, alive. I know it is fear that I fear the most, and the unknown will always be the greatest phobia any person can face.

Franco is waiting in the hallway to escort me to the appointment in London. I overheard snippets of conversation between him and Dante, but they always speak in Italian and I only understood a few words. I don't know if it's to purposely exclude me or to protect me from information that will only worry me further.

"Are you ready Mrs Rossi?" He asks.

He can clearly see the anxiety written all over my face. I'm petrified of walking out that door, driving through those gates. Franco interprets my look of fear and adds in a lower tone.

"I will look after you."

Nodding my head in thanks, we walk out into the cold air. December will be here too soon. Christmas. The first of so many events that Alex will miss. The despondent thought carries me to the car. It's then I notice the convoy of vehicles. With a frown I look to Franco for clarification.

"I will ride with you and the driver in this vehicle." He indicates with his head. "We will be accompanied by two guards in that one." He points to the car behind.

So many people, just for me. I feel safe in the knowledge, but I also feel wasteful of their time. Franco seems to be a mind reader today as he goes on.

"It is our job to ensure your safety. We are all happy to do it."

With a smile I thank him and enter the car door he has opened.

The ride to the clinic is quiet, and my fellow passengers are ever vigilant. Occasionally I hear Franco whisper into his sleeve, check a mirror, and speak again before resuming his usual observations. I try not to look at all the people out of the windows, it's hard, I really do try, but I find myself scanning the faces of strangers on the streets.

As we pull up to the clinic, Franco orders me to wait before he exits the car. The driver constantly scans the areas surrounding us.

After he has spoken with the passenger from our tailing car he opens my door, placing his body directly in front of me.

"I will lead you inside, please stay close."

Rising from the car we walk towards the entrance, and I feel the other guard behind me. My body safely ensconced between theirs.

The receptionist doesn't appear shocked at our unorthodox arrival, or that my bodyguards have checked me in. She smiles at me and asks me to take a seat, indicating the waiting area with her hand. It's pretty obvious what and where it is due to the number of chairs and magazines arranged jauntily.

Taking a seat, the guard positions himself on the wall nearest the door. He has a view of the whole waiting area, clinic doors and the entrance. Franco walks me towards the chairs and indicates the seat he would prefer I took. I don't argue. This is his job, and I assume he knows what's best.

The wait is relatively short and an older lady in navy blue scrubs comes from one of the clinic doors. She speaks to the receptionist, who hands her a folder and indicates towards me with a nod. The older lady walks towards me, completely ignoring Franco, and smiles.

"Mrs Rossi?" She asks in the gentlest voice.

I nod, and she smiles brighter.

"Please could you follow me?"

I rise from the chair and Franco begins to follow too. I'm just about to say something when the nurse stops outside the room and steps aside slightly. Turning to Franco she speaks.

"We will be using this room today."

Franco nods and enters the room. I can see him checking the area, windows, and even under the desk, before he exits and nods to the nurse.

"Please Mrs Rossi, after you."

In shock, I enter the room and turn to wait for the nurse. I can see Franco has positioned himself outside of the door as she begins to close it.

"Please take a seat Mrs Rossi." She offers, indicating the very comfy looking chair by the desk.

Slipping my coat off I go to lay it over the back of the chair when the nurse smiles and takes it from me before hanging it up on the coat-stand by the door. I sit down and await her return.

The room is nothing like a hospital or clinic. It was clearly designed by a lady. Every consideration for comfort has been, well, considered. There is medical paraphernalia but more as an afterthought. The whole room is relaxing, my tension begins to subside.

"My name is Ruth and I will be your midwife for the remainder of your pregnancy if that is suitable to you." She says.

Her voice is so gentle it's like a calming wave washing over my soul.

"How are you feeling today Mrs Rossi?" She asks as she takes a blood pressure monitor from the desk.

I roll up my sleeve and place my arm on the desk, she places the cuff over my arm and presses the button to measure it.

Her gentle smile flicks to me before she reads the numbers, a slight frown flits over her face before it drops away.

Looking at me, she removes the cuff.

"It's a little on the high side."

That's an understatement.

"Life's a little stressful right now." I offer.

Ruth nods her understanding, I doubt she could fully comprehend the magnitude of it all.

"How are you feeling in general?" She asks, scribbling notes in the folder.

I don't know how to voice it all without saying my life has gone to hell and I don't know what I can do about it.

"As I said, things are really stressful."

Her kind face offers me a sincere smile, and I don't know what possesses me, but I start to open up to this stranger.

"My husband died over three months ago in a car accident leaving me with our two boys. We didn't really know his family and we've recently been introduced to them, which was nerve-wracking in itself. We're having to stay with them whilst improvements are being made on my home to install a full security team to protect us from an unknown threat, and then last week I discovered I was 4 months pregnant at the age of 39 when I thought I was starting the menopause, and to top it all it's a girl and my deceased husband didn't know about her before he died."

It's at that point I see the tissue she has procured and is gently placing in my hands.

"It's all been a bit much hasn't it." She says, and I can only nod my head in agreement.

"Firstly, I am truly sorry for your loss Mrs Rossi. Losing your husband is one of the hardest things you will ever have to face." By the sympathy in her words I know she's a widow too.

"Secondly, you are not old enough to be menopausal. More women have babies over the age of 40 now, and with proper care and attention they deliver a healthy baby. So, don't worry your mind on that."

I had read about the average age of mothers rising. With the constant battle women have in the professional market they can't afford to take time off to push a baby out and still be able to return to their original position. It's so unfair.

"Thirdly, your boys are a gift, as is this little one. They will be your constant reminder of the love you and your husband shared. Their faces will bring you joy for many, many years to come."

I like Ruth a lot, I could listen to the softness of her voice all day.

"And think how lucky you are to escape the mess and chaos at home. Let someone else help you. You need their help because your number one job right now is keeping this little one safe."

With her beautiful smile before me, I wipe away the tears, as she pats my arm affectionately.

"OK, today I would like to take some standard blood samples. We have the results from Dr Manessi, but we need to take our own, then I would like to listen to the baby's heart and we can have a look at her growth too."

With her ever-present smile she goes about taking blood and then escorting me to the bed. Laying down I adopt the usual routine in these exams and roll up my top and roll down my jeans. I won't be able to wear them much longer as they are already too tight. I lost a lot of weight after Alex died, and now it's piling back on, but in a good way.

She takes the doppler and finds the heartbeat almost straight away. Years of practice she says.

The sound is a comfort to any expectant mother. Hearing her for the first time reduces me to yet more tears. That amazing noise filling the room with the sounds of her life.

Ruth moves on to the ultrasound next and finds her straight away. I'm happy to lay and watch her dance on screen as Ruth expertly takes measurements.

"I'm sure Dr Manessi spoke with you concerning the risk of Downs."

I nod my head and before she can continue I tell her that it doesn't matter to me.

She gives me her smile and carries on with her measuring. Occasionally I hear the printer when she finds the baby laying in a particularly good position.

"OK, that all looks amazing. You are actually one week further on than Dr Manessi said. You are now 21 weeks and 3 days. Can I ask your history with birthing your boys please?"

Laying on the bed the image of my baby is still on screen and I happily watch it as I babble away. Both boys were born naturally. I fill her in on a few of the complications I had with Marc, which Ruth scribbles down a few notes, occasionally asking me questions about the hospital and if I could remember any of the doctors. I give her what I can but most of it's a blur.

Smiling she passes me a warm cloth to clean myself before I reset my clothing. Making our way back to the desk she finishes her notes and places her pen down to give me her full attention.

"Is there anything you would like to ask me? I know practices have changed since your youngest but in essence it's still the same."

I smile at her words. I was a little apprehensive.

"Where will I give birth?"

This has been on my mind. We live at least an hour and half from here, and on a bad day that could be considerably more.

"The plan would be to birth here at the hospital attached to the clinic. It is a completely private hospital. You will be assigned a doctor to your care, but it will be myself that is on-call when your time comes."
The relief must be evident on my face as her smile gets even brighter.

"I would need to move closer when the time is near then?"

I think through the options, and the only solution would be to stay at the Rossi house. Would that mean I have to go back there after the birth, I know I can do it on my own with the boys but sometimes you just need an extra pair of hands for the first few weeks.

"We don't need to worry with the details now. We have a few months to write your birthing plan. As I will be your assigned midwife I would like you to take my number, you would call me and not the clinic if you need anything, or maybe just to chat. It's my job to care for you while you care for the baby."

I really, really like Ruth.

"Well in that case, I beg you to drop the Mrs Rossi. Please call me Kate."

And with that Ruth's beautiful smile makes me smile.

## Chapter Twenty-two

Armed with the multiple images and the next appointment booked, plus a care bag, book on pregnancy, iron supplements and various other additional vitamins, we exit the clinic. Franco takes the lead with the other guard behind me. The door is opened to the outside world, and I'm so happy I can't be concerned right now. Looking at the pictures in my hand I don't see Franco stop till I barrel into his back. I go to step back but I instantly feel the guard behind me. Looking up quickly I see the other two guards are out of the car's watching a potential threat. The car is parked opposite the building and the men inside aren't trying to hide their intense watch of me.

The door to our car is quickly opened and I'm carefully, but forcefully, pushed inside. Franco shuts the door, and almost instantly the sound of the driver's door opens, I immediately swing my gaze from the threat to see who is entering the vehicle, when I see my own guard get in and start the car simultaneously. Franco gets in, his eyes trained on the car opposite. Talking into his sleeve, he issues instructions in Italian as we pull away from the curb. Looking through the rear window I see the threat remains stationary and so does our escort car.

"What's happening?" I ask.

I can't take my eyes off the scene behind. Nobody is moving, no guns blazing, no physical violence. They are just sitting there, watching.

Franco continues to speak into his sleeve as the driver manoeuvres safely but at speed away from the clinic.

It feels like an age before Franco answers my question. Turning in his seat he nods to my lap.

"Seatbelt."

I quickly grab the seatbelt and yank at it, but it locks in place. I try it again, with the same effect.

"Slowly."

Franco's calm words sound through the car.

Taking a deep breath, I release the seatbelt, letting it fully retract and then slowly, calmly, pull it till I can reach it around my body and click it into place. Looking up I see Franco nod his approval.

"Who was in the car?" I ask him.

I can see the look pass over his face, he's not sure what to tell me.

"Was it anything to do with Colombo?"

The look of surprise tells me he didn't know I knew.

He nods his head.

"Yes, they were two of Lorenzo Colombo's private men."
"By private I assume they aren't part of the Colombo syndicate. They're not family approved?"

I remember everything Benni said about Lorenzo going against his family. If he is stalking me without their knowledge he could hardly use the official Colombo men.

Franco nods again. Shock still evident on his face.

"Is Dante and Benni, or the other families, aware who these additional men are?"

By the delay in his response, he's not used to being asked questions, and probably not by females. The only other lady in the Rossi family is Maria, and I doubt she asks, she tells.

I remember at the funeral that all the Rossi blood relatives were male. Females married into the family. The thought hits me even harder. I place my hand over my growing bump. This will be the first female to be born to the Rossi line in generations. That's why they called her a princess. She truly is a special gift.

"We suspected but hadn't seen for ourselves. Now we can identify them and use the information against Colombo himself." Franco says breaking my little happy party over my daughter.

Thinking for a moment I look through the side window, Franco thinks we're done talking and turns to face the front.

"Will that help? With this and the evidence Alex acquired on his extra-curricular activities , is it enough to take him down?"

I don't know what they need to get him dethroned or thrown out or whatever it is they do to the head of a family. Is it enough to free us and the other families from Colombo?

The shocked gasps from the front seats are all I hear as we travel in the silent car.

As we approach the Rossi house the doors open and Bear barrels out. I see in my peripheral vision the guard flinch in response to his exuberance. Heading straight to me I lean down slightly and hug his thick neck, placing a kiss on the top of his head.

"Hey big fella."

The boys come out no less slowly, firing questions at me as they descend the steps. Pulling the pictures from my bundle of goodies, they literally snatch them up to inspect them closer. Looking at me Leo beams.

"Is everything Ok with her?"

I nod and smile.

"She's perfect, and she may be arriving a little earlier than we expected."

With a questioning look from them both I fill them in with all the details from the midwife.

Franco begins herding us indoors, and it's only then I realise we're all stood exposed in the open. I'd forgotten the potential threat from earlier for a moment.

Franco catches my concerned look.

"It's a little cold to be standing out here Mrs Rossi."

I appreciate his professional concern for our precarious position and the ability not to show his unease in front of the boys. I don't want them finding out about the incident earlier.

Safely inside we move to the lounge where Maria sits with afternoon tea. I note she has coffee though. The cakes all look amazing. Sitting down she serves us all whilst asking questions about my appointment with the midwife. When the subject of the due date comes up I begin to fret. Should I ask her now if we can stay here nearer the time? It would be much more convenient. My thoughts are interrupted by the entrance of Benni.

"Boys." He says jovially. "I hope you've left some cakes for your favourite uncle."

As he sits on the sofa he grabs a fruit tart. Shoving it in his mouth whole. I look at him with raised eyebrows and mock disgust at his lack of manners.

"What?" He says around a mouthful of pastry. "I'm hungry."

"You're always hungry!" I quip.

After the boys have stopped laughing at his antics their attention turns back to their grandmother.

"Dante would like a quick word." Benni whispers.

I turn to him and silently ask why.

"About this afternoon." He answers my silent question.

Glad that the boys, or Bear for that matter, haven't upset him, I nod my OK. As I rise from the seat, Benni follows.

"I need to get changed." I tell the room, but they're all focused on the pictures and pregnancy book, looking at the details for this week.

Walking up the first flight of stairs there is yet another guard on duty. Benni nods to him and the guard knocks once before he opens the door.

"Howdey Dudey Dante."

I swear Benni does it to get a rise from him.

"Good afternoon Kate. How are you?"

Dante totally ignores his brother, his focus trained completely on me. I take my usual seat before I answer.

"Good thanks. The midwife, Ruth, is amazing. She's due the end of April." I say running my hands over my bump.

Dante looks down at the paperwork on his desk.

"Ruth Norris. 56 years old. Widow. No children. Qualified over 25 years ago as a midwife. Clear criminal history. No known associations.:

My jaw just hit the floor in shock. He's still reeling off information about the woman I only met a few hours ago.

"She's all clear. We checked before the appointment." Benni says. Not to me. To Dante.

"Good." Dante says.

Glad they've cleared that up then.

"Does someone want to fill ME in?" I ask sarcastically.

Both their heads turn to me.

"Well?"

Benni tries to hide his smile and Dante looks confused.

"Why do you have a full dossier on my midwife?" I ask slowly as if I'm talking to a child.

Benni's smirk get bigger and Dante just frowns.

"To ensure you are safe." He says

It's a women's clinic for god's sake.

"Colombo could have got to you through her."

That didn't even occur to me. Just goes to show how unprepared I am for this life.

"People are bought off all the time Kate. Offer them enough money and they would sell their own mother."

I sit in silence, chastised by Dante's words.

Benni reaches forward and places his hand on my arm in comfort.

"We're just being cautious." He offers.

I nod my head. This is all so new to me.

"She's really nice." I offer.

I know I don't have a folder of information on the woman, but in my heart, I felt her goodness.

"Good." Dante says closing the subject.

"What can you tell me about the incident after?"

I knew this conversation was coming and I've tried to retain as many details as possible. For the next half an hour I run through every aspect I can remember. A few new points pop into my head, the colour of their hair, other vehicles I saw, people in the waiting room.

Dante and Benni question me further on these details. Thankfully the driver recorded the incident which Dante and Benni view. I don't need to see it, I was there. Although they weren't threatening me, their presence was scary and intimidating. Once they've viewed the video twice I ask the question that's been burning inside.

"What did you find on the other phone?"

Dante knows what I'm asking and after a few minutes of deliberating, he finally responds.

"It contained Allesandro's video evidence."

I wait for him to elaborate but he remains quiet. Looking at Dante now, I can see how much it pained him to see his brother. I didn't think they were close, but the man sitting in his throne is hurting just as much as me.

I nod in understanding. For the relief they still have the evidence and in compassion for our mutual loss.

Deciding to lighten the mood I broach the subject of the baby's sex. Gently rubbing my belly, I look at them both as I ask.

"When was the last female Rossi born?"

The smile on Benni's face is infectious as Dante relaxes back with his own version.

"It is believed that our great-grandfather had a sister, but she sadly died at birth."

Thinking backwards that would have been late 1800's I assume. As sad as it was, it wasn't unusual to lose a child at birth.

"So, little Angel Allesandro will be the first Rossi girl to be born in a very long time." I say on a smile.

I didn't think it was possible, but both their smiles grow even bigger.

"Yes, she will." Dante says with true affection in his voice.

"She really is a Principessa." Proud to use that word.

"She'll be the first Principessa in over 200 years." Benni announces.

"Wow!" Rubbing my belly. My little Angel. I just wish Alex was here to share in our joy.

The atmosphere over the weekend changes drastically. Gone is the usual calm and tranquillity, replaced with an apprehension throughout the household. The guards are more vigilant which gives everyone a sense of unease. I suggested that the boys stay out of their way as they appear distracted with more pressing matters. I have my suspicions that this is related to Lorenzo and when I questioned Franco, he avoided answering and recommended I stay indoors for a while.

Both Dante and Benni have been absent from the house. When Leo asked Maria where they were she gently brushed him off and said they were busy with family business. Her anxious behaviour and the look she darted my way, told me she was lying. My imagination is running riot. The man is a loose cannon.

On Monday I called the school again to arrange more homework. I explained there was a delay to the repairs, due to the builders finding asbestos. It was the only excuse I could think of. I remembered seeing a programme about a family who had to vacate the property when it was found in their house. The head teacher didn't question it and was happy to extend their leave of absence. As Dante is still away from the Rossi house, I couldn't get an update from him. I have no idea what is actually happening in my own home. Franco is overseeing everyone's security in the compound, and the tensest I've ever seen him. It would be impossible for him to manage our renovations when everyone's safety is clearly a priority right now.

As the week moves on the tension in the air begins to dissipate. You can feel it evaporating. The staff in the house appear more relaxed and the guards seem to have stepped down a level too and I've been stuck in the house for too long. The boys are occupied upstairs with their studies and I'm bored. Bored of being waited on. Bored of my every need being taken care of. I sound spoilt, but I'm used to doing it all by myself.

I need to do my Christmas shopping, but I become distracted with the finer details like where we will be. I still haven't spoken to Dante on that subject as he's still mostly absent from the house, but I wanted to go home for Christmas. It's our first major event since Alex died. Surely, we should spend it in his home.

I haven't left the compound in a few weeks, so I don't know if there are still potential threats out there. After the sudden atmosphere change last week I'm assuming there is. Would there be more if we left? Would I be putting everyone in danger with my selfish desire to go home?

Sitting in the sunny garden room I think about my garden. I miss the freedom of just pulling on my boots and walking whenever I want with nothing and no-one to stop me. Sighing to myself I'm being unfair. Would it be that difficult to stay here for a while? After Alex died I was so lonely. I know I had the boys, but I missed him so much. I know I can never get the feeling of familiarity back, but being here with the boys, sharing our time with his family I feel close to Alex again. Rubbing my belly, I still feel him in my heart, but I realise now that it must be because of Angel. His heart grows within her, and she is safely cocooned inside of me.

I know if we stay here our lives won't be our own. Dante expects Leo to take over the family business and as his mum I just can't correlate it in my head. Neither Leo nor Marc know the true nature of their business and I know from a teenager's perspective it would all be amazing. He will only see the glamour of this lifestyle. What he won't see is how that lifestyle is retained. The legal operations would be a lot for any one person to manage, and add into that the responsibility of hundreds, thousands of people dependant on you. On the other side of the Rossi Syndicate they are affiliated with illegal activities. I can't even begin to understand fully what they are involved with. The conversation about the drug imports nearly blew my mind. I know Benni said their only real threat is Lorenzo Colombo but surely there are others. My head is going round and round and round when Maria walks in followed by a maid with a tray.

"Please." She indicates to the maid.

Placing it on the table the maid smiles to me and then leaves.

Maria takes her seat and begins to pour tea, placing sandwiches and fruit on a plate before passing me them both. All carried out without a word.

I nod my thanks as I take her offering.

"When I married my husband, I knew some things of his family."

OK, where's she going with this?

She sits back in her chair, holding the saucer in her left hand whilst raising her teacup to her lips in her right. Taking a dainty sip, it's obvious she prefers coffee.

Setting the cup back down, she lowers it to the arm of the chair to look at me.

"I did not know how the business worked. My husband, he tell me I don't need to worry."

A little chauvinistic, I think.

"He says his job is to run the business and my job is raise his sons."

Yep, definitely a chauvinist.

"He did not like it when I tell him no."

I've just mentally shuffled to the edge of my seat. Taking another sip of her tea, I wait anxiously for her next words. She slowly places the cup down before she continues.

"He show me how it all works. We spend our nights together, he teaches me. We did not tell anyone."

She waves her hand behind her towards the door.

"We did not tell the boys."

Giving me a stern look, I read her unspoken message.

"They still do not know."

I nod my head in agreement at her silent request.

"I tell my husband I do not like some of our business, we change it. I do not like the unsavoury partnerships, we change it. I do not like the guard's violent behaviour, we change it. His father did not want to move with a new plan, he was set in the old ways. My husband and I wanted to lead our children into a better life."

She takes a slow sip of her tea before placing it down again.

"Women are not accepted as the top of a family, but it is a woman who shaped it this far." She says giving me a pointed look.

"You are a strong woman Kate. Leonardo will listen to you. Dante will teach him the business, but it is his mamma that will guide him in the right direction."

Looking at this amazing woman before me I'm in complete awe. She is responsible for shaping the syndicate into a more legal business. It is because of her they are so successful. Yes, they are involved in some illegal activities which may be inevitable and probably left over from the previous ruler, but if Leo did take over he would have the power to make changes for the good. As I'm musing through her words and my thoughts, Maria places her cup on the table with a disgusted look.

"I do not like this tea. I think I will change that also."

My laughter follows her as she leaves the room.

After my conversation I make the decision about Christmas. I need to get organised.

## Chapter Twenty-three

That evening as we enter the dining room, Maria is sat with Dante and Benni, all talking rapidly in Italian. When they notice our entrance their conversation stops immediately, instantly putting me on high alert.

"What's wrong?" I don't give a damn about protocol or appearing rude.

Both Benni and Maria look to Dante, but he remains quiet. Whatever it is, it's not good.

"What's happened?"

Dante rises from his seat and straightens his cuffs as he begins to approach me.

"Would you please accompany me to my study?"

Posed as a question, I know it's not.

Smiling at the boys I exit and follow Dante up the stairs and into his study.

Indicating to the chair he says, "Please, sit."

I take the seat as Dante moves around the desk and pulls open a drawer. After extracting something he walks back around and sits in the other visitor's chair. Holding the item under his hands on his lap, I can't see what it is. It looks like an envelope, but I can't be sure.

Dante takes a deep breath before looking me straight in the eye.

"You received a letter."

OK why's that so bad?

"With the on-going threat, Franco screened it before passing it to me."

Surely if it's addressed to me I should have opened it.

Taking another heavy sigh, his fingers begin to pluck at the edge of the paper in his lap.

"I am glad he took this precaution. The item is a card meant to distress you."

I'm starting to worry because of Dante's reaction. Passing the envelope to me face down, I see the seal is still intact as someone has used a knife to slice the top open.

Turning it over in my hand I see them shaking. The letter is clearly addressed to me, but I don't recognise the handwriting. The post mark over the stamp is dated yesterday.

I look up to Dante, although he looks nervous, he gives me an encouraging nod.

Grasping the edge of the card I pull it free of the envelope. Placing the envelope in my lap I turn the card over to see the front.

### Condolences on your loss

I look up again at Dante. Strange to be getting a card now. Alex died months ago. Dante closes his eyes as he nods again, pain evident on his face. Opening the card, I read the standard words.

### We are so sorry for your loss

But handwritten underneath someone has added:

### Of your Principessa!!

The gasp of shock falls from my mouth. Why would anyone do this? The card isn't signed. Just those 3 menacing words.

With shaking hands, I pick up the envelop from my lap and hand them both back to Dante. I don't want to see them, touch them. This is someone's idea of a very sick joke. Placing my hands on my bump to reassure myself, I hold my baby. I can feel her. She's safe. Why would anyone do this?

Looking up I see Dante carefully placing the card back in the envelope and laying it face down on his desk. His actions slow and precise, but I can feel the anger bubbling in him. This card has declared intention to harm my baby and probably me too. The card is a direct threat to both our lives. Whoever sent it knows who I am, where I am, and the sex of my baby. It feels too close. I won't panic, I need to stay calm.

"Who do you think sent it?" I ask.

Dante doesn't answer.

"Lorrenzo Colombo?" I suggest

This time Dante nods reluctantly.

"How did he find out?" I mean the sex of the baby, Dante interprets correctly as he answers.

"The clinic."

It can't have been Ruth, I'm sure.

"They would have hacked into their system after your visit."

Relief falls over me.

"What happens now?" Even I know that a direct threat on a family member doesn't go unpunished.

Dante is weighing up his words before he begins.

"Firstly, please know that you are safe here."

I know I am.

"I have called a meeting of the families, here."

I start to panic at the thought of Lorrenzo coming here. Dante holds up his hands to halt my spiralling thoughts.

"I have asked Colombo Senior, his father, to attend. Without his son."

Slightly relieved I listen as Dante continues.

"Colombo Junior has become uncontrollable, unstable."

Slight understatement.

"Benito and I have met with the families who have connections with the Colombo family. It has been difficult, but the meetings were successful. Each family has been affected directly by his actions. He has escalated from mere threats to kidnapping. They are all concerned."

Great so the pyscho isn't just after me then.
"It appears Colombo has become deranged. There are rumours that he killed his own underboss. The remainder of the Colombo family have asked for help from all the families affected as he has become powerful by using mercenaries and not Colombo men."

"That's not good. What do they want you to do?" I ask.

"As the famiglia potente, the Rossi Syndicate will lead the other families in taking Colombo down."

"What literally?"

"Yes Kate. Literally. He has become so deranged with power he is a danger to everyone."

I know he's a sick individual but surely it would be better to pop a straight-jacket on instead of popping him with a gun.

"Do you have a plan?" As soon as the words leave my mouth, I realise he won't divulge any more.

"Yes, now we must return to the dining room."

Rising from the chairs we move towards the door, as he goes to open it he hesitates for a moment.

"I trust the information I shared will not be divulged."

I nod my answer. If I ever spoke with anyone outside these four walls about it they would think I'm delusional, and I'd end up in the mental home with Lorrenzo Colombo.

Dinner was slightly subdued last night after my meeting with Dante. Benni kept us all amused with his antics and stories, but when we went to bed the boys asked me what was said during my meeting. I lied to my children. I'm not proud of it, but I had to.

They're both busy with their school work and I've spent the morning ordering Christmas presents for everyone on-line. I flew through it. I don't know why I've never done it like that before. My biggest dilemma was, what does one buy for ones very own personal bodyguard? It's not a question I ever imagined I'd ask myself. Everyone else was easy to buy for, and I especially liked the gift for Sofia. I figured if I liked it so would she.

Bear is laying in his usual position by the fire as I look out to the bluest sky I've seen for a while.

"I'm going for a walk!" I declare.

Both boys look up from their studies, give a half-hearted nod and look back down at the table again. Bear springs up, which should be impossible considering his size, and starts pacing between me and the suite door, clearly excited. Grabbing a warm coat, scarf, gloves, my hat and boots, I leave the boys to it.

Sitting on the bottom step I start lacing up my boot, my head down trained on the task. My baby bump is growing quickly and in this position I have to lean slightly around her. Picking up the other boot I see Franco striding towards me with a questioning look. I wiggle the boot I'm holding at him, indicating my intentions.

"Don't worry. I'll stay close to the house." I say as I put my foot in the boot.

Tying the laces, I hear him talking in a low voice. Finally finished I rise from the step slowly, I don't want to get a head rush.

Franco stands before me, clearly wanting to say something.

"Spit it out Franco." I say as I feed my arms into my coat and wrapping the scarf around my neck. I start to button up and flick him an expectant look.

"I cannot escort you myself Mrs Rossi. A guard will be close by, they will not disturb you."

My shoulders sag. Really? My look to him says it all.

"We have a number of visitors today. I would prefer you to stay inside." Then adds in a lower voice. "But we both know you won't."

Smiling at him I go to walk past and reach out to pat his arm affectionately.

"You're learning." I say, trying to hold in my laughter. "Come on Bear."

Bear obediently follows and I can still hear his chuckle as we exit the door.

The sun is so beautiful in December, everything feels clean and fresh. Pulling my hat lower over my ears I put my gloved hands in my pockets. Bear and I are walking haphazardly, wherever we please. The formal gardens soon become large expanses of grass which leads on to woodland. From time to time I catch a glimpse of the perimeter wall, and my guard is respectful in giving me space to roam. I love being outside, it allows my mind to rest from stresses and pressure. It's the one time you don't have to think. Every other activity requires you to concentrate, but with walking your mind is completely free.

Following Bear through the trees I spot various animal tracks, they have used this path too. There are also the occasional size 11 footprints spoiling their pretty patterns in the mud. The leaves are either laying on the forest floor or ready for a gust of air to knock them down, leaving the naked branches exposed. Taking huge lungful's of air, I feel restored. It's safe here, I can relax, unwind some of the tension wound tightly inside of me.

Eventually we make our way back to the house, both of us invigorated from our walk. As the guard opens the door for us, he stops our shadow to speak with him. Ignoring them both I sit on the step again and begin to unlace by boots, I look up as I hear my shadow approach.

"Mr Rossi would like to speak with you in his study please Mrs Rossi."

I nod my head to confirm I heard him and finish my task. My boots are muddy, and I go to take them back outside to leave on the doorstep.

"I'll take them for you." He says, relieving me of them.

Smiling my thanks, I turn towards the stairs. Stuffing my gloves in my pocket I pull my hat from my head, attempting to tame my static hair. Approaching Dante's study there are two guards outside. The one I recognise nods at me and turns to knock on the door before he opens it. Walking forward I begin to unbutton my coat; the heat indoors feels extreme compared to the garden. Somehow, I've managed to button my coat with my chunky knit scarf trapped in between the button and the buttonhole. Carefully pulling the button through, I disentangle the wool from around the button. There, done it. I look up and find six sets of eyes all watching my antics. On seeing Benni, Bear barrels into the room and suddenly four sets of legs are quickly knocked aside. He's like a bull in a china shop. Benni laughs as he quickly grabs him by his collar. Casting a sideways look at Dante, I can see he's not impressed with our entrance.

"Sorry Capo." The guard appears next to me. "I'll take him out."

He grabs his collar as Dante spits, "Si." Tersely.

Bear is reluctant to leave, I bend down and give him a hug and whispers in his ear.

"Where're the boys? Go find them." I don't have to ask him twice.

Turning quickly, Bear shoots out the door with the guard desperately holding on for dear life.

Removing my coat fully, I chance a look at the four imposing men watching me intently.

"Here, sit." Benni says quietly from behind me.

Looking over my shoulder, I smile my thanks and sit as instructed, draping my coat over my lap. Dante doesn't look very happy with our unorthodox entrance to his domain, taking his gaze from me he addresses the strangers in the room.

"Gentlemen, I would like to introduce you to Mrs Allesandro Rossi."

All four sets of eyes swing to me, surprise evident on their faces.

"Kate is English, and I would ask you to continue our conversation thus out of respect for her presence."

Still surprised, each man nods his approval.

"Good." Dante says. "Kate, these gentlemen are from the four prominent families we are connected with."

With his left hand he goes along the row, indicating each seated man.

"Romano." We nod to each other.

"Gallo." Nod.

"Moretti." Nod

"Colombo." Hesitant nod, as I slide back in my seat. My action doesn't go unnoticed.

Colombo looks to Dante, who nods his head in silent confirmation, before turning back to me.

"Mrs Rossi, by your reaction I am to assume it is the name you fear, not me?"

Swallowing the lump in my throat, I nod.

Turning back to Dante he says one word in question, "Lorrenzo?"

Dante nods on a sigh.

Colombo turns to his companions and says something in Italian quietly.

"Gentlemen, in English if you please."

"I apologise." Colombo says with a heavy sigh.

"It appears my son," he spits the last two words, "has reached a new level of depravity. We, the family, have heard of his dealings with these mercenaries and their actions. He is not teaching them honour. They steal, kill, maim, destroy and all for pleasure."

The men in the room all offer their sad nod in agreement. It appears Lorrenzo really has gone off the rails.

"His mother, god rest her soul, warned me he would turn out bad."

Looking to me he offers a sad smile.

"For a mother to say such things about her only child, he must have been bad. I did not see it. I chose not to see his actions."

That poor woman must have seen the evil in him, her own son, her flesh and blood.

Turning back to Dante, Colombo Senior looks older after his confession.

"Lorrenzo is no longer my son. He must be stopped. Permanently."

I desperately try not to show outwardly the shock from his words. Sitting in my seat I try to put myself in his shoes. He's a brave man to disown his only son, a demonic child that turned into a psychopath as an adult.

Raising my head, I hear one of the men talking of a compound Lorrenzo has built. A new empire independent of the Colombo family, whilst using their money to fund it. This compound is the most likely location to find Lorrenzo and his men. The rumours about his underboss dying in suspicious circumstances is confirmed. It seems Lorrenzo killed him himself. They also discuss the likelihood of two family members that disappeared some months ago being held there. One Romano guard and one Gallo lady, from what I can work out she was a 2nd or 3rd cousin. The man is sick. He has no loyalty to anyone.

Apparently, the compound has been fortified, and there is a stockpile of guns. They list endless supplies that have been spotted going inside. He's got everything there he needs to start a war. The question is, who's the enemy?

The discussion continues, and they begin to plan their combined attack. I'm surprised I'm allowed to witness these plans, no-one questions my attendance.

They will attack simultaneously. I'm intrigued with the level of detail they have to cover, and their minds fully comprehend every aspect that is required for a safe strike.

Romano will organise disabling the security. He will ensure all cameras and communications are taken off-line. If they can't see or hear I suppose it would make it difficult for them to co-ordinate their defence. His men will enter from the east-side. I hope they all wear the black vests you see on films.

Gallo will attack from the south. How do they know the east from the west? They don't have a map. His men will take down the security office and adjoining bunk house where the off-duty guards will be. I have no idea how many men he has, but apparently there are only four guards inside the house itself. The house staff will all be on the upper floor, which Moretti will access from the north wall next to the servant's entrance. I'm glad they all agree to spare the house staff. Those poor people probably had no idea what a sick individual he was when they took the job.

Colombo senior is being used as bait. He's going to enter through the main gates on the west side. When he says enter, I'm not sure if he will ring the bell or just steam straight through them and I'm too scared to ask for clarification.

Dante is leading the Rossi family through the gates after Colombo has entered. Our men will fan out across the compound and eliminate Lorenzo's men. A shiver runs down my spine at that word. I just hope none of our men get hurt.

It's in that moment that I realise I called them our men. I actually feel like I belong. By including me in this meeting Dante has unofficially accepted me as a Rossi. It's like I'm sitting in for Alex, but we all know he's not coming back.

The details are finetuned and everything is clarified, checked and confirmed. No detail is left to chance. They will storm the compound at 0300 on Sunday morning. The last few details are discussed when I hear Colombo confirm their meeting place.

"Ummm, excuse me sir, but where are you meeting?" I hesitantly ask.

Colombo looks at me the same way Dante does when I question him. Reluctantly he responds.

"Water's End Road in Grafton."

Turning back to Dante effectively dismissing me.

Dante notes my reaction and halts his conversation with Colombo and the other men.

"Kate?" He asks, stern but kindly.

"Grafton, you're meeting in Grafton." I ask him as clarification.

"Yes." He says on a frown.

"Grafton is next to Honiton."

Realisation hits him instantly. His nostrils flare, his anger palpable.

"Fottuto inferno!" He says in a low menacing voice.

The guests look from me to Dante and then to Benni.

"Spiegare." One of them demands.

Benni takes a deep breath before he can speak.

"Our brother, Kates husband, Allesandro was killed there."

Dante sits in shock, the same as me. Is that where Alex was going the day he died. Did Lorrenzo run him off the road? Was it a car chase? The police found no evidence of any other cars involved. But if they weren't looking for it, would they have seen it? Surely, he wouldn't have gone there alone. Looking to Benni I can see he's having the same thoughts, and judging by the look on his face, he doesn't have any answers either.

"He is mine." Dante's menacing voice halts the mumblings of the four family heads.

All eyes turn to him.

Sitting straighter in his chair he looks Colombo Senior directly in his eyes.

"Lorrenzo is mine. I will be the one to eradicate him for what he did."

The force of his statement shows emotion he's trying to hide.

There is no evidence to confirm that Lorrenzo was involved but there is no doubt in these men's minds that he is guilty of the crime they accuse him of.

Colombo leans across the desk and offers his hand, Dante takes it instantly without hesitation.

"I apologise to you and your family Capo."

Turning to me he does the same, his large hand engulfing my small one.

"To you Mrs Rossi I offer my sincerest apologies. My family have wronged yours and for that we will remain your servant and offer our total protection."

I can see the words he offers are sincere. I have no idea what his statement means but judging by Benni's reaction, and the other men in the room, it is a huge honour to be afforded.

With a curt nod to his hosts, Colombo and the other three gentlemen exit the room. I see the unfamiliar guard from the door way stand to attention before escorting the men down the stairs with Dante's own guard.

"Well that has never happened before." Benni exclaims with a look of total shock.

Dante sits nodding his head absentmindedly.

"What?" I ask looking from one brother to the other.

This is all foreign to me, I have no idea what just happened.

"Colombo." Benni waves his hand towards the door he just exited. "He has offered you, Kate, the protection of the whole Colombo family. You are in effect untouchable by anyone."

That's nice, I suppose. I still don't really know what that means so I just smile politely.

Shaking his head, Benni looks dumbfounded by my response.

"Kate, the honour he has bestowed places you higher than any other member of their family. They are bound to protect you. No-one would ever dare harm you. The Colombo family have many, many affiliates and that protection would be honoured by every family in their association."

Lovely. I sigh, unsure how I'm supposed to respond.

Benni stands in front of me with a smile as he shakes his head.

"That was nice of him." I think?

## Chapter Twenty-four

The boys have finished with their school work early so they're in the pool, Maria is off somewhere in the house organising the staff for Christmas no doubt, and Dante and Benni have been closeted in his study since their meeting with the families a few days ago. With the fire blazing in our suite, I curl myself up on the sofa with my tablet. I really need to buy maternity clothes, and as I'm not comfortable leaving the compound, and I doubt Dante would allow it, I decide to browse on-line.

Scrolling through the internet I find a company that specialise in maternity wear, an added bonus is I actually like their style, so I navigate to the page and begin viewing the items on their pages. I start filling up the on-line basket with essentials, jeans, tops, underwear, jumpers and of course more jeans. I quickly become distracted with their baby clothes selection and before I know it my shopping total is over £500. Hesitating for a moment at the cost, I decide to throw caution to the wind and buy it all. I've always been frugal, not because we couldn't afford it, simply because I loved the challenge. Some of my favourite items are from charity shops. Just because you can buy it all in one shop takes the fun out of shopping. Being part of the Rossi family officially, I should change my style to fit in more with their style, but that's just not me.

A knock sounds at the door just as I'm putting my card details in.

"One minute." I call as I finish paying.

Checking the invoice has gone to my e-mail, I put the tablet on the sofa and go to answer the door.

Franco stands there looking slightly flustered, which is unusual for him.

"Everything OK?" I ask, quickly turning to check Bear is still in our suite, and not causing his normal mayhem. Bear is laying in front of the fire on his back, legs in the air, snoring.

"Um there's been a delivery for you Mrs Rossi." He says.

I'm instantly on alert after seeing the card that Dante showed me.

"Could you come downstairs for a moment please?"

I nod my head and shut Bear in our rooms.

Following Franco down the stairs we walk to the back of the house and through the kitchen to another room with a door which leads outside. In the room are two guards and a very nervous delivery driver.

I smile warmly at the driver and look back to Franco with a frown. I've never met the man before and I'm at a loss as to why he's bought me down here.

"There appear to be a large number of parcels all addressed to you Mrs Rossi. It seemed slightly suspicious." He says the last part in a lower voice so only I can hear.

Has Lorrenzo gone mad and sent me threatening items, my imagination is running riot as to what it could be until I spot the first few parcels on the table. The logo is instantly recognisable, realisation hits home straight away.

"Wow, they arrived quickly." I say with a huge smile.

Franco looks confused by my reaction.

"Christmas presents for the boys." I inform him.

Understanding fills Franco's face.

"Is there somewhere we can hide them?" I hesitantly ask.

I didn't really think this through, I haven't even spoken to Maria yet. I hope I haven't made a monumental mistake.

"We will need to check each parcel before we store them." He gives me a knowing look as I slowly nod my understanding.

Franco instructs the guards to help bring each package in to the room.

Passing me a knife, I shudder at the thought of what it's been used for and start opening each package slightly to ensure it is what I ordered.

Box after box, package after package, the process goes on for ages in an ad-hoc production line. I really don't remember ordering this much. I feel sorry for the driver as he looks petrified. I bet this wasn't on his job description.

With the last 2 boxes checked I turn to Franco and motion for him to come closer. He bends slightly so I can whisper in his ear.

"Do you have any cash I could borrow please? I will pay you back, I promise."

Straightening back up I see his smile as he reaches into his pocket and opens his wallet towards me in offering. Plucking out two £20 notes, I smile my thanks and hand it to the delivery driver.

"Thank you for your patience sir. We just needed to check they had sent the correct items."

The driver accepts the offered money with a beaming smile.

"Anytime Mrs Rossi."

Turning to the guards I smile as I speak.

"Thank you too gentlemen for your assistance. Could you do one last thing please and help this gentleman find his way to the gates. It can be a little confusing and quite a long way."

The guards nod their understanding. The three exit the room as I turn back to the mountain of boxes, damn I forgot to buy wrapping paper. I catch Franco watching me and I lift my eyes to him in question.

"Well played, Mrs Rossi, well played."

Coming from him I will take it as a compliment, maybe I am learning how to live this life.

The guards soon return, and Franco leads us all to a storage room which currently houses a few old pieces of furniture, they would look amazing either distressed or with a blue crackle glaze, I think to myself. We decide to store the presents in here as the door locks, and teenage boys can't resist being nosey.

Returning to the outer room I'm instructed not to carry anything but to organise the piles in the storage room instead.

It takes them 15 minutes to carry it all in, and we soon have three distinct piles, Leo, Marc and other. Happy, I close and lock the door and pass the key to Franco for safe keeping, as I know I will lose it.

I'm excited for dinner tonight as I've decided to raise the subject of Christmas with the family. Sitting in our usual seats I'm just about to speak when Dante does.

"I understand there were a number of parcels delivered today." Is he trying to stifle a smile?

I nod my head, but I can't hold in my beam.

"Yes, I may have gone a little over board." I say as I hold my thumb and index finger in the air, almost touching.

Maria looks confused, so do the boys.

With a deep sigh I decide to jump right in.

"I know it's a little presumptuous, but I was hoping we could stay here and celebrate Christmas with all of you."

I'm nervous as hell. This isn't my home and I've just invited me and the boys, and of course Bear, to stay with them over one of the most important celebrations of the year. I thought I wanted to be in our own home, but right now I would prefer to be here with these people. I feel safe and loved, and right now that feeling is helping the boys and me to heal.

I shouldn't have worried as the look on all of their faces is pure delight.

"Really?" The boys ask in unison.

I nod to them both.

"As long as it's OK with your nonna and uncles, then yes."

"Our celebrations are a little different to yours." Dante says, bringing my celebratory mood down a notch.

I'm just about to say we'll fit in with whatever their plans are when he goes on.

"But this year, I would like to celebrate with your traditions."

Emotion hits me directly in the chest, he couldn't have said anything nicer or kinder. I'm grateful for his thoughtfulness. The look on the boys faces at this moment makes life worth living. I can see how happy they are at Dante's words and he looks equally pleased by their reaction.

"We need to plan. What do you do?" Maria asks flapping her hands in a mix of hesitation and excitement. She is fit to burst with happiness.

The remainder of the meal we tell them how we celebrate. Everything from the decorating of the Christmas tree, which chocolate tins, obviously an essential, decorating the house, how we open our gifts on Christmas day, the crackers that I make, and how each has an individual table gift, the music, the laughter. I can tell they are avoiding the parts that Alex does. They need to remember their dad.

"I know it's a little difficult," I swallow down the sob in my throat, "but maybe you could ask one of your uncles to help  with the things you did with dad. They could take you to pick out the tree, take you shopping for my gifts, help you find the right Christmas sweaters." I say on a grin.

It's a tradition to have a really ugly jumper and Alex always took the boys to choose them. "I'm sure Uncle Benni would love to help, if he has the time that is." I cautiously say.

Benni smiles, obviously loving the plan.

"We will both take you." Dante pipes up with a genuine smile on his face, shocking us all.

Over coffee in the lounge, Maria takes pages of notes on how we celebrate and even enlisted two of the maids to help her. They scurried off to research further, no doubt typing in 'Typical English Christmas' in a search engine. Maria is relentless with her questions, but my yawn overtakes me, and Maria looks on with affection.

"I need my bed." I inform the room.

Rising from the seat I kiss the boys on their heads before leaving them with their grandmother. I climb the stairs to our suite contented. I haven't felt truly happy since Alex died, and right now it's a nice feeling to have.

Saturday morning brings with it a tense atmosphere to the house. I know why, which keeps me on edge. Dante and Benni are ensconced in his study with a number of guards. Numerous men arrive and are escorted upstairs and closeted behind the study door. From my view point in the lounge I can feel the tension emanating from each new visitor.

The boys are playing video games in the suite. Benni bought it in early this morning with the latest games. He said it was his, but I have my suspicions. As a distraction it's the perfect gift, they've been playing it for hours already.

I can see the guard numbers have tripled in size, many of the faces I recognise from the compound, the others are strangers, and from what I can work out, they are all Rossi men. The Rossi house appears to be the main head-quarters for the syndicate. The rest of the family live in similar properties to this, dotted around the UK. Each house is run by a cousin or uncle or some other relative bearing the Rossi name. It's amazing what you can learn by watching and listening, and Sofia is a font of knowledge too.

"How long have you worked here?" I ask her as she brings in yet more tea.

Laying the tray on the table, she fusses with the teapot and cup, ensuring both handles are facing the same way. Straightening again, she looks at me with a smile.

"Umm, I've been here about 10 years now."

She really doesn't look old enough, and she interprets my look correctly. Laughing slightly, she goes on.

"Mr Rossi was good enough to give me my first job, here. I will always be grateful to him."

Pouring my tea, she hands over the cup before continuing.

"Originally I tried to get a job at one of his clubs." She says self-consciously.

Patting the seat next to me, she casts a quick look to the door, before perching on the edge and smoothing down the skirt to her uniform.

"Mr Allesandro caught me trying to apply for a job at their dancing club."

The shock must register on my face. I thought she was talking about Dante, or even Benni. It never occurred to me she meant Alex.

"I lied about my age, I told him I was 19, but I had only just turned 16. I thought, stupidly, that I could get a job as a dancer and no one would question me."

She doesn't look directly at me, clearly embarrassed by her confession.

"Mr Rossi arrived as the manager was interviewing me. I saw him watching as we talked. I was so naïve, I thought he liked me."

She drops her shaking head, her blush rising up her face.

"Go on." I encourage, gently rubbing her arm.

She takes a deep breath to compose herself.

"The manager noticed Mr Rossi and they spoke before he dismissed the manager. He just sat there, looked at me and asked if I was in trouble."

Sofia pauses for a moment, clearly re-living the memory.

"I tried to lie and say no, but he just kept looking at me till I broke down and told him the truth."

I smile to myself as I'd seen him do that exact technique with the boys. It worked every time. Turning to me, she smiles a beautiful smile.

"I told him I was 16 and I needed a job. My mum was a drug addict, probably still is. Her boyfriend at the time, he, well.." I can see she's struggling but after a moment she finds the strength to go on.

"He was getting more and more friendly. It was disgusting and made me uncomfortable. My mum didn't give a damn as long as she got her next fix. I was only 15 at the time and even at that age I knew what he wanted. So, on my 16th birthday I packed my bag walked out of home and straight into the club."

I know I had a rubbish childhood but at least I was safe from predators.

"Mr Rossi asked me lots of questions and told me to wait. He walked off to make a phone call and I was scared as I thought he was phoning my mum to send me back."

Shaking my head mentally, that poor child, what she went through to survive. Giving her an encouraging smile, she continues.

"When he came back I was a nervous wreck, Mr Rossi just smiled, told me he had a job that would suit me better, but I would need to leave London. I didn't have to think about it, I jumped at the chance."

Laughing she adds.

"I didn't realise at the time how dangerous it could have been, he could have been a human trafficker for all I knew."

She shudders slightly at the thought, then tips her head in contemplation.

"I trusted him though."

She looks at me with sympathy.

"He was an amazing person, if I may say so Mrs Rossi."

I nod my consent, never a truer word spoken.

Shaking her head from her reverie she continues.

"He bought me here," she waves her hands around the room, "and I've been living here since. He saved me."

Tears float in my eyes. Taking her hand, I say the only thing I can.

"Yes, he was amazing. He was the best."

Sofia produces a tissue for me to dry my eyes. My husband saved her and for that she will remain loyal to the Rossi family for life. Her story isn't lost on me. How many other people who work for them are loyal because they saved them? I'm proud of my husband, for the man he was beneath the suit.

Voices from the hall shake us both from our private thoughts of the man, Sofia stands and looks at me with a genuine smile.

"Can I get you anything else Mrs Rossi?"

I shake my head.

"No thanks Sofia."

With another smile from her she leaves the room and me to my reflexions.

I hear through the open door the men still arriving. I begin to understand the hierarchy by observing their body language. Each group has one boss, and he appears to have two underbosses. The underbosses talk directly to their guards and issue the orders given by the boss. Each boss talks directly to Benni as he greets him at the entrance, Dante doesn't come down at all. When they leave Benni sees them out and they put any questions they have to him before they depart.

It didn't occur to me before my observations that Dante sat so high in the pecking order. I thought he was just head of this house and these guards on the compound, when in fact he is the boss to every boss that walks through the door. I swallow down my alarm when I think of how I've spoken to him, how I've questioned him. I cringe when I remember defying him and refusing the money he thrust at me. I can't change that now. I am who I am, Dante will have to live with it while we're staying here. Hopefully after tonight it will be safe to go home, and Dante will be free of my defiance. No wonder Benni finds me so amusing, I bet no one else has ever spoken back to a Capo like me.

# Chapter Twenty-five

I've been sat in the lounge for hours now, watching the comings and goings, when Maria walks in catching me spying on the men.

"Would you like to join me for lunch?"

As soon as she mentions food, my stomach responds for me.

Nodding, I rise and follow her to the dining room. I'm surprised to see the boys have been dragged from their video game.

The four of us sit down to share platters of meats and cheeses. The bread is divine and so are the sun-dried tomatoes. Our conversation is light-hearted, and I know Maria is using lunch to distract the boys from the goings on in the house. Unfortunately, she has underestimated them.

"What's going on nonna?' Marc asks confidently.

Since being here Marc has really started to come out of his shell. The people in this house appreciate his uniqueness, Benni has been working closely with him and his Italian has really improved.

"Who are all of these men?" He pushes.

Maria doesn't even bat an eyelid.

"They are your uncle's men. They need to meet with him to discuss business."

Maria continues eating, thinking that's the end of the conversation, but I know differently.

"What all on the same day?" Marc presses.

Maria hides her shock well.

"He has many businesses to run."

Marc picks up more bread and cheese, but I know he's formulating his next question.

"Who's Colombo?" He asks, whilst buttering the bread in his hand.

Leo sits back and watches Maria's reaction to his brother's question. If I didn't know better, I'd think they'd planned this.

Maria carefully lays down her cutlery, clearly trying to buy herself some time.

"Colombo senior is the head of a family the Rossi family work with."

Marc's not finished, I can see it in his face.

"What like Romano, Moretti and Gallo?"

Maria looks to me for support.

"Where did you hear those names darling?" I ask as she looks like she needs saving.

Marc turns to me, but Leo keeps his vision trained on Maria.

"I was listening to the guards talking."

He can understand them, even if I can't.

"Yeah, and what else did you hear?" I'm fishing for information.

Marc flashes a look to his brother quickly then back to me. He hesitates because he knows I know that he knows something. Before he can say a word, Leo speaks, not to me, to Maria.

"What's a combined attack nonna?"

I admire Maria's poise. Gracefully she raises her head to meet her grandsons questioning look.

"It is when all the families work together as one."

"Is that what's happening tomorrow morning?" He fires back, this time looking from Maria to me to gauge my reaction to his question.

"Yes Leo, it is." I answer him honestly.

Maria looks to me, silently asking if I'm sure I'm doing the right thing. I have no idea, but my gut is telling me to be honest with them both. Leo looks at me, slightly miffed, but I know it's not from my response, it's from being kept in the dark.

Laying my knife and fork down, I push my plate away, mentally preparing myself for what's to come. I breathe deeply, trying to take in the courage I need.

"Tomorrow morning there is a planned attack on a man."

I take another breath, in, out.

"His name is Lorrenzo Colombo. This evil man has done some pretty horrendous things. The families here today are working together to.." I hesitate for a moment as I see Maria nod a 'yes', "eliminate him."

The boys stare at me, not in shock but in rapture.

"He was part of one of the families here today, but he's branched out on his own and become very dangerous."

"Is that why we're staying here?" Leo asks.

"Yes." I clearly hear from behind me.

Turning quickly, I see Dante and Benni standing inside the closed door of the dining room. Benni looks at me with an encouraging smile and Dante is focused solely on his nephew. He doesn't look upset, more intrigued.

"Are we in danger? Is mum in danger?" Leo asks his uncle directly.

Dante moves towards the table and straight past his usual seat opting for the one next to Leo.

"No Leonardo. You and your mamma and brother are safe here."

Leo digests his words as Marc pipes up.

"What's a Capo?"

Dante looks to his other nephew, but no shock is evident at his question.

"A Capo is the person who is the boss of all the other bosses."

Marc nods at his answer, he already knew, he was testing him.

"So, you're the Capo of all the men here today?"

This is the true question, the test. Will Dante pass?

"Yes Marco, I am their Capo."

He passed.

"How many are involved in the combined attack today?" Leo asks.

Turning in his seat, Dante faces Leo again.

"We estimate 150 men with 50 as back-up."

"How many are inside the compound?" Leo fires back.

Dante calmly allows his question while I'm sitting here sweating with the stress.

"The reconnaissance has reported 25 guards, 10 house staff plus Colombo himself."

Leo thinks this through for a minute.

"The odds are in your favour then."

I'm shocked how well they're taking this.

"Yes, they are. When a soldier goes into battle, he needs to assess those odds and any risks he may encounter." Dante steadily responds.

"You will let the house staff go?" Marc asks.

"If they are innocent, then yes."

How are they so calm? I look from one to the other, both in private contemplation.

"Tell me what's going on in your heads boys." I gently say.

Leo looks up to me first.

"Just thinking it all through mum." He says on a shrug.

"You don't seem very shocked." I offer.

Both boys look to each other, then to me.

"Umm, that's because we're not." Leo says as if I'm stupid.

"Look around you mum." He waves his hand around the room, then pointing to Dante and Benni. "Have you met our uncles??" He finishes sarcastically.

I frown at his response, and I see Benni smirking from the seat at the head of the table.

It appears my sons were a little smarter than me.

"I would like to continue this conversation, but sadly I cannot right now." Dante looks to both boys in turn then to me.

"We came in to say goodbye. We need to leave in order to prepare."

Maria hides her fear well as her sons rise and both kiss her in turn. They then kiss the boys on their heads before approaching me.

"Would you walk us out please Kate." Dante says.

I'm shocked at his request and automatically rise from the table. Once we leave the dining room, Dante issues orders to the men in the hallway to ready the cars. When it's just the three of us they both turn to face me.

"Please stay in the house until we return. The guards will take the dog out when necessary. I have left a small staff of guards on the grounds that will keep you safe." I see Dante swallow and look at Benni before he continues.

"If, and only if, you are in danger, mamma will lead you to the secure room. The entrance is behind a panel in the lounge. The staff are aware of the protocol if we are under attack."

I hadn't thought of the possibility of a retaliation attack on us while all the men are so far away.

He looks like he wants to say more but dismisses it and leans forward and awkwardly kisses both my cheeks before he leaves. Benni approaches me and pulls me in for a hug before kissing both my cheeks too. As he pulls away he smiles down at me.

"Hasta manana piranha." He says before he walks out the door backwards.

Teaching Maria how to use a video game was difficult enough, but the driving game they're playing in the suite is hilarious. She doesn't understand that the car has to stay on the road. So far she's run over a cow, driven through a church, across an eight-lane highway and is currently in the sea. The laughter echo's around the room at the look of concentration on her face.

"It is unfair."

Trying to dampen down his laughter Leo asks her why.

"I have never sat in the front of a car before. This view is new to me."

Realisation sets in that she has always been chauffeured which sets us all off again. Secretively she looks to me with a smirk on her face while the boys are doubled over.

They've had a fantastic afternoon playing games with us both. The boys have informed me that I'm useless. I know I am. My hand eye co-ordination is rubbish. I'm surprised by Maria's dexterity with the hand controls. I have a sneaking suspicion she's played video games before.

The day has flown by and dinner time is approaching. I don't know about the others but I'm not really hungry and I can't be bothered with the formality of the dining room.

"Maria, would you mind if we had a picnic style dinner in here tonight? The four of us?"

Maria finishes driving through a crop field before she answers, not taking her eyes from the game.

"I like that idea. We can play the game more then."

I'm a teensy bit worried as I've managed to corrupt Mrs Rossi senior in just one afternoon.

I leave the three of them to their game and wander down the stairs with Bear in tow. If I can find a guard they can let him out for a wee. At the bottom of the stairs a man walks forward to greet me with a smile.

"Good evening Mrs Rossi."

I smile back at him; his face is vaguely familiar.

"Could you let Bear out for a minute please?"

The guard nods and calls him along as he walks towards the front door. Bear has gotten used to our new living arrangements and is happy to go with him.

Turning at the bottom of the stairs, I make my way towards the kitchen. Inside there are a number of staff all busy at work, I begin to feel guilty. They've gone to a lot of effort to prepare tonight's meal and an idea begins to formulate as I look for the head cook. Walking towards her I smile in vain hope that my next words won't be too much of an insult.

"Good evening Mrs Rossi, can I help you with something?" She asks, clearly perturbed at my appearance in her kitchen.

"Good evening." I say on a huge smile.

I have no idea what her name is, and I don't want to be rude and ask.

"I wondered if we could change this evenings plans slightly?"

She gives me a frown as she nods. "Of course."

"Instead of eating in the formal dining room could we have dinner in my suite please. Just a small selection of food would be amazing, something similar to lunch."

The cook turns to look at the food already prepared and what's still cooking on the stove, with disheartened look.

"When do the staff get to eat?" I ask, disrupting her perusal.

"After the family have eaten." She answers, a little shortly.

Placing on my biggest smile I move forward with my plan.

"Perhaps tonight as both the Mr Rossi's are away from home they would like to eat earlier. The food you have prepared looks amazing and you have all put so much work into this meal, you should all sit and enjoy it."

Her look is apprehensive as she gives a tentative smile.

"I believe that we are all in need of some merriment." I say with a raised eyebrow.

I know the staff are aware of the true nature of the Rossi house, and probably more aware of their plans for tonight.

"You could all take this evening as a sort of sabbatical." I suggest.

Her smile begins to grow.

"Why don't you have the maids lay the table," I point to the large table off of the kitchen, "and perhaps find a bottle of wine or two." I don't want them getting plastered and I have to trust they won't drink Dante's rare or expensive wines.

"That would be lovely Mrs Rossi. Thank you." Cook beams at me.

"I'm sure you would all appreciate a night off to enjoy this amazing fare." I indicate to the dishes.

I see Sofia in the kitchen and she gives me a nod of understanding.

In a slightly lower voice I add. "Please just make sure no-one drinks Mr Rossi dry."

Her laughter can be heard throughout the kitchen.

"I will arrange for your meal to be brought to you Mrs Rossi, I hope you enjoy it as much as we will."

With my task fulfilled I walk back to the hall as the front door opens and Bear saunters in with a red-faced guard. Frowning at him I wait for him to approach me.

"Everything OK?" I'm on high alert after Dante's words earlier.

With a few puffs and pants, the guard finally gets his breath back.

"Yes, sorry Mrs Rossi, he ran away from me and wouldn't come back. I had to chase him."

Trying not to laugh, I pinch my lips and nod my head.

"Thank you." Is all I manage to say before I turn and head back up the stairs with Bear following closely behind.

Our lighter dinner arrives as the boys are trying to teach their grandmother a shooting game. Apparently, you have to kill the zombies, but they're not just in human form, they can be plants, cars, animals. It all seems a bit gory for my taste, but Maria is surprisingly accurate. Everything she aims at she hits.

"Go nonna." The boys shout as the maids enter the room.

They lay the trays on the table and turn to look at the tv screen, then to Maria. She is completely oblivious to their entrance.

Thanking the maids, I escort them to the door.

"I hope you enjoy your evening ladies, and I trust you will ensure the guards receive a plate of food each too."

They both offer a sort of curtsey nod before the taller of the two speaks.

"Thank you Mrs Rossi, your suggestion was very much appreciated, by all the staff."

Her genuine smile tells me she's not being facetious.

I'm glad they're happy. They all work so hard.

Dragging Maria away from the console is more difficult than I would have thought. It gives me an idea of what the boys can buy her for Christmas. Eventually sitting down, we avoid the elephant in the room and talk about the game, Christmas, traditions, anything and nothing. The smaller setting in our suite is more to our taste. Our preferred meal is in front of the fire while we lay around and chat or watch movies.

"Do you fancy watching a film?" I suggest between a mouth full of sun-dried tomatoes. I think I've found my new favourite food.

The boys both look at me for suggestions. With a grin I suggest a Christmas movie. They both know which one it is, and Marc scrolls through the television to see if it's available to view. It's an old movie but hysterical. A true feel good film, and one that I think we could all use right now.

Grabbing our plates, Maria looks at us almost horrified when we leave the table.

"Come on nonna." Leo calls from the sofa. "You can have the chair."

Maria hesitantly gets up from the table with her plate and sits in the assigned chair. We all pile onto the sofa in our usual arrangement of legs over legs and place our plates on whatever surface we can.

"Press play then Marc." Leo calls.

A contented bliss settles over us when the upbeat music of the open credits begins. Maria wanted to learn about our Christmases, and the scene here tonight is definitely one of them.

## Chapter Twenty-six

Lying in bed I know it's early still as it's still dark outside. Checking the clock, it reads 4.35. I'm so pleased we shared last night with Maria. When she left us after the closing credits I could see how much she enjoyed her time with us.

Plumping the pillow, I turn it over so the cold side is up and lay back on my side. Gently rubbing my bump, I can feel her moving about. That must have been what woke me up. My pyjamas have twisted around and are really uncomfortable. Thankfully the new clothes should be here soon as everything is really tight now. If I use an elastic band I can fashion an extra-long button hole for my jeans, and my tops were a bit baggy from the weight loss, but they're stretched quite tight now.

Turning from side to side I try to get comfortable and my mind begins to wander. I think about Alex. I still dream about him every night, but I don't usually remember them. The grief and pain still cuts me in two and can overwhelm me, but I'm glad I can still feel him in my heart. Feel the rhythm in sync with mine. Gently caressing my bump, she begins to settle down. I will cherish the feeling while I carry Angel, because I know once I've given birth that feeling will leave me too.

A knocking at my bedroom door wakes me from my dreams, automatically I look to the clock. 6.55. I must have fallen back to sleep.

"Mrs Rossi." I can hear somewhere calling gently.

"Yes." I say as I go to get up but lay back from a head rush.

I reach over and turn on the switch, temporarily blinded by the light, I wait for my eyes to adjust as I hear the knocking again.

"Mrs Rossi, Kate."

The voice sounds more urgent this time.

"Yes." I say a bit louder.

The door opens, and I can see the outline of someone standing in the doorway. My brain is still foggy.

"Mrs Rossi, I need you to wake up please."

I know the voice instantly.

"Franco?"

What's he doing here at this time of the morning. Oh no don't tell me the dogs got out.

Bringing myself to a sitting position. I throw the covers off and swing my legs round, desperately trying to keep my head from swimming.

"What's wrong? Is it the boys? Bear?" I fire questions at him.

"Please Mrs Rossi I need you to come downstairs quickly."

His nervousness is making me uneasy.

Standing without face planting, I look around the room for the sweatshirt I wear instead of a dressing gown. Franco bends down and retrieves it from the floor where it had fallen off the end of the bed. Pulling it over my head, I feed my arms in the sleeves and somehow get one caught in the hood instead of the sleeve. Taking it out I try again and find the sleeve on my second attempt. My vest is all twisted up over my bump now, so I straighten it and pull my jimmy's up slightly, they instantly slide under the baby again, there's not a lot I can do about that right now. Feeding my feet into my sliders, I blindly follow Franco from the room. As we walk through the suite I see the door to the boy's room has been shut, I assume Franco did that before waking me. I go to check on them, but Franco reaches out to stop me.

"I've checked and they're both asleep. I left Bear in there with them." He whispers.

I nod my thanks and he ushers me from the room as he quietly closes the door behind us.

We descend the stairs in silence, but I can hear mumbled voices from the lower floor. It all comes slamming back into my brain. The combined attack, it's already happened. Thoughts start to race through my mind, were they successful, did they get in, did they eliminate Lorrenzo, did any-one get hurt?

I stop and turn to look at Franco.

"Did any-one get hurt?"

I see his Addams apple bob up and down as he swallows.

"Please Mrs Rossi, we need to go downstairs quickly."

His response instantly puts me on high alert. He won't answer me, I know something terrible has happened. Turning I begin to descend again and as we pass the first floor I glance over to Dante's study, it's not in use, turning back I head straight down the stairs.

The lights are all ablaze on the lower levels and men dart from room to room in a hushed silence, all intent on their mission. Reaching the bottom step a smell permeates the air, the smell of sweat mixes with an acrid smoke stench. A guard stops as he passes, turning to me he bows his head "Mrs Rossi" he offers before he moves on. Moving through the throng of bodies a second man stops, bows his head and offers the same salutation, "Mrs Rossi".

I turn to Franco, but he won't look at me, he's looking directly over my head.

"In here." He offers, with his arm extended, guiding me to a lounge I saw when we first arrived.

The masculine vibes weren't appealing to me, too austere. I've tended to use the room at the front of the house. With the lighter décor and the sun shining through the windows, it bathes your soul.

There are more men on the threshold of the room who part as we approach, creating a path allowing me to enter the room.

"Mrs Rossi" is offered again and again and that feeling of dread is building higher inside of me. I sense that feeling of despondency in the room. Frantically looking from left to right I try to find either Dante or Benni in the mass of bodies.

Crossing the threshold my eyes settle on my doctor, Dr Manessi. What's he doing here? The gasp of shock escapes my mouth as the realisation that someone is hurt. His shirt sleeves are rolled to his elbows as he vigilantly tends to the patient laying on the sofa. With its back to the entrance I can't see who is stretched out on the brown leather couch. He manoeuvres with efficiency, issuing various instructions to the men surrounding him. I watch as two guards drag a tall brass standing lamp closer, ripping off the shade to place a bag of fluids, the tube trailing to the IV needle in the doctor's hand. A sense of urgency is in his actions as he inserts the IV line into the man's arm. Surely, he should be in a hospital, why did they bring him here?

Looking about the room I see their helplessness permeating in their faces. They don't know what to do to help their friend. My heart beats in my chest but I feel it slowing with each step I take closer to this poor helpless man.

Anxiously I scour the room again in search of Dante and Benni, whipping my head from side to side. They may have only been in our lives for a few months, but I've come to love them like the brothers I've never had.

My breath stutters as I look through the throng of people. Sitting in the wingback chair is Dante, his demeanour desolate, his body showing the distress his mind is clearly feeling. The men move, and I lose sight of him for a moment before a gap appears again. His elbows are sat on his knees with his head placed firmly in the grasp of his hands. His fingers pulling at his hair tightly. Blood stains his arms, his shirt smeared with red. I'm alarmed by the sight of him, I've never seen so much blood. My head whips to the sofa and back to Dante again. Looking round at the other men in the room, they all wear the same despondent look. The man on the sofa is clearly in grave danger. Turning quickly ,I try to find Benni. My heart slowing with each turn. I can't see him, he's not here. Looking again I stand on my tip toe in vain hope, but I can't see over the men. I look towards Dante again, I have to talk to him, I have to know where Benni is. The man in front of me steps to the side and I finally see him. Benni. He looks unharmed, but his clothes are also covered in blood. So much blood. Picking up my leaden feet I walk towards him, sidestepping men left and right, checking constantly he's still there. Benni turns from his conversation as I approach, the look on his face difficult to read. He looks happy but sad too. I'm relieved to see he and Dante are both alive and well. Walking towards me he grasps my shoulders with one arm, tightly hugging me to him. His other hand goes to the back of my head, his hand splayed across my hair. Pulling me into his chest, his grasp is tight. The smell from earlier is stronger on his clothing, the smell of smoke with a metallic odour.

I feel the thumping of his heart against my cheek laid on his chest. His hold on me tightens as he places a kiss to the top of my head, before laying his cheek to my scalp. His breath moves the strands of hair as I feel him go to speak, hesitate and then tries again. Nothing comes out.

I hear the mumbling of men around me suddenly halt as the doctor demands quiet. Preparing to move from Benni's clutches but he seems reluctant to let me go.

"Every-one out. NOW." The distinct sound of Dante's voice is low but clear.

The reverberation of movement follows his command as men vacate the room. I hear Benni say 'Stay', as he lifts his cheek to speak to someone behind me.

The feel of another pair of hands surrounds me as Benni disappears from my clutches to be replaced by Dante. Holding me close in a similar fashion to Benni, he too places a kiss upon my head.

"I am so sorry Kate. I am so, so sorry." I hear him whisper into my hair, over and over.

"I've got a pulse!" The doctors voice breaks through Dante's chant.

"It's weak but it's there."

I go to pull away and Dante allows me to, but only so he can grasp my upper arms. Bending slightly to get to my eye level I see tears in his eyes.

I'm confused by his display of affection and the evident emotion. My heart starts to beat stronger as panic creeps into my body. What's he sorry for? What's going on?

Leaning down he presses a kiss to both my cheeks before looking me directly in the eye. I feel like he's assessing me, but I don't know what for.

Gently, ever so gently, Dante turns me from his body, holding the tops of my arms tightly till I'm turned fully. Bracing his left arm across my upper body and his right lays across the baby. I'm effectively held up by the strength in his arms. My heart starts to beat faster. What's happening? What's going on?

I see the doctor currently knelt on the floor, his stethoscope placed lightly on his patient's chest, listening intently. The man lays half naked on the sofa, blood masks the multitude of injuries he has clearly sustained. His feet are covered in filth and the hair on his legs is matted with blood. A towel has been laid across his naked torso to retain his dignity, but it is clear how emaciated he is. The shock of his half-starved body makes me gasp. How can anyone survive the injuries he has sustained when his body is so weak? I feel Dante tense at my gasp.

Gently Dr Manessi moves the stethoscope not pressing hard, listening intently. Removing it from his ears and draping it around his neck he removes a small torch from his shirt pocket, leans further over the man, I assume to check his pupils as the light moves from left to right and right to left.

Clearly pleased with his findings, the doctor sits back on his haunches with almost a smile. As his body lowers back the movement reveals more of the man. I feel bad for standing here, watching as he lays in his incapacitated state, but I can't stop my eyes from straying. I need to know who this half-starved creature is.

As they stray finally to his face my mind can't accept what my eyes are seeing. He may have sunken cheeks and months of facial hair, but my heart instantly recognises him. My breath stutters from my body, I can't breathe, I can't take in any air. Dante's support of me has tightened, holding me up. Tears begin to fall landing on his arm that is banded around my body like a vice. I must be wrong. I'm hallucinating, delusional. My heart misses him so much it's an apparition, a mirage.

His chest rises and falls, the effort clearly a strain for his weakened state. I need him to breath. He needs to breath. Please god make him breath.

"Alex." The word whispers from my lips.

My husband lays before me, alive, barely. It's not possible, but I know it's him. My heart knows it him. Instinctively I move forward, I need to touch him, feel him, reassure myself that he's real. I need to feel the beat of his heart beneath my hand, my cheek. Dante holds me tighter against his body, restricting me, stopping me.

"No." I say grappling at his arm, my fingers desperate to escape the prison of his constraint.

"No, I need to feel he's real. Please." I start to beg but Dante just holds me tighter. Placing his lips closer to my ear, his voice is calm, gentle.

"Ssh Kate, ssh. It is him, believe me, it is him."

I can't believe his words, and I can't trust my eyes. They told me he was dead. They told me I had lost him forever. How can he be laying here, now?

"Please Dante, please." My please turn into sobs.

"Please, please…" I can feel myself sinking down into the darkness, the black abyss surrounds me, wrapping me in a heavenly blanket.

"Alex." I need him.

Alex.

"Hold her, do not let her fall."

I hear as my body becomes heavy with the weight of the dark cloud that has swallowed me whole.

The feel of a hand gently brushing the hair from my face brings me up from the depth's darkness, and Sofia's blurry face comes into view.

"Mrs Rossi, Kate, I need you to open your eyes." Her voice softly intones.

My vision begins to clear as I take in her unbound hair. Looking at my surroundings, the dark austere room comes into view. My mind awakens as my vision clears and instantly takes in the image of my husband's prone body.

"Alex." My dry lips form the word.

"She's waking up sir."

The sound of movement permeates the silence in the room as Dante's face leans in to my field of sight.

"Please allow me." I hear Dante's voice as he assists Sofia to stand. Dr Manessi perches on the edge of the sofa, instantly taking my wrist to take my pulse.

"Kate how are you feeling?" he asks as he begins to count the seconds down on his watch.

"I know this is all a shock, but I need to know you're well."

I gingerly nod my head and attempt to sit up but the pressure of his hand to my shoulder ensures I stay flat.

"Kate, I need you to talk to me."

Looking at him I can see the weariness in his face.

"Alex?" I ask.

Am I hallucinating, is this all real?

A look passes over his features before he replies.

"He's alive, just."

I did see him, he is real. He's alive.

"I know you want to go to him but he's weak, very weak. Please, I need to trust you to lay here a while longer."

I nod my head slightly to indicate my submission in the matter.

"Sofia, can you please get Mrs Rossi some sweet tea." He orders as he rises from my sofa to return to the other.

I hear Sofia acknowledge his request before the distinct sound of someone leaving the room.

Turning my head, I lay completely still and watch my husband fight to stay alive. Why is he here and not in a hospital?

The question burns through my brain over and over.

"He needs to be in a hospital." I speak quietly to the silent room.

The silence that greets me is deafening. I can't understand why they can't take him.

Watching from my prone position I see the gentle movement of my husband's chest, his arm laid out next to his otherwise motionless body. The IV feeding him vital fluids to help his body fight. He needs to fight.

I feel the tears slide from my eyes, landing on the cold leather of the sofa and roll down and away. I hope more than I've ever hoped that life isn't rolling away from Alex in the same way.

Dante and Benni stand and watch their brother, their eyes pleading that he's strong enough to survive. We've all lost him once, I don't think I could endure his loss a second time.

Sofia returns with a tray, pouring me a tea before she approaches. Placing the cup on the floor she takes a pillow from the wingback chair and slowly helps me to sit up. Perching on the edge of the sofa she passes me the cup, watching my movements until she's satisfied I'm stable. With a quick nod she stands and returns to the tray, pouring a second cup and placing it by the doctor who is knelt on the floor. Collecting two glasses of amber liquid from the tray she passes them to Dante and Benni. They both accept her offering without detection, their eyes not straying from their brother.

Returning to me she perches on the sofa again and gently brushes the stray hairs from my face. With the kindest eyes I've ever seen she smiles down at me.

"Is there anything I can do for you; can I get you anything Mrs Rossi?

I start to shake my head when the boys jump into my mind.

"The boys?" I say quietly.

With a reassuring nod she smiles again.

"They're OK. She sighs deeply. "Franco is keeping them and Mrs Rossi senior distracted."

Relief fills me for a moment. I couldn't face the boys right now, and clearly Dante doesn't want his mother to know yet.

With a gentle squeeze to my hand she rises and quietly leaves the room, silently shutting the door as she goes.

The room remains hushed except for the movements of the doctor, and the occasional rasping from Alex's chest. With each sound he delivers we individually hold our breath in morbid anticipation before his breathing eases and we exhale in relief. The sun has risen and taken away some of the darkness of the room. The house is silent.

Moving myself to a more comfortable position, I draw my legs up beneath me and pull my sleeves over my hands as I hug myself and my baby.

The question is still burning in my mind.

"Why is he here, why can't we take him to a hospital? Surely they can help him better?" My voice sounds loud in the silent room although it came out in a whisper.

Dante shakes his head in despair as his shoulders drop. Benni walks towards me and sits down on the sofa, his body rigid with tension.

"We can't Kate. There is too much at stake."

I'm amazed they would risk his life like this.

"There would be too many questions and it may be connected to another offence." He says more quietly, shooting a quick look to the doctor before he turns back to me again.

I assume he means the combined strike. If they take him to the hospital, they may find evidence linking the family to the atrocities that happened there last night. I understand their need to keep us all safe, but I still struggle with it.

"How is it even possible?" I quietly ask Benni.

His understanding of my question clear.

With another in-take of breath he leans back into the sofa. He's not relaxed, it's to keep his conversation between the two of us.

"After we entered the building," he flashes a look to check if the doctor is busy, with his stethoscope in his ears again he can't hear our words, "we questioned a member of the house staff."

He looks slightly guilty, but I can't feel sorry for Colombo's people right now.

"He directed us to an area of the house we weren't aware of. There were no plans, so we didn't know about the underground rooms."

I can see it's difficult for him, but I need to know.

"Please Benni." I say to encourage him on.

With a visual swallow he continues.

"Inside we found two men that had been taken a few weeks ago, Gallo and Moretti thought they had both deserted their families." He stops to take a breath the pain evident in his eyes.

"Their injuries were bad but not life threatening. There was a young female who will survive, but I doubt she will want to." The look on his face shows the disgust at Lorenzo's acts toward her. The poor woman must have suffered at the hands of that maniac.

"We found Alex in a cell. I didn't even recognise him." He says clearly upset.

"When one of my men turned him over I knew it was him instantly." I can see he's reliving those moments, clearly traumatised.

Looking to me he checks to see how I'm taking his words. I nod to reassure him. I know this will be difficult to hear but it must have been a thousand times worse to see.

"He has been tortured over the last few months." On a huge sigh he looks up to the ceiling, not for inspiration but to hold in the tears.

"The houseman we questioned had cobbled together what he thinks happened."

Looking to his brother he is clearly not happy about something.

"Unfortunately, Colombo couldn't answer for himself." He says through gritted teeth before calming himself enough to look back to me.

"Remember Colombo senior said his son had killed his underboss, well it appears he was nearly right. The houseman said he had heard about a car chase. Colombo's underboss was chasing Alex that day. They both lost control on the bend which resulted with the other car flipping over, and Alex hitting the tree. The impact caused serious injuries to Alex, but obviously not enough to kill him." He says ironically waving a hand towards his brother.

With another sigh he continues.

"Colombo's man was killed instantly. Apparently, Colombo had Alex dragged from the wreckage intent on maiming him. When he saw he was still alive his depraved mind stepped in and the underboss was put in Alex's car. Colombo had his towed away to be disposed of."

The man clearly is sick in the head.

"Hang on, they identified Alex from his dental records." I say confused.

Nodding his head, he gives a mocking smile.

"Remember Kate, people can be bought off. Everyone has a price."

The dentist, he must have lied to the police. The police.

"But the investigation said that no one else was involved."

I remember asking the question.

With raised eyebrows he just purses his lips.

The police were paid off too. Is everyone so corrupt in this world? Is this the society we really live in where any-one's loyalty can be bought at a price?

"He's been alive all this time." I say shaking my head.

I knew subconsciously in my heart he was still out there somewhere. Turning back to my husband I place my hand to my heart. I need it to keep beating, while it's beating I know he is alive.

## Chapter Twenty-seven

A gentle knock from the door sounds around the room and Sofia enters dressed in her uniform carrying a tray of drinks and food. Laying the tray on the table she pours coffee for the three men, handing the cup and saucer to them each in turn before handing me my tea, she smiles lightly as I note the mug instead of the preferred house china.

Placing sandwiches on a plate she presses it into my hands with the word "eat." Passing the platter between the men, who are all stood watching vigil over Alex, they each take one without realising she's even there. Covering the platter on the table, Sofia collects the old cups before leaving again, just as quietly as her entrance.

The hours tick by and it feels like nothing has changed. That's got to be good?

Dr Manessi sits in the chair with his head back resting his eyes, Benni and Dante are both stood by the window talking in hushed voices. From the snippets of conversations I overhear, no-one was left alive. The compound was left ablaze before they departed, destroying all evidence connecting the Rossi's or any other families to the crime.

With my eyes fixed on Alex I blink for a moment to moisten them. When they open again I catch the tail-end of a movement. I'm not sure if I imagined it. Making sure I'm not seeing things I stare at him more intently when his hand flexes. It's not much but he definitely moved. Waiting an eternity, it happens for a third time.

"He moved." I whisper to the room.

Dr Manessi sits bolt upright and Dante and Benni spin on the spot. All eyes are trained on him, waiting for evidence of my words. We wait, and we wait. I begin to doubt myself when it happens again.

The doctor physically sags in his seat, relief evident in his action. Both brothers release a breath of air. Carefully rising from my seat, I approach his body and carefully crouch down by his side. Gently I take his hand and place a kiss to the back. The contact long overdue.

The stench emanating from him overwhelms me, but I feel the warmth of life.

"Please Alex, I need you to fight." I whisper to him.

Holding his hand, I place my cheek to the back trying to pour my strength into him through our contact.

Sitting on my knees I feel the baby moving inside of me from where she's momentarily squashed in this position. Distracted by her movements I almost miss the flex of his hand against my face. Turning it gently I push my cheek into his palm.

"Please Alex. I need you. We need you so much."

His movements become a little stronger and the thrill empowers me.

I sense Dr Manessi crouch down beside me.

"He's responding to your touch."

I nod my head as I feel him twitch again. The look of relief on the doctor's face encourages me.

"Thank god." He says under his breath.

Turning to Dante he makes his request.

"Can we have some warm water and cloths please?"

Dante instantly pulls out his phone and issues his commands in Italian.

A few moments pass as I remain in position before a knock sounds at the door. Sophia quietly enters before closing it again. Placing the tray on the floor she hesitates a moment.

"Would you like me to help, or would you prefer to do it?" She asks kindly.

Not removing my eyes from Alex, I shake my head. He's my husband. This is my job.

"Thank you Sofia but I would prefer to do it."

Sofia rises and exits just as quietly.

Placing his hand gently on the sofa I see it twitch and flex at the loss of my touch. The movement fills me with joy.

I dip the cloth into the warm water and the smell is a welcome break from that of Alex. I begin cleaning his face, running it gently over his forehead and cheeks before wiping his facial hair. Dipping the cloth in the bowl again I run the edge over his mouth and I swear I see his tongue pass over his lips. Continuing to refresh the cloth I meticulously make my way across his body, washing what I can reach. My ministrations take time as I'm careful with my touch. Wherever my hands make contact I feel his body move in response.

The water is stained with the blood and grime and he appears more rested now as opposed to the comatose state he was in.

Rising from the floor, Benni instantly assists in helping me stand, I stretch my body, I feel hopeful. Alex is strong. He may be weak bodily, but his strength runs deeper.

After visiting the loo quickly to refresh myself and relieve my bursting bladder, I'm eager to get back to the room. Back to Alex, I'm pulled to him. My heart knows where it needs to be.

As I enter I catch the tail-end of the doctor's conversation.

"If we bring the bed in here, it would be more comfortable for Allesandro." He says.

Looking to Dante I see him nod his head in agreement, before taking his phone to issue his demands. I look to Benni to fill me in and as he walks towards me he smiles before taking me in a fierce hug. It feels more for him than me.

"Manessi wants to turn this room into a make-shift hospital. Dante's issued the command and they're no doubt currently robbing the local hospital." He jokes.

Smiling up at him, I'm glad to hear his usual jokey tone, more like the Benni I've come to know and love.

"Mamma will need to know soon, especially if the men are removing furniture from rooms." He quips with raised eyebrows.

The thought of the others hits me hard.

"The boys, Maria." I say quietly.

The world outside of this room has ceased to exist in my mind.

"Let's get Alex settled before we tell them." He says.

I have no idea what they've been told.

Before long there's a knock on the door, Benni disentangles himself from me to answers it.

I hear his words spoken quickly in Italian before two men enter quietly.

Together they lift the empty sofa I had been lying on and place it against the wall. Clearing the path, they open the door fully to reveal 2 further men stood waiting, holding a bed. The four of them manoeuvre the bed silently and place it precisely before going out the door and returning with fresh bed linen. Immediately I begin to make the bed when Dante places his hand on my arm to stop me.

"Leave it. A maid will do it."

I can't explain, but I need to do this small thing for him. I need to see to his comfort. Dante must see something in my look as he lets my arm go. He nods his head in understanding. Making the bed with my baby bump isn't easy, but I'm more than happy to do it.

When the bed is made to my liking, Dante instructs the men, who have all stood patiently waiting, how he wants them to lift his brother. Each man respectfully lifts and carries Alex to the softer haven. Once settled and the IV drip is changed for a full bag, I begin to tuck him in and place a gentle kiss to his lips. A kiss I never thought I would ever feel again. The connection between our tender touch ignites my soul. That one small caress reawakens my heart and I feel complete. My other half has returned to make me whole again.

Dr Manessi left earlier, and I have a list of strict instructions for Alex's care. He said I could call him anytime I'm concerned. I'd rather he'd stayed but on a positive note he wouldn't leave him if he was worried. He'll be back later tonight to check on him again.

Dante informed me they had business that needed immediate attention, and with my look of concern at their departure too, he placed his hand on my shoulder and told me I would be fine. Benni gave me a hug before casting a glance to his brother who hadn't moved since they placed him in the bed.

The guards kindly placed a chair by Alex's side where I am currently curled up with a blanket. My eyes have grown sore and dry from staring at his prone body for so long. I can see his colour has improved vastly. The IV line in his arm is still feeding him the life-giving nutrients.

Despite the beard, and obvious weight loss, he looks like he's sleeping peacefully. I can't stop my mind from running through all the times I'd laid in our bed watching his chest move with each breath, placing my hand on his heart just to feel it beating. Sometimes he'd wake but he'd allow me to finish my perusals. I wish I could lay in that bed and do those very things now, but the doctor warned me he's too weak.

My eyes begin to close of their own accord, I'm exhausted. Every emotion one person can feel has hit me today, my mind and body need rest, but I'm not prepared to leave this room, I can't leave him.

Laying my head to the side of the chair back, I allow myself a few minutes respite.

A knock at the door brings me from my much-needed nap. The sun set a long time ago judging by the darkness through the windows. The door opens quietly as Sofia enters bearing a tray of food.

"I thought you might be hungry." She says quietly closing the door behind her.

Carefully she balances the tray on her hip as she lifts a small side table and places it by my chair and lays the food on it. I see she's bought all my favourite foods, picnic style, a large glass of juice and a selection of sweet fruit tarts. I really need the sugar hit right now.

Smiling my thanks, she turns to look at Alex.

"How is he?" She asks gently.

With a sigh I uncurl my legs from under me and stand to stretch my aching limbs.

"He seems more settled now." I say looking down at him.

He does look much better. His colour has improved during my nap.

"I'm pleased for you." I sense she means more than just his improvements.

Turning from Alex I feel her looking at me .

"Can I get you anything Mrs Rossi?" She says despondently.

I understand her sense of helplessness, I feel the same. I shake my head as I answer.

"No but thank you Sofia, you've been amazing today."

She really has.

"How are the boys?" I ask quietly.

A small smile touches her lips.

"The guards have kept them distracted most of the day."

I have no idea with what, but I'm grateful for their thoughtfulness.

"Mr Rossi has just taken them and Mrs Rossi into his study with Mr Benito." She adds more solemnly.

I feel guilty for leaving the task to Dante, but I don't have the mental capacity to deal with it right now.

With a heavy sigh I take my seat again and start picking at the food. I'm not hungry but I know I need to eat for the baby's sake. I need the strength to get through all of this.

"I'll leave you alone." Sofia says from the doorway before she exits.

From the sound of the commotion outside the temporary hospital room, Dante has told them all, Maria's cries can be heard through the solid wood door. There is the sound of her gently being coaxed away before silence returns again. The door opens and Benni walks through casting a look directly to his brother. Seeing the change to his pallor, a smile brightens his face.

"He's looking better." He says, confirming my own thoughts.

I nod my head in agreement.

Walking over he perches on the edge of the bed, watching Alex breathing steadily.

"How are you Benni?" I ask.

As the happy go lucky member of the family, sometimes his feelings get overlooked.

It takes him a few further moments of observation before turning to me.

"Don't lie to me, please." I say.

His shoulders sag slightly as he responds.

"Happy but sad, and angry, really, really angry."

I can see the anger hidden behind the small smile.

"How did this happen?" He says shaking his head. I know the question is rhetorical.

We sit in comfortable silence before we see Alex's hands moving where they lay on top of the covers. It stops suddenly, before it happens again. The movement looks like he's trying to grasp something, or someone.

"Has he done that before?" Benni asks, a frown furrowing his brow.

"No." Is my immediate response. I've watched him twitch but not to this degree.

Taking his phone from his pocket he calls Dr Manessi. With rapid fired Italian he soon finishes and replaces his phone.

"He's on his way." By the tone of his words, I don't think the doctor had much choice.

"You've spoken to the boys." I say rather than ask. "How are they, what did you tell them?"

"They're shocked, understandably." He responds.

I can't imagine what's running through their heads.

"I need to see them." I say before looking at Alex. " But I can't leave him."

Benni looks at me and gives a firm nod. Rising from the bed he walks straight for the door and instructs someone outside to find them, before returning to his brother again.

We sit in silence watching his chest rise and fall, grateful for the sight of the monotonous movements. A gentle knock brings us both from the trance we're in.

"Enter." Benni calls in a low voice.

The door opens to reveal the boys. Their body language screams apprehension. It's obvious they're reluctant to cross the threshold. Their uncles have given them hope to dream and stepping into this room that reality may be realised, or it will shatter their hopes turning their lives back into a living nightmare.

Rising from my chair I move towards them, my smile genuine, and I see the relief on their faces instantly. Reaching out I put an arm around each of them hugging them fiercely to me before placing a kiss to both their cheeks.

"Is it true?" Leo asks quietly.

Evidence of his tears still on his lashes.

I nod my head and I hear a stutter of breath release from them both.

"He's very weak though." I have to pre-warn them as Alex looks very different from their memories of him.

I hesitate before I ask, but I know now my boys are more astute than I gave them credit for.

"Did your uncles tell you what has happened to him?"

Their sorrowful nods are synchronized. I just hope that Dante didn't go into too much detail.

"Remember he is strong inside." I say with vigour before taking them both by the hands and lead them into the room.

The last time I held their hands like this they were still in primary school, mere babies, but now, stood beside me, are two amazing young men, trusting me, their mum.

The guard leans in to close the door as I hear the distinct sound of Bear running towards us. I can't risk him jumping on the bed, I'm grateful for his quick reactions. His whining sounds in the room through the closed door and it breaks my heart to exclude him, but his love for Alex is too dangerous right now.

With hesitant steps we approach the bed and Benni rises, revealing their dad to them, their shocked gasps sound in the room. Benni immediately moves towards us and places an arm around Marc's shoulders.

"We need to be quiet, but I think your dad would like to hear your voices." He says encouragingly.

I urge them forward and both boys stand like statues, staring in awe at the man lying in the bed. I hear a gentle crying from one of them and I allow them time to process it all. Benni stands back too and I appreciate him not commenting on their reaction. The shock is huge.

"Hi dad." Leo says before he tentatively reaches out and gently touches his hand.

Alex's hand flexes from the contact and Leo reactively retracts his own. Turning to me quickly with concern in his eyes.

"I didn't mean to hurt him." He says quickly with tears evident in his eyes.

I walk forward and hug him tightly to me.

"You didn't darling, you didn't."

Pulling away from his fierce hold on me, I smile up at him and copy his movements and touch Alex's hand with my own. Alex responds in the same manner.

"See, he knows we're here."

Relief washes over his face.

"Can I, can, umm, can I touch him too?" Marc asks quietly, his eyes trained on his dad.

"Of course you can." I say encouragingly.

Marc reaches out and strokes the back of Alex's hand.

"Hello dad, we missed you." He says, as Alex instantly reacts to the contact with his son.

Both boys wear a look of elation.

I hear Benni behind me before I see more chairs being placed next to the bed.

"Sit boys before you fall on him." He jokes.

The level of his voice feels a little loud for the room and I turn to check if it disturbed Alex. I see his eyelids flicker from the movement of his eyes beneath,

"He moved his eyes." I say in shock.

All four of us watch but he doesn't repeat the action.

"Come on let's sit for a few minutes." I propose.

We take our seats and Benni perches on the end of the bed again. The silence is stifling, uncomfortable.

"Why don't we tell dad about nonna playing video games." I suggest, the memory making me smile.

The boys are hesitant at first but soon become comfortable talking. Occasionally I have to remind them to keep their voices low and they're more than happy to comply.

Time flies by and the atmosphere in the room becomes lighter, less morbid, when a knock on the door halts our laughter and Dr Manessi walks in.

"Hello boys are you looking after your dad?" He asks jovially.

The boys nod and immediately rise from their seats to allow him space to tend to their dad. Their manners make me so proud of them.

"Come on you two, I think I need to see what nonna can do on that zombie game."

Benni places an arm around each of his nephews and leads them to the door.

The doctor begins his ministrations, so I take the opportunity to go to the toilet. On the way back I pass a maid and ask for tea for Dr Manessi and me. He looked like he needed something stronger though.

As I approach the guard automatically opens the door without knocking.

"Thank you." I say on a smile as I enter to see the doctor changing his IV line. I don't know how many he's had but they are working miracles.

"How do you think he's doing?" I ask hopefully.

With Alex's hand in his, the doctor sees and feels his movements. Looking to me with a frown he says.

"Say something else."

My mind goes blank. Dr Manessi nods at me encouragingly.

"Hey Alex, the boys were so pleased to see you. They've missed you so much. We all have." My words don't even cover the depths of despair we reached at his loss.

The doctor turns to me with a huge smile.

"Your husband can hear you Mrs Rossi, he's mentally very strong. It's his body that needs time to heal."

His confirmation of my thoughts is a joy to hear.

The rest of the evening I talk gently to Alex, the feel of his hand in mine is one of the greatest feelings in the world. I purposely avoid talking about the baby. His mind may be strong, but the shock could be too much and it's a conversation we need to have when he's fully compos mentis.

Fatigue is taking over but the thought of leaving him scares me. Dante enters the room as a huge yawn leaves my mouth, I quickly cover it with my hand, thankfully he's too polite to comment. Taking one of the chairs the boys vacated earlier he sits in silence for a while, just watching his brother.

The sound of his voice in the silence comes as a shock.

"How is he?" He asks hopefully.

"Dr Manessi is hopeful. He told me to talk to him as he responds to the sound of our voices."

A smile covers Dante's mouth at the same time I cover mine to hide yet another yawn.

"You need to rest." He commands.

I know I do.

"I will stay with him."

Dante must interpret the look of fear on my face correctly.

"I will send someone to wake you if there is any change."

I trust that he will, but I'm still loathed to leave. Letting him from my sight scares me, but my body is fighting exhaustion, and I'll be good to no one if I'm sick.

Nodding my tired head in accord, I lean down and kiss Alex's lips, because I can, and leave my husband in his brother's hands.

## Chapter Twenty-eight

Alex has been home for a week now, back in our lives, and I'm still stunned by it. Dr Manessi is encouraged with each visit he makes.

"He needs time." He says when I ask him yet again if he knows when he'll wake.

The boys and Maria sit with him each day, and I allow them their private time. It would be unfair of me to hover in the room when they have their own private words they want to share with Alex. I have caught snippets of conversation the boys have had, the love for their father is immense and they told him over and over. Maria spoke quietly in Italian but the emotion on her face and her overall demeanour showed her happiness at her son being returned.

Sitting in my usual seat I hold a book in one hand and stroke my growing belly with the other. Angel reacts to the sound of my voice when I read to her dad. The new clothes arrived which are so much more comfortable, and I was glad to see them in my bedroom. I hope Franco was nice to the delivery driver.

Reading the book out loud I'm consumed with the plot and momentarily forget and begin to recite the words in my head. Taking my hand from my belly to turn the page I gasp at the outcome of the fight. I'm so engrossed as the words depict the sound of clans clashing, defeating their sworn enemy in a prolonged battle, sword against sword, when I hear the most magnificent sound ever.

"Kate?"

The voice is gravelly from lack of use. The question in his voice shows his confusion.

Throwing the book to the seat I rise instantly and lean on his bed.

"Alex." I say quietly.

I pray I heard him, and it wasn't my imagination.

"Can you hear me?"

The fluttering of his eyelids is the first sign of response other than his hands twitching.

"Alex." I say again, encouragingly.

Slowly, painfully slowly, he begins to open his eyes. I'm grateful we're in the darker lounge as the light would be too much for him to bare.

Momentarily opening his eyes he then begins to close them again, the effort clearly draining him. Running to the door, I fling it open, startling the guard on duty.

"Get Dante, quickly." I throw at him before rushing back to Alex's side.

Sitting on the edge of the bed I gently take his hand in my right hand and stroke the fingers of my left across his brow.

"Alex." I say again, and I feel the squeeze he awards me.

"Please open your eyes." I plead.

His eyelids flicker slightly before I feel the effort it takes through my fingers at his forehead, and he offers me the beautiful prospect of his eyes.

"Hello handsome." I say smiling with tears trailing down my face.

The elation I feel at seeing him, the connection lighting a fuse, breathing life back into us both is beyond measure. My smile is so wide, I feel my unused cheek muscles pulling tight.

A frown begins to mar his face and I can see the confusion and disbelief, it's heart breaking.

"It's me." I say as I take his hand and place his palm to my cheek.

Turning my head, I press a kiss to the centre and put it back to my face once again. His fingers flex, feeling the texture of my skin.

"Kate." His voice low and raspy.

"Yes, it's me." I say as he catches a tear with his fingertip.

"Kate?" He questions again, confused.

His head remains still as his eyes take in his surroundings.

"You're at the Rossi house." I say while he continues his perusal.

"You're safe now." I add in a lower voice.

Slowly his eyes return to mine as I hear someone rush through the door.

"Kate?" I hear them ask.

Not denying myself the vision in front of me I reply over my shoulder.

"He's awake Dante." Happiness evident in my elated voice.

Dante quickly moves to the other side of Alex and half kneels half stands.

"Allesandro." He says quietly, in astonishment.

Alex appears confused and reluctantly moves his eyes to his brother.

The smile that lights up Dante's face is dazzling.

"It is very good to see you brother." He says with glistening eyes.

"Dante?" Alex questions before looking back at me. "Kate?"

Alex is clearly confused by us both being here. I don't know what's safe to tell him without sending him back into a comatose state.

"Dante rescued you. You're safe." I offer as explanation.

"Safe." Alex breaths as exhaustion takes over and his eyes shut, denying me my pleasure.

Taking out his phone Dante calls Dr Manessi, hanging up he dials Benni immediately after.

I catch some of his words, but I'm too happy to care what he's telling them.

Placing the phone back in his pocket he stands and looks down at his brother.

"Benito will be here shortly. He is not on the compound at present."

I nod my head to his words.

"He spoke." I say elation in my voice.

Dante takes a seat on the bed, relief evident.

"He did." Is all he manages in response, trying to suppress his emotions.

We both sit in companionable silence and watch Alex sleep. His rest now is clearly more peaceful.

On the doctor's arrival he is shown straight in, and we both reluctantly rise.

"So, he spoke, did he?" He asks checking his pupils with the torch.

"Yes, he seemed confused though." I tell him.

"Not surprising considering." He says absentmindedly.

He's right, it's not surprising, I shudder to think what he has endured. The scars may heal on his body but there are others that never will.

Once he has finished his ministrations he stands at the end of the bed and smiles.

"Well, I think your man will make a full recovery. He will need to take things slowly." He says more to Dante than to me.

Dante nods his immediate agreement.

Going through a strict list of do's and don'ts before he leaves to return to his clinic.

Dante orders the specified foods, water, a straw, scissors, beard trimmer, a mobile bath, who knows where they'll find one, but I guarantee they will, clean clothes, I suggest fresh bed linen too. He orders our lunch to be brought in before putting away his phone and we continue our vigil.

Most of the items are delivered, and still we wait. And wait and wait. The position I'm sitting in is getting uncomfortable and I stand to stretch my aching limbs, sore from holding them tight with tension. I go to release Alex's hand, but his grasp becomes tighter.

"Don't." He says quietly.

Smiling I lean down and kiss his lips.

"I need to stretch a minute." I whisper into his mouth.

Alex begins to open his eyes again as I release his hand, ensuring I won't leave.

Standing I stretch my arms and neck out as Benni walks through the door. He hides his shock well at seeing his brother finally awake.

"Hey, hey sunshine, how are you?" He asks jovially.

Alex moves his head, which was trained on me, to look at his new guest. Stepping to the side to allow his brother access, Alex suddenly looks panicked. I can't bear to see the look on his face, so I plonk myself at the head of the bed by his pillow facing his approaching brother. I wrap my right arm over his head and my left rests gently on his chest, feeling the beat of his heart which matches my own. Alex appears to calm instantly with my nearness and Benni takes my original spot on the bed with a huge smile for his brother.

"Welcome home." He says, the last note rising in pitch betraying his happy appearance.

Alex moves his hand to grasp mine to his chest as he distractedly plays with my wedding and engagement rings, moving his head to take in Dante then Benni and back to Dante again.

"What happened?" He asks.

His voice is croaky, so I make to get up to pour water but his strength surprises me when he holds my hand tighter stopping me from leaving, he doesn't want to break our connection.

"Benni could you pour some water please?" I ask, nodding towards the tray with my head. "And the straw too." I add.

Alex squeezes my hand in silent thanks.

Benni returns with the water and with a bit of negotiation he sits up resting his back against the headboard, with me still wrapped around him, and drinks deeply.

Benni looks to Dante before he begins.

"Colombo junior took you after the car crash. He's kept you hostage for months." He hesitates before he goes on. "From what we can establish the sick bastard tortured you for fun."

I feel Alex flinch, clearly reliving a memory.

"You were declared dead at the scene of the crash." Benni informs him.

The gasp is audible plus I feel his chest move with the sound.

"Colombo's underboss died. He swapped his body for yours."

Benni lets that settle around us all for a moment.

"He bought both the police and your dentist."

We definitely need to find a new dentist now, I can't believe he faked the dental records, and the boys liked him.

"We buried you." Benni adds solemnly. "Allesandro Rossi is officially dead."

Alex squeezes my hand as he turns his head to look at me.

"I'm so sorry." The pain I feel inside is evident in his eyes.

I shake my head, too scared to speak. I can't trust the tears not to fall. Squeezing his hand back I offer the best smile I can as I mentally relive that day.

"What has been done?" Alex asks turning to his older brother.

"It has been dealt with." He answers looking to both Benni and me, before returning to his brother. "No one was spared."

The fierce look on his face shows his disgust at Colombo and his men.

"What about the house staff?" I ask.

He said if they were innocent they would survive, but they were part of the house that kept my husband captive, they knew he was being tortured.

Dante looks to me and shakes his head.

"Good." I say with venom in my voice.

Alex moves his head quicker than I would have expected and looks at me with a frown.

I hear Benni laugh before he speaks.

"Oh, a lot has changed around here my man!"

While Alex looks at his brothers, I shake my head with widened eyes to them each to let them know that I haven't told him yet. My message is received and understood.

"Sapevo che era forte." Dante says firmly with certainty.

"What?' I ask on a smile.

I have a vague idea what he said.

I feel Alex begin to shake his head in dismay.

"Allesandro did not think you could handle our life. I think he may be a bit shocked." His says with laughter in his voice.

"Well maybe Alex should have given me the choice." I say firmly, as both Dante and Benni laugh heartily.

The bath is brought in and with the help of his brothers Alex relaxes in the warm water. I can see he's embarrassed but I know he will feel much better once he's clean. I've finished stripping the bed and I put on clean sheets before kneeling down next to the bath. Thankfully my long flowing top hides my secret.

Taking the scissors to his beard, I slowly unmask the beauty hidden beneath. I set the beard trimmer on a higher setting to leave a sexy amount of stubble. He's not ready for a wet shave and I'm quite liking the look on him. Quite a lot actually!

Rubbing the bristles in his hand I see mischief dancing in his eyes. Wiggling his eye-brows he says, "You like?"

My smile is huge at being caught ogling my husband. Nodding I lean forward and rub my cheek to his, the hair is softer that I expected, laughing I go to pull away, but he grabs my shoulders trying to rub his face on me some more. The smile on his face is amazing, and I have to catch my breath at the sight of it. Sitting back on my knees I catch both Dante and Benni observing our antics with a loving look in their eyes. They've never seen us together like this, this is our normal, and I am grateful to be able to live it again.

The guard bought in food for all of us once Alex was dressed and back in bed. I can see he's exhausted but his body needs food. The soup smells amazing but the strange looking drink I'm a little dubious of, but I'm sure it will help him to recover. With my sandwich half way to my mouth I see Benni furiously nodding towards my lap with his eyes, and I realise my napkin is accentuating my bump, I surreptitiously move it and pull my top looser. I will tell him, but not yet. I want to enjoy this moment first. Eating lunch together feels amazing. The simplicity of being able to share the same space with Alex and his brothers has my heart soaring to the highest height.

The reunion with the boys brings a tear to everyone present. Franco, who escorted them in, tries to hide his emotions, and Dante and Benni are suspiciously wiping at their eyes.

"Come on in boys." I say waving them closer.

The awe on their faces is beautiful to see. We never believed we would have him back with us and the boys have taken the news amazingly showing their true maturity. I see Leo swallow down his emotions, but Marc doesn't care who sees. The tears track down his face at the sight of his dad, his hero sitting up in bed. The sound of Marc's sniffle breaks Leo's resolve as he looks on at the miracle before him.

"Dad." He chokes out before hurrying forward.

The boys sit on either side of the bed, gentle as they lower themselves. They are conscious of their movements, and I can see they just want to throw their arms around him and hold him tight, never let him go.

Holding out his hands they each take one and I see the glistening in his eyes matching everyone else in the room.

Words are useless right now. We all need to soak in the atmosphere of love and phenomenon that is Alex. A vision we could only ever dream of. I know they will have questions, but I'm grateful for their speechless state as I don't think Alex has the strength to answer them.

Not once do they remove their eyes from their father. I can see Marc running his thumb backwards and forwards across Alex's hand, and Leo has his father's hand held tightly between both of his. Both need to feel the warmth emanating from his skin, to feel the blood rushing through his veins, feel of his heart beating, to hear the sound of his breathing. Only with this evidence will they allow themselves to believe that this is all real.

Minutes pass in silence until Marc looks up from his dad's hand with a smile.

"I'm really glad you're not actually dead dad."

The smile that crosses Alex's face is a wonder to behold.

"So am I Marc, so am I."

We have had to practically drag the boys away to allow Alex time to rest. I can see how quickly he tires, and his mother needs to reassure herself too. Maria requested she spend time with him alone. From one mother to another I understand her heartache and pain. She thought she had lost him, just like us, and lived through the grief of burying her son, her baby. I can't even imagine the pain a mother goes through when she buries her child. The emotional drain from seeing her son again has been too much and she has returned to her room for the rest of the day.

Today the boys are keeping Alex occupied with their antics and the smile I see on all their faces is unbelievable. The sheer joy the boys get from simply basking in his presence lights them up. He does the exact same thing to me. I feel truly alive again. No longer suffering the half-life I thought I was resigned to live with his departure from this earth.

Whilst Alex is busy talking with the boys I speak to Franco to discuss a few issues. Bear has managed to get out a few times, plus a number of parcels have arrived, hopefully the wrapping paper, and a few other gifts for Alex. I'd nearly forgotten with all the excitement, that Christmas is just around the corner. We couldn't have asked for a better present. If I told the boys that they only had their dad for Christmas for the rest of their lives, they would be euphoric at the prospect. I know it's cheeky, but I ask if anyone is free to help me wrap the boy's gifts. Franco was with me when we separated them out and I always use one colour wrapping paper per child. This year Marc has dogs wearing Santa hats, and Leo has dancing elves. I've hidden his and Sofia's presents upstairs in my room for safekeeping, when I wrap the few bits I have for my husband, I'll do theirs too.

I can feel Alex watching me as I discuss my appointment tomorrow with my personal guard.

"I need to see the midwife tomorrow." I all but whisper to him. "We need to leave by 7.30am."

Alex is usually asleep till 10am so I should be back by the time he wakes.

Franco nods his understanding before looking over my shoulder. Glancing back myself I catch Alex glaring at Franco. Turning back to my friend, I smile an apology and he smiles at me before taking his leave.

The boys stay for another half hour before I remind them they need to finish their school work. With grumbles from them both they trudge out of the room. When they get to the door they both turn and check their dad is still there. Their smiles are brighter than the sun and his is too.

"You need to rest." I say, going to get my mug from the side table.

I might have a nap while he does, I think about maybe having a soak in the bath too.

I can feel him thinking so I turn to look at him. With raised brows I'm waiting for him to say whatever is on his mind.

He hesitates before he speaks.

"You seem very friendly with Franco."

There is no accusation in his tone, but I can clearly hear what he isn't saying.

"Yes, I am very friendly with Franco." I reply deadpan.

I see the torture evident on his face from my words.

I stand at the end of the bed for an eternity, but he doesn't say any more. It's clear he has misinterpreted the situation with Franco.

"He was assigned as my personal body guard." I say, "By Dante. Your brother." I add.

He doesn't look any happier with my explanation, he just looks exhausted.

"You need to get some sleep." I say softly.

Approaching him I lean down and kiss his lips gently.

"I love you so much Mr Rossi. Never forget that." I say as I place another kiss to his lips.

Alex tries to deepen the kiss, but I can't let him, not yet. He's too weak still to take this any further than a loving kiss and I can't run the risk of his hands wandering and discovering the secret I hide.

Pecking him on the end of his nose and then his forehead I look him deep in the eyes.

"I love you more than you will ever know."

The look of love I see in his eyes is overflowing.

"Not as much as I love you Kate." He says, sealing our hearts together again for eternity.

The ride from the clinic is far less stressful than the last time. My blood pressure is now in a more normal range and my blood results have all come back healthy. I still have no desire to have an amniocentesis. What will be will be. The scan showed how much she has grown, and the due date is set for April 22nd. The measurements all look good, and Ruth was more than happy with her development.

We discussed the birth and the different options available now. Apparently in the birthing room, that I will have assigned for my own personal use, I can choose the music, colour of the curtains, birthing pool, warm bath, the list was endless. I'm sure when the time comes I'll just be screaming blue murder and I won't give a damn who's crooning softly in the background to relax and ease her through the birth canal, allowing my body to open and deliver her into the world. Her words, not mine. I took the pamphlet she gave and said I would think about it. She asked me if I had any questions and my mind went completely blank. I will need to start jotting things down as I think of them. We've set the next appointment for mid-January and again she offered her number if I ever needed to call.

Ruth is everything kind and gentle you could hope for in a midwife, and I know when the time comes this amazing woman will transform before my eyes and become the motivator I will need to deliver Angel safely.

The gates swing open into the grounds of the Rossi house, and I catch a glimpse of Bear playing with the guards. I think he's playing. I hope he's playing. Franco catches me leaning forward to get a better view and laughs lightly.

"He's the best trainer we've ever had."

Trying not to laugh I keep my eyes on Bear, who is now chasing a man in a suit and wow he can jump really high, he almost made it to the safety of the tree,

"He hasn't actually hurt anyone has he?" I'm really not laughing, honestly.

I hear a chuckle emanate from the driver before Franco responds.

"No, he's just a big cuddly teddy bear, it's the newer younger guards that he likes to play with. Plus, it's good for Bear to learn more."

I appreciate his response. To us he is a soft cuddly dog, but to people that don't know him, he is a little intimidating.

Pulling up to the door, Franco gets out and opens my door. I nod my thanks and we walk up the stairs together. I smile to the guard at the main door as he opens it.

"Thank you."

When we reach the hall, I start to unbutton my coat and remove my scarf.

"I have two men working on the project downstairs." Franco says in code, standing at my back and helping me out of my coat. "If they have followed my instructions then they should be finished later today."

I smile my thanks as I turn around to him and place my hand on his arm.

"Thank you Franco, I really appreciate your help, and your kindness."

"You are more than welcome Mrs Rossi. Can I get you anything before I deliver this to Sofia?"

"Yes, I do." I say remembering what I need and rifling through my pockets and finding what I'm looking for. I put it in my back pocket and look up to him with a smile.

"Thanks again Franco. I will talk to you later."

Turing to walk away I can see directly down the hall towards the room that Alex is in and I catch a movement. Whoever it is, isn't very fast. I won't call him out on it in public, I'll wait till I close the door where he can't escape me.

As I'm just about to enter I see a maid and order tea and a snack to be delivered, I'm starving. With a smile I continue on my mission.

"Good morning gentlemen." I say to the guards as I approach.

The delay in them opening the door answers my question. They're no doubt giving him time to scurry back into bed by delaying me.

I raise a brow at them and go to open the door myself.

"I'll do it myself then." I mutter under my breath.

They both drop their heads in embarrassment.

"Sorry Mrs Rossi, he asked us to delay you."

"I know." I say softly with a smile and their shocked faces meet mine.

I nod towards the door and it is opened immediately.

"Thank you gentlemen. Please let me know when the tray of tea arrives. After that I would rather not be disturbed for a while."

"Yes Mrs Rossi." Is offered in unison from their smiling faces as the door is closed again, sealing my husband in the room. It's long past due, and we are going to have a talk.

"Morning Alex. How are you feeling? You look a little out of breath." I say with mock concern in my voice.

I look him deadpan in the face. I can stand and wait all day. As a mother of boys, you learn certain techniques, and this is one of them.

Alex lays back on the pillows, a light sheen to his brow, but in no way out of breath. His health has improved vastly, and he is demanding the doctor lets him out of this room and into our family suite. I think that day might be today after we've had a little chat.

"Where have you been?' He asks.

"Sorry I didn't tell you, I thought you would still be sleeping."

The knock at the door sounds and I call for them to enter.

"Thank you, if you could leave it there please." I say indicating the small side table I use.

"Of-course Mrs Rossi."

The guard leaves the tray and goes to leave.

"And if you can keep us from being disturbed for a while I would really appreciate it."

The guard turns and offers a brilliant smile before nodding his head and leaving us alone with the click of the latch.

"Tea?" I ask, automatically pouring.

Standing straight I'm aware that the outfit I chose today reveals my growing bump. Walking toward the bed I pass him the cup and sit in my usual chair. Not once do his eyes stray from my face. It's like I'm an enigma he's trying to work out.

Taking a sip and a quick nibble of the pastry I place it all on the table and look at him.

"I think it's time we had a chat, don't you?" I ask in mock seriousness.

Alex looks a little uncomfortable as he chews on his lip. I haven't specified what the chat is about, I will let him lead with what he thinks I should know first. I feel like we're at the beginning of the game truth or dare as I have no idea where this conversation will start but I do however know how it ends, and it is currently sitting here with us, although he isn't aware yet.

"I couldn't tell you Kate." So that's where we're starting, at the beginning.

He hesitates a moment before looking at me.

"Your life was so different to mine. I couldn't help it, I fell in love with you the instant I saw you." The look that passes over his face holds the joy that we both feel.

"You tangled me with your beauty and I couldn't let it go." He sighs heavily before he continues.

"I tried to leave you alone but the thought of life without you was too distressing. I spoke with Dante and he said if you were the person I believed you to be, then we could make it happen."

He sits in silence for a moment staring at nothing but clearly remembering all those years ago.

"I'm not embarrassed of the life I grew up in, but I didn't think you would understand." He says more quietly.

"You never gave me the option to try." I state.

Shaking his head, he realises his error.

"Why didn't you trust me Alex?" I have to know.

Looking up at me sharply he seems hurt by my words, but not as hurt as I was at finding out the truth.

"I did trust you, I always will, but you have to understand this life isn't easy. I couldn't put you in danger. I couldn't risk losing you."

"Maybe not, but I lost you." My words don't even cover the pain I felt.

It's killing me sitting here but I need to maintain this distance to keep a clear mind.

Looking down again he looks defeated.

"As a Rossi I will always be in danger to some degree but once we married I chose to take less risks, I helped Dante with the more legal side of the business." He looks slightly uncomfortable as he speaks.

I can see he's trying to gauge my reaction to his statement, but there's no shock there, I'm already aware of the two sides to the Rossi syndicate.

I decide to put him out of his misery.

"Dante has told me a lot, as well as your brother and mum."

He doesn't look as relieved as I thought he would.

"Your boys guessed before I did." I state.

I can't help the smile that appears on my face.

With a reluctant sigh he looks defeated.

"How much do they know?"

I think about it for a moment.

"I'm not sure how much but they are aware of the more unusual aspects of the business." Laughing to myself, I remember their reaction at the dinner table.

"Your youngest son is currently learning Italian and listened to the guards speaking before the combined attack." I say with pride and at the same time dumbfounded.

The shock on his face is comical.

"Really?" He asks with pride in his voice.

I nod my head.

"Clever little sod." He quips.

I need him to understand my mindset on it all.

"While I can't fully comprehend the life you lead here, and your family syndicate, I can begin to understand the why. I've seen for myself the good that you can do, and the loyalty that is borne of that goodness. On the other hand, I can see the evil that exists in this world of yours and I comprehend why you wanted to keep us away, separate your two lives, and the need to keep that evil in control."

Alex sits looking at me like I'm a rare creature he has just discovered.

"You can't continue to live these two lives Alex. I won't have you lying to me and the children any longer. We are either a part of your life fully or not at all."

It kills me to say those words, but he needs to know how this has affected us all.

"I would NEVER ask you to walk away from your family. Since you died." I have to take a breath in to stop the emotion before I can continue. "Since you were taken from us your family has shown me nothing but kindness, loved us, cared for us, protected us when we needed it."

The frown of anger appears on his forehead. I flap my hand at him to dismiss my words.

"That's in the past and besides I've been given complete protection and some servitude thingy from all the families through Colombo Senior apparently." I still don't fully understand what he meant.

The look of shock on Alex's face makes me sit back in my chair a little.

"What did you say?" He asks quietly.

"Oh, Colombo said he was my eternal servant and the entire family and their affiliates or something will honour complete protection of me, and I assume the kids too." I respond, flapping my hand a bit more, saying the last part more to myself. Maybe we can get back to normal life if nobody is trying to hurt me.

Alex still looks a little shocked.

"Are you OK?" I hesitantly ask.

Alex just moves his head up and down like a nodding dog with the largest eyes I've ever seen on him, they really are an amazing colour.

"Anyway, as I said I won't ask you to choose, so the decision is yours. We either all stay a part of this family together or you do it alone. What will it be?"

I can see the relief on his face. I don't have any family and being a part of his has felt amazing, I'm not prepared to give it up any more than he is.

The smile spreads across his features.

"When did this happen? When did you get even more beautiful and courageous?"

I laugh lightly at him.

"I fully understand there will be changes to our lives, and Franco currently has the alterations underway at our house. The loft over the garage is being transformed into a security room and accommodation for the guards. I'm happy to keep him as my personal security guard, but I would like to avoid the need for the boys to have someone following them in school."

At the mention of Franco's name, I see his face sour instantly.

"And while we're at it, get over the jealous mister." I raise my eyebrows waiting for his retort, but it doesn't come.

"When all of this was first forced onto me, after I buried you, he showed me kindness and friendship, and as he wasn't a Rossi, I felt I could trust him, and Sofia. They have both looked out for me and helped in more ways than you will ever know."

The contrite look satisfies me.

"I'm sorry, it's just, well you looked so cosy."

I raise my eyebrows in mock anger just before a smile breaks out.

"Besides, I'm going to need them both more in the next few months if you don't hurry up and get out of this sick bed."

The look of confusion on his face is adorable.

Standing up I retrieve the item from my coat pocket, before sitting on the bed facing him. With my legs crossed, I begin to open the envelope and I can see him trying to see what I have. Flattening them out I lay them on his lap for him to see.

He immediately looks down and for a moment doesn't understand. Picking them up he studies them further, before looking up at me and back to the images again.

A number of emotions display on his face before reality begins to set in and then a look of anger, then hurt, then distress.

"She's due April 22$^{nd}$." I say quietly.

It is evident from the show of anger that he momentarily thought it was someone else's and I'm temporarily insulted.

When he looks at me this time the smile is huge and a look of disbelief in his eyes.

"You're pregnant, really?"

I nod a yes.

"But how, you thought you were going through the change, and your age Kate, is it safe?"

"Bit rude." I return, and a remorseful look comes over him,

"Sorry but you know what I mean."

I can't be upset with him, as I had the same thoughts myself.

"Yes, it's all safe. I've been checked out several times, and my midwife is amazing. They have offered an amnio, but I've declined."

He knows my thoughts on this already.

"Wow." Is all he manages.

"The boys know, and the rest of your family too, it was Dante who arranged for my medical care. It needed to be checked it was safe to attend."

Just another example of how complying I've been with his family. If that doesn't show my acceptance, I don't know what will.

Alex sits and stares at the images in his hand for an age, gently running his fingers over and over, almost caressing her. I stand from the bed and lift my top to expose the bump beneath. I'm surprised he hadn't noticed, but sometimes when it's just the two of us, nothing else matters.

I walk towards him as he turns and sits on the edge of the bed. He pulls me to stand between his legs and holds my top up as he places his warm hands either side of my bump and lays the gentlest kiss to the centre.

"Hello Baby." He says in the softest voice.

I'm not sure if he feels it but she automatically responds to the vibrations of his voice.

Looking up at me with a huge smile, he felt it.

The look of love in his eyes connects us and I lean down to place a kiss to his lips. The electricity travels from his lips to mine and creates an unbreakable circuit. An everlasting circle for infinity. Lifting from his lips I look at him as his smile suddenly turns into a perplexed frown.

"You said she's due in April. She, a girl?" His face is contorted with confusion while I look on.

I can't help the beaming smile as I nod my head.

"Yes, she. Angel Allesandro Rossi. The first girl to be born to the family in 200 years. Your daughter."

I see the tear roll down his face as he looks at me in awe before turning his loving eyes to my bump, where he places another gentle kiss.

"My daughter."

His smile is huge.

"My Principessa."


THE END

## EPILOGUE

The sight of my beautiful wife takes my breath away still after all of these years, even more with her belly rounded with our very own Principessa. A girl. I'm still in shock. I still can't quite believe I'm going to be a dad at 45 but mostly because it's a girl. A female hasn't been born into the Rossi family since the 1800's. I remember my grandfather talking of a curse, no-one knows the whole story and he was very superstitious.

Sitting at the table in the home we created together, I watch as she gracefully manoeuvres her way around her dream kitchen. The happiness she emanates surrounds her like a cloud, touching everyone who comes into contact. I love watching her. She's completely oblivious and my observations of her natural self, go unnoticed. Her gentle caress to the dog, smoothing of a wrinkle in the tea towel, re-positioning of a pot plant on the kitchen window sill. The house is sparkling clean and these final touches are all signs that labour will be starting any day now.

My admiration for Kate can't be measured with any tangible force. She adapts and moulds to any given situation and I regret now not telling her the whole truth 20 years ago. She didn't turn her back on me or show any form of repulsion at the life I was born into. My fear of losing her overtook my sensible brain, as I couldn't bear to be without her, but my fears weren't manifested and the love she has always shown me was unwavering. I didn't realise I could have both Kate and my family life and live in harmony. I chose to separate the two most important aspects of my life. Living a double life was draining, it felt like I was being unfaithful to her, in some respects I suppose I was. Lying to the one you love eats away at you and begins to crush your soul. Some nights I wanted her to hold me and reassure me that my actions weren't beyond redemption. I know I can always turn to her for affection but withholding the reasons why slowly ate away at me. I needed Kate to keep me sane, keep me whole. Both Dante and Benni urged me to open up to her, they saw what it was doing to me, but I couldn't take the chance I would lose her. I know I was selfish, but I couldn't risk losing my reason for breathing.

After I woke in my childhood home I felt panic rising knowing the whole truth would spill out. I had no idea of what they knew, what they had been told, but my whole life was in that house and it broke my heart thinking their opinion of me had shattered. The thought of Kate walking away with my boys seared dread in my veins. Terror that I could lose them because of my own stupidity. I totally fucked up that day. My family grieved me. I died to them. They buried me for god's sake. I'm normally so rational but Colombo's man was following me, and I couldn't risk exposing Kate and the boys to him if he followed me home. I knew there were murmurs about my private life, but I've fought so hard all these years to keep them hidden. That day when I saw the car I knew evasive action had to be taken. I didn't know anything about his compound, and the chances of crashing there were simply bad luck and timing for me.

I'm not embarrassed to be a Rossi but trying to explain Syndicate life to an outsider is almost impossible. Preconceived ideas borne from overdramatised films and books paints our lifestyle either with rose-tinted glasses or as perpetrators of heinous crimes. In reality our life is a mix of both and a bit of neither. We control large portions of the entertainment business, all legally, but we also have a hand in the illegal party trade, mostly the latest drugs. In reality the legal aspect of our business takes up most of our time but offers a smaller return than the regular shipments we land, cut, distribute and sell through our trusted contacts. We have no interest in human trafficking or arms and the families loyal to us don't either. It's an unwritten rule, I suppose we could be classed as gentlemen criminals in some respects.

When the Syndicate was passed to my father he inherited the old ways, which were quite frankly unsavoury and distasteful. He changed our direction quite drastically bringing us more in-line. I suspect mamma was integral to the advancements of the Rossi name.

The feud with the Colombo family was the final clean up from the old ways. It was left over from previous generations. No-one knows where it transpired but Dante was determined it would end with him. Eliminating Lorenzo Colombo settled that feud and subsequently saved my life. The fact Dante chose to act on the threat to Kate is ultimately the reason why I am sat here today. The fact that Kate has the total protection of the Colombo family still staggers me. She doesn't quite understand the honour they bestowed, but I know that she is safe, truly safe.

I don't allow my mind to ruminate on my time being held at the compound and what that sick bastard did to me. The visible scars are healing but any person with a weaker mind would have broken by now and allowed the darkness to consume them and the demons to take control. I'm not weak. That woman standing in front of me makes me strong.

I'm in awe of her strength and ability to adjust to a lifestyle she previously had no knowledge of. She takes everything in her stride, nothing seems to faze her. Kate's total acceptance has blown my mind. She has proven me wrong so many times as to my decision to keep her and the boys separate from my Syndicate life. She will listen to my reason for an action to keep them safe, consider it from different angles and adapt my suggestion to fit in with our family life. Evidence of that is currently living above our garage.

The relationship she has with Franco at first was uncomfortable for a husband to witness but eventually I saw it for what it is. With a little help and persuasion from my brothers, and my wife of course, I overcame my jealousy and removed the green-eyed monster from the equation and saw a platonic friendship. I trust Franco with one of my most precious jewels, my wife. If I can't be with her then she takes him, and not once has she complained about the intrusion on her privacy or the impact it has had on our lives. The fact they are such good friends has eased my families transition into the Syndicate lifestyle.

My boys have been truly phenomenal. Once they were reassured I wouldn't be taken from them again they began to relax and enjoy their childhood. They both matured massively the months I was held captive and I'm so proud of them both. Their excitement at having a baby sister almost rivals mine. With her pink palace all ready, they're eagerly awaiting her arrival into the world.

Dante, Benni and mamma are either on the phone or dropping in almost daily. The enhanced relationship is a new dynamic we are all adapting to, and I can see Kate thrives under the umbrella of their undying love. Leo has grown close to Dante, and Marc to Benni and the harmony this affords us all is a balm for the storm I can feel coming in the years ahead. The boys are aware of most of the intricacies of the Syndicate and Leo looks set to take on Dante's role when the time comes. Kate isn't happy, and I foresee her moulding and manipulating him into running the business more within the legal parameters that she is inherently used to.

The ringing of my phone wakes me from my thoughts and I see my eldest brothers name on the screen. I haven't fully returned to work, only running Gia and taking on light Syndicate duties. I'm not at full physical strength yet to resume my usual role.

"Buon giorno Dante." I say as I spy Bear hovering closer to Kate. Today he has been her permanent shadow.

"Allesandro, how are things?" He asks casually.

His tone doesn't fool me. He's as anxious as I am awaiting Angels arrival.

As I prepare to respond the sound that leaves Kate's mouth stops me in my tracks.

"AAARRRGGGHHH."

Clutching one hand to her rounded belly the other has a death grip on the worktop. Her knuckles are white, matching her dress. The look of intense pain on her face tells me everything I need to know.

"It's time." I say down the phone before disconnecting the call and quickly dialling another number. The phone answers on the first ring.

"Yes sir?" Franco asks in his usual composed manner.

"Bring the car round, it's time." I say the words calmly before pressing end.

Placing the phone in my pocket I walk over to where Kate is bent over double in pain.

"How bad?" Simple questions will give me the answers I need.

We were meant to have the baby in London but judging by the intensity she's feeling right now, I don't think she'll make it that far. Panting in short bursts as Ruth showed her, Kate begins to straighten as the contraction subsides.

"Seven."

Shit, that's not good.

Quickly dialling her number Ruth answers immediately.

"Mr Rossi is everything OK?"

Her voice is a calming influence on me.

"Kate's gone into labour. Pain is at a seven already."

Her light chuckle annoys me.

"I thought this might happen. You need to take her directly to the local hospital. I will meet you there."

"I don't think you'll make it in time." I respond tersely.

"I anticipated this sir. I've been staying close to the hospital for the last few days."

Kate had an appointment at the beginning of the week and Ruth must have sensed she was imminent. The woman is amazing. I breath out the stress, grateful for her foresight.

"We'll be there soon."

"Take it slowly sir. I'll inform the hospital you'll be arriving. I have a private suite reserved for us."

Ruth disconnects the call before I have a chance to thank her.

Manoeuvring Kate into the car is a slow process. Franco instructs one of the guards to collect the boys from school immediately and the other to fetch Kate's bag then stay and look after Bear. He drives carefully but efficiently to the hospital as I sit in the back and time each contraction, panting along with Kate and doing whatever I can to ease her during the journey. The pain she is feeling breaks me to pieces. Seeing the one you love suffering is the hardest thing to witness.

Pulling up to the maternity ward Franco jumps out of the car and retrieves a wheelchair before opening Kates door. Climbing out of my side, I run around the back of the vehicle and help her from the car.

The pain is becoming more intense and the wet stain on her dress indicates Angel is eager to enter the world.

"I've called your brother regarding the change in location sir." Franco says as I push the foot pegs down on the chair and place her feet gently on them.

I thank him with a nod as I straighten. Her panting is getting harder and scarily closer.

"Good luck." I hear him say as I race through the doors.

Pressing the intercom to the delivery suite the doors open automatically and the sight of Ruth in her scrubs eases my nerves instantly.

With a knowing smile she indicates the direction to go and I follow her hurried footsteps. Ruth opens the doors to a comfortable but sterile room, and I see she has everything ready.

Carefully we help Kate stand and I pull her oversized t-shirt from the bag hanging on my arm. I see Ruth shake her head at me when Kate drops hers as another contraction rips through her.

"No time." She mouths, before tending to my wife.

'OK Kate are you ready to meet your daughter?" Ruth asks in her gentle voice once Kate is lucid again. "Let's get you comfy and I'll take a look."

Helping Kate on to the bed, I fluff her pillows and use the damp cloth to cool her down. Ruth removes Kates underwear and snaps on a pair of gloves before checking her progress. Another contraction hits and then another almost immediately.

"I need to push." Kate throws out on an exhale, pain evident in her voice.

Her magnificence is astounding. The poise she has even in the direst of situations never fails to astonish me. Kissing her head, I hold in my emotions and give her my unguarded words of admiration. Kate needs all of my strength right now, she can have anything she wants of me. It all belongs to her anyway.

"On your next contraction, I want you to push Kate."

We don't have to wait long to meet Angel Allesandro Rossi. After only a few pushes she entered the world and invaded my heart. My instantaneous love for her almost bought me to my knees. Weighing a healthy 8lb 3oz, a thick mop of dark curls and dark eyes like liquid pools of melted chocolate, I fell in love instantly. She is the image of her mother. I never believed I could love anyone as much as Kate or the boy's, but the little girl cradled in my arms owns my heart, and from this day on I will forever be her slave.

Printed in Great Britain
by Amazon